MW01518908

The Code Of The Order

MATTHEW B. GIBSON

Dedication

There is evil in this world. This novel is dedicated to those who choose to stand up to it in all its forms – sometimes at great personal cost.

Acknowledgment

An effort such as this does not occur in a vacuum. Many people helped me along the way in this, my first novel.

First, I want to thank my wonderful family. I love you all so very much, thank you for supporting & believing in me.

Thank you to Crystal, Scott, Andy, Andre, Norton, and Catherine. Thank you for pushing me to be a better writer.

To Fun Zone & SKYKING:

Uncle Moe, Cynthia Ramain, Biernutz, Sparty, Revolution, Guy Smith, JoAnn, LeightonKing, CHIP, Cuebacca17, Bullzeye, nchia, Andre YMKYMFOI, Richard the Saint, Athiest4sure, Pjays14, ARB bf... YMBM!, RipofTruth, Mermaid Miss K, Joan Miller, thomaspainesghost, Quantanamo Bae, CatTheGreat, DumbOlDad, Keanu A, Blueeyesftlaud65, DigiSoldier, Donna, Russoutdoors, StevenCocoa, Dr. Zaius, C3POwn, Michael Austin, I Killed The Bank, Spuds1964, B MC, Lynette King, MrsSpartanAltsobaPatriot, Wendy, Ariane, THoTH Altruism, Kratom_Spoon, Igo, 13th-GEN_PATRIOT, Randle, Zooms Mom, vDarkness Falls, Wobble Hypotenuse, Smokyjoky, Ghost Face, & Legitimaximus

Thank you all for encouraging this budding author, and believing I could grow into something more.

Contents

About the Author

Matthew B. Gibson has always wanted to write a book since an early age. He makes it a point to read (or re-read) as many books as he can. Other hobbies include cooking, studying history, Bible study, and competitive shooting. He lives in Northern California with his family.

Prologue

June 12, 1798, Port of Valetta, Island of Malta

The naval guns were silent. After two days of intense fighting, the island of Malta was his. He pulled his cloak around his small frame and adjusted his uniform. *"Perfect,"* he thought, *"now to end this irritation from these troublesome knights and secure means of resupply for my fleet."* As he stepped outside his quarters on board the French Ship of the Line L'Orient, two soldiers snapped to attention. Their boots clicked on the teak deck, the noise echoing off the still water in the harbor. The smell of the sea filled his nostrils as he gazed out across the harbor. Fires burned between the buildings and smoke crept skyward. His crew had already prepared the skiff that was set to transport him across the harbor to Valetta where he would meet with Grand Master Ferdinand von Hompesch zu Bolheim and negotiate the Order's surrender. Not that there was much to talk about; his expeditionary forces could defeat the holdouts in the fort city of Valetta, but a siege would take time, and with Lord Nelson and the Royal Navy nipping at his heels, time was a commodity that had run short.

The skiff slowly slid across the inky waters of the bay, leaving General Bonaparte alone in his thoughts. The fires on the island had died down but still glowed between the buildings in colors of red, orange, and yellow. Long shadows from French garrison patrols stretched across ruined buildings, their images distorted from firelight and the heat. The scene cast an image in his mind as though he were sailing into hell. The general shrugged off the thought. Still, the resistance was greater than anyone had expected. Before tonight, these knights were known throughout Christendom as a charity rather than a fighting force. Their order began as a military arm that defended the holy land but also gave its soldiers medical training. As the ages wore on, the order turned to caring for the sick over training for war, but some of its members chose to follow money rather than God. The trappings of wealth led some to resort to piracy to maintain their lifestyle, and ever since, they have been an irritation to merchant traffic crossing the Mediterranean. General Bonaparte and all his staff officers believed they were dealing with do-gooders and perhaps criminals, not professional soldiers. That assumption proved to be a fatal error. They took the beach without incident, but once battle formations were mustered and the assault began on the city itself, his soldiers met resistance unlike anything they had yet encountered.

The defenders used the city to their advantage, funneling French troops into a warren of narrow streets and ambushes. The terrain of the city absorbed the assault like a sponge, and the defenders would attack long enough to inflict sufficient casualties to demoralize the French soldiers, but then the knights would suddenly withdraw, only to mass at another location. This happened over and over. General Bonaparte ordered his captains to fall back and regroup so his naval artillery could pound the city into rubble.

It took an hour. Apparently, the knights had decided that they had had enough and requested terms. Still, General Bonaparte could not shake the nagging feeling that he was again making an assumption he would later regret. Nothing about these knights was what it seemed. Soon, he could see a party waiting for him on shore. Among the officers were General Louis Baraguey D'Hilliers and General Claude-Henri Belgrand de Vaubois. These men led the invasion, which encountered stiff resistance on the island. The skiff made ground, and General Bonaparte stepped off the bow and onto the dark sand in one fluid stride. General D'Hilliers appeared at his side. "Mon

General, all is ready. The Grand Master is waiting for you this way, si vous plait."

A garrison of two hundred soldiers formed ranks to escort the General into the city of Valetta and to the seat of government where the Order of St. John had ruled this island for generations.

The garrison marched as one, and the sound of their boots echoed off the alleys. Every now and then, he would see a wretched shadow peeking out from the alley, hoping not to be noticed. Yes, the civilian population was sufficiently cowed, even if the knights were defiant to the point of foolishness. The narrow cobblestone streets stretched on forever. Soldiers stationed on the roofs of the buildings lining the streets looked down at their general. Any attempt to assassinate him from a window or doorway would be immediately met with steel and fire. General De Vaubois had made certain of this. The men were tired, but General Bonaparte could feel their pride in their victory. They would need it once they crossed swords with the Royal Navy. That battle was coming. As they approached the palace doors, two knights in ceremonial battle dress crossed their halberstadts, blocking entry. Now this was indeed rich! A surge of red-hot anger flashed within General Bonaparte at the sight of this arrogance, but he suppressed the urge to order his men to cut them down and force the doors open. He could use force, but it was far better to show restraint. In that way, one truly dominates a vanquished foe. He smiled, then nodded to General D'Hilliers, who then walked up to within an inch of one of the knights and said, "The General has arrived to see the Grand Master. Stand aside." The knight stared right back and did not move. This game lasted for another half a minute before the knight barked a command to his junior, and they both hoisted the Halberstadts and stood aside as ordered.

The doors opened, and a frail man stepped out of the shadows. "Good evening, General. I am Adolf Vogel, herald to his Excellency the Grand Master of the Order of St. John. I will show you to his Excellency's office." The officers and a few of the soldiers continued inside the palace. The room they entered was a large hall with a grand fireplace as a centerpiece. The smell of ash and a fire long since burned out could just be made out. The room was dark, and a small light slid inside through the window slits and the open door. Overturned furniture littered the room, and evidence of an artillery hit in the corner of the room could be seen. The shell must have penetrated the wall and floor but not gone off; if it had, the explosive charge would have brought part of this building down. It would have resulted in General Bonaparte meeting with a corpse instead of a defiant old man with noodles in his brain. They continued around the furniture to the back of the room, down a corridor, and up a narrow staircase. Alcoves were set along the walls of the staircase, but they were empty. It was as if this once grand palace had sold most of its finery at auction long ago. At last, the frail old prime minister brought them to a door with one knight standing guard. The knight opened the door, stepped inside, and held it open. Once the French officers were inside, he shut it behind himself. The French junior officers of the general staff waited outside with the knight.

The French officers entered the office – if one could even call it that, an old desk, bookshelves stuffed full of scrolls and documents, a Persian rug on the floor, the smell of old paper and leather, it looked like a priest's study rather than that of a senior military officer. A man of unextraordinary stature stood to meet his guests. He had silver hair and was well groomed. All three of the French generals noticed that this man did not possess the demeanor of a defeated commander; not...at...all...

Instead of a routed adversary all too willing to beg for terms that would avoid the gallows or a firing squad, a royal presence greeted them. Everything about this Grand Master radiated confidence and control. The only thing Napoleon could compare it to was a prince holding court. No, it was more than that. With the ferocity with which these knights fought in the streets and the near suicidal bravery with which they conducted themselves on the field of battle, this silver haired man was far more than he appeared.

This man held the leash of Cerberus in his hand.

Pleasantries were exchanged, and brandy was offered and accepted. The French officers were invited to take seats facing the Grand Master's desk. Once everything was settled, the negotiation of terms began. "Ah, good evening, gentlemen," Grand Master Hompesch announced. He gestured towards General Bonaparte and said, "You must be the brilliant flag officer I keep hearing so much about. Your men fought well; we were impressed."

Bonaparte smirked and nodded to General D'Hilliers, who started in German, "Greetings, your excellency, we are here to negotiate the terms of your surrender. We offer safe passage for you and your surviving men into exile if you..."

Hompesch interrupted, "I'm sorry, General, but I am having trouble following your German; perhaps we may continue in French?"

General D'Hilliers began again, "Indeed. We offer you and your men exile and safe passage if you cease hostilities immediately and surrender all port facilities and provisions over to our fleet at once."

Hompesch shifted positions in his chair. "I see. And will some of your men be staying behind?" He asked.

"We intend to leave a small garrison here, of course. And we will make sure that this Island cannot continue to make war or resume its habit of piracy," the General said with a sneer. "You and your soldiers must leave, or we will set fire to this city. We do not intend to give quarter if this would be your choice." *"Dangerous,"* Napoleon thought. *"Didn't D'Hilliers see the hazard in threatening this man?"*

Napoleon's eyes glanced at General De Vaubois who shared his look of concern. *"De Vaubois saw it too. We will see where this goes; I can always intervene if necessary."*

The Grand Master said not a word, but his gaze bore right through General D'Hilliers. *"Hmm, this man had his emotions under control,"* Napoleon said to himself. *"Good."*

D'Hilliers continued, "Furthermore, you will surrender all of your artillery, powder, and small arms under the supervision of my junior officers. Once your men have disarmed, they will be permitted to leave the island."

D'Hilliers took a small sip of brandy. "Any other terms?" the Grand Master asked.

"No. And I might add that these terms are to be considered final and absolute." General D'Hilliers added curtly.

"Very well, General. But you are forgetting a few items," The Grand Master countered.

"Oh?" Replied D'Hilliers.

"Yes. If I may continue, my order intends to leave the island as is, and if you wish to have our weapons, you may have them," the Grand Master continued. "However, we ask that estates in France be given to the order and that you provide safe passage to Trieste."

Bonaparte shifted in his chair. *"This was a reasonable accommodation,"* he thought. *"Estates were easy to come by, and if these fools wanted land that France could then tax, they were welcome."* As to the location of their disembarkation, he could not care less, just so they were out of the way.

The Grand Master then looked General D'Hilliers right in the eye and said in a firm voice, "Furthermore, you will finance the remainder of your campaign in the Orient through our financial institution. We will expect France's finance ministers in Zurich by the end of this month to make the necessary arrangements."

A quiet settled over the room. The French officers were not sure if this man was serious or if he was patently insane. "I must not have heard you correctly," General D'Hilliers offered.

"No General, you heard me just fine," Hompesch said.

"Enough of this!" D'Hilliers roared. "This negotiation has no place for games! Accept the terms as stated or face annihilation!"

Napoleon put a hand on his subordinate's shoulder. General D'Hilliers complexion was still flushed, but he stopped at the suggestion of his superior officer. Putting aside his anger, he excused himself and let General Bonaparte continue. "Grand Master, please forgive us as we are weary from the voyage and fighting your men," Napoleon started. "You have good fighters under you, some of the best I've seen. However, the terms that you are suggesting are unusual and, frankly, quite preposterous under the circumstances."

The Grand Master took a thoughtful sip of his brandy, savoring the amber liquid. Flavors of caramel and chestnut were significant; this was a good year; the best. He gently set his snifter down and calmly began once more, "General Bonaparte, I understand your subordinate's feelings on this, but neither of you have thought this matter through sufficiently. You come into my office and threaten me and my men with death, yet you haven't considered the consequences of such an action."

This statement surprised Bonaparte "Consequences? What Consequences?" He asked.

"You have not considered what I will do to France if our terms are not met," the Grand Master stated menacingly.

A chilly silence slithered through the room.

The Grand Master continued, "You will recall that the priories of my order have long cared for the sick and dying. One hundred fifty years ago, we cared for the victims of the black plague. During this time, when all of Europe was consumed with fear and suffering, we made a discovery. We learned how the plague can jump from one man to another and that it is, in truth, a living creature. The plague burned itself out, but we have carefully kept that creature alive all these years. If you cast aside my terms or harm any one of us, men loyal to me will release that creature in Paris." An icy chill crept up Napoleon's spine. He felt like this man could kill him just by uttering a word. *"He means it,"* Napoleon thought. *"None of this is an idle threat. D'Hilliers pushed this man too far, and the man is gone. What we see before us now is a determination to achieve a result, no matter the cost. A human? Not anymore."*

"But we don't need to walk down this path, gentlemen," the Hompesch continued. Gone was the thing, once more veiled by the shape and polite manners of the silver-haired old man. "I have come to know many things. I know that France is not a match for England in industrial output. Your surviving nobility has fled your borders and taken most of its wealth with them, leaving France starved of tax revenue while the nobility of

England is as strong as ever, as are their pocketbooks. I know that France is having difficulty securing lines of credit with other countries, while England purchases idle armies from non-belligerent nations to fight you. Do not underestimate the treasure that England will spend to stop you from victory. I offer you a chance to even the scales financially," Hompesch argued.

It was incredibly quiet in the office. All the French officers were bone pale. The Grand Master made no mention of this and held up his glass. "More brandy, anyone? It's a particularly good year that I've been saving for the right occasion. I can think of none better than to celebrate the chance to assist France in her time of need," he said.

"That was an interesting way of looking at it," thought the general. General Bonaparte got his emotions under control. He said in a calm voice after pausing for a minute to keep from shaking, "Grand Master, we are tasked by France to make war against England and her allies. We are not involved with financial matters..."

The Grand Master cut him off, "Rubbish. You have influence at the highest levels of French power. If you speak, they will listen. I make an offer that is mutually beneficial, and all of what I say regarding France's financial position in this war is true. Stop stalling and give me your word that you will make this case before your government. I will settle for that now that we both know who is in Paris at this very moment and the monster that he carries with him." The Grand Master looked right at General Bonaparte and asked, "Now sir, what is France's answer to my counter-terms?"

The General's mind took all the data into account: the war with England, the financial situation, the threat of plague, and the curious way that the Grand Master put that last question, as if he were addressing France through him. The risk of supporting the order was low; the consequences of defying it, however, were too large to calculate. It was an easy decision. "Oui, we have an accord," the general said as he stood up and offered his hand to the Grand Master. Ferdinand von Hompesch zu Bolheim took the offered hand of Napoleon Bonaparte, and the fate of nations aligned in a quiet office on an island in the Mediterranean Sea.

"Wonderful, General. I'm delighted that France is willing to accept our help. Our representatives will have everything ready for your finance ministers when they arrive in Switzerland. I have a draft of the financial agreement and instructions on how to contact us in this letter I give to you now." The Grand Master extended a leather document portfolio with a sheaf of documents bearing the seal of the Order of St. John. The Grand Master said in parting, "Fortune and safety be with you, General. Please excuse me while I arrange the order's departure from Malta. I thank you for your visit."

Prime Minister Vogel saw the officers out, and the Aides-de-camp waiting outside took note of the expressions worn by their superiors. The expressions did not do the look justice. *"Odd, I thought we won this battle…"* the junior officers thought to themselves.

The surrender and journey to exile went smoothly. Every surviving knight followed the Grand Master's orders to the letter and surrendered their weapons and equipment without incident. The Grand Master was the last knight to leave Malta. He looked back at the city one last time before stepping onto the skiff that would take them to the Italian ship that would take him to Trieste. The Italian ship set sail for home at once. The merchant sailors knew that it was dangerous to be so close to the French war fleet; it was far better to be at sea, alone, and safe. As the Grand Master watched Malta in the wake of the ship, Prime Minister Adolf Vogel stepped beside him. Both men watched their former island home disappear into the boiling mirage of the horizon. A time passed, and Vogel asked, "Sir, May I be so bold as to confront you with something?"

Hompesch turned to him and answered, "Of course, Adolf. What troubles you?"

Vogel swallowed and said, "Master that conversation back there, in your office... Was it true that a member of our order had the Black Death at the ready?"

The Hompesch paused for a long moment and replied, "No. But I was successful in convincing France that someone was." He continued, "And Vogel, please stop calling me Grand Master. That was for fooling the French Generals, and we can dro   p that subterfuge now that we are safely away. Tell me, how is the real Grand Master?"

Vogel responded, "The same ever since we arrested him days ago; he's scared to death."

"Excellent," Captain Aleksander Zajac said, relieved that he could quit pretending he was the cowardly Hompesch. That fool of a man provoked General Bonaparte over something as trivial as a resupply issue. Had he not been there to arrest Grand Master Hompesch and take control of the situation, the order would have lost the island for nothing. Fortunately for the order, Zajac was able to secure financing for the French campaign and estates for Hompesch, so it appeared the Grand Master betrayed the order for money. Vogel let out a sigh. "But what about financing a war? You know our treasury cannot cover that kind of expense... And those French officers might not have known the first thing about money, but I assure you the Swiss will."

Captain Zajac let out a roar of laughter and told his old friend, "Vogel, not to worry! The priory of Poland arranged with the Emperor of Russia when he moved us to St. Petersburg. Once we land in Trieste, I will contact my friend Emperor Paul I for the financial assistance he promised. He despises France and cannot wait to hurt them financially. Once General Bonaparte realizes how badly he's been cheated, he might be foolish enough to invade Russia. We can only hope." And thus, we would remove a future threat to all of Europe. The last thing the continent needed was another

Roman emperor. Much needed to be done, and both men knew that they needed to exercise the utmost caution when dealing with France, but for now they rested in the comfort that the financial future of the Order of St. John was secure. They pondered the vastness of the sea as the Italian ship sailed towards the Eastern horizon.

Chapter 1

Monday, January 26, 2015

London School of Economics, UK

"On July 6, 1799, Grand Master Hompesch dispatched a letter to Emperor Paul I of Russia. The purpose of his letter was to abdicate his title of Grand Master to the Emperor. In Russia, this set about..." the history professor droned on and on. *"I wish a knight could save me from this class,"* thought Victoria. She glanced at the clock; there were five minutes left. The one redeeming quality about this professor was that he was a stickler for starting and ending his lectures on time. A gifted student, Victoria took her notes, being careful to record dates and situations that she would research and commit to memory later during her study time. She looked up, only to see a male student immediately look away. *"Too bad, he was kind of cute,"* Victoria thought. 5'-9" with blond hair, blue eyes, and an athletic figure, she was used to men quickly looking away when she chose to notice. Although she was from Idaho, she could have been one of the **California Girls** that Brian, Dennis, and Carl Wilson sang about when they captivated a generation with their music decades ago. Three minutes to go. Victoria could almost taste the coffee she planned to get on the way to her next class, English Literature. The smell of vanilla, smoke, and earth, followed by rich, hot cream and... "That's time, class," the professor said. "Please keep in mind that there will be an examination this Thursday on Napoleon's Italian campaign. Please remember to bring a blue book for the essay portion, and you may view a study guide on the department's web page. Dismissed."

Victoria had time for a coffee to go, but not anything else. She knew there was a gap in the morning rush at the Starbucks around the corner, and she was going to exploit that lull. She quickly put on her London Fog coat, Burberry scarf, and patent leather gloves, grabbed her messenger bag, and began to walk down the hallway to the door of the old LSE building that would place her on Houghton Street. Victoria's family was privileged. Her father owned a vast cattle ranch, and her mother came from old Texas oil money.

As Victoria exited the building, she braced herself for the cold; London was frigid in January. A brisk walk down Houghton Street brought her to a dead end on Aldwych. The heels of her boots clicked on the old flagstone street before they made their familiar tapping sound on the more modern concrete sidewalks of the main London streets. A right turn, then one hundred paces, would take her to Kingsway, where she turned right once more. Starbucks was just ahead on the right side of the street. It was time to get out of the bite of the frosty morning. She walked through the door to a familiar smell; roasted coffee, caramel, and chocolate all at once. The barista recognized her immediately and said, "Good mornin' love! I'll get your order ready! Nigel, could you fetch up Victoria's order for me please?" Meg, the barista, was a kind woman, although a bit chatty. She made an excellent latté, though. It was piping hot and perfect every time. As the espresso machine hissed and vented steam, Meg was a tornado of activity. She had the latte ready within two minutes. Victoria picked it up in a swoop as she headed out the door. As she was greeted by the freezing, damp air, Victoria took a sip of the rich liquid to chase away the chill. The latte warmed her belly, and the heat from the coffee radiated out from within her torso. Another half block, and she would be able to cross Sardinia Street to the location of her next class.

There is sometimes a grave hazard to having a routine. Routines made certain jobs easier and far less risky. Victoria did not notice the man in a tracksuit sipping his tea. A slim man of average height, he was the type of man you could look at but never remember; that was intentional, and he worked extremely hard to practice that skill. He was along the wall, where it was difficult to see if a person was talking to the baristas or picking up a drink. The choice of his table was not an accident; he arrived at Starbucks twenty minutes before Victoria did. As she walked out the door, he clicked the push-to-talk, or PTT, button of a civilian-band radio twice. This radio signal set everything in motion.

35 seconds out.

The van had already made its left turn onto Kingsway from Remnant Street. Two other men, one massive in size who could have been a linebacker, the other a frail man who looked like an Egyptian librarian, readied themselves, waiting on Sardinia Street. One more man across the street on Kingsway was watching Victoria walk. He too had a radio; his thumb hovered over the PTT button.

20 seconds out.

The man across the street on Kingsway pressed the PTT button three times. This was the signal to the two-man team on Sardinia Street to get moving. They walked at a brisk pace, talking to each other. The radio signal was to alert this team that Victoria would come around the corner in five seconds. She did, right on time.

10 seconds out.

Contact. The smaller of the two men ran into Victoria and looked up in surprise. A full second passed before this man started offering an apology to Victoria for bumping into her and spilling her coffee. The frail man pulled out a handkerchief and moved it briskly on Victoria's coat; again, the movement was fast and intended to distract from the slower movements the larger man was making. The van slowly made its left turn onto Sardinia Street and turned on its hazard lights as though it were making a delivery. The driveway ramp was directly ahead. Victoria began to accept the man's apology when she looked at his massive companion, who was slowly moving towards her. Something was wrong.

5 seconds out.

Too late. The small man's big companion had already drawn a stun gun. In a flash of brutal but precise movement, his strong hand grabbed

Victoria's arm as he forced the stun gun into the side of her neck and activated it. Victoria did not even have time to cry out. The electric current from the device surged through her body. Her muscles locked up and tensed. She was imprisoned in her own body, which refused to follow the frantic commands from her brain. Three seconds later, the man deactivated the stun gun. Victoria would have fallen to the sidewalk had the big man not held her by the arm. The smaller man who bumped into her and the larger man grabbed Victoria, picked her up off her feet, and moved her into the waiting van, which already had its side door open. Both men muscled Victoria inside and pushed her to the floorboard of the van. The driver gently pulled away from the driveway as the smaller man closed the door. The larger man could handle Victoria. He gave her another shock from the stun gun as he produced a set of handcuffs and restrained her. As she sobbed with fright, a pillowcase went over her head, and Victoria's world went dark. The van's driver whistled a tune as he turned left onto the road that encircled Lincoln's Inn Fields. Another left, and he turned back onto Remnant Street. A right turn brought the driver onto Kingsway. The motorway was to the Northeast. It took twenty minutes to get onto the M1. There was no rush. The men had a safe house waiting, and no one had seen the kidnapping.

At an altitude of two hundred feet above the street, a quadcopter drone slowly began to move. The drone was all but invisible from this altitude thanks to its grey paint. Although it was true that no person had seen Victoria's abduction, the drone's mechanical eye saw everything. As the van got further away, a powerful zoom camera locked in on its license plate, and the operator was able to freeze and capture an image.

GF64 DLX

The drone operator was in a shipping container outfitted as an electronic intelligence center. Carefully distressed with paint and dents on the outside, the unremarkable exterior of the shipping container gave no hint as to what was inside. The only abnormality about the shipping container was a larger than usual refrigeration unit installed at one end, but one would have to be in the international shipping trade to know that. The shipping container served a dual purpose: first, it was easily overlooked by the public, and second, it could also be picked up by a truck or a helicopter and moved anywhere. The drone operator was a small man with neat blond hair. His code name was Echo, for he was the "eyes" of any operation and a critical member of the team. He swiveled in his chair away from the piloting console for the drone to a computer hooked up to a compact but powerful rack of Dell R930 servers. These monsters had a combined 12 terabytes of random-access memory (RAM) and could chew through encryption like a hot knife through butter. A remote query over the internet to a compromised computer at the Driver and Vehicle Licensing Agency provided every detail about the van and the registered owner.

The owner of the van was a contract delivery company that did overflow work for companies like Amazon and DHL. This company was in London and was owned by Iraqi immigrants. Many people from that part of the world migrated to Europe during the global war on terror. Another internet query to yet another compromised computer at the Metropolitan Police mainframe allowed Echo to view London's system of surveillance cameras. One of the most extensive in the world, the cameras picked up the license plate of the van within ten seconds. Echo watched the van weave its way through the morning traffic and proceed to the M1 motorway. Echo then placed a cellular call to an unlisted number. The phone rang once.

"Field office"

"This is Echo, Authentication; x-ray delta tango."

"Foxtrot acknowledges, Echo. Challenge code?"

"Bravo two, Mike."

"Go ahead, Echo."

"Captain, you have a white Ford Transit van heading towards your position on the M1. The license plate is GF64 DLX. Speed is seven zero miles per hour; ETA your position, five minutes."

"Copy that, Echo," the Captain said. There were two cars parked at a petrol station near an on ramp to the motorway several miles outside London. Captain Jan Luczac led a team of five other men. He was tall, well over six feet tall, jet-black hair, and had piercing blue eyes. Not only handsome with chiseled features, Jan was also monstrously strong; he and his team did calisthenic exercises together every day. While most elite soldiers could do ten pull-ups at a minimum, that was not enough to be on this team. On Jan's team, each man had to be able to perform fifteen pull-ups with one arm. So too, with push-ups, squats, and handstands, all the exercises were required to be done with one arm or one leg. The logic of this superhuman standard of strength was that they always worked in small teams, and if one arm or leg were to be injured in an operation, the injured soldier usually had to get themselves out of trouble. The exercises used to progressively build up to this fitness standard were secrets handed down from ancient times through the generations, and he and his team were the latest beneficiaries of this knowledge. One day, they too would pass it on. But today, they had an operation to execute.

The unexpected kidnapping of the LSE student had forced them to accelerate their plans. Jan signaled to the driver of the second car: get ready. The phone rang again; it was Echo. "Captain, target vehicle is three-zero seconds from your on-ramp; speed is seven zero miles per hour."

"Copy, Echo. The team is rolling now," Jan said as he ended the call. The cars left the petrol station and accelerated smoothly onto the M1. The white van had passed the exit a short time ago. The colors of white, brown, and grey streaked by the cars as they merged into their tail positions one kilometer behind the van. With the M1's traffic surveillance, a physical tail was not necessary, and the cars could keep their distance, but once the van got off the highway, camera coverage was spotty. The team had to be certain the van went to the farmhouse.

The driver of the van was careful and drove under the posted limit, always mindful of being a considerate and passive driver. He watched the frost-covered rolling countryside stream by as he drove North. The work van, one of thousands in the island nation, slowed off the motorway and took the A5183 exit towards Flamstead. Instead of going to Flamstead itself, the driver turned right onto Old Watling Street, past a marshaling yard for trucks. Up ahead, the road narrowed, with hedgerows flanking either side of the street. Here the driver turned North, away from well-kept country farmhouses with large gardens. This street was Chad Lane, and the van climbed a little hill before leveling off onto a narrow country lane. The lane was narrow, covered with snow, and barely wide enough for one automobile. The driver slowed a bit. A collision here with the girl in the back simply would not do. A few more minutes of careful driving brought the van to a cottage at the end of a long gravel driveway. The cottage was secluded, with hedgerows surrounding the perimeter of the property. Once inside the grounds, though, the hedges were trimmed to waist level. The owner liked to see the whole of his property and only kept the hedges high on the perimeter to keep the cows out.

Jan saw the van turn onto Chad Lane and ordered his driver to terminate the tail. The second car had sped ahead to the next exit and was deploying a drone. Echo took control of the drone once it was set up. This drone was not a quadcopter; it was more like a model airplane, but with greater endurance and equipped with powerful observation cameras. Echo wagged the ailerons twice and set the throttle to maximum. The men who set up the drone pulled a cord attached to the spring-loaded launcher, and the drone surged forward. It dipped in altitude a bit, then began to climb rapidly. Painted in the same grey camouflage motif as the quadcopter, the drone was invisible past three hundred feet. The drone made its way towards the farmhouse and began to circle the structure at an altitude of 3,000 feet. The drone had a perfect view of the happenings below.

The van came to a stop, the icy gravel popping under the tires. The sliding door opened, and the large man picked Victoria up to take her out of the vehicle. She tensed at first, but the large man activated the stun gun, letting Victoria hear the cracking sound for a full five seconds before saying in heavily accented English, "Obey, and I'll be kind to you. Resist, and I'll hold this on the back of your neck until you soil yourself. Either way - you're coming with me."

Victoria nodded and relaxed. She was terrified of the big man and what he might do.

"Good," said the big man. He and his smaller companion each took one of Victoria's arms and led her up the path to the farmhouse. The farmhouse was old, with grey stone walls two feet thick and a shake roof. Outside, there were bare trees. The frost on the lawn crunched beneath their feet as they walked around the side of the farmhouse. On the side of the house, there was a concrete staircase that led down to a cellar door. The cellar was cold and damp. It smelled of earth, old wood, and musty grass; of things rotten and turned to dust long ago. In an alcove, the men had made a holding cell out of lumber. They opened the door, pulled the hood off Victoria's head, and pushed her inside. The door shut abruptly behind her, and Victoria heard three locking bars secure the door. She stood up and pushed on the door; it was so securely shut, it was like it were nailed closed. Escape was impossible.

Inside the cell, there was a cot and a single light bulb in a fixture in the ceiling. In the corner, there was a small camera. The same camera was in the opposite corner. The men did not need bars to see Victoria's every move; in fact, they could watch her from anywhere on the property. Victoria looked at the cot. There was a jumpsuit neatly folded on top of the blanket. It was orange in color. The surge of adrenaline was gone from Victoria's system. The fear of injury had subsided, and with nothing to do but think, the enormity and grave peril of her situation hit her all at once. Victoria crumbled to her knees and fell to the floor, sobbing uncontrollably.

The small man's features were illuminated by the pale grey glow of the LCD monitor. His gaunt face looked hard at the image on the screen. He watched Victoria cry for a moment before pushing back from the table where the monitors for the farmhouse's surveillance system were set up in the dining room. The house was vacant, save for a few items in the kitchen and some military-issue cots in the bedrooms. Their cell was small, only eight men. Right now, two men were walking the perimeter; two dozed, waiting their turn to perform sentry duty; and the other three were down the hall, where they were setting up the cameras for the livestream to the internet. The small man, Khalid, had been fighting the infidels since the US Marines invaded his home city of Fallujah, Iraq. Back then, he and his brothers in arms were called the Fedayeen. ISIS came later. Khalid walked down the hall and opened the door where the other three men were working on the cameras. He nodded to the big man, Fahad. Fahad was a professional wrestler from Damascus. He was a giant of a man with a barrel shaped chest. He had a huge jaw and forehead, along with a dark beard. One fateful morning, Allah spoke to him in his daily prayers, and he left to find ISIS that same day. He was aggressive and a natural fighter. Khalid once saw Fahad kill an Iraqi policeman with his bare hands. Fahad's fury in battle was a remarkable sight. "Yes, brother?" Fahad asked once he saw Khalid. "Is everything ready, Fahad?" Khalid asked in response.

Fahad said, "Yes. We just finished the system test, and our brothers in Iraq have said our signal is good. We will be ready to broadcast on time." The other two men finished their work and left the room for a cigarette outside. Fahad watched them leave and said to Khalid in a quiet voice, "Brother, are you sure you can trust these two? They do not come from the battlefield like you and I; the Imam recruited them here. There is not a one of them who's seen blood like what is going to be spilt later."

Khalid answered, "I know. The Imam vouched for them, though."

This was not making Fahad happy. "Yes, brother," Fahad said, unconvinced.

Reassuringly, Khalid said, "Fahad, if they are to carry out jihad with you and me, then they will see violence at some point. It is better they see it now rather than later when we are conducting an operation. Allah will strengthen them, brother. You will see." And that was that. Fahad pushed his doubts aside and instead did his duty. The others would see his example and follow. It was the same with men in combat all around the world. He walked to the kitchen. He had put some water on the stove earlier for a cup of tea. Tea would calm his doubts. It always did.

Jan was on the phone with Echo again after ordering his driver to return to the M1 and drive north to rendezvous with the rest of the team. The driver, Aleksy, carefully merged off the motorway and drove to the old factory building, where the other team members were waiting. Aleksy brought the car to a gentle stop in a free parking space in front of the factory. Aleksy was much like the others, born in Poland at a hospital run by the order. He could hear Jan on the phone with Echo say, "No doubt about it, Captain. The drone saw the kidnap victim get taken to the farmhouse by way of the basement, and we confirmed the van's plate; GF64 DLX."

Jan nodded, "I copy all, Echo. Is there any increased internet activity from our target?"

Echo replied, "Yes, Captain. I have increased social media activity, and ISIS is performing bandwidth tests on their servers. They're going to stream video data soon; it matches activity we saw last August when James Foley was murdered."

"Now they're going to try it on English soil..." Jan thought aloud, "Echo, can you give me any idea where we sit on their timetable?"

Echo had an answer: "Captain, based on the internet traffic patterns I'm seeing from ISIS, you've got about 10 hours before they murder that young lady and stream it around the world."

"Where every psychotic terrorist and internet troll with a fetish for gore will watch the fear and suffering of another human being with lurid fascination," he thought. Echo ran into these ghoulish people all the time when monitoring internet chatter for the

purpose of intelligence gathering, and their behavior made him sick.

Jan sighed and said, "Copy that, Echo. I want you to keep monitoring the farmhouse with the drone. Bring it back here to the industrial complex only for fuel. Start analyzing enemy force deployment and patterns. We are going to hit the farmhouse tonight." That was a change. The old plan was to attack the farmhouse later that week. They have been monitoring the place for two days now. The fact that they had seen the kidnapping was pure luck, and only because they were following the van. Echo understood why Captain Luczac had moved up the attack. It was against everything they swore loyalty to and stood for to let that girl die. Every man on that team, Echo included, would risk their lives and die if necessary to prevent that girl's murder, so the assault plan was moved up, and that was that. Echo finished with, "Echo copies, Captain. I have six hours to bingo fuel on the drone. Will keep you informed of any changes in enemy strength or patrol patterns. Echo out."

Jan put the phone away and got out of the car. He and Aleksy walked a short distance from the car to the front door of the old brick building. It was an ancient structure, built in the late 19th century as a machine shop and foundry. One century ago, this building was an advanced blacksmith shop that supported the newly industrialized farms that dotted the region. If your steam-powered tractor broke, a place like this was where you took the damaged part, and the 'smiths would fashion a replacement. This building had been unoccupied for years. Aleksy creaked the door open, and one could smell the echoes of industry that once flourished here. The aroma of old metal and dust, with a faint chemical smell from the nitriding pots, was quiescent. Aleksy and Jan walked to the end of the now vacant building, where a large tent had been set up by the team. This was the kind of tent you would find at a wedding or outdoor event where rain was expected. In this case, it kept the dust and leaks from the roof away. Jan gestured to the sentry outside the tent flap as they stopped to go inside. He wanted all his men to hear about the change in plans.

Jan spoke in a loud and clear voice, "Soldiers of the Order, we have a fragmentary order!" All his men formed ranks in a flash and stood at rigid attention. "At ease, men. It is my duty to inform you that the ISIS cell we have been shadowing has now kidnapped a female LSE student. I've spoken with Echo, and we are certain that the ISIS cell intends to kill her on an internet stream this evening." The other five men did not move, but their eyes hardened as they heard the news. The captain went on, "As you know, we were going to attack the cell later this week. However, now that they have a hostage, we will attack the cell tonight. Get some food and rest, men. There will be a briefing and then kit selection at 16:00. Dismissed."

Jan's men looked at each other. Aleksy, the driver, looked at Lew and Kuba, the two other assault team members. Lew was thin, like a runner, and had sandy blond hair that he wore with a part and steel blue eyes. Kuba was a massive black-haired man with a moustache that could do more push-ups than the whole team put together. These two men, along with Aleksy and the captain, made up the four-man assault team. The two other team members made up the sniper element. Anatol, the smallest team member at 5'-9" was the sniper, and Olek was his spotter. Olek was well over six feet tall and as strong as Kuba. Both Aleksy and Olek had similar features and red hair. Jan sat down at a field desk and began to finalize his assault plan.

Chapter 2

Abandoned Factory

Jan stood at a large LCD television screen as he delivered the briefing. His team was seated in front of him at tables, quietly paying attention. The room was dark; illumination came from only the harsh light of the screen and the softer yellow of the desk lamps that were placed in front of each man to make it easier to read their briefing documents. A map of the farm and a floor plan of the farmhouse were included.

Three additional men had joined the assembled team. Stefan, the helicopter pilot, was a wiry man with greying hair. Filip, the co-pilot, was larger, almost six feet tall, but younger than Stefan. Lastly, at the end of the table sat Igor, the crew chief and door gunner. The flight crew was performing a practice run in the EC155 Dauphin helicopter when Echo told them about the Fragmentary order, or FRAGO. They raced the dark grey helicopter back to the airfield and drove a car to the factory. The Captain continued, "Echo, has there been any change in patrol patterns for the sentries in the last five hours?"

Echo's voice came in clear over the teleconference phone: "Negative, Captain. There are always two sentries patrolling the area outside the house. Every three hours, they switch. There's been no change to the patrol patterns since their hostage arrived."

"Very well, gentlemen. Anatol, I want you to engage the sentries when we are ready to approach the house," the captain ordered. Anatol nodded. This was going to be a tricky shot. A miss would alert the sentry and blow the mission, as would anything besides a fatal shot to the brain stem. It was not a far shot, and wind would not be a factor, but Anatol knew that he had to hit a playing card-sized target as it slowly moved.

He had a suggestion: "Captain, I recommend that I engage the sentry as he turns the corner and moves away from my position. The head will be relatively stationary and easier to hit. The body will also be concealed from the other sentry until he turns the same corner."

Jan nodded approvingly, saying, "That makes sense to me, Anatol. That first shot will be critical; we might as well give you the easiest shot possible." Jan always listened to suggestions from his soldiers, especially his specialists. Jan could run a sniper rifle if needed, but he was not the best.

That distinction belonged to Anatol and Olek. Each of those men could put every round they shot through a playing card at three hundred meters - regardless of position or circumstances. Wet, cold, hungry, either hand, any position; it did not matter; both men could land round after round through that playing card-size target. For this engagement, the shooting position would be deep inside a hay barn, about ninety meters from the farmhouse. The terrain blocked anything but a standing position. This wasn't an ideal hide, but it was all that was available. The sniper rifle for this mission was going to be a bolt-action rifle chambered in a new cartridge, the 300 AAC Blackout. Anatol followed the development of this new cartridge and had a rifle built for it. The base rifle was a Tikka T3 hunting rifle, but Anatol had one of their armorers change a few parts on the rifle, add a chassis for ergonomics, and shorten the barrel.

The barrel was now only nine inches long but had an integral suppressor built around it. The 300 Blackout didn't need a barrel longer than nine inches to achieve its full subsonic velocity; anything longer was waste. This allowed a short, easy-to-hide rifle that was very quiet. Most suppressors don't sound like the ones in movies, but this one did. The report from the rifle was impossible to hear any further than fifty feet, and the sniper's hide location was more than three times that distance from the enemy. No one would hear a thing once Anatol took the shot.

"This leaves the assault team," Jan went on. "Lew, Kuba, and Aleksy, you'll be with me. We will crawl along this low stone wall, and when Anatol eliminates the sentries, we will go over the wall and advance on the house in staggered column formation. We will quietly make entry at the kitchen door after looking through the endoscopic camera. There should be two men in the living room or kitchen. We will eliminate both before continuing. Aleksy, Kuba, you will eliminate the two sentries inside the house while Lew and I cover the hallway."

Every man in the assault team nodded his understanding as Jan spoke. "Yes, Kuba?" Jan said as he saw Kuba's hand go up.

Kuba asked, "Sir, to be clear, once we cross the entry door, we are weapons-free?"

Jan answered his team member, "Yes, Kuba. And we go for a burst to the face; we don't expect the enemy to be wearing TATP vests, but they are wearing web gear with rifle magazines, so we take no chances. Headshots only." ISIS was known for wearing bomb vests on missions. Triacetone Triperoxide or TATP was a very unstable and dangerous explosive that was easily made with common household chemicals. The explosive was so unstable that a bullet could set it off; if that happened, everyone inside the front of the house would be dead. The other problem was that the sentries were seen on the drone feed with short AK-105 rifles and web gear to carry extra magazines on their chests. These chest-mounted magazine carriers would stop a subsonic 9mm round for sure. Headshots would be difficult in a CQB environment, but his men were up to the task. Every member of the assault team could fire four rounds from their MP-5 submachine guns into a head-size target in under a second.

The MP-5 was easy to find in Europe. All the armed Metropolitan Police carried them. With the help of their client, these guns were written off from a police inventory after the records on the guns were fudged by an agent to show excessive round counts. The bureaucratic process then placed these guns into inactive status and marked them for destruction. They were placed in a crate and were supposed to go to the metal shredder, but were instead driven by another agent to one of the order's armories.

Once at the armory, each MP-5 underwent a full arsenal rebuild by an armorer trained by the Heckler & Koch factory. During the rebuild, the barrel was changed, a support weldment was added to the receiver, and an integral suppressor was added. When rebuilt into the SD or Schalldämpfer variant, the new MP-5SDs were so close to a factory unit that only an expert could tell the difference. Practically speaking, the suppressor quieted the guns down significantly, so much so that the noise from the action cycling was far louder than the noise from the shot. The MP-5SD was also fast. The gun used a roller-delayed blowback action that used recoil and the pressure from the fired round to cycle the bolt. This allowed the reciprocating parts to be far lighter than a normal blowback submachine gun and allowed a higher cyclic rate. It was the perfect weapon for an aggressive direct action mission against a group of terrorists. Kuba thought about that for a moment. All this waiting and watching was part of the job. Such careful work was professional and assured the best chances for success, but he'd be lying to himself if he weren't looking forward to the actual assault. "Make sure that if you drop a terrorist, you also follow up with an anchoring shot," Jan added. Kuba nodded at this. Anchoring shots were a tactic of African big game hunters. Once the hunter shot the animal he was hunting, he moved to a spot where he could anchor the animal with another well-placed shot. An experienced hunter never approached a wounded animal; he always made sure the animal was dead before he moved in to collect the trophy.

No trophies would be taken tonight, but the assault team would also take no chances. The concept of anchoring shots in missions against ISIS was quietly adopted by counter-terrorism teams all over the world. No one wanted to be shot in the back or blown up by a man who was supposed to be dead. Rules and best practices were good but having them take root required watering with the blood of less careful men, so the assault team would kill the bad guys, then kill them again - just to be sure. Jan looked at the flight crew and said, "Stefan, I want you to fly a racetrack pattern south of the farm. We will call you in case air support or emergency medical evacuation is needed," said Jan. He continued, "Callsign for the helicopter will be 'Rattler'."

"Understood, Captain," Stefan told his superior.

"Captain," Stefan said, "if we need to respond, we must avoid a collision with the drone. I recommend a flight ceiling for the helicopter of 1,000 feet, and a hard deck for the drone of 2,000 feet. That spacing will allow for evasive maneuvers if needed." Jan nodded, "Echo, is this flight altitude acceptable for good resolution from the drone's camera systems?"

Echo replied, "Yes, Captain. More than acceptable." "Team," Jan went on, "the assault frequency will be 140.252 MHz. Aerial frequency will be 141.150." The captain was ready to dismiss the meeting. "Soldiers of the Order, any questions?" Jan's call was answered with silence. "Very well, kit up. We leave in six zero minutes."

Farmhouse

Fahad walked down the steps to the basement. It was time to give their prisoner her last meal. Fahad put the tray down and removed the bolts that secured the door to their prison cell. Inside the cell, Victoria heard the door being unlocked. As it swung open, she ran for the door. Fahad was ready for it, lowered his shoulder and stepped in front of her. Victoria was fast, but a swift 120-pound female will simply not overpower a 235-pound male athlete. Victoria bounced off Fahad like a ping pong ball off a paddle. She landed in a pile on the floor. As she rolled, she could smell the damp concrete; it was cold. Fahad said to her,

"You must be hungry. I have food for you if you'll calm down. Escape is simply not possible; I will not allow it."

Victoria heard his words. She knew he was right. This monster of a man could bench press three times her body weight. Victoria nodded, and Fahad smiled at her and said, "Good. Please sit on the bed." Fahad turned slightly and got the tray. He placed the tray of food next to her. There was bread, hummus, fresh vegetables, and a plastic cup of cold water.

Fahad said to her, "In four hours, I will return. We will be filming a propaganda video."

He gestured to the orange jumpsuit, and said, "You will be dressed in that garment when I return."

He left and bolted the door to Victoria's cell. Inside the cell, Victoria looked over at the plate of food. She could smell its fragrance; she hadn't eaten in hours, and the aroma was nearly intoxicating. Sitting on the bed, alone with her thoughts, Victoria began to understand. She had heard about ISIS in Iraq. They kidnapped people, dressed them in jumpsuits like this, and then killed them. The maniacs filmed every minute of it to distribute as propaganda. With nowhere to go and no one else to turn to, Victoria felt she needed to do something she had not done since she left Idaho. Victoria felt a need to pray. What to say? Victoria tried to remember those days in mass, back when she was a girl in Idaho. Her mother was Catholic and took her and her siblings to mass every Sunday. She tried to remember something, a priest's sermon that would bring her calm. Her mind raced as she tried to remember. *"So long ago,"* she thought, *"I can't even remember verses in the Bible."* It was at that moment of desperation that Victoria noticed a feeling of calm pass over her. She heard a still, small voice whisper words of encouragement into her soul. In that moment, she remembered the Catholic liturgy spoken every Sunday and chose to talk to God and recite part of it from the heart.

I believe in one God, the Father almighty, maker of heaven and earth, of all things visible and invisible.

I believe in one Lord Jesus Christ, the Only Begotten Son of God, born of the Father before all ages. God from God, Light from Light, true God from true God, begotten, not made, consubstantial with the Father; through him all things were made.

For us men and for our salvation, he came down from heaven, and by the Holy Spirit, he was incarnate of the Virgin Mary, and became man. For our sake, he

48

was crucified under Pontius Pilate, suffered death, was buried, and rose again on the third day in accordance with the Scriptures. He ascended into heaven and is seated at the right hand of the Father. He will come again in glory to judge the living and the dead, and his kingdom will have no end.

I believe in the Holy Spirit, the Lord, the giver of life, who proceeds from the Father and the Son, who with the Father and the Son is adored and glorified, and who has spoken through the prophets.

I believe in one holy Catholic and Apostolic Church. I confess one baptism for the forgiveness of sins, and I look forward to the resurrection of the dead and the life of the world to come.

Amen.

She finished the Nicene Creed, spoken by Catholics throughout the world each Sunday, and felt the fear and doubt melt away with each word. She was then moved to tell God the whole truth and ask for help.

And Lord, you know me, and you know my heart. I'm scared of dying, and I do not know if I measure up. But you told me through your words that you listen to the cries of your children. I want you to send me an angel to defend my life in my time of need. But if it is my time to go, let me come home to you without fear.

It seemed the proper thing to do.

The image of the farmhouse slowly turned on the screen as the drone orbited overhead. Echo watched the image inside the cargo container. He could also see the team advancing to their positions. The IR strobe lights attached to their ballistic helmets were easy to see on the drone's FLIR camera. Jan ordered his team to halt at an old shed. This was the waypoint where the sniper element would break off and advance to their firing position. The assault element that Jan was leading would advance to the farmhouse by crawling next to a stone wall. They would wait at the end of the wall until the sniper team gave the all-clear signal on the radio. The men were dressed in stone-gray uniforms. A patch of the Maltese Cross of the Order of Saint John on their right shoulder and their name on their breast were the only adornment on their uniforms. Each man wore a grey vest-like plate carrier that held body armor that could stop a rifle bullet fired out of the enemy's carbines. The plate carriers had pouches for extra magazines, and each man wore a Heckler & Koch USP 9mm on their belt. The pistols were used when things went very wrong; a jam for instance. The team could have chosen any sidearm they wanted, but they went with the USP because the environmental conditions were harsh that night. Jan had a stripe of reflective IR tape stuck down the back of his helmet. The last time the world was at war, this stripe meant "officer" to American soldiers who walked these very hills on training missions seventy years ago. The sniper element peeled off the main group and began to sneak towards their shooting position.

Victoria heard the bolt to the cell door click. Fahad stepped through the door and saw Victoria sitting on the cot. The tray was next to her, the food on it had been eaten. Victoria's clothes were neatly folded in the same place where the jumpsuit was placed. He said to her, "Thank you for getting dressed as I ordered. We will go upstairs to film a short video. I don't think it will be long - no more than fifteen minutes. After we're done, I'll bring you back down here, and you can rest."

Victoria looked up at him, she knew he was lying. It was his eyes, they darted all over the place as he spoke. Victoria was frightened, but at peace too. She would be seeing Jesus soon, just as Paul had written about in his second letter to the church in Corinth. Victoria held on to those words as Fahad took her by the arm and walked her out of the cell. They climbed the stairs together, the old timber creaking under their combined weight. They entered the main floor of the farmhouse and walked down the hallway to the back bedroom. Victoria suppressed her natural fear. *"That's the flesh talking,"* she thought. Eternity with her Lord and Savior awaited. Victoria felt peace grow inside her with each step. By the time she and Fahad stepped inside the room, Victoria had grown past her fear of dying; she felt only calm.

Anatol and Olek slowly moved past a parked tractor on their way to the hay barn. Before they left the concealment of the tractor, Anatol did a slow scan of his surroundings. He was looking for any movement or something that did not belong; his ears were listening for any sound that would reveal the presence of an enemy. The world took on a pale green hue through his PVS-31 night vision goggles. He repeated the scan once more and signaled Olek to cover him as he moved to the hay barn structure itself. Anatol kept low and covered the distance quickly; he did not want to be seen in the open. Still, he had to be extremely cautious about noise. Noise traveled far on a cold night, and there is no sound quite like the rhythmic noise of a man running. Once Anatol got to the wall, he turned and looked at Olek.

Olek repeated the scan Anatol did just a moment ago, then hurried across the open area. Olek stacked up behind the sniper and put his hand on Anatol's shoulder, giving it a squeeze. Anatol moved slowly along the wall towards the exterior door, with Olek right behind him. When both men got to the door, Anatol slid an endoscopic camera under the door and slowly moved it around. On the small screen attached to the other end of the camera wire, Anatol watched for any dangers waiting for them on the other side. Running into a sentry that was missed by their intelligence assessment - or worse, running into a tripwire attached to a mine, could blow the mission. Seeing nothing, Anatol placed his hand on the door and turned the knob very slowly. The door gently opened, and both men stood and moved purposefully through the door to minimize their time silhouetted on the threshold. They blazed inside the barn, MP-5SDs at the ready. They ran in opposite directions for about ten feet and then swung their muzzles back to the center of the room. There was nothing.

The hay barn was an a-frame type of building, with large barn doors open at one end. Every twelve feet, there was a 6x6 column that supported the ceiling joists and rafters. Anatol moved to one of these columns and slung his MP-

5SD. He reached around and opened his backpack. Anatol extracted his compact Tikka T3 bolt-action sniper rifle. He flipped up his NVDs, took the weapon off **INACTIVE** which disabled the firing pin and locked the bolt in place, and put it on **SAFE**. He tapped the magazine with the palm of his hand and manipulated the bolt, slowly chambering a live round. Anatol trapped the rifle's sling between his hand and the column, as if he were making a stop gesture. He placed the butt of the rifle into his shoulder pocket and leaned into the rifle. This put tension on the sling and took all the slack out of his firing position. The rifle's weight was now fully supported by the sling and his own body weight; he could hold this standing position comfortably for a long time. Olek unpacked a large sheet of cheesecloth from his pack. He used pushpins to secure one end to the barn rafters and used a pair of pails he found to secure the bottom of the cloth to the floor.

When stretched, this cloth would block an enemy from seeing the sniper team but would allow unobstructed viewing of the target area. This technique was a simple trick of physics that would make the sniper team disappear in plain sight. Olek did not break out his spotting scope. He wanted the widest field of view possible in case an unexpected enemy came into their target area. It was too easy to get tunnel vision when performing a task like this, and survival meant seeing the enemy before they saw you. Olek smiled. *"If things do happen to go downhill, I brought a little surprise with me,"* he thought as he glanced down at the large, heavy bag he had brought with him. Anatol flipped the caps off the lenses of his scope and activated the clip on his NVD in front of his Kahles rifle scope. The whole farmhouse in front of him glowed a pale green. Anatol turned the magnification dial on the scope to **6X**. Higher magnification would not be necessary. He could hear Olek whisper to him, "Sniper, right front yard to edge of house, Sector one. House edge to house edge, sector two. House edge to backyard, Sector three." The spotter divided up their view from the hide into sectors. The sectors would be used to quickly identify targets and threats. Both men settled in and waited.

Movement.

He saw the sentry. Olek whispered, "Sniper, enemy contact sector three." Anatol swung the rifle, so the scope crosshairs centered the man's head, and Anatol began to track him. He whispered to his spotter, "Enemy Contact Front, Sector Three. Enemy wearing a black coat, armed with an AK-105." Olek responded quietly, "Roger, sniper. That's your target." Olek pushed the **ILLUMINATE** button on a laser rangefinder. Through the NVD he was wearing, a green laser streak appeared momentarily as it shone through a hole cut in the cheesecloth. "Sniper, target range is ninety three meters. Set parallax and mils." Olek read off the data from his rangefinder. Anatol looked up and gave his elevation turret 1/10 of a mil of adjustment from the ninety meter zero. He twisted the parallax knob to bring the image in the scope into perfect focus.

The bullet would fly true. It was time. Anatol pushed the safety lever forward to **FIRE** and waited with his finger just in front of the trigger. Anatol whispered to Olek, "Call it in."

Echo waited at his console, watching the assault team creep forward. They were almost in position. He heard Olek say over the communication system, "Echo, sniper team ready. One enemy in sight. Standing by to fire." "Echo copies the sniper team," Echo said, "waiting for the assault team to get in position. Continue to track targets and hold fire."

The sentry Anatol was tracking disappeared from Sector 3 around the back of the farmhouse. Anatol swung his rifle to sector one and waited. There. Anatol saw the sentry's head come into the crosshairs of his rifle scope. He watched the man's head slowly move up and down as he walked. It was always the same. His targets never knew he was there, stalking them. These men were a particularly nasty lot, and it brought feelings of humor to the sniper that tonight, a far more dangerous predator hunted this territory. This man in the crosshairs would soon learn that sometimes dark corners held the brilliant fury of the righteous.

Almost there.

He was the end of the wall. Jan gave his assault team a hand signal to *"make weapons ready."* All four men rotated their MP-5SDs slightly to the side and flipped the selector from **SICHER** to **FEUERSTOß**. They kept their fingers outside the trigger guard. One trigger press would send a full auto burst down range. Jan pressed a PTT button on the microphone, clipped his plate carrier, and called Echo on the com system, "Echo, assault team in position. Do you see any changes in enemy strength or positions?"

Echo said, "No, Captain. Two enemy sentries are circling the house. No changes to patrol patterns or additional enemy units."

Jan took a slow breath and pressed the PTT button on his communication system. He whispered, "Sniper, weapons free."

Khalid looked up. He saw Fahad bring their prisoner into the room. *"Odd,"* he thought, *"She doesn't look like the terrified girl we threw in the van in the morning."* Khalid put this aside, he had work to do and the broadcast time was approaching. Fahad brought the girl over. Khalid said, "You will kneel here. We will be making a short propaganda film to inspire Muslims suffering under the rule of the infidel. You will be silent for the broadcast. When we are finished, you can go back to your room to rest."

Victoria stared at him the whole time, her face impassive. She wasn't really listening to Khalid; her thoughts were occupied with the throne room of heaven and all the wonders she would see there. Khalid went on, "For the video, you will wear these." He produced a set of handcuffs and locked her wrists behind her back. Fahad led her to an X marked with tape on the floor and helped her sit down.

Fahad spoke to Khalid in Arabic, "Are we ready, brother?"

Khalid answered, "Yes. We will broadcast in five minutes. Get ready with the others." Fahad nodded and began putting on a balaclava and throwing a chest rig onto his shoulders. The other men were ready. These two, the ones from the local mosque, were looking at him. One was running the camera equipment and monitoring the video streaming portal; the other was dressed the same as Fahad, ready to take his place on screen.

Fahad said to them in Arabic, "Be strong now, brothers. You serve a higher purpose with us today." Both men nodded. Four minutes to broadcast.

"Sniper, the enemy sentry is about to enter Sector Three," Olek whispered to Anatol. Olek had flipped up his PVS-31 goggles and was using a 6x NVD to better see the shot placement. Anatol got ready to break the shot. He saw the sentry pass the edge of the farmhouse, about to go to the back side. He whispered, *"Ready."*

Olek was fast with his response, "Sniper, kill zone clear, wind zero value, send it." Anatol applied pressure to the rifle's trigger. It broke like a glass rod.

PFFFTT

The rifle sounded like a pellet gun being fired into a pillow. Olek watched the sentry's head snap back. The sentry dropped like a marionette with its strings cut. Olek whispered, "Enemy down, rotate to sector one." Anatol quickly swung his rifle to wait for the next sentry. There. Anatol saw the sentry's head come into the circular, green-hued image he saw through his scope lens. Olek saw it too; he whispered, "Sniper, wind value still zero, kill zone clear, send it." Anatol pressed the trigger once more.

PFFFTT

Two thousand feet above, Echo saw the second sentry fall on the snow-covered ground. Through the infrared camera looking down, he could see the man's blood on the ground. It was still warm, and looked white on the screen. "Captain, both sentries eliminated. No other movement," he said over the radio.

Jan motioned with his hand to the assault team: "Rally point one, go." The assault team stood up as one and jogged silently to the first spot near the door to the kitchen. Here they grouped up in single file, with Aleksy in front, followed by Kuba. Jan was third in line. Lew covered the rear. Aleksy flipped up his PVS-31 goggles, opened up a pouch on the side of his plate carrier, and removed an endoscopic camera. He slid the lens under the door and scowled at the screen. One of the off-duty sentries was sitting at the kitchen table, cleaning his weapon. Looking a bit to the right, Aleksy could see the other sentry sleeping on a cot in the living room. Okay. Aleksy put the camera away and held up two fingers. He then made the hand signal for enemy unarmed. Jan turned and whispered to Lew, "Stack up for entry."

Relieved of his rear cover duty, Lew turned and gave Jan's shoulder a squeeze. Jan repeated the gesture to Kuba, and Kuba did the same to Aleksy. Aleksy thought, *"Okay. Let's go."* He put his hand on the doorknob and slowly turned the knob. The off-duty sentry had just finished cleaning his weapon. He had reassembled the bolt carrier when he saw the kitchen door swing open. *"Odd,"* he thought. *"We aren't supposed to relive the men outside for at least another hour...Is something wrong?"* His question was answered with what came through the door next. A soldier dressed in grey. Death had come calling, and he felt a bolt of fear pulse through his nervous system. Aleksy was through the door in a flash. He was already bringing his MP-5SD up as he saw the enemy's shocked face. He saw the red reticle from the EoTech optic trace up the enemy's torso as he applied pressure to the trigger.

TAC-TAC-TAC-TAC-TAC-TAC-TAC

He held low on the man's neck and walked the rounds from his SMG into the terrorist's face. The terrorist's head broke apart from the impact of the Federal HST 9mm hollow points, and his lifeless body slid out of the chair onto the floor. Kuba was right behind Aleksy and turned quickly to the right. There. His target had just been jarred out of his sleep by the action noise from Aleksy's MP-5SD. The enemy sentry was struggling to get up and grab his weapon - too late. Kuba leveled his own MP-5SD at the back of the terrorist's head and squeezed the trigger.

TAC-TAC-TAC-TAC

The enemy's head came apart like a water balloon. Skull fragments danced around the air like confetti. As the sentry fell to the floor, Kuba was already scanning for more threats in the living room. Aleksy was doing the same, and the Captain and Lew had already come into the kitchen, covering the hallway to where the captive was held. Finding no threats, Kuba swung his SMG down to what remained of the fallen enemy's head and fired three more rounds. He could hear Aleksy doing the same ten feet to his left.

Enemy sentries eliminated.

Aleksy and Kuba came back to the kitchen to regroup with Lew and the captain. Jan signaled Aleksy and Kuba to move down the hall. The team could hear a man shouting in Arabic behind a closed door. They smoothly moved down the hall, sure of their footing and careful not to betray their position with an errant noise. Aleksy stopped when he reached the closed door. He held his hand up and made the gesture for demo up. Lew, the combat engineer, moved forward in front of the door and secured the detonation cord to the door with tape. He quickly attached two blasting caps to the detonation cord and attached electrical leads to the caps. Only one blasting cap was needed to detonate the det cord; the second one was insurance. As Lew strung the electrical leads out of a pouch in his vest, Aleksy slowly and with utmost caution slid the endoscopic camera under the door. He was careful not to let the lens protrude past the door frame. From the awkward angle on the viewing screen, four men could be seen. One was seated at a table facing away from the door. The others faced the door but were looking at the camera. The terrorist's captive knelt at the feet of the man speaking Arabic to the camera. Good. The hostage was not in the line of fire. Jan squeezed Aleksy's shoulder. It was time to breach. Lew's thumb hovered over the detonator lever.

Khalid was speaking in Arabic with all the passion of an imam. He remembered his family, how they were killed by the Baathists years ago. He remembered the US Marines moving about his city with impunity. He remembered the anger and rage he felt in his heart and poured them out to the world through the camera attached to the internet. It was time to show the world his resolve. He removed a combat knife from its sheath clipped to his belt and held it high as he spoke. He grasped the back of Victoria's hair with his left hand and lulled her head back to expose her neck. She looked up with a peaceful expression. *"She must be a Christian,"* he thought. *"All of them die like this."* Very well. He moved forward with the knife and shouted, "Allahu Ackbar! Allahu Ackbar! Allahu Ackbar!" The door to the room disintegrated in a flash of yellow, encircled by a wreath of oily smoke. The flash was followed by a deafening roar.

Chapter 3

The assault team looked away and braced themselves for the blast. Once it arrived, Aleksy had his MP-5SD up and moved forward towards the smoking hole that used to be a door. He entered the room and moved towards the left corner. Kuba was right behind him, but he turned and went right. Both men saw there were no threats in their corners and pivoted their SMGs back to the center of the room.

Contact!

Each man saw a dazed terrorist. They snapped their MP5-SDs to bear and pressed the triggers. The heads of both enemies snapped back, and the bodies went limp. Jan was the third man through the door and saw two terrorists in front of him. He pressed the trigger of his MP-5SD and sent a burst of 9mm hollow points into Khalid's face. Khalid fell to the ground in a crumpled heap. There was one more terrorist directly in front of Jan. He lowered his SMG in a flash and pressed the trigger once more. The terrorist's body spasmed and went slack. It was over. "Soldiers of the order, report in!" said the captain in a booming voice.

"Clear!" replied Aleksy.

"Clear!" replied Lew.

Kuba was last with his report. In the excitement, he let his English slip back into Polish, "Jasny, Kapitan!!"

The Captain ordered his men, "Secure the room! Well done, soldiers!" There was a radio call to make: "Echo, assault successful. No team casualties; eight tangos eliminated; one hostage rescued. Continue to monitor the surrounding area."

Anatol and Olek looked at each other briefly and nodded. *"Well done, gents!"* Anatol thought. A few more minutes out here, and they would move back to the rally point. Their job was technically complete, but the sniper team would cover the farmhouse until the assault team ordered them off their hide.

Aleksy and Kuba continued to move forward and put a burst of 9mm into the head of each terrorist. These evil men would never hurt anyone ever again. Finished, Aleksy and Kuba pulled the charging handles back to the locking notches on their MP-5SD's, stripped the magazines from the receivers, inserted fresh magazines, and slapped the SMG's charging handles home with the palms of their hands. The reloading of their weapons was fluid and practiced thousands of times. Finished, they each slung their weapon. Jan moved forward and picked up the female hostage with his strong hands. She was limp in his arms as he lifted her off the ground like a child. Jan held her close as he carried her to a corner of the room and gently set her down on the floor. Lew was collecting intelligence. He called to Jan, "Captain, the blast took out the camera and the laptop that was handling the internet connection. Their video stream was interrupted." Jan nodded. "Echo, can you confirm loss of their stream?"

"Roger, Captain. The stream was interrupted on the ISIS website," Echo responded. Echo let out a slow breath. *"Thank God we got there in time,"* Echo thought. "Another five seconds, and they would have killed her." There were more important matters that demanded his attention. Echo returned to monitoring the IR feed from the circling drone.

Jan looked the hostage over. She had passed out from the overpressure from the detonation cord, and she wouldn't be able to hear anything for a while. He took out a vial of ammonium carbonate, broke it, and placed it under her nose. Victoria was instantly awake. She tried to push him away, only to lose her balance and fall back down. Jan held up his hands and pointed to his ear. Victoria slowly realized she was unable to hear anything. In a panic, she thought, *"Am I deaf?"* She suppressed the surge of adrenaline and looked up at Jan. He was holding a small notebook. She read:

You're safe. Hearing will come back soon. Are you hurt?

She shook her head, no. She could start to hear distorted sounds and men talking. Jan wrote her another message on the pad:

Wait here. Don't stand; the explosion made you very dizzy. We will take you home.

She nodded and sat up, leaning her back against the wall. She had a roaring headache, so she closed her eyes and tried to will the pain to go away. Jan stood and walked over to Lew. "Lew, were you able to recover anything from the laptop?" he asked.

Lew answered, "No, Captain. We need to get this back and get at the hard drive to see if we can pull any intelligence out."

Jan nodded and turned to the others, saying, "Get what you can; we exfil in five minutes." Next, Jan called Anatol on the radio, "Sniper team, copy?"

Anatol and Olek heard the captain's voice through their tactical headphones, "Roger Captain, Sniper team copies, go ahead."

Jan said to them, "We exfil structure in five minutes; get ready to abandon hide."

"Sniper team copies, Captain," Anatol answered over the radio. He looked at Olek and nodded. Olek nodded in return and began to remove the cheesecloth from the ceiling joists. Anatol put his rifle on **SAFE** removed the live round from the chamber, closed the bolt, and flipped the selector to **INACTIVE**. He slowly got out of his shooting position. He slung the rifle and stretched his shoulders and back.

Victoria's hearing was slowly returning. She looked over at the armed men and thought, *"Who were these guys?"* She looked at the floor and saw the dead terrorists, *"They killed them all?"*

She looked over at the man who wrote her the messages and said, "Who are you?" Jan walked over and knelt by her side.

"Who we are doesn't matter now; all that matters is that you're safe. We are going to take you out of here, and then we will drive you to a hospital." Victoria nodded, still not sure what was going on.

Echo's voice over the radio interrupted the team. "Attention, Captain! I have enemy QRF inbound to your position! ETA two-zero seconds!" Echo saw the two vans in close formation turn off the main road and accelerate down the driveway. That could mean only one thing: that an enemy quick-reaction force was responding to the assault.

Anatol and Olek heard the warning on the radio. They could hear the vans roaring down the gravel driveway. They froze mid-task and shared a thought. The assault team was going to be overrun. They could not fight off what had to be twenty or more members of the QRF. Anatol shoved a fresh magazine back into his rifle, worked the bolt to feed a round into the chamber, turned the magnification ring down as far as it would go, and flipped the selector to **FIRE**. He began to scan for targets as Olek unzipped the bag he brought with him. He lugged this heavy bag along just in case the mission went sideways. Olek reached inside the bag and extracted an FN Herstal M-249E3 squad automatic weapon. This was the paratrooper model, with a short barrel and collapsible stock. He lifted the machine gun's top cover and extracted the belt of ammunition from the bag slung beneath the weapon. He placed the belt across the pawls on the feed tray, slapped the top cover closed, and charged the action. He made sure the weapon's selector was set to "SAFE" and activated the AN/PEQ-15 infrared laser. The laser was invisible to the naked eye, but it had the appearance of a continuous green beam when seen under NVDs. Olek looked at Anatol and whispered, "Ready."

The QRF team members dismounted from the vans as they came to a stop. Twenty-five men dressed in black tactical clothing and plate carriers armed with 5.56mm M4 rifles jumped out and began to take positions. They saw the dead ISIS sentries lying in the snow as they ran to their positions. One of the men, a lieutenant, began to give orders and direct his men. They would assault the house and kill anyone inside.

"Captain, the enemy QRF has dismounted and is securing the area," Echo said over the communications net. "I'd say you have about thirty seconds before they try to breach."

Jan responded, "Copy, Echo. Enemy strength?"

Echo answered, "Twenty-five men, Captain." Jan paused for a second to get his breathing back under control. He knew that they were going to have to fight their way out of this. He thought for another second and then called Echo once more, saying, "Echo, I need air support. Call Rattler and get them moving to our location."

"Copy that, Captain," Echo told his commander. Echo changed the frequency on his tactical radio. "Rattler, this is Echo; how copy, over?"

Stefan heard the call through the speakers in his helmet and keyed the PTT button in the Eurocopter EC155's cockpit. He spoke clearly: "Echo, this is Rattler; I copy you five by five."

Echo took a deep breath and said, "Rattler, Assault team has encountered enemy QRF and requests immediate air support."

Stefan pushed the cyclic to starboard and gave the aircraft a bit of right rudder. The EC155 tucked into a fast right turn as Stefan swung the nose of the aircraft to bear on the farmhouse, ten kilometers to the north of their position. Stefan looked at Filip, his co-pilot, and at Igor, the door gunner. Igor gave the pilot a thumbs-up gesture as he opened the sliding door of the EC155 and swung the FN MAG out the door on its pintle mount. He lifted the top cover of the 7.62 NATO machine gun and fed the first links of the ammunition belt into the feed tray. He then slapped the top cover closed and pulled the FN MAG's charging handle. He swung down the night vision goggles attached to his helmet and activated the PEQ-15 infrared laser mounted to the weapon. Igor said over the helicopter's communications system, "Gunner ready."

Stefan hit the PTT button and said to Echo, "We are Oscar-Mike, Echo. ETA farmhouse two minutes."

Echo responded to the pilot racing North in his aircraft, "I copy all, Rattler. Switch your radio frequency to the assault channel: 140.252 MHz."

Stefan looked over at Filip, who had already set the radio to the new frequency. Stefan hit the PTT button once more and said, "Assault team, this is Rattler. En-route to your position, ETA: one minute, forty-five seconds. Make sure your IR strobes are active."

Jan smiled; things were about to get exceedingly difficult for the enemy. "Copy, Rattler," Jan said to the pilot over the radio, "The assault team is inside the farmhouse, and the sniper team is inside the barn. All personnel outside are enemies. Coordinate with Echo for enemy positions once you get on station."

"Be there soon, gents," Stefan thought to himself. "Rattler copies, assault team - ETA 90 seconds," Stefan said as he eased his grip on the cyclic control a bit. The air was dead still on this

cold January night, and that made his job easier. *"One more minute, and then we eat the enemy alive,"* Stefan thought as he glanced at Igor. Igor was a surgeon with the FN MAG.

Jan radioed Anatol, "Sniper team, I want you to drop the enemy officers. Olek, fire at will with the SAW after Anatol takes his first shot."

"Copy, Captain," Anatol said, "I've already got a bead on their officer; stand by." Anatol had found the leader of the QRF.

Lieutenant Aubert saw his men stack up at the front door of the farmhouse. The third man in line, the team leader, looked at him. Lieutenant Aubert raised his hand above his head to give the signal to breach when a 200-grain bullet entered his skull. The lieutenant dropped to the frozen ground where he stood. There was no sound at all. *"What the hell?"* the assault team leader thought. He looked away for one second, and now the boss was lying down. *"Did he fall?"*

Olek already had his M-249 leveled at the assault team. When he heard the quiet shot from Anatol's rifle, he flipped the selector to **FIRE** and pressed the trigger. The weapon roared and pushed against his shoulder as it poured fire down range at 1,100 rounds per minute. Acrid smoke filled his nasal cavity, and his eyes burned. The QRF team getting ready to breach did not have a chance. They were cut down by machine gun fire in two seconds; each man was shot more than once. Olek held the trigger down on the fallen men for one more second before swiveling towards a man trying to run away from the machine gun fire. Olek put the laser beam just in front of the runner and shot him mid-stride.

Anatol saw another man who was barking orders and waving his hand as he ran to cover. *"He will do,"* Anatol thought as he pressed the trigger. The bullet quietly left the rifle and struck the man in the hip, shattering his pelvic girdle. He screamed as he fell mid-stride onto the snowy ground. Two QRF soldiers ran to their wounded comrade. The wounded man frantically waved at them to get back when the first man fell to the ground with a bullet in his head. The rifle report could not be heard; the only audible sound was like someone throwing a wet tennis ball against a wall. The second man froze, realizing his mistake in running to a man wounded by a sniper on the battlefield. *"It was a trap..."* The man could not finish his thought as the world went black.

"Regroup on me! Stay out of the line of fire of that machine gunner!" Sergeant Fournier shouted into his radio. Not even one minute in, and the mission had gone to hell. He still had one team of ten men in the last van. "Corporal Petit," he called on the radio channel, "get away from the van and flank that machine gunner. Breach the door to the barn and use frag grenades."

The junior man answered his commander, "Roger, sergeant!" To his men, "Okay boys, advance on that barn to the west and hold at the door - MOVE!!" The squad quickly moved in formation to the barn and stacked up near the door.

Corporal Petit was ready with orders: "Leferve, you will kick open that door. Dumont and Lambert, right behind him with frag grenades. We wait for the detonation and then we breach. Weapons are free, boys; let's get those devils!"

"Echo, tell me where our guests are," Jan said into his radio.

"Captain, what remains of the main group is behind the farmhouse, East side," Echo said over the communication net.

"There are three men remaining. Be advised, another element of ten men is advancing on the barn and is trying to flank the sniper team," Echo added.

Jan replied, "I copy all, Echo."

It was time for Anatol and Olek to leave. Jan asked them, "Sniper team, did you hear that?" Anatol cycled the action of his rifle. Another enemy soldier was down. He looked at Olek and said, "Time to go, brother." Olek nodded and adjusted the M-249's sling so he could shoot it on the move. Anatol and Olek stood up and turned around when they saw the door to the barn fling open. An explosion thundered through the barn.

The entry team kicked open the door and threw two M-65 fragmentation grenades inside the barn. Dumont and Lambert had cooked off the grenades by popping the grenade handles a second before Leferve kicked the door open. Dumont rushed inside the barn, with Lambert right behind him. They were met with a barrage of automatic gunfire from Olek's M-249. Olek and Anatol saw the door violently open and instinctively dove into the animal stalls that lined the walls of the barn and hit the floor. Their ingrained reactions saved them, as they were far away enough that shrapnel from the grenade explosions impacted harmlessly into the wooden walls of the stalls. Fighting through the fog of the overpressure from the explosion, Olek fired a twenty-round burst of 5.56 NATO where he thought the door was. He shakily got to his feet and stumbled back to better cover, firing three- to five-round bursts at anything that moved. He could not see Anatol. No matter - he had to hold these men off until Rattler got on station. Olek threw two M-84 flash bang grenades back towards the door. The instant they went off, he started to reload the M-249; he had done it many times before, but this repetition was so fast, it must have been a world record. He lay down and deployed the M-249's bipod. He had a perfect sight line to the door and the surrounding area.

"Okay," he thought, *"now let them come."*

He pushed the PTT button on his tactical radio. "Captain, this is the Sniper Team," he called into the radio. "We've been cut off from you; I cannot see Anatol; we need help over here."

"Uh-oh," Jan thought. "Rattler, when you arrive, I need you to hammer any enemy personnel outside the barn," he told Stefan over the radio. Stefan hit the PTT button and said, "Copy Captain. Hang on, lads, I'm almost there!" Stefan pulled back on the collective, and the EC155 rocketed skyward. Once Stefan reached an altitude of 1,000 feet, he leveled off and pulled back on the

stick a bit to slow the aircraft down. He also moved the pedals to turn the aircraft slightly so it could orbit the target area. Igor was looking down, scanning for targets.

Outside the barn, there was chaos. Corporal Petit had three men down. Dumont, Lambert, and Leferve had been hit by automatic gunfire the second they rushed inside the barn. Petit did not know if they were wounded or dead; regardless, they were out of the fight. Petit knew his assault force was exposed here, stacked up on the side of the barn. He did not believe for a second that the exterior walls of an agricultural building would provide cover from a light machine gun. He had to withdraw fast.

"The stone wall," he thought.

"Bravo team!" Petit called to his men, "Over the wall!" The remains of the Bravo team scrambled over the low stone wall that Jan and his team followed to the farmhouse minutes earlier. Petit looked over at one of his men.

He ordered, "Leon, go back to the van and get the RPG! The rest of you, spread out along this wall and hold!" Petit could hear an odd sound overhead, a low whistling.

The sound he heard was the EC155's Fenestron, or fantail tail rotor system, developed by Eurocopter decades ago. Igor saw a man break away from the group, hiding behind a low wall. *"Where are you going?"* Igor thought.

"Pilot, I have multiple targets below, ready to engage," he said over the aircraft's intercom system. Stefan had slowed his aircraft to a crawl right at 1,000 feet, just to the south of the farmhouse property. Stefan held the PTT down and broadcasted over the assault channel, "Rattler on station, Gunner, weapons free!"

Leon ran as fast as he could. He had to get to the safety of the van and out of the line of fire of that light machine gun and that sniper. He felt as though he were being watched, and he ran even faster. Almost there, just another few meters, and...

Igor put the laser beam just ahead of the runner and pressed the spade trigger on the FN MAG. Every second, fifteen bullets rained down from above. Igor saw the runner fall and put another burst of automatic gunfire into his body. He then immediately swung the machine gun back to the wall and began shooting at the enemy huddled behind the wall. Stefan had effectively flanked the enemy's position with the helicopter, allowing Igor to pick off the enemy at will. Igor thought, *"This was so unfair; it's like shooting fish in a barrel."* And it was. Proper planning and careful consideration of outcomes in combat deliver situations just like this to professional operators. The last man behind the wall tried to stand and run, but Igor cut him down with another two-second burst from the FN MAG. "Pilot," Igor called, "enemy forces eliminated!" It was time to reload the FN MAG. Igor performed this task quickly and got his gun back into the fight. Stefan was already on the radio with Echo: "Echo, this is Rattler. Enemy forces have been eliminated by the barn; do we have any additional targets?"

Echo radioed back to the pilot, "Rattler, we have three more enemy personnel taking cover behind the farmhouse, east side." Echo added, "Echo to assault team, move away from the rooms of the house facing east." That was all Jan needed to hear; "Roger that, Echo. Rattler, I'll call you when we are out of the room."

He looked at the assault team and said, "Gents, time to move. Fall back to the kitchen." He looked down at Victoria and said, "We need to move away from the walls." He pointed to the wall and said, "The enemy is on the other side." Victoria looked at the wall, stood, and nodded at Jan. Lew looked at her and motioned for her to step over to him. He said to her, "Stay right behind me." Victoria nodded as Aleksy and Kuba raised their MP-5SD's and exited the room back towards the kitchen.

Lew looked at Victoria, pointed to the handle on the back of his plate carrier intended to pull an injured man to safety, and said, "Hold onto this. Go where I go." She nodded, and Lew led her out of the room, his MP-5SD at high ready. Victoria could hear her footsteps echo on the old wood floors. The hallway was cold. Lew led Victoria into the kitchen, and from there she saw the two dead terrorists the assault team eliminated earlier. Victoria thought to herself, *"What on earth? Who were these guys?"* Jan was the last man to step into the hallway when he called Stefan on the radio, "Rattler, this is assault team. We are clear of the East rooms of the structure."

In the orbiting aircraft above, Stefan heard the transmission from Jan below. *"Okay, now we finish the job,"* he thought. Stefan pressed the PTT button on the aircraft intercom once again as he guided the EC155 above the property below: "Gunner, weapons free on East side of structure."

Igor's voice responded back through Stefan's helmet, "Roger, Pilot. Stand by..." This shot was a bit trickier than the one by the stone wall. Igor had to account not only for the aircraft movement and the downwash of the rotor blade, but he also had to ensure his fire would not stray off target and accidentally strike the hostage or a member of the assault team. He saw the group of enemies below him, and he held his aiming point at a spot above and just behind where he wanted his fire to go. He pressed the spade grip on the FN MAG, and the gun roared again. Igor saw a line of tracers streak down to the cold ground below.

On his IR feed 2,000 feet above the ground, Echo could see the carnage through the rotor blades of the helicopter. He saw the three figures blazing white on the screen, and then white blobs and pieces started to come off the once well-defined figures as Igor started shooting. Echo heard on the assault frequency, "Echo, this is Rattler; do you see any other enemy forces?"

Echo told the pilot, "Negative, Rattler. All enemy forces eliminated."

In the kitchen, Jan let out a slow breath. He had orders to issue. "Assault team to sniper team," Jan said over the radio.

The reply came quickly: "Copy that, Captain," Olek said. "There has been no contact with the enemy since the last transmission."

"Copy," Jan said, "enemy QRF eliminated; start looking for Anatol; we will come to you, and then we move to the LZ." Olek stood up and slung his M-249. He shouldered his MP-5SD and began cautiously moving forward towards the bodies of the QRF team. He moved to each man, making sure they were dead. Satisfied, Olek turned to look for his brother. "Anatol," he whispered. "Here," came the reply. Olek moved quickly to his brother's side. Anatol was sitting in one of the horse stalls with his MP-5SD trained at the door. Olek looked down at him and said, "Time to go, brother."

Chapter 4

Schloss Drouin, Federal Republic of Germany

The dark pine forest flew by as the dark blue Mercedes-Benz sedan carved its way up the road. Cradled in the warm embrace of the heated tan leather seat, the driver was troubled. He had to deliver the news of a failed mission to a man not known for his patience. The driver slowed for a corner, then buried the throttle of the Mercedes. The car accelerated out of the turn like a cheetah, the big V-8 engine roaring under the hood. *"This posting did have its perks,"* thought the driver as he smiled and marveled at the performance of this amazing car.

He had been driving on this road for the past fifteen minutes. Outwardly, the road appeared to carve through a national park, the type of road that vacationers would use to travel to a campsite or vista point, but it was nothing of the sort. This road was privately built and impeccably maintained. The forest was not a national park, but a vast estate owned by one of the wealthiest families in Europe. One could not simply wander onto this forest drive; there was a gate at the only entrance to the road staffed by armed guards. Anyone not on the list of approved visitors was politely but firmly turned away.

The driver was reminded of his training class at the infamous spy school for the Central Intelligence Agency (CIA). A section of a military base in eastern Virginia had been transformed into a CIA training facility where all field agents underwent instruction in the arts of spy craft and were subsequently assigned postings upon graduation.

While most of his classmates were sent to the Middle East, Afghanistan, or Southeast Asia for counterterrorism missions; he and one other student achieved high scores and were chosen for postings in Europe. *"Only the CIA's best went to Europe,"* he thought. *"After all, that's where all the world's conflicts began."*

He couldn't believe his luck when, less than a year after graduating, the station chief in Paris approached him with an assignment. Initially, it seemed like he was given an agent to manage. However, the initial meeting took an unexpected turn. He met an older man from an aristocratic background with immense wealth. Instead of seeking to provide information, this man expressed his desire to partner with the CIA. His goal was to politically destabilize Europe through terrorism, utilizing ISIS fighters who were blending in with the influx of people migrating to Europe from Syria and Iraq.

Recognizing the gravity of this revelation, the driver promptly reported it to his superiors, believing he had uncovered a significant source of funding for Islamic terrorism in Europe. The response to his report was even more peculiar:

Request from agent approved – furnish any CIA assets or resources requested without delay.

Money was not a concern in this arrangement. Instead, the CIA made available its equipment, relationships, and highly classified intelligence. Some of the intelligence he received exceeded his clearance level and came dangerously close to revealing the identity of sources—the most closely guarded secrets within any intelligence agency. Additionally, the CIA provided its technology and analytical resources to a private citizen in a foreign country. The arrangement violated every rule his instructors taught him at the "farm."

None of his training at the CIA facility could have prepared him for this unique situation. The involvement of the Director of Central

Intelligence and potentially even the Executive Office of the President of the United States added to the mystery. He couldn't fathom how this geopolitical puzzle fit together, but he had received the authorization to carry out his operation and was instructed to handle requests and approvals without asking questions.

He was too junior to be involved in the why's or the how's of such a sensitive operation; his focus was solely on his participation and the opportunity it presented for his career. The benefits of working for the wealthy man were extraordinary, as demonstrated by the recently gifted Mercedes sedan that now served as his transportation. The car had been personally delivered by a Mercedes employee from the factory in Sindelfingen, who handed him the key and departed, silently emphasizing the older man's power and influence. *"The turn is coming up,"* he reminded himself.

He slowed the car once again to throw the vehicle into a tight corner, this time a hairpin turn. He was sure to heed the posted sign advising a maximum speed of 30 kph; any faster would send the car off the road. Exiting the turn, the road stretched out into a long straightaway, but he refrained from opening up the throttle. *"One does not drive fast here,"* he thought. This part of the road was under constant surveillance. Ahead, a brightly illuminated gate came into view. Bringing the car to a smooth halt, he rolled down the window.

Approaching the vehicle, a tall guard dressed in a black uniform requested his identification. Annoyed, the driver tapped his fingers on the steering wheel as the guard cross-checked his identification against the list. *"Didn't we just go through all this twenty minutes ago?"* He thought to himself, growing impatient.

The guard looked up from his clipboard and addressed him, "Mr. Jason Pogi? You're all set. Please proceed to the main entrance, and a valet will assist you with your car." Jason retrieved his identification card and rolled up the window.

"Valets, 24-hour security, an estate the size of Connecticut," he mused, finding it hard to grasp the sheer opulence of the place. The term "billionaire" hardly captured the extent of the older man's wealth. While his official holdings may have been in the billions, when accounting for all the additional assets tied to ancient aristocratic agreements and royal privileges, his net worth easily surpassed the low trillions of dollars. Regardless of how many times Jason had

been summoned to this place, he couldn't help but be awestruck by its grandeur.

Once past the gate, Jason was greeted by the familiar sound of gravel under his tires. He skillfully maneuvered the Mercedes towards the front entrance, although calling it a mansion would be an understatement—it was more akin to an 18th-century German palace. The wings of the house extended from the grand entrance, adorned with numerous windows and chimneys. With over 200,000 square feet of space, the palace exuded a lavish atmosphere. It felt as if the old German Dukes were still present, engaged in plotting land annexations and negotiating trade tariffs. Bringing the car to a halt, Pogi watched as the valets swiftly opened the driver's door and trunk. He exited the Mercedes as the valets took charge of the car. Pogi then proceeded to the palace's entrance, accompanied by a valet who carried his attaché case.

As the doors swung open, the palace butler stood before him, poised to receive the house master's guest, even at such a late hour. "His Excellency Count Drouin is expecting you, Mr. Pogi," the butler announced. "Please allow me to escort you to his Excellency's chambers." With the butler leading the way, they traversed through the expansive and cavernous rooms of the residence. Ascending a grand staircase and traversing a gallery adorned with larger-than-life portraits, the journey continued. Jason's gaze lingered on the final portrait in the gallery, depicting a short-statured nineteenth-century French general. Finally, they arrived at the imposing, tall doors of the west wing. As the doors swung open in unison, two servants revealing the entrance to the east wing, and the butler gestured for Pogi to step inside.

"Come in, Mr. Pogi," a voice inside beckoned, "please come and tell me what went wrong tonight." Pogi took a deep breath and walked over to the chair. The room was a library. A table with maps was at one end, and desks were at the other. The chair where he was ordered to sit was one of two on either side of a great marble fireplace. The whole library was bathed in soft light from lamps, and the orange light from the fire cast an ominous glow in the room. A thin man in his fifties was sitting in the chair, patiently waiting for Pogi to deliver his report. The older man was impeccably dressed in the finest suit that his private tailor had to offer and wore a beard that was neatly trimmed. Everything about this older man's appearance was perfect and carefully put together. This man was one of the unseen rulers of the world. He extended his hand towards his guest.

Pogi took the offered hand and gave a bow, as one does in the presence of royalty. "Of course, Count Drouin," Pogi said, "May I sit?"

Drouin withdrew his hand and said, "You may."

With the intolerable European protocol complete, Pogi sat down in the chair and began, "Your excellency, as you know, we are implementing the plan to carefully insert ISIS operatives into Europe. The Flamstead cell had set up a safe house, and this was the first day of their operation, kidnapping civilians in the UK and executing them on an internet livestream."

The Count interrupted, "Before you continue, Mr. Pogi, please understand how disappointed I am with the outcome of tonight's...failures." He went on, "Our operation had been carefully planned for months, to drive fear into the population and to make Britons shake with terror. Be aware that there are other operations underway in addition to this one that must now be put on hold due to what happened tonight. Choose your next words carefully, Mr. Pogi."

Pogi took a full ten seconds before continuing, "The stream was interrupted at 20:34, your excellency. We radioed the farmhouse to report that the stream was interrupted, but we received no response from Khalid, the sentries, or anyone else." The Count listened as Pogi continued, "As per plan, the QRF was called and attempted to secure the area. Lieutenant Aubert radioed that he was going to enter the structure with an assault team when things began to fall apart."

Drouin nodded and gestured for Pogi to continue. "We had to piece together what happened from monitoring the QRF channel; preliminary reports indicate that the assault team fell under attack from a sniper and a machine gunner. When the second team attempted to breach the structure that concealed the enemy troops, the second team came under machine gun fire and was then attacked from above by a helicopter, which eliminated the QRF. The identity of the enemy troops is currently unknown."

Count Drouin leaned back in the chair and asked, "Was any footage recovered from the web cams or the body cameras worn by the team members?"

"As a matter of fact, yes," Pogi replied. "We recovered only a few frames, but what we saw was an adult male soldier wearing a grey uniform with body armor and night vision equipment. We saw no insignia on the uniform except one, a white Maltese Cross."

Count Drouin took a long breath and slowly stood. He carefully walked to the mantle and thought for a long moment. While facing the mantle, he spoke, "Mr. Pogi, you've just told me the single most important piece of information I've ever heard. Well done."

Pogi was bewildered with this turn of conversation. *"I thought Drouin was going to dismiss me,"* he thought. *"Now I'm being congratulated?"* Pogi had given up on ever understanding this man.

Drouin walked across the room to a desk, where he pushed a book aside and pressed a button on an intercom device. He spoke clearly into the speaker, "Send Major Aubert in." Drouin paused for a moment and then walked over to the map table. A drawing of the floor plan of the farmhouse was laid out on the table, as was a survey map of the farm property and a topological map of Flamstead and the surrounding area. Drouin checked the topological map and retrieved four other maps from the map drawers stacked behind the table. The doors to the library opened once more, and a serious man with close-cropped brown hair walked in. He was dressed in black fatigues. His clothing had a patch that showed his last name and another sewn to the uniform's sleeve with a blue shield and eagle embroidered with gold thread.

Aubert walked to the map table and saluted Drouin. "Ah, Major," Drouin said, "come look." Aubert walked around the table to get a better view of the maps. Drouin began, "I am sorry for the loss of your younger brother tonight; he was a good officer."

Aubert's face betrayed none of his emotions as he thanked his employer. Drouin went on, "I know you have trained yourself and drilled your men to be professional; the mission comes first. However, it's my pleasure to tell you that fate has delivered us an opportunity." Drouin looked at Aubert and smiled as he said, "We must eliminate the team that interrupted tonight's operation, but in doing so we can avenge the death of your brother... and restore my family's honor."

Major Aubert's eyes widened as he replied in surprise, "You can't possibly mean..."

Drouin folded his arms as he answered, "Yes, the Order has survived to this day; we just got confirmation."

A thought occurred to Drouin, and he turned around to look at Pogi. "Mr. Pogi, my apologies; it slipped my mind that you were there. Will you excuse the Major and me for a moment?"

"Of course, sir." Pogi stood and walked over to the library doors, which opened once more. Once they were shut, Drouin continued, "Look here, Major. Where would Soldiers of the Order go?"

Aubert looked at the topographic maps and said, "They took the hostage with them, and it makes sense that they used the helicopter." Aubert studied the maps, looking for likely destinations. He began again: "Your Excellency, the most likely landing areas are Cranfield Airfield to the north or Watford General Hospital to the south."

Viscount Drouin said, "The hospital. They'll go there."

Aubert smiled and commented, "Know thy enemy." He continued, "I'll get an assault force together and annihilate them."

Drouin nodded and went back to the intercom. He spoke into the device, "Send Mr. Pogi back in." Drouin was halfway back to the map table as the library doors opened and Pogi walked in once more. The three men stood at the map table as Drouin addressed Pogi: "Mr. Pogi, I will need the help of your CIA again. The assault team that attacked the farmhouse must be eliminated before we can proceed with our operation."

Pogi took in Drouin's words as he continued, "Our adversary has sought refuge in Watford General Hospital. We will attack them inside, but we need a fabricated cover story to conceal what we are doing."

Pogi remained silent, inwardly worried about what he was going to hear. "The Major and I have decided that we need to fabricate a mass shooting at this location. We need you to create a false identity for a disgruntled employee who got access to a rifle. We also need you to intercept the 9-9-9 call and relay our story to the police. Once we have these two fabrications in place, follow up afterward with MI-5 to make sure the outcome of the investigation yields that this was a mass shooter and that the mass shooter was killed by responding police units. This will provide camouflage for the presence of the assault team the Major will be sending and will explain the reason for the gunfight that will occur when we eliminate the adversaries."

Pogi thought to himself, *"My God...that will work...was it really that easy? Control the narrative, and you control reality. Unreal."*

He answered, "Yes, your Excellency. Anything further?"

Drouin walked to the intercom one final time and spoke, "Send Greta in."

Drouin walked back to the other two men as Greta, a sleek blonde woman in her late thirties, walked in with a stunningly athletic younger woman in tow. The younger woman looked down at the floor. She was dressed in a short silk robe and spiked heels. The silk robe was closed, but it was obvious there was not much else she was wearing underneath. Drouin smiled at the young woman approvingly and said, "Thank you, Greta. Mr. Pogi, the hour draws late. May I entice you to spend the night with us?"

Pogi's jaw almost fell open, but he managed to control himself and replied, "Of course, your Excellency."

Pogi could not believe his luck. *"This posting sure had its perks indeed,"* he thought as Greta gestured for him and the young woman to follow.

Chapter 5

Airspace North of Watford General Hospital, 2,500 feet AGL

The lights of Watford blazed below the EC155 as it slid through the frozen night air. Jan had a blanket over Victoria, who was holding his hand tightly. Aleksy was busy collecting the MP-5SD's and spare magazines from each team member. The weapons and magazines went into a large bag that had cushioned dividers to keep all the equipment sorted. The rest of the assault team was pulling out white lab coats to cover their grey uniforms and body armor. Victoria looked around and thought, *"That's odd; they all look like doctors."*

Stefan's hands were gently moving the controls of the EC155, his thumb pressed the PTT button as he spoke into his helmet mounted microphone, "Control, this is air ambulance Victor Four, approaching the pad, requesting traffic advisory, over."

A reply came, "Uh, Roger Victor Four, this is Control; I see you to the North; no traffic in the area, confirming one casualty on board?"

"Roger Control," Stefan said, "This is a trauma six patient, repeat a trauma six patient, over?"

Inside the control structure, the radio operator looked over at his senior and asked, "What the bloody hell is a trauma six patient?"

The senior man looked at the operator and said, "Never mind that, it's a special case. Give them clearance to land, I will ask Doctor Roberts to take this one," he picked up a phone and started dialing an extension. Confused, the radio operator said to the strange aircraft, "Roger Victor Four, we copied a trauma six patient. Pad is yours; wind is five knots from the South."

Stefan smiled and replied, "Roger Control, Victor Four, entering final." Stefan slowed the EC155 down from its cruising speed and brought the aircraft into a hover five hundred feet above the landing pad. As the landing gear unfolded from the fuselage, the aircraft gently descended and touched down on the pad. From the warmth of the control structure, the radio operator could see the dark grey helicopter's door slide open and out stepped four men in white lab coats with one woman wrapped in a blanket. One man was carrying a large black bag. The radio operator could see one of the hospital doctors race out to meet them.

The doctor spoke to one of the men and they all quickly walked back inside. The helicopter pilot's voice came in over the radio, "Control, this is Victor Four, on the pad requesting departure."

The operator said into his microphone, "Roger Victor Four, wind still five knots from the south, no traffic in pattern, you're cleared for departure." The dark grey aircraft lifted off once more and disappeared into the dark January sky, leaving the radio operator with nothing but unanswered questions.

Dr. Roberts led the group off the freezing helicopter pad and into the now calm winter air. "We will have to take the stairs," he said. "The lift leads directly to the surgery wing." Dr. Roberts opened the door and held it open, letting it swing shut behind him as he stepped inside after the group.

He caught up with Jan as they descended the staircase. "One wing of the hospital is under renovation," he began, "I thought that would do, there's a recovery room in that section with beds."

"That will do fine, Dr. Roberts," Jan responded. The group continued down the stairs and got off on the third floor. They passed through a hallway with hospital rooms on either side, then passed a nurse's station without a glance from the staff. The hospital activity got less frequent, and the atmosphere grew still as the group entered the wing of the hospital that was undergoing renovations. Only one or two lights were on in the hallway, enough to barely illuminate the floor, but leaving dark shadows in between the overhead lights.

All the rooms on this floor were dark, and the nurse's station was enveloped in plastic used by construction crews. The scent of paint, adhesive, and freshly cut lumber hung in the air. Tool cabinets and ladders were neatly stored in the hallways, and electrical cords were coiled and hung nearby.

Dr. Roberts pulled out a set of keys and unlocked a door just down the hall from the nurse's station. The room was long and rectangular, lined with beds draped in plastic on one side. "This is the recovery room," the doctor said. "This part of the hospital isn't used by staff now that it's under renovation, so you won't be disturbed by the custodial staff or orderlies bringing patients in here." Dr. Roberts continued, "If you need me, dial this number." He handed a scrap of paper to Jan.

The Captain took it from him and said, "Thank you, Doctor. We defend civilization."

Dr. Roberts answered him with the second half of the line, "...And we care for the afflicted." Dr. Roberts slipped out of the room as Jan walked over to his team. He had a call to make. He dialed a number and activated the speaker.

The phone rang in the shipping container. Echo picked it up before the first ring died. "Captain?" Echo asked over the line.

"I copy you, Echo," Jan replied, "Echo, we have a problem."

"The QRF. Yes, Captain, that was an unpleasant surprise," Echo said.

Jan went on, "Echo, report to the client's representative; MI-6 needs to know about what happened before the news reports an infantry engagement occurred near Flamstead." Jan thought a moment and said, "I've got a few questions to ask our guest; I'll get back to you soon, out." Jan disconnected the line and looked over at Victoria.

Lew was examining her and making sure she was uninjured. Everyone on the team had medical training, it was one of the oldest tenants of the order for a Knight to be able to care for the wounded. Jan walked over to Lew and Victoria and asked her, "How are you feeling?"

"My head hurts," she said, "Who are you guys? Police?"

"No," Jan answered, "We are soldiers of the Order of Saint John."

"Soldiers? Order of Saint John? That doesn't make any sense," Victoria countered, "That sounds like a charity."

Jan looked at Lew and smiled. He continued, "We've been with you a long time. For now, please accept that we work as paramilitary contractors for the British government."

Victoria shut her eyes and said, "I need to sit down." Lew came over with a chair for her. Exhaustion set in as she let her body relax in the chair.

Jan asked her, "What is your name?" She looked up at him and gave a tired smile, "Victoria, what's yours?"

"You may call me 'Jan' or 'Captain' if you wish," he said. "Victoria, this is very important; do you know why you were taken?"

She shook her head and said, "No. I was on my way to class when these two Middle Eastern men used a stun gun on me and threw me in the back of a van. My parents have money, but I don't think the men who took me were trying to collect a ransom; I think they were going to kill me."

Jan nodded, "Let's not worry about that now, those men cannot hurt anyone ever again," he said. Jan had to get her thoughts on something else besides a near-death experience. He asked another question, "Have you noticed anything out of the ordinary, like someone following you or strange phone calls?"

"No, I can't think of anything like that, sorry." She said this as she lifted the corner of her mouth to accentuate the word.

Jan smiled and ended the conversation, "*Victoria needs to rest, as soon as we can arrange transport, we will get her to MI-6 for debriefing,"* he thought.

Echo had been on the phone with John Archer, their MI-6 contact. Archer was nearing retirement and had risen to a director position within MI-6. His team was responsible for tracking ISIS incursions into Europe, and they had decided to contract tactical services with the Order to avoid the bureaucratic entanglements of operating within Britain. This way, Archer could make one phone call and order a commando raid, rather than go through traditional channels and risk missing an opportunity to strike. The telephone conversation started out cordial enough, but the intelligence man became more concerned as the description of the evening's events went on. "So how many enemies?" Archer asked.

Echo explained again, "Eight ISIS personnel were in the actual cell, and then an enemy QRF responded to an unknown trigger event. The QRF had a strength of twenty-five men, so thirty-three enemy dead total."

Echo heard a low whistle on the other end of the phone as Archer replied, "And no team casualties, with a successful hostage rescue? Incredible."

Echo had one last thing to add, "Sir, the enemy QRF forces are of great concern. We need to know who these men are, and why they were supporting the ISIS cell. They certainly weren't Middle Eastern; they were European, well organized, and heavily armed with U.S.-made weapons."

Archer nodded understandingly and said, "I agree. Echo, tell the assault team to stay put while I get to work on this. Thank you for telling me about the mess at the farmhouse. I can get in front of that business and encourage the local constables not to look too deeply into the incident. Do be so kind as to call if there are any further developments." The line clicked off, and Echo was alone in the shipping container once more.

English Channel, British Airspace

A Dassault Falcon 7X private jet cruised over the English Channel at 25,000 feet. The aircraft's tail was decorated with a blue shield and golden eagle. Inside, Major Aubert was hard at work on the aircraft's sky phone. "Correct, Lieutenant," he said. "I want fifty men ready to deploy against a ground and aerial threat within 10 minutes after I land."

Lieutenant Lapointe's voice came through the sky phone speaker, "Oui, Major. I will have the men, weapons, and vehicles ready for you. How far out are you?"

Major Aubert glanced at the digital readout in the aircraft's cabin that displayed the remaining flight time and said, "Fifteen minutes, see you on the ground, Lieutenant."

Aubert ended the call. He could feel the aircraft begin to descend from its cruising altitude so it could enter the traffic control pattern. Everything was ready. The Order of Saint John had caught them by surprise earlier, but the order had no idea how large a threat they faced. He chuckled as he thought back to the Schloss and how he grabbed that little CIA weasel by the arm and ordered him to task agency assets to build the identity of the fictional disgruntled hospital employee. Aubert also made him call and set up the arrangements with the Special Branch of the Metropolitan Police before he let Pogi run upstairs with his new companion. *"People were so easy to control when one knew the right levers to pull,"* Aubert thought as he heard the pilot's voice come over the intercom and announce the updated arrival information. *"Five minutes,"* he thought, *"Almost there."*

The warehouse was a flurry of activity as Lieutenant Lapointe prepared for the Major's arrival. Men were putting on their kit, man portable air defense systems (MANPADS) were being loaded onto the vans, and floorplans of Watford Hospital were being posted to large bulletin boards set up in the warehouse. A black BMW 535i sedan stopped right outside the warehouse's open bay door. Major Aubert stepped out of the front passenger door and walked inside with purpose. Lapointe and two of his sergeants snapped to attention and saluted the Major as he approached. Aubert returned the salute and remembered their time together in the Foreign Legion; he had served with all three of the men at an earlier time when the climate was hot and the conflict intense. Welcome, Major," Lapointe said, "We are ready for the briefing. Sergeants, have the men fall in."

Terse orders were shouted in French, and the ranks of security personnel formed in front of the bulletin boards. Major Aubert began the briefing, "At ease. As you all know, 25 men were lost tonight on a counterattack mission. Many of you lost friends, I lost a brother. Our intelligence has found the men responsible for this massacre, and we are going to hit the enemy back – hard."

Eyes narrowed at this statement. The crowd of assembled men was dead quiet. The Major continued, "The enemy force is taking refuge in Watford General Hospital, likely in a sparsely populated section of the building. We will clear each area until we find the enemy. There is a cover story for our operation. We will issue you all **POLICE** insignia, and if anyone asks, we are a police tactical team looking for a mass shooter. We expect opposition strength to be between four and eight men plus one female. This is a kill mission; all these people are to be shot on sight. We will have two, three-man teams armed with MANPADS positioned in the car park near the helicopter landing pad. Once we engage the opposition, enemy air support is expected. Let the MANPADS teams handle the helicopter, do not run outside the Hospital to assist. Are there any questions?"

His query was met with silence, "To the vans, men. We leave in five minutes."

The ride to Watford Hospital was quiet as the black vans roared towards their destination. The vans had blue strobe lights fitted, so they gave the appearance of emergency vehicles. Traffic pulled over to let the five vans pass. Major Aubert sat in the front passenger seat of the lead van. He was alone with his thoughts. *"My younger brother was only twenty-eight. He had just found a nice girl."* Major Aubert swore, he was going to have to write both his parents and the young lady a letter. *"Such a waste,"* he thought. He saw on the van's moving map display that they were approaching the hospital. *"Steady now; make sure your thoughts are on the mission and your men,"* the Major thought. He had seen combat with the French Foreign Legion all over Africa and the Middle East. He put the thoughts of his brother out of his mind; he had a job to do and fifty men to try to bring home safely.

The vans screeched to a stop in front of Watford Hospital's emergency entrance with their emergency lights still blazing. The sudden presence of fifty heavily armed men dressed in blue uniforms was quite the spectacle. Major Aubert opened the door and walked directly towards the entrance. The automatic doors parted as he walked into the building. As one, every staff member in the Emergency Room looked at the Major. As the staff saw the forty strong heavily armed assault team follow him, jaws began to drop, and some people scurried away. Others froze where they stood. The major strode right up to the head physician and said, "There is an active shooter threat that has been called in against this hospital. I need you to get your staff together and have non-essential personnel evacuate the building. My officers and I will search the building."

The doctor stammered, "Officer, we have critical patients that cannot be moved without..."

The Major cut him off: "I said non-essential personnel, sir. I understand the critical patients and the staff caring for them cannot be easily moved at a moment's notice. We will guard them, give the orders to your staff, please help us protect this building and the people here under your care...MOVE!" The head physician's shaking hands picked up the phone, and he began making calls to department heads.

Echo looked up from his console at the alert. The Dell server rack had a custom Artificial Intelligence program that was used on missions to pick up tactical intelligence in real-time. It drew data from radio, cellular, and internet sources and constantly scanned this data for repetitive words or images. The AI took a few minutes to get the general baseline of an area, and once this was established, it looked for any data anomalies. Multiple anomalies were catalogued by the AI program and once they exceeded a user-set risk threshold, the operator was alerted. The AI was warning Echo that "Watford Hospital" was beginning to rise above the baseline of the normal communication and internet "noise" in the area.

The phone rang in the recovery room. Jan picked it up to find Echo on the other end: "Captain, I'm seeing a lot of attention from social media and law enforcement radio frequencies being focused on Watford Hospital."

"Copy, Echo, what do you think it means?" asked Jan.

"Not sure yet, Captain. The AI is set to scan social media, cellular communications, police, and emergency radio frequencies. It just alerted me that Watford hospital is a word that's being repeated in your area."

Jan had another question: "Echo, could this be explained by a disaster or medical emergency somewhere nearby?"

"No, Captain," Echo said. "The AI will scan for such an event and filter it out. Right now, the AI needs more data to develop any specific threats, but the word "Watford Hospital" is being used enough in radio communications and internet traffic that the risk threshold has been exceeded. This usually means some kind of threat is forming."

Jan took a deep breath and said, "I copy everything, Echo. Let me know right away if we must move."

At that instant, Dr. Roberts burst through the door of the recovery room and said, "Captain! A police SWAT team is searching the hospital for an active shooter! They are going room by room, starting with the unoccupied areas."

Jan looked at Dr. Roberts, then down at the phone in his hand. A heavily armed police force and the AI giving Echo warnings could mean only one thing.

They were under attack.

THE CODE OF THE ORDER

Chapter 6

Watford General Hospital

"Echo, get into the hospital security system and start monitoring the surveillance camera feeds," Jan ordered through the phone, "switch to tactical communications on the assault channel, and call Rattler for an immediate dust off."

Jan ended the phone call and turned to Dr. Roberts, "Doctor, how many men?"

"I don't know their full strength, but I saw at least twenty men on their way to the Basement. They were breaking up into smaller teams," said Dr. Roberts.

Jan asked, "How were they armed?"

"Captain, I saw these men armed with 5.56mm M4 rifles and body armor. They also had pistols and fragmentation grenades on their belts," Dr. Roberts answered him.

Jan thought for a minute, *"Not police – police don't carry frag grenades."*

Jan turned to his team, "Soldiers, we are going to get hit; we need to get out of this room and on the move so Rattler can pick us up. Aleksy, what do we have for weapons?"

Aleksy looked at the bag he carried off the helicopter, "Captain, I've got six MP-5SD sub-machineguns, and I have four Benelli M4 12-gauge shotguns. We had them in the bag in case we had to breach a door on the farmhouse, but they weren't needed earlier. Everyone still has their USP, of course." Jan thought for a minute.

The fighting, if it occurred, was going to be up close and fast – against men armed with rifles. The SMG was not a wise choice. He looked at Aleksy, "We go with the shotguns. How many shells do we have?"

"I can give every man 30 rounds of 00-buck and five rifled slugs," Aleksy said.

Jan nodded and looked at Lew, "What explosives do you have on you?"

"Nothing heavy, Captain," he answered, "all the bang is on board the helicopter. We have four flashbangs with us, and I have three feet of det cord and four blasting caps."

Jan looked at the team, "Everyone give Lew your flashbangs. Let's get kitted up. We leave in sixty seconds."

He hit the PTT button on his tactical radio, "Echo do you copy?"

The reply from Echo was distorted with static, "Yes, Captain – barely. Your radio transmission is not good from that location in the building. Rattler reports his ETA is two-zero minutes to your position."

"I copy all, Echo. I'll call you when we are ready to move," Jan said.

He looked at Victoria, "Victoria, the men who attacked the farmhouse are back. We need to leave. You will come with me."

Victoria nodded. She knew this soldier would protect her, even if he died trying. Jan looked at his team; Aleksy, Lew, and Kuba had already extracted their Benelli M4 shotguns and had loaded up the magazine tubes with 12-gauge shells. These shotguns were the "Entry" model, which had a short barrel, collapsing stock, and a Trijicon RMR micro red dot co-witnessed with the iron sights. Kuba handed his captain the last Benelli, loaded with five shells in the tube and "ghost loaded" with one shell in the chamber and another on the lifter. The weapon was on "SAFE," Jan noticed. Jan slung the weapon and began placing fabric shotgun shell "cards" onto his body armor. Each one of these cards held seven shells and had Velcro backing, so they stuck to his plate carrier or to the side of the weapon. All the men had put on their helmets and ditched their lab coats to reveal their gray combat fatigues underneath. Jan called Echo again on the assault frequency, "Echo, can you see the hallway outside the recovery room?"

Echo looked at the surveillance cameras and said, "Hallway clear, captain."

Jan looked at Dr. Roberts, who nodded and left the room down the hall, going back toward the Emergency Room. Jan knew the doctor would distract any enemy soldiers he came across and give his team time to escape. It was brave, and Jan would expect nothing less from a former soldier of the order.

Lew and Aleksy led the way with their shotguns at low ready. Lew and Jan trailed several meters behind Victoria. The group had reached the end of the hallway and was ready to enter the stairwell. Aleksy gently opened the door and looked up and down the stairwell. He saw nothing as he signaled

Kuba to join him on the landing. Together they began to move down the stairs; Kuba covered the stairwell going up while Aleksy quietly made his way down to the next landing in between the floors. As he reached the landing, he saw an enemy soldier coming up the stairs – fast. Too close. He pulled the shotgun stock over his shoulder, aimed down the barrel, and fired a round of 00-buck into the man's face. The weapon roared in the enclosed space of the stairwell. "CONTACT!" he shouted after the weapon fired. As the man Aleksy shot fell, he could see two more men bringing their M4 rifles up to engage. Aleksy was on the landing and could lean back to safety where the stairs provided cover. As he did so, he fired two buckshot rounds at the wall. The shot skipped off the concrete wall, wounding the men trying to get up the stairs. The men fired their M4 rifles in response, the rounds disintegrating harmlessly into the reinforced concrete walls of the stairwell, doing minor damage but making lots of noise and dust. Jan and Lew had already ducked back into the hallway, pushing Victoria toward safety. Kuba and Aleksy were right behind them, and together the team ran deeper into the construction zone.

Back at the landing one floor below, Sergeant Fontaine called in the contact over his radio, "Major Aubert, we have enemy contact, third floor, Northwest stairwell of the building – the construction zone. I have one man dead, and myself and one more are hit."

The Major swore at the news, "Sergeant, hold there. I'm getting you some help."

Aubert switched frequencies and said, "All search teams, all search teams, enemy spotted at Northwest stairwell, third floor, all teams converge on the construction zone!" Major Aubert left the Emergency Room at a run. He had the enemy cornered, and his teams could prevent their escape if they moved fast enough.

Jan's team ran down the hallway. Aleksy and Kuba led the way. Jan could see Aleksy pushing shells into his shotgun as he ran. A doorway dividing the construction zone from the rest of the hospital was ahead, and the team was quickly closing the distance to it. Suddenly, the door opened, and a man dressed in black armed with an M4 rifle stepped out into the hallway. Aleksy and Kuba fired their shotguns at him, and he collapsed, not dead but incapacitated. Jan and Lew grabbed Victoria and forced their way into a hospital room to their right. Kuba and Aleksy did the same, just one door further down the hall. Jan looked around; they were stuck. These rooms were adjoining, but the only way out was back into the hallway where the enemy was waiting for them.

Sergeant Clement saw the point man fall. "Hold your positions!" he yelled.

The men behind him hugged the walls of the hallway. He got on his radio and said, "Major, we have enemy contact near the Northeast corner of the building, third floor. If we get men up the Northwest stairwell, we can trap them in the North hallway!"

The Major heard the radio transmission as he ran towards the Northwest stairwell, "I copy you, Sergeant! Hold that position!" He called his Lieutenant on the radio, "Lieutenant Lapointe, how close are you to the stairwell?"

The Lieutenant's voice came back over the radio in less than a second, "This is Lapointe; I'm ascending the stairs now. I have a force of ten men with me."

Major Aubert slowed his pace, and there was no need to sprint to the front line. Sergeant Clement and Lieutenant Lapointe were competent tactical leaders and would make the right decisions, even under fire. *"No need to micromanage them,"* the Major thought as he walked briskly to the stairwell ahead.

Lapointe reached the landing where Sergeant Fontaine was wounded with the other man in his search team. It looked like Fontaine caught a glancing hit in the arm from the buckshot. The other man's thigh was bleeding. The wounds were painful but not serious. "Fontaine, can you fight?" the Lieutenant asked.

"No, sir," Fontaine said, "We held this position, but I was worried that if they tried to force their way down here, we couldn't hold the stairwell with two men."

Lapointe pointed back down the stairwell, "Make your way back downstairs to the Emergency Room. We will take it from here. My men on me; let's move up there!" One or two of Lapointe's men glanced at the corpse of the man that took the round of 00-buck to the face. They put the grisly image out of their minds as they ascended the stairway. Lapointe had one of his men slowly open the door and look down the hallway, covered by the doorframe – the hallway was empty. He saw the door down the hall where Sergeant Clement held with his men.

The man leaned back inside the stairwell and told his Lieutenant, "Hallway clear, sir, no enemy contact."

Lapointe nodded and called on the radio, "Sergeant Clement, this is Lapointe. Hold your fire. We will move across the hallway and around the corner at the end. I'll get a ballistic shield sent up to you, and we can finish the enemy off."

Major Aubert heard everything over the radio. He called his MANPADS teams, "Missile teams, we have the enemy cornered, be ready for incoming enemy air support." The two missile teams had made their way to the car park near the landing pad. They extracted their FIM-92 Stinger missiles from the bags they removed from the vans.

The Stingers were a gift from Pogi and his CIA. Corporals Simon and Blanc, the missile team leaders, had found a spot where they could cover the landing pad and a small field near a hospital exit. Corporal Simon Responded to the Major, "Copy, Major. We are ready for him." Simon looked over at Blanc and the men setting up the Stingers. He knew some of the men that had died in the helicopter attack earlier that night. He looked forward to the chance to avenge them by blowing that aircraft out of the sky.

Inside the hospital room, Jan called Stefan on his radio, "Rattler, what is your position and ETA?"

Stefan hit the PTT on his control stick, "Copy Captain, we are fifteen clicks Northeast of Watford Hospital, ETA five minutes."

Jan said, "Rattler, we are pinned down here inside the hospital; we are going to try to get moving again."

Stefan and Fillip shared a look, and they could not help the assault team escape from the EC155. They only had a door gun; no ordinance was mounted to the helicopter. Stefan looked behind him into the cabin. Olek and Anatol had grim looks on their faces. Olek had put on a rigger's belt and was getting ready to sit next to Igor at the side door. Together, they would double the firepower of the EC155. *"Good,"* Stefan thought, *"I just hope it's enough."* A nagging feeling was telling him that the LZ was going to be a hot one.

Echo called Jan on the tactical radio channel, "Captain, I'm monitoring the surveillance camera feed. You have a group of nine men to the East of you and another ten to the west by the stairwell. They have taken up blocking positions, and I see ballistic shields being brought by still more men on the first floor." Jan paused for a minute. Whatever they were going to do had to be done now. "Lew," Jan said, "I need a way out of here. I need a large detonation to clear the enemy position ahead." Jan chose the hallway doors over the stairwell. It was closer, and his men had the advantage up close with their Benelli shotguns. The stairway was too far, and the enemy was massing there.

Lew turned and looked at Jan, "Captain, my options are limited. I don't have enough explosives to give you the detonation you..." Lew's voice drifted off as he looked into the hallway. The ceiling tiles had been removed for the renovation, and one could see the overhead utility piping. In addition to pipes that had to hold water and electrical cable, there was another pipe painted green and marked with a single word:

OXYGEN

Lew realized he had all the explosive potential that he needed. "Captain," he began, "I have a solution. It's going to hurt, but it will work. I recommend that we fire a rifled slug into that oxygen pipe. As soon as we rupture it, we toss two flashbangs down the hall, shut the room doors, and get under the mattresses in this room."

"How big will the detonation be?" asked Jan.

"Captain, I can't tell you for sure," Lew answered, "but a high oxygen atmosphere will detonate once it reaches 19.5 percent. The force of the flashbang grenade detonation will be greatly amplified, and there's a high probability a fire will start."

"What about patients on the floor below us," Jan asked, "Is there a risk of structural collapse?"

Lew replied, "Yes, Captain, there is. However, Dr. Roberts told us that the wing of the hospital was under renovation. The risk of innocent casualties is minimal, but we must do this now."

Jan looked at the team. "Aleksy, load a rifled slug into your shotgun," He ordered, "Kuba, you and I will pull the mattresses off the beds and put them in the corner of the room. Once Aleksy puts a hole in the pipe, Lew will throw two flashbangs down the hall. You both will have three seconds before they go off. Understood?" The three soldiers nodded as one.

Jan turned to Victoria, "We need to create an explosion. This will hurt. Please plug your ears with these." He handed her a set of earplugs. He pulled a mattress off one of the beds, and Kuba did the same. Victoria lay down, and Jan got on top of her to shield her with his body and armor plates. Kuba put a mattress on top of them and got under another. Aleksy cracked the door open and took aim at the oxygen pipe as far down the hall as he could. He could see the door frame where the soldiers were hiding.

Aleksy looked at Lew and asked, "Ready?"

Lew nodded and pulled the pins on two of the M84 flashbang grenades. Aleksy took a breath and let some of it out as he applied pressure to Benelli's trigger. The weapon bucked hard against his shoulder as it sent a 1-ounce lead slug streaking toward the oxygen pipe at 1,350 feet per second. The slug easily penetrated the pipe and tore a one-inch hole in the steel. The hallway was filled with a deafening hiss as the oxygen gas rushed out of the hole with 50 pounds per square inch of pressure behind it. Once he heard the gas escaping, Lew moved his thumbs to let the grenade spoons fly off under spring pressure, and he threw the flashbangs down the hall as hard as he could.

ONE...

The M-84 flashbang sailed through the hallway as Lew pulled the hospital room door shut. Aleksy was already running toward his mattress. Aleksy dove to the floor and pulled the mattress over him as Lew followed him.

TWO...

Sergeant Clement heard the report from the shotgun, and his men were behind cover; he was not sure what the enemy was shooting at, and then he heard the hiss from the oxygen gas. *"What is that?"* he thought as the noise from the escaping gas overwhelmed every other sound in the area. Clement did not hear the M-84 grenades as they bounced off the floor.

THREE...

The grenade fuze was already burning as the delay reached the primer. It detonated, igniting the main charge, and sent fine metal powder rushing out of the grenade body, which ignited. This burning magnesium entered a highly oxygenated atmosphere that was well above the lower explosive limit of oxygen. The oxygen gas began to react violently, burning and expanding rapidly as a pressure wave began to form.

BOOOOOOOOOOOOMMMMMMM!!!

The whole building shook on its foundation as the oxygen exploded. Major Aubert was knocked on his back as the building moved underneath his feet. Even here, two floors down from where his soldiers had contacted the enemy, the overpressure hit his sinuses hard enough so it felt as though he had been struck in the face. Aubert got to his knees as he called his men on the radio. There was no response.

Inside the hospital room, the force of the explosion ripped sheetrock off the wall and physically moved furniture in the room. The pressure wave struck the mattresses like an automobile, but the cushioning kept the team from being hurt or killed. The tactical headsets that they were all wearing saved their hearing. Jan could hear the building steel groan and fail. He got to his feet with the others, and they looked out into the hallway. The third floor that they were on had collapsed and formed a ramp of wrecked steel and concrete to the second floor below. The hole that Aleksy had put into the oxygen pipe with his shotgun now had a flame coming out of it like a four-foot blowtorch. Beyond the flame, the hallway on the third floor was engulfed in fire. Jan went back to Victoria and helped her to her feet. She was a little dizzy from the explosion but otherwise unhurt. Aleksy and Kuba mounted their shotguns once more and moved out of the room, followed by Jan, Victoria, and Lew. The team drew no gunfire from down the hallway. The team of soldiers massing there would have caught the overpressure wave as it ripped down the hallway like a bullet coming out of a gun. The team ran down the wreckage of the hallway and came out onto the second floor. Lights blinked on and off, and exposed electrical cables sparked from the force of the detonation. The air was heavy with the smell of ozone and dust. The team ran as fast as they could to an exit. They had to get outside before the enemy soldiers realized what was happening and moved to stop them. Jan called Stefan over the radio.

The EC155 cut through the night air. The Helicopter was one mile away from Watford Hospital when the entire town skyline was illuminated by a giant orange explosion. A second later, the aircraft shuddered. *My God...* thought Stefan as he realized the explosion had come from the hospital.

They were nearly on station when he got a call from Jan over the radio, "Rattler, this is the assault team. Do you copy over?"

Stefan sighed in relief as he responded, "Rattler on station, I copy you five by five. Are you all right? We saw a large explosion from up here."

Jan answered the pilot, "We're ok, Rattler. We are getting ready to exit the building on the East side. Is there a place to land?"

"Captain," Stefan said, "There is a football stadium 100 meters to the Northwest of your position. Can you get there?"

Jan looked at the team as he ran towards the exit, "You bet, Rattler. Be advised we have encountered heavy resistance inside the hospital, and we have an unknown number of enemy troops outside."

Stefan hit the PTT button on his control stick, "Copy assault team. We will orbit for a while and sprint in to land at the stadium when you call us." Stefan moved the cyclic control stick to port and gave the helicopter some left rudder to put the EC155 into a wide orbit around the hospital. Stefan kept his distance at 1,000 meters and his altitude low because the terrain would shield his aircraft from enemy fire.

Jan and his team had reached the exit stairwell and had gone down the stairs to the first floor.

They were on the East side of the building, ready to open the door and make their way to Vicarage Road Stadium. Jan looked at his team, "Gents, reload with slugs. We will have to cross open terrain, and we will be encountering the enemy where their rifles have the advantage. We need to get to the cover of the stadium as fast as we can."

The team began pulling back the charging handles of their Benelli M4's and inserting a rifled slug into the chamber. The slugs would make their shotguns behave like a rifle out to about 150 yards – but unlike a rifle, the slug projectile could incapacitate or kill an enemy with even a poorly placed hit. Jan looked at his team, and they nodded. Aleksy opened the door and peered out. He saw a few soldiers in black uniforms looking in the opposite direction. He looked at Jan, who nodded, and Aleksy and Kuba ran across the street. They ducked behind a parked car, and they aimed their shotguns at the enemy, who were still facing away. Lew, Jan, and Victoria followed them. The air was cold, and Jan could hear his footsteps echoing down the street. They made it to the car; the enemy still had not turned in their direction. It was time to move again. They had to move 20 feet from the car to the alleyway, where buildings would shield them from view. Aleksy and Kuba Sprinted the distance to the building corner that led into the alley and took cover behind it. Kuba trained his Benelli on one of the black-clad soldiers as Aleksy motioned for the rest to come with a hand signal. As the group left the protection of the car, the soldier turned around and saw them. Kuba put the glowing dot of the RMR right on the soldier's sternum and pressed Benelli's trigger.

The shotgun bucked hard as it sent its rifled slug down range. The one-ounce projectile struck the soldier in the neck, effectively decapitating him and showering his companions with blood and tissue. Both soldiers dove for cover. One got on the radio, "Major Aubert, this is outside security team three, East side of the building. We have enemy contact!"

Major Aubert had made it to the third floor and was looking at the carnage the oxygen explosion had wrought on his soldiers. There was no sign of Sergeant Clement and his men. They had caught the worst of it. Lapointe's team had two men down with serious injuries, but the rest had recovered from the effects of the explosion. Major Aubert responded, "Security team three, do not engage. Where are they going?"

"Major," the team leader answered, "the enemy has crossed the street on the East side of the hospital. They are making their way to the stadium."

"All teams, all teams," the Major spoke into his radio, "the enemy has escaped the blocking position and is moving East towards the football stadium. Everyone get to the front of the hospital and load up in the vans." The Major's command sent all the soldiers who could make it running back to the front of the hospital past a shocked chief physician and nurses. They had already begun to treat some of the more seriously wounded soldiers.

Major Aubert got to the vans and watched his soldiers get in the vehicles in the light of the carport. He saw Sergeant Fontaine walk up to him, "Thirty-six men present and accounted for, sir," he said.

"Sergeant, you're wounded," Major Aubert said, "Get yourself inside."

The sergeant looked at the Major hard, "I can drive, sir."

Major Aubert nodded and replied, "Mount up, sergeant."

The Major got into the passenger seat of the lead van; Fontaine got into the driver's seat next to him. *"I'm the luckiest man alive,"* he thought, *"To have the privilege of commanding such men as these."* Fontaine put the van in gear and raced off towards the East side of Vicarage Road Stadium.

"Rattler, this is assault team. Do you copy?" Jan said on his radio.

"I'm here," Stefan said, "I can be on the ground in one minute, Captain."

Jan said, "Rattler, we have enemy contact; this will be a hot LZ. I'll call you again once we are one minute from the pickup."

"Copy that, Captain," Stefan said. He said over the aircraft's intercom, "Igor, Anatol, Olek, we are expecting a hot LZ, be ready to engage enemy forces on sight. Weapons are free once we get inside the stadium." The three men in the EC155's cabin looked at the pilot. Igor had his FN MAG loaded and ready with 7.62 NATO ammunition. Olek was ready to rush out and cover the assault team with his M-249. Anatol was ready, too, with a Heckler & Koch G36K rifle with an EOTech holographic red dot sight mounted to its rail. The helicopter crew kept these rifles stowed in the cabin in case the EC155 was shot down, and they needed to fight. He chose the borrowed G36K over his Tikka sniper rifle because the need for silence did not exist, and he wanted the fast follow-up shot capability of the G36K and its select-fire action. Anatol would not need to take a shot over 100 meters anyway; the need for extreme accuracy was not there. Stefan increased the speed of the EC155. When Jan called him, he would have to dart towards the stadium and land quickly, and he did not want to be on the ground any longer than needed. This was going to be more dangerous than the farmhouse. Above the farmhouse, pouring fire down at the enemy was safe and easy flying. Here, under these circumstances, the enemy could get an advantage over him very quickly. His only path to safety was speed. He looked back at the men in the EC155's cabin, *"Those boys were in for a real ride,"* he thought to himself as he concentrated on flying the aircraft through the still night air.

Sergeant Fontaine fought through the pain; his shoulder wound ached every time he moved the steering wheel. Two pellets of 00-buck had slid off the concrete wall of the stairwell at a shallow angle and penetrated his shoulder. He was lucky. The corporal with him caught four pellets in the leg. He would be in the hospital for a while with that wound. When Fontaine served with the Major in Africa, the two of them had seen (and treated) their share of combat injuries. Although he would not be going into the stadium, he was happy to drive the men back there so they could give back a portion of what the enemy served up.

Fontaine Made a hard left onto Occupation Road and brought the van screeching to a stop in front of the stadium entrance. The van hit a bit of ice and slid another twenty feet before it stopped. The soldiers barreled out of the van, and Major Aubert gave his old comrade-in-arms one last look and a smile as he ran off to join his men. Fontaine chuckled; that one look from his officer was a conversation. It was, *"Thank you, I'm proud of you, I hope we meet again, and look what I get to do!"* all unspoken, all at once. Such fellowship is known only to men who have shared hardship under the threat of death. Fontaine was happy to have done his part, but he wished now more than anything in the world that he could go into that stadium and wager his life on a toss of dice one more time.

Jan's team was almost inside the stadium. It was time to make the call. "Rattler, this is the assault team," Jan radioed, "we are one minute out. Start your run."

"Finally," Stefan thought as he pushed the cyclic to starboard and turned the aircraft to line

up with the stadium. He was coming to the stadium from the North so he could take advantage of the shape of the field and give him more space to land.

The stadium was approaching quickly, and he was pushing the EC155 as fast as it would go. "Be ready, gents," Stefan said over the intercom, "I'm going to bring her down quickly, and this is expected to be a hot LZ."

Stefan waited until the last minute and pulled back on the cyclic firmly as the aircraft's momentum whipped the EC155 up and over the stadium wall. The men in back fought against the g-forces as he pushed the collective down, and the helicopter began to descend. As the last bit of forward momentum was overcome by the vast quantity of air the rotor blades were pushing, Stefan eased the stick forward to drop the nose and bring the EC155 into a perfect hover. Phillip flipped a switch on the instrument panel, and the landing gear began unfolding from the fuselage. Stefan then pushed the collective down further and let the aircraft drop. He fought through the ground effect and brought the EC155 to a gentle landing on the perfectly manicured grass of the football stadium. The instant the EC155's gear touched the grass, Olek and Anatol ran out of the helicopter and stood ten meters from the open left side door, scanning for targets. Igor scanned the right side of the helicopter, mindful that the assault team would be approaching from this side. Their weapons were ready as they waited for the assault team.

They did not have to wait long. Kuba, Lew, and Aleksy ran to the helicopter. Stefan had the aircraft at full power, and both Rolls-Royce turbines were screaming as the helicopter tried to force itself into the grass of the stadium. Jan and Victoria waited for the other three to cross the twenty-five meters to the safety of the helicopter. Jan saw his men get inside the helicopter's cabin and saw Igor waving at him in a "come here" gesture. He looked at Victoria, gave her hand a squeeze, and set his boot onto the grass of the football field.

Major Aubert could hear the shriek of the jet turbines. The noise reverberated off the empty seats and concrete of the stadium. He and his men poured out of the stadium's East tunnel. They saw the helicopter on the ground at full power. They instinctively fanned out and dropped into a prone position. Several of them squeezed the triggers of their M4 rifles, shooting at the standing figures with controlled bursts of automatic fire. The figures dropped to the ground and returned fire. The black-clad soldiers could see movement inside the helicopter's cabin as a bright flash from a light machine gun appeared both on the field and inside the helicopter's cabin. One of the soldiers was able to hit the light machine gunner on the ground with a well-placed shot. The gunfire from that position stopped abruptly. The man who scored a hit was immediately shot by the other figure, but the incoming rounds impacted his armored helmet, and he collapsed onto his rifle, knocked out with a concussion. As incoming fire from the helicopter grazed over the prone men, they stopped shooting and hugged the ground even further. The second figure helped the wounded man to his feet, and together they ran the ten meters back to the helicopter and jumped inside the cabin. The withering fire from the helicopter's door gun continued.

Stefan could hear the incoming 5.56mm rounds impact the skin of the helicopter. He had to get off the ground before something vital was hit, but he still had troops on the ground. He saw Jan and Victoria only one meter from the stadium tunnel, and it would take them a relative eternity to reach him. No matter – Stefan would stay here on the ground no matter what.

Jan looked across the field at the helicopter and knew that he and Victoria could not make the distance in time. Even at a full run, the helicopter would be damaged by gunfire by then and unable to fly. He stopped and turned Victoria around by the arm as he radioed Stefan, "Rattler, we can't make it to you in time. Get out of here, and we can try for a pickup somewhere else."

Reluctantly, Stefan pulled up on the collective, and the helicopter lifted off and disappeared into the inky night sky. The staccato noise from Igor's mounted machine gun faded as the helicopter gained altitude. Jan ran with Victoria to the safety of the West stadium tunnel. They had to get out of the sports arena before the enemy soldiers realized what was happening and that the helicopter was missing two passengers.

Major Aubert watched the helicopter climb. This engagement was costly, he had three men wounded, but it was successful in one aspect. He had driven the helicopter away from the stadium, and now the enemy was in one place. He got on his radio, "Missile teams, the target is passing over the South end of the stadium, be ready."

Corporal Simon and Corporal Blanc had heard the radio call. While the rest of their comrades rushed off to the stadium in vans, they made their way with their teams to the roof of the hospital. They had watched the helicopter approach the stadium, and they now had their Stinger missiles ready to deploy. When the black-clad soldiers engaged the enemy inside the stadium, Simon shoved his battery coolant unit into the bottom of the missile launcher. This provided cryogenic cooling of the unit so the infrared tracking system would work properly. He started counting to forty-five. When he got to thirty, Blanc shoved his BCU into his launcher. The coolant only lasted for forty-five seconds; this way, the teams could provide air defense coverage continually. When Simon got to thirty-seven, they saw the helicopter. Both men trained their launcher's rudimentary sight on the EC155 and were rewarded with a shrill warbling from the stinger missile's seeker head. The men depressed the firing triggers on the launchers, and the five-foot missiles shot out of their launch tubes.

A short distance away from the launch teams, the missiles ignited their main rocket motors and began to accelerate quickly. Each missile could see the heat from the helicopter's engines and tail fan gearbox. They streaked toward their target, quickly accelerating past Mach one.

Igor saw the launch. "Pilot!" he called over the intercom, "two missiles in the air on your four-o-clock!"

Stefan heard the frantic call from the door gunner. He pushed the cyclic over to the left and swung the tail around. He had no flares, and he hoped he could move fast enough to confuse the missile seeker heads, maybe even get behind terrain. One missile was too close and overshot the helicopter; it rocketed away from Watford at Mach two. The second missile saw the sudden maneuver and adjusted its course. The second missile would have overshot as well, but the onboard computer made the decision to detonate its one-kilogram warhead two meters from the right side of the helicopter, peppering the airframe with shrapnel. The aircraft shuddered as Stefan fought for control. The cyclic felt sluggish, and he could feel ominous vibrations through the collective. The instrument panel was lit with multiple caution and warning lights, and the EC155's computer began saying, "Engine fire...Engine fire..." in an oddly calm female voice.

Stefan killed power to both turbines, one engine was wrecked for sure, and he did not trust the other. Stefan and Fillip went through the emergency landing and autorotation procedures for the EC155; they had done this a dozen times in their training work to prepare for the mission, and their movements were automatic. Fillip spied a landing site directly in front of them, and it was a grass field used by a school. He relayed the information to Stefan, who adjusted the aircraft's course slightly. Stefan had already buried the collective to prepare for the autorotation, and he traded altitude to keep momentum in the main rotor. The vibrations got worse as the ground rushed up at them, eerily visible through the phosphorescent green display of their night vision goggles. Stefan had about three seconds to flare the aircraft and try to land before the EC155 became a greasy crater. He called out over the intercom, "Passengers and crew...BRACE! BRACE! BRACE!"

At the last possible instant, he pulled up on the collective and flared the aircraft hard, using the momentum in the main rotor he had built up earlier to slow the aircraft. At this moment, something broke in the control linkages that moved the swashplate, and suddenly Stefan had no control over the cyclic or the collective. Without a way to slow the descent, the aircraft impacted the grass hard and bounced back up in the air slightly. The impact ripped the blades off the rotor and collapsed the tail boom, sending fan tail blades flying like pieces of shrapnel. Stefan felt the second impact of the doomed aircraft as it contacted the ground again, his helmet struck the instrument panel, and the world went black.

Chapter 7

Vicarage Road Stadium

Jan and Victoria had just exited the stadium when they heard the missiles behind them. Jan turned and saw the smoke contrails streak towards the helicopter. He winced as he heard the low boom of the missile's warhead detonation. A few seconds later, Jan heard the distant noise of something mechanical crashing. It sounded like a car hitting a wall, but there was no noise of tires sliding across the pavement, as is usually heard when an automobile wrecks. Jan froze in his tracks. He knew in his core that the sickening sound of metal crumpling and turf being dislodged was the funeral song of the men on his team. A quiet "Noo..." escaped his lips as he loosened his grip on Victoria's hand. She looked at him and saw the confidence in the man run away from his face. Her thoughts returned to the soldiers in black, who had to be nearby. "Captain," she called.

There was no answer. *"CAPTAIN,"* she repeated, this time more forcefully. He snapped out of his thoughts and looked at her.

"Right," he said, "We need to go." They ran to Vicarage Road, just a few feet away. They saw a vehicle approaching. Jan boldly walked into the street directly in front of the oncoming car. "Halt," he shouted as the vehicle screeched to a stop. The driver's side window came down, "Look mate, you off your rocker? Get out of the bloody road!" the driver shouted.

Jan woke up to the man hanging out of the window and began to raise the Benelli M4. "Out," he said to the driver, who began to panic and desperately clawed at the door pull to comply with this soldier in a grey uniform. Jan had to open the vehicle door to let the shaking man out. "Easy," he told the driver, "I won't harm you; I just need the car." The driver did not even nod in understanding as he scampered away and down the street, visibly shaken. Jan motioned to Victoria, "Get in," he said as he pulled the driver's door shut and put the car in gear. Jan let off the clutch, and the vehicle eased forward. They were safe for now, but they had to get rid of the vehicle and find shelter. "Captain, this is Echo," came the call over the radio, "I've lost contact with Rattler."

Jan answered, "Echo...they didn't make it. Make ready to break down the TOC and go dark for a while."

"Captain, who is with you?" Echo asked.

"Only Victoria," he replied, "The rest of the team got on the helicopter, and it was shot down with missiles."

Echo winced, "I copy Captain, Echo out."

They started driving West; Jan knew where they had to go; there were places he had memorized in case something like this happened during the mission. In fact, there was a network of them all over the world. "Where are we going?" Victoria asked.

"We're going to a friend," he said. "At least, I hope so." Victoria looked at Jan. She could see that he was gripping the steering wheel hard and slamming the shifter as he worked up through the gears.

"Jan," she began, "I'm so sorry. Thank you for helping me to get away." Jan was experiencing a flood of emotions and could not answer. His mind reeled as he felt many opposing emotions at once. Pride, despair, sorrow, joy, guilt, and relief assaulted his soul as he drove. The mission and the deep-seated will to keep going when he had nothing left was the only thing that kept him functioning. He saw another vehicle identical to the one he stole approaching on his left. He stopped and got out of the car, extracting a collapsible screwdriver as he did so. He quickly exchanged the license plates of the cars, so the parked car now wore the plates of a stolen vehicle. Jan gently pulled away and turned at the end of the street. He looked in the rearview mirror to see if anyone was about; no one was seen. Jan turned left onto the A410, which took them out of the town of Watford. "Where to now?" asked Victoria.

He looked at her with one of the most troubled expressions she had ever seen as he said, "Chesham."

140 Saint George Lane, Chesham UK

Mary Walker was in her kitchen. She had warmed up a pot of water for tea and was preparing to steep some herbal tea before bed. Mary was a pensioner, having spent a career in the NHS as an OR nurse. Her husband had passed away two years earlier, and her children had moved away long ago. She had planned to travel with Timothy, her husband, but he had fallen ill shortly after retiring from Rover Company Limited. She had taken up the unplanned duty of being a nurse once more, but the cancer was aggressive and took her husband at the age of sixty. At fifty-nine, she sometimes wondered aloud if death would come calling when she reached the age of her husband. Some days were easier than others, but the life of a widow with her children gone could be lonely indeed. Still, she kept a regular physical activity regimen, walked daily, and was careful to eat healthy. The tea was ready. She placed the teapot onto a tray and carried it to the living room, where she was going to watch television for a few minutes. She was engrossed in a variety show when she heard someone knock on her door. *"At this hour?"* she thought. The knock came again, the same pattern as before. Realization jolted through the synapses in her memory. This was not just a knock; this was a code and one that she was duty-bound to answer. She closed her eyes and slowly walked to the front door.

Jan repeated the sequence again. Before beginning the operation at the farmhouse, every team member memorized the locations of nearby homes that were owned by people loyal to the Order. No. 140 Saint George Lane was one of those homes. The door opened, and Jan was greeted by an older petite woman in her late fifties dressed in a robe. "We defend civilization..." Jan began.

"...And we care for the afflicted," Mary replied. "My name is Mary; how may I be of service to you, soldier?"

Jan let out a slow breath. The locations of these safe havens were always discussed in mission briefings, but this was the first time Jan had to use one. "Mary, we need a place to hide for a few hours," he said, "You may call me Jan. The woman accompanying me is Victoria."

"Well, better come in out of the cold," Mary said as she ushered Jan and Victoria into her cottage home. The home was old, with wood floors and plaster on the walls. But it was warm, and Victoria could feel the heat return to her flesh.

"Victoria, I need some time alone now that we're safe," Jan told her, "I..." The words drifted off, and for the first time in his life as a soldier of the Order, he did not know what to say or do. All he knew was he needed time alone to think and to get his emotions under control. He looked at Mary, "Is there a place I can be alone?" he asked.

"There is, Jan," Mary said, "You may use my bedroom for as long as you need."

"I'm sorry to impose further," he said again, "But can you stay with Victoria for a while?"

Mary took his hand and looked him right in the eye, "It's no bother, Jan. I hope you can find rest." As he went to the bedroom and closed the door, Mary looked at Victoria. "Fancy a cuppa, dear?"

Jan sat on Mary's bed and stared at the wall. The passage of time melted away. A minute, an hour? They were all the same to him. Now that he was alone, the thoughts he had forced down came flooding the front of his mind. He placed his head in his hands, and the tears came. Never, not once in his life did he feel so adrift. *It wasn't supposed to be this way,* one side of his mind would say. *"But it is this way...and it's your fault,"* the other side would answer. *"No... I made the right decision,"* he thought defensively. Then a cruel reply said, *"No,*

YOU should have DIED with them. Some captain you turned out to be."

Jan drank from a bottomless cup of anguish as he fought through this negative thinking. *"Stop it; you MUST pull yourself together; Victoria needs you,"* he told himself. The accuser in his mind was quick to answer, *"You're going to get her killed too."* "ENOUGH," he said aloud. He looked over at the bedside table and saw a well-used bible. He picked up the old King James Version and looked at its gold edge gilding, with many ribbons marking favorite passages. He turned to an Old Testament book he knew well; 1 Samuel. Only this time, he turned to chapter twenty-two.

"18 – And the king said to Doeg, Turn thou, and fall upon the priests. And Doeg the Edomite turned, and he fell upon the priests, and slew on that day fourscore and five persons that did wear a linen ephod.

19 – And Nob, the city of the priests, smote he with the edge of the sword, both men and women, children and sucklings, and oxen, and asses, and sheep, with the edge of the sword.

20 – And one of the sons of Ahimelech, the son of Ahitub, named Abiathar, escaped and fled after David.

21 And Abiathar showed David that Saul had slain the LORD's priests.

22 – And David said unto Abiathar, I knew it that day when Doeg the Edomite was there, that he would surely tell Saul: I have occasioned the death of all the persons of thy father's house.

23 – Abide thou with me, fear not: for he that seeketh my life seeketh thy life: but with me, thou shalt be in safeguard."

"I know how that feels," Jan thought as he read. He felt the same guilt David must have had thousands of years earlier. Earlier in the chapter, David seeks refuge in the town of Nob and meets with the priest, Ahimelech, who aids him and his men. Later, Doeg learns of this and tells King Saul, who, in a rage, orders his men to kill all the priests of the synagogue. When Saul can find no soldier to carry out the deed, Doeg volunteers. Doeg then leads an assault against Nob and murders everyone in the town, along with every ox, donkey, and sheep. Only Ahimelech's son, Abiathar, escapes, and then David tells him that he knew beforehand about Doeg. Jan could only imagine what Abiathar felt when David shared that bit of information. "You knew and told no one??" Abiathar must have said to David. *"Yet,"* Jan thought, *"The LORD was with David, wasn't he?*

It says there, 'Abide thou with me, fear not: for he that seeketh my life seeketh thy life: but with me, thou shalt be in safeguard.' Indeed, Abiathar should have no fear so long as he is with David because David had the LORD with him." Jan read on, and a thought came to him out of nowhere, "*This too shall pass...*" Jan stopped reading and looked up from the scriptures. The voice that accused him earlier was silent.

Victoria drank the hot liquid from the cup. The mint aroma filled her nostrils as she sipped. She did not realize how tired she was until she sat on Mary's couch. She felt like she could sleep for a week straight. Mary looked at her, Victoria's blond hair was out of place, and her borrowed scrubs were torn in places. "So, what's your story, dear?" Mary asked.

"All I know is that earlier this morning, I was kidnapped by some middle eastern guys while walking to school," she began, "They took me to a farmhouse, and I think they were going to kill me, but then Jan and these soldiers burst in and killed everyone..." Victoria's words drifted off, and she took a sip and continued, "...Now we are being hunted by these other soldiers dressed in black, they were at the farmhouse, and now they came to the hospital. Jan lost his whole team when their helicopter was shot down."

Mary thought for a moment and asked, "What do you know about the Order of Saint John?"

There it was, that odd organization that sounded like a charity. "Nothing," she answered, "I've never heard of that organization until... wait," the memories of her studies earlier that morning came flooding back. "I read about them in school," she started, "The Knights Hospitaller or later, The Order of Saint John, were Catholic knights that fought in the Crusades, then wound up with an order in Poland and another on the Island of Malta. The group in Malta were forced out by Napoleon Bonaparte, and the group in Poland allied with the Emperor of Russia." She stopped suddenly as a realization came to her. *"We've been with you a long time..."* Jan had said in the hospital. Victoria looked at Mary, "These can't be the same people!" She exclaimed.

"Why not?" Mary offered, "Is it so hard to believe what you see? In addition to being soldiers, the Knights Hospitaller invented institutionalized medicine. The Order pioneered the modern system of dedicated hospital facilities, the system of triage for prioritizing patients, and the top-down military-style organization of most hospitals. The first institution dedicated to treating the wounded and caring for the sick was in Jerusalem and was founded by the Order during the Crusades. Knights Hospitaller is where we get the modern word, hospital."

Victoria could not believe this... actual Knights in 2015? But that would explain why these soldiers sought refuge in a hospital, and Dr Roberts had said the same thing to Jan that Jan just said to Mary, *"We defend civilization, and we care for the afflicted."*

Victoria was beginning to realize the depth and size of this secret Order. "Also," Mary continued, "I don't know if you realized, but the soldiers who rescued you are all Poles; did you notice the slight accent?"

Victoria set her cup down and stared off into the living room. "Today, the order exists within the field of medicine as a secret society, and there's also another part of it that steers human events towards good; sometimes that requires a soldier with a weapon to go fight," Mary said, "Many doctors are retired soldiers of the Order. One of those doctors recruited me as a nurse long ago."

"Wait," Victoria began to ask, "When medical charities recruit doctors and go to war zones..."

Mary smiled, "That's right, dear. Those doctors and nurses loyal to the Order are the support infrastructure that assists knights on missions when they are called to intervene in a conflict; We defend civilization *and* care for the afflicted." Mary refilled Victoria's cup and then hers.

"Thank you," Victoria said, "Thank you for taking us in."

Mary smiled, "It's all in a day's work, dear."

Jan felt better and more grounded. The ache of losing his team was there, but it was distant, under control. Most important, that voice of self-doubt and incrimination was gone. He stood; it was time to stop and return to the living room. Jan found the two women talking back and forth, *"I probably should have told her more,"* he thought, thinking about Victoria, *"She must have many questions, and she's a part of this now."* That was one thing that bothered him. Victoria was dumped into this unrelenting combat operation, and although he had the training to deal with the stress, she had none. *"At least none I'm aware of,"* he thought, *"She is handling herself well."*

"Good to see you again," Mary said as Jan stepped into the room, "I've told Victoria a bit about us."

Mary gestured towards an easy chair, "Please join us, Jan. May I pour you some tea?"

"Yes, ma'am; two lumps, please," he said. He turned to Victoria, "I'm sorry I haven't told you more. You've been through a lot, and you deserve to know." Victoria set her cup on its saucer, "Jan," she started, "Mary told me you're a knight..."

"Yes," he said, "I and the rest of my team members are. The order recruits out of orphanages and trains us from the age of seven. We begin with physical strength training, military discipline, and history; this education is not unlike attendance at a military academy. Later, at fourteen, these former children become squires in a religious ceremony that involves giving the squire a sidearm consecrated by a priest of the order."

"Wait," Victoria exclaimed, "You give teenagers firearms?"

"Of course, this is a custom that reaches back across time into ages past," Jan said, "And you must understand that these young men come up in a radically different culture than the typical person today. By fourteen, these young men are no longer children and are ready for adult responsibilities, including handling weapons with wisdom. It's been this way for most of human history; the idea of young people being large children is a modern fallacy. Shortly after receiving his sidearm, the squire moves on to weapons training and small-unit combat. By the time he is twenty-one, the squire is ready to be sworn into the order as a knight. Each year, on Christmas Day, squires accept knighthood in a high mass that is intended to communicate the huge importance of what it means to be a knight of the order. Christmas Day is chosen because as the day celebrates the birth of Jesus Christ as the savior of mankind, the mass so too celebrates the birth of a new warrior to defend civilization until Christ's return. Once the former squire is sworn into the Order as a knight, he is given title, swears loyalty to the order and the Grand Master of his Priory, and then sent out for service around the world."

"And this has been going on since the Middle Ages?" she asked.

"It has," Jan said, "We are the latest soldiers in an ancient Order that goes back to the time of the

Crusades. We go where others fear to tread, volunteer when no one else will, and will do what is right even if it costs us our lives."

"You mean chivalry," she said.

He answered her, "That's the old word for it, yes. When a knight is sworn into the Order, they take vows of chastity, poverty, and piety. These vows sound alien to modern western culture, but to knights of the order, this rigid social structure keeps soldiers focused on their missions and their brothers-in-arms beside them."

"And the network of hospitals?" Victoria asked. "The hospital network we depend on to operate consists of two branches," he explained. "The first are doctors and nurses that keep their allegiance to the order secret but allow us access to their hospitals and medical services in time of need; that's who Dr Roberts was. The other branch operates within the Saint John of Jerusalem hospital network as a charity that provides medical services worldwide. This second branch operates the recruitment network of orphanages and most importantly allows access to conflict zones around the world. This allows the Order to quietly insert soldiers into these areas to shape world events for good."

Victoria shook her head, "Wait, so you're interfering in government policy?" she asked.

"Not exactly," he said, "Sometimes we are asked by various intelligence agencies to intervene on their behalf; that's what we were doing when we rescued you."

Victoria stiffened, "So you were working for Britain?"

"Well, let's say unofficially," Jan answered with a smile. "We were asked by some in Britain's intelligence service to monitor and persecute ISIS trying to get a foothold in the United Kingdom; that's how we saw your kidnapping. We thought we were going to simply eliminate the ISIS cell, but the arrival of those enemy soldiers has made this whole operation much more complex. The fact they found us in the hospital is troubling, very troubling."

Their conversation was interrupted by the news program on the television. The variety show Mary was watching earlier was interrupted by a breaking news report.

"This is Huw Edwards with the BBC. We interrupt this program to bring you breaking news. Tonight, at Watford Hospital, a crazed man with a gun came to

the hospital intent on violence. Fortunately, the Metropolitan Police were able to anticipate the suspect's actions and deployed to the hospital. A gun battle ensued, and police were able to subdue the suspect despite heavy casualties. Details are few, but the suspect is believed to be a disgruntled employee at the hospital. It is currently unknown if any hospital staff or patients were killed. We will be updating this story as it develops..."

"That's not what happened," said Victoria, "How could the news report be so wrong?"

Jan's thoughts wandered at that a bit. *"That could mean many things,"* he thought. "What that tells me is either the BBC is engaged in wild speculation to break the story first, or someone in the Metropolitan Police is intentionally feeding the BBC a false narrative," Jan said to them, "My suspicions tell me that the latter scenario is the truth, but why?"

"Jan, your team was engaged in combat, correct?' asked Mary.

"Absolutely," Jan answered, "A big fight. We were forced to destroy a part of the hospital, and our helicopter was shot down. We eliminated at least ten enemies..." His thoughts drifted off for a minute as he remembered something else, "Also, the enemy soldiers we fought were dressed in black and had **POLICE** markings on their armor."

"You're sure of that, Jan?" Mary asked.

"Yes," he said, "But that would mean the story of the crazed gunman was pre-arranged and intended to provide cover for the engagement. It also means that the police are involved in this somehow." Jan's thoughts swirled like a tornado in his mind. The three of them discovered something particularly important, something that ties the QRF response at the farmhouse with the attack at the hospital, and now this false story about a gunman to cover the gunfight at the hospital. That meant whoever was orchestrating these events knew that Jan's team would fight if engaged and knew that his team would seek refuge at the hospital.

"Jan, what do we do now?" Victoria said, pulling Jan back to the living room and away from his thoughts.

Jan answered her, "We rest here tonight, and then we go visit friends tomorrow."

Chapter 8

CIA Headquarters

James Carver paced the seventh-floor carpet of his office as the afternoon sun streamed in from the windows. This operation in Britain was going off the rails. *"What on earth was Drouin thinking?"* Carver thought as he slowly walked the breadth of his office. First, the farmhouse attack where the responding security force stumbled into a dug-in and well-equipped foe, and now they destroy half of a hospital trying to get some bit of revenge? He was tasked with trying to knock Europe out of its stability, to shake things up so the U.K. citizens would fear for their safety and hastily adopt rash and restrictive measures that would make the population complainant and easy to control. Instead of accomplishing this mission covertly through an intermediary funding and equipping ISIS cells, he was now talking to his counterpart at MI-6 and assuring him that no US-backed operations are being carried out on British soil! That business, with the request coming in from Pogi earlier to plant an identity inside the NHS for a fictitious gunman, was inconvenient. Overt moves like that were sure to be noticed by MI-5 and made it much more difficult to conceal CIA involvement.

Carver asked aloud, "Why couldn't we have found a more experienced field officer?"

He knew the answer to that, of course. No experienced field officer wanted the job. He asked a few trusted men he knew in Europe to do the assignment. When no one volunteered, he called in favors. When that did not work, he even resorted to threats. Even being leaned on by the Deputy Director of Operations did not budge these men's convictions; one even said he would retire rather than take the assignment. That left Carver with Pogi, an ambitious young field agent who did not have the sense to say no, but that also meant that he did not have the experience to kick off a color revolution in a Western nation without attracting attention. Pogi also did not have the experience to handle a man like Drouin. *"Drouin will manipulate that poor kid fifty different ways before this operation is over,"* Carver thought. He didn't want to involve Drouin in a CIA operation, but orders were orders. Besides, Drouin had control over a private military company that had worked with the CIA for years, allowing the CIA to keep a much lower profile.

The CIA pioneered the use of these private armies back in the 1990s. The President back then was reluctant to commit U.S. troops after a few failures, and the CIA could no longer rely on Army Special Forces or the Marine Corps being available when requested. A new source of combat resources was needed, and companies emerged in the 80s and 90's where one could simply purchase these resources when needed. As long as the dollars kept flowing to these companies, the CIA could have all the soldiers it wanted. As an added benefit, these mercenaries did not wear a U.S. flag on their arm, thus providing the CIA with instant plausible deniability.

At least he had the French station chief on board with the operation and could at least keep an eye on Pogi. *"And keep my involvement with this to a minimum,"* Carver thought. The DDO position was a political one, as were many senior civil service positions in the U.S. Government. One did not rise to the director position without some help along the way, and he was wise enough to know that operations to destabilize "friends" were fraught with opportunity and peril.

For a man like him, it was best to stay on the margin of the operation; that way, he could claim the credit if it were a success but deny involvement if it became a failure. *"The President was no help either,"* he thought. Carver remembered the day he was asked by the Director of the CIA and the National Security advisor that the National Security Council, through the Executive Office of the President, was ordering ISIS cells activated in the United Kingdom. *"That's how you order Europe destabilized, but keep your hands clean,"* Carver thought.

The President wanted no part of this, so he used the EOP to issue orders instead of an executive order. The CIA had carefully created the terror group in the years prior, in the same way, they had created the Taliban through the Mujahedeen when they allowed the more radical elements of the group to take over Afghanistan after the Soviet Union left in 1989. After a decade-long campaign in Afghanistan and Iraq to support the "Global war on Terror," the CIA was behind the Arab Spring uprising in early 2011. Back then, the purpose was to destabilize the Middle East, which would accomplish two things; one, there would be a refugee crisis that would put a strain on Europe, and second, it would allow more radical elements to take over weakened governments.

There was room on the earth for only one superpower, and America felt that the European

Union was growing too big. The plan worked beautifully, and the CIA was able to create ISIS with seized funds from nations like Tunisia and Egypt and arm them with weapons seized from the Gaddafi regime in Libya. The color revolutions drove civilians out of the region to Europe in the hope of a better life and a more stable environment to raise their children. That mass migration put a strain on the immigration services of European Nations and allowed ISIS operatives to slip into the E.U. unnoticed. Once inside the E.U., they could travel freely anywhere in Europe. Four years later, after the initial uprising, the destabilization plan was ready to begin; only now it was threatened by a loose cannon of a billionaire and an inexperienced field agent. Carver swore, he had to get Pogi to exercise more restraint and keep the CIA's involvement in this to an absolute minimum. He picked up the phone to dial the French Station Chief in Paris.

The cell phone rang in Randy Campbell's apartment. He reached for it blindly as he woke up. Calls after midnight usually meant something bad was happening. One look at the caller's I.D. confirmed that suspicion. "Campbell," he said into the phone.

"Randy, It's Jim Carver," Campbell swore in his thoughts as he wondered what this was about. A personal call from the DDO qualified as bad.

"Yes, Sir. What can I help you with?" Campbell said.

There was nothing else he could really do; Carver occupied a far senior position to a mere Station Chief. "Randy, I'm worried about the op underway with Pogi. Call me back on the STE."

The call abruptly terminated. Campbell got out of bed and went to his home office, where the NSA had installed an STE secure telephone system. These all-digital units replaced the older analogue STU-series phones and were much better. He called the DDO using the proper extension. He did not have to wait long. "Randy?" The DDO said into the phone.

"What's got you worried about Pogi, sir?" Campbell asked.

"He's using the CIA resource system too much. First, we get a requisition for communist-bloc arms shipments. A week later, we got a request for U.S.-made small arms, then an urgent request for FIM-92 stinger missiles. The arms shipments can be concealed easily enough. The problem is he's now asking MI-6 to intervene in police investigations to provide an excuse for a huge gunfight that occurred at Watford Hospital earlier today. The U.K. is part of FVEY; if Pogi isn't more careful, MI-6 is going to discover our operation," Carver said.

Campbell cursed again. FVEY was an abbreviation of FIVE-EYE, which was the name of an intelligence alliance between The United States, Great Britain, Australia, Canada, and New Zealand. This alliance had been advantageous to the CIA historically, but that also meant it was exceedingly difficult to conceal an operation from a FVEY member nation. Pogi making these requests, no doubt the suggestion of Drouin, did not help. Carver was right to be concerned about Pogi; he did not have the experience for this kind of delicate operation. *"This is what happens when you staff European stations with experienced field agents close to retirement and ask them to take a career-buster of an assignment,"* Campbell thought with a smile, *"They all turned you down and left you with no one to turn to but a field agent long on ambition but short on experience."* It was time to get Carver to relax.

"I'll talk to Pogi, sir," Campbell said, "If you can keep MI-6 from digging too deeply into this, I think we can salvage the operation." Carver let out a long breath on the other end of the security line. This is exactly what he wanted to hear.

Schloss Drouin

Drouin sat at his massive desk enjoying a late-night brandy. The study, like the rest of the palatial home, was richly appointed. The desk itself was made from a dozen different trees from African and Sumatran rainforests. Woods chosen for their beauty and rarity were chosen for the desk's construction. Drouin was a man who liked to keep fine things. Pogi was enjoying one of Drouin's fine possessions now, and Drouin smiled at the mental image. *"People were so easy to control,"* He thought, *"Most want to be led by a ruler."*

Drouin steered his thoughts to the evening's events as he took another sip of the brandy. He had just ended a phone call with Major Aubert. Thanks to the CIA's missiles, he was successful in ending these irritating Knights of the Order. Aubert thought that the girl the knights rescued was not on the helicopter. He also thought it was possible a knight was with her and survived. No matter – if either of them were foolish enough to show themselves, Drouin had already decided to have them killed. Aubert had also said he was going to use a social media app to try to find them. Aubert had told him the name of the app and how it worked, but that was the business of servants; Drouin did not really care.

The re-emergence of the Order of Saint John was an incredible stroke of luck. He had heard rumors of their existence all his life, but to have actual confirmation was something rich indeed. He thought back to his ancestor and the port of Valetta that night two hundred and sixteen years ago. General Bonaparte had stumbled into an economic ruse that cost France dearly. When he tried to exact revenge against those in Russia who were responsible, it cost him the Gran Armeé and the throne of Europe. Long before the Renaissance in Italy, Drouin's family had carefully positioned itself to grow its wealth and power. When Napoleon I was crowned emperor of France but could not sire an heir with Josephine, an opportunity emerged to grow the family power beyond anything believed possible.

The House of Drouin worked quickly once prenuptial negotiations fell apart with the Emperor of Russia and offered one of their eligible daughters as an alternative. Eager to cement his royal position as ruler of France through marriage to a royal European family, Napoleon I accepted the offer.

Despite objections from the House of Drouin, Napoleon I began his great campaign into Russia and squandered a great opportunity to rule the continent of Europe for a century. The House of Drouin reorganized after that doomed military adventure and again positioned itself to benefit from the chaos. The family went silent in major military adventure once more until an opportunity once again presented itself once all of Europe plunged into conflict on July 28, 1914. House Drouin worked on both sides of the war, funneling arms and financial assistance to the Kaiser and the Hapsburgs while sending sons to fight in the French and Russian armies. House Drouin stood ready with eligible royal daughters to wed the victor's sons and would then be able to rule Europe unopposed.

The Russian Communist revolution in October 1917 changed the calculus of geopolitical events in Europe, and with the Treaty of Versailles all but ensuring a future conflict between the victors of WW1 and a humiliated German Empire, House Drouin began to realize that their plans for ruling Europe through a political or military opportunity were a fool's errand. The age of the old royal bloodlines as rulers of Europe ended as East and West squared off to fight a conflict by proxy in the far-flung corners of the world. Drouin's father, Friedrich, had dedicated himself to the pursuit of peace and of intellectual study. His vision was to transition the House of Drouin from a major royal player in European court politics to a force for philanthropy. Drouin remembered how angry he was at his father when he returned from university only to hear him talk about feeding the hungry and trying to broker peace deals. The old man was a traitor to his heritage and was unworthy of the family name, Anton Drouin had thought back then. Fortunately for Drouin, he did not have to wait long, as in 1977, the elderly Frederick passed away when Drouin was only twenty-two. Drouin worked quickly to cancel his father's foolhardy philanthropic ventures and aggressively consolidated the family's wealth and power. Realizing he could not do this alone, Drouin appealed for support from the young heirs of old European royal families.

Most of the heirs turned him down; they had bought into the toxic thinking of having European commoners rule themselves while the European aristocracy was destined to assume a quiet role in European art and high culture. Drouin despised these soft princes of the once-strong families.

Five hundred years ago, such weaklings would be sent to languish in asylums or exiled. To Drouin's delight, he was able to find like-minded heirs from two of the old network of families. Baron Von Muller from the House of Sion in Germany and Archduke Martinez from the Duchy of Cordoba in Spain answered Drouin's call.

All three men shared the dream of a united Europe under one all-powerful dynasty, and all three were committed to the task. In an ancient ceremony that dated back to medieval times, the three formed a triumvirate and pledged their families' fortunes and futures to the shared goal of a European feudal empire. Drouin took another sip of his brandy and savored the rich bouquet of the priceless liquid. When the House of Sion and the Duchy of Cordoba unified under the banner of House Drouin, the three men knew that they lacked the military strength or the political influence to seize power through conflict. They did have money and the ability to issue titles of nobility, and they found that ambitious politicians in Europe were all too willing to accept both. Drouin chuckled, *"That was a benefit of operating in a culture that placed great importance on titles of nobility and who could trace their family line back centuries,"* he thought.

Despite recent experiments with representative government and democratic elections, Europe was still a feudal system. The triumvirate realized they could exploit the democratic system and simply purchase the loyalty of politicians and government officials or appeal to their vanity by secretly issuing them a title that would allow privileged access to the upper crust of European cosmopolitan society. In truth, the titles did not instill noble lineage onto the bearer of such a document, but a few calls to the right families in Europe created the illusion as though they did.

In a way, the triumvirate created the largest title of nobility scam the continent of Europe had ever seen. In return for money or privilege, these governmental vassals to the triumvirate would be expected to answer when called. The network of financial support in exchange for favors had spread to the new world as well, specifically to the United States. Through subtle politicking and injections of capital when necessary, the triumvirate had even been able to co-opt the loyalty of the President of the United States. It was easy. Drouin had spent one hundred million dollars on the election, and in return the U.S. President did whatever he wanted. Drouin had tens of billions of dollars in liquid cash, and the sum he spent on the election was inconsequential. With the support of the President and some of his senior cabinet members, assistance from the CIA had become available, which made the triumvirate's task easier. The great irony was that the CIA did not even know it was being used. Here was the great intelligence agency of the United States, being played like a flute by European aristocracy who knew the fine art of wielding power. *"Animals,"* Drouin thought, *"The common people are like animals and want to be ruled. Even more so when you fill their hearts with terror and provide vivid examples of danger."* Like a young student's head being removed from her body by religious fanatics.

The LSE student was but the first kidnapping that was planned. Other abductions and murders would soon follow from the two other ISIS cells that Drouin was funding. These murders were intended to make the flock fear their neighbors and live in constant terror that any one of them might be abducted and slaughtered next. *"Yes, once frightened, the flock will run into the corral I've set for them,"* Drouin mused. In fact, the laws rescinding freedom of travel and initiating harsh curfews were all prewritten and ready for consideration in parliament. Still, other legislative proposals were set to control banking and cash flow under the cover story of strangling terrorists' access to funding networks. In practice, these laws were so restrictive they would implement quotas on what Britons could buy and when. This new financial system was the WWII British rationing system on overdrive. Penalties for noncompliance were numerous and severe. Hard times and extreme peril called for harsh ways.

These laws were the foundation for the implementation of similar legislative proposals across the parliaments of Europe, where ISIS cells would unexpectedly pop up again and again and again. The kidnappings would keep happening until the triumvirate got the laws it wanted passed. It was easy, really. Dangle the promise of safety in front of the herd of commoners in times of peril, and they will happily hand over their freedom for the promise of normalcy. Drouin set his snifter down and looked at the fireplace. The embers were dying, and he had a desire to retire for the evening.

Drouin stood and exited the study. He walked the hallway of the master's wing of his palace. There were nearly ten thousand square feet of living space set aside for Drouin here. There were dressing rooms, private baths, and even a small satellite library that servants could stock with Drouin's favorite books and maps. Drouin lived like one of the eighteenth-century rulers of Europe here. An army of staff supported his lifestyle, though he never saw any of them unless he specifically called for one to appear before him.

There was a network of passageways in the palace that staff could use to move about unseen. In addition, there was a strict code of conduct for staff that, if violated, would result in immediate dismissal. One of those rules was to never be seen by the master unless specifically called. To a visitor who had no knowledge of how an ancient imperial household operated, beds made themselves, meals appeared when requested, and clothing was laundered and put away once worn. Drouin entered his massive bedroom and saw that his bed was turned down and ready, and the maids had pre-warmed the sheets minutes before he came into the room. He removed his slippers and robe and slid into bed. Drouin closed his eyes and had the most restful sleep he had experienced in years.

Chapter 9

London

Jan and Victoria were on the London Underground's Metropolitan Line on the way into the city. They had an opportunity to change clothing once Mary took their sizes and went shopping that morning. Jan was dressed in slacks and a sweater, with a large grey field jacket that concealed his Heckler & Koch USP 9 pistol. Victoria wore tan riding pants and boots with a white blouse and a navy-blue barn coat. As Jan had said last night, they were on their way to the city center to meet with friends. The suburbs and row houses streaked by the window as the train reached its destination. Victoria was surprised she got any sleep last night, but her body was exhausted from the physical exertion, and her mind was spent from so many close brushes with death. She looked over at Jan from her seat by the window. He was focused on the environment around him, appearing as though he were bored or disinterested, but his eyes were constantly moving. He had a paperback novel he was using to hide his intentions. He was not reading a novel to pass the time; he was scanning for threats.

Victoria was deep in thought, *"What are the odds,"* she mused, *"That a knight from the very order I was studying in my European History class yesterday is sitting right next to me?"*

She examined his handsome face and his piercing blue eyes. *"Not only a real knight,"* she thought, *"But a tall, dark, and handsome one as well."*

He towered over her, and she knew he was impossibly strong from when he carried her after she momentarily passed out when his team saved her last night. She felt her heart flutter at the thought of this man, only to have her conscience interrupt her thoughts. *"Oh, come on,"* she thought, *"Can't I have at least one impure thought without being disturbed?"*

"No." came the reply inside her head. She forced her mind elsewhere as the train entered the tunnel that would take it under the city streets.

The window went dark as the train car's overhead lights gave a soft glow to the cabin. The air pressure changed as another train sped by them, and Victoria popped her ears by opening her mouth. Jan glanced at a station map mounted in the train car. Their stop was coming up ahead,

Euston Square. "We will be at our stop soon," Jan said.

Victoria nodded as the train closed its doors and smoothly accelerated from Baker Street Station. "Next stop, Euston Square," the operator's voice came over the intercom. The train smoothly came to a stop, and the sliding doors opened. Jan and Victoria rose and exited the train, just like another couple on their way this early afternoon. They rode the escalator, coming up to street level inside a glass-walled station foyer. They left the station together, and the pair stepped onto the sidewalk of Gower Street. An aggressive panhandler saw them. Thinking he had an easy mark, he stood up from his spot and walked towards the well-dressed couple.

Jan saw him coming. He put himself between the panhandler and Victoria, rising to his full height, and put out his left hand. In a booming voice that could be heard across the street, he addressed the vagrant, "I can't help you." The panhandler stopped in his tracks. He saw Jan's right hand casually slip inside his field jacket and decided these two were not the kind of people to rob. He said an obscenity to Jan and walked back to his spot, grumbling. Jan watched him the entire time; only when the vagrant sat back down did he remove his hand from the USP 9. Jan relaxed his body as he turned to walk away, his left hand gently taking Victoria's right as he moved. Three steps later and it was as if nothing had happened. One block later, an immense five-story red brick building appeared on their right. Jan looked both ways as he stepped into the street, Victoria's hand in his. She felt the penetrating heat from his hand as they reached the opposite sidewalk and ascended the entry steps to the building. A sign-out front read:

Saint John of Jerusalem School of Medicine

Jan stepped ahead to open the door for her, and the two went inside the building. As they stepped across the threshold, warm air greeted them. Jan looked at a map of the building, which was built in the shape of a cruciform. Jan committed the map to memory and told Victoria, "The department we need is this way. We can find a friend there."

The medical school was another one of those "safe places" where knights could find refuge in times of need. They walked the white tiled halls together, up a staircase, through an arch, and past a warren of hallways and rooms. They passed students scurrying about, making their way to a lecture or a laboratory session. Finally, they arrived at the Pathology Department, and Jan looked at the directory. "Room 432," he said aloud. The name next to the room number read:

Dr. Robert Turner – Professor of Pathology

Dr. Turner was in his office, having just finished answering a question from one of his medical students. He was past sixty years of age, with a white Quaker beard. He was thin, dressed in a lab coat with his signature bow tie. Dr. Turner looked over the graded exam papers. Those had to go back to the students tomorrow, and there was also a lab class to prepare. He would ask his lab assistant if everything was ready for... He stopped his train of thought when he saw a figure at the door to his office. He looked up and recognized the face immediately. "Jan!" he exclaimed and rose to his feet. The two men embraced in a bear hug. "My goodness! I wasn't expecting to see you, son," He looked over at Victoria, "Oh, excuse me, my dear." He looked back at Jan, noticing the pistol on Jan's hip.

"This isn't a social visit, is it?" Doctor asked.

"No," Jan replied, "It's not. We need your help."

Dr. Turner nodded and picked up his phone, "Mildred?" he called his secretary, "Hold my appointments for the rest of the day. I need to attend to a personal matter." He offered Jan and Victoria seats in his office as he got up and shut the door. "Now," he said, "How might I help?"

Jan told Dr. Turner everything. He described Victoria's kidnapping, the farmhouse raid, the inexplicable response by the soldiers in black who were supporting the ISIS cell, and the death of his team in the helicopter crash. Dr. Turner winced at that last point, "Son, I'm so sorry. I have lost men under my command, and it's never easy." He looked over at Victoria and her confused expression. "I wasn't always a doctor, dear," he said with a wink. "Jan, tell me about these soldiers who attacked you, who always are following you like a shadow. They are the key to understanding what is going on."

"They are Caucasian," Jan began, "They move and respond to threats like they have had formal military training. They have identical clothing and weapons. There's a clear command structure; there are officers and NCOs for sure. Lastly, all of them had the same patch on the left sleeve of their uniforms."

Dr. Roberts took an interest in that last point. "The patch," he said, "Tell me about the patch. Was it a unit insignia? Once you recognize?"

"I don't know," Jan answered, "But I can tell you what it looked like. It was a blue patch in the shape of a shield with a gold eagle embroidered on the shield. The eagle held something in its talons, but I'm not sure what it was."

Dr. Turner smiled, "That's the key to this, son. Jan, Victoria, my dear? Please come with me to the library. We need to meet with the Historian of the Order."

Dr. Turner walked through the halls of his medical school as Jan and Victoria kept up. They walked deeper and deeper into the interior of the red brick building. The tiled hallways gave way to wood-paneled walls and oak bookshelves. Dr. Turner approached the librarian's desk with authority. A stout woman with glasses looked up from a ledger illuminated by the soft glow of a green desk lamp. "Good afternoon, Alice," Dr. Turner addressed her with a smile.

Alice beamed; Dr. Turner was a charming individual and one of the most adored professors at the school. "Good afternoon, Robert!" Alice replied.

"Alice, I need to see the historian." The smile was gone; this was a serious matter indeed. Alice looked over at the man and woman who came in with Dr. Turner. One look at Jan confirmed her suspicions; *order business.* "I'll ring him right away," she said, "Go on ahead. He will be expecting you."

Dr. Turner led Jan and Victoria through the library to a small door between two bookcases. He unlocked the door with a key and held it open for them. Jan and Victoria entered the landing of a narrow spiral staircase. Dr. Turner closed the door behind them and walked deeper into the floors beneath the library's main level. There was an oak door down here, at the base of the wrought iron staircase, the door illuminated by a small sconce light fixture above. There was a brass plate on the door, it read:

HISTORIAN OF THE ORDER OF SAINT JOHN

Dr. Turner opened this door, and the three stepped inside the room. The walls of the long rectangular room were brick, and the ceiling was not remarkably high here. Steel cabinets lined the walls of this room; each had a small green LED on the door. The cabinets were a temperature-controlled archive environment for documents, old documents. In the center of the room was a large square table with a leather top. At the opposite end of the room was a series of reading desks, each with a green desk lamp the same as the librarian had above. From around a rolltop desk, a diminutive man appeared. He was small, about the size of Victoria, and not a pound heavier. He wore horn-rimmed round glasses and a mustache. His hair was greying, and he wore a tweed jacket. He walked up to Dr. Turner, shook his hand, and asked, "What brings you down here, Doctor?"

"A question about an insignia," Dr. Turner gestured towards Jan, "Tell him, Captain."

Jan began, "We need information on a patch found on the sleeves of enemy soldiers." Jan described the blue patch with the golden eagle to the Historian.

"That's not a military unit. It sounds more like a coat of arms. We have detailed records of heraldry. If a coat of arms matches, it should not be difficult to find." The Historian walked over to a computer terminal and opened a search application. He set filter parameters and let the computer run a search of its database. Seven coats of arms came up. He looked at Jan and asked, "Do any of these coats of arms match what you saw?"

Jan looked hard at the screen and pointed, "That one."

"Come with me to the main table," the Historian said. He walked over to the table and touched the leather with his delicate hand. The table's surface was not leather at all but rather a high-definition touch-sensitive LCD screen. The blue coat of arms with the gold eagle appeared on the screen. The group gathered around the table as the Historian began to speak. "Here we have a coat of arms, Azure Escutcheon, Old French in shape, with an 'Or' eagle displayed overt with a thunderbolt in its talons. Captain, this is the crest of the house of Bonaparte."

It got noticeably quiet in the room. Jan asked, "As in Napoleon I, the emperor of France?"

"Yes," the Historian answered, "Napoleon I adopted this coat of arms in 1804. It was changed in 1808, and again in 1813."

Jan had more questions, "Did the order ever cross paths with Napoleon?"

The Historian continued, "Yes, in 1798. But this was the Order on the island of Malta." The Historian brought up more information on the table. He touched a file icon, and a scanned document appeared. "Look here, there's a report from Captain Zajac," the Historian said. "It's in Polish; let me find the translated document...there. It says that Captain Zajac and his men landed in the port of Valetta for routine business and communication between the various priories in Europe one month before the French war fleet arrived. He reports that Grand Master Hompesch provoked the French fleet into attacking the city over a re-supply dispute. Zajac then arrested Hompesch and organized a defense of the city. Once the French invasion force had been bloodied a bit, Zajac ran up the white flag and requested terms from the French."

The Historian read on, and the others listened to him convey the story about how Zajac tricked General Bonaparte into thinking he was Hompesch and carried out financing negotiations between the Order and France. He also secured estates for the real Hompesch to provide the excuse to name Hompesch a traitor and allow the Priory of Saint Petersburg to take over the Priory of Malta. He also planted the offer of financing the campaign in the Orient through the Order's financial institution, which was merely cover for capital supplied by the Emperor of Russia. The Historian brought up another document on the table. This one was a report from a spy in France. The report said that Napoleon I, discovered that the Order had played a role in extracting a significant amount of wealth from France. The discovery was made sometime in January 1810. The discovery may have played a role in Napoleon's decision to pull out of marriage negotiations with the Empire of Russia. The Historian added, "The Order of Saint John did fight when the French army invaded Russia, but that was the last time the order had any direct contact with Napoleon."

Dr. Turner placed his hand on his chin, deep in thought. "Are there any surviving descendants of Napoleon today?"

"Not directly," the Historian answered, "Napoleon had three brothers and three sisters, and although Jerome Bonaparte has surviving descendants, the House of Bonaparte does not use the heraldry you saw the soldiers wearing."

"Dead end," thought Jan. A thought occurred to him, "Who did Napoleon marry?" The Historian brought up more documents on the table, "Napoleon I married Josephine in 1796 when he was still a general in the French Army. He divorced her on December 14, 1809. Napoleon remarried Marie of House Drouin on March 13, 1810, although the actual wedding took place in April." "Drouin," Jan said aloud. "Does the house of Drouin exist today?" The Historian moved his hands over the display and brought up the order of succession for the House of Drouin. "Yes," the Historian answered, "The House of Drouin's current heir is Anton Drouin, aged fifty. He currently has no children, and his father Friedrich died in 1977." "List known assets of Anton Drouin," Jan asked. The Historian recited the assets of the family. These were mostly corporations and trusts formed by wealthy families to minimize tax liability. The Historian placed each corporation on the screen and had the computer automatically search for company assets and sub-assets, nesting the results on the large table screen like a corporate family tree.

"Filter results by company type," Jan told the Historian, "Look for any military contractors, security companies, or anything defense related." Those filter parameters narrowed the results significantly. There was one company that stood out, Legion Services. The company logo was the herald of House Bonaparte. "That's it," Jan said, "That's the company."

The Historian brought the website for Legion Services up, filling most of the table with the webpage. "This company provides secure transport, executive protection, infantry training, and armed security anywhere in the world," the Historian said.

"It sounds like a mercenary company," Victoria said.

"It is," the Historian went on, "The company hires most of its employees from Legion Entrangere or the French Foreign Legion."

"That would explain how they reacted to combat," Jan thought, *"These men had obviously been trained by someone."*

"But why are people from this company trying to kill me and Jan?" Victoria asked, "Why did they kill Jan's team?"

"That's a question for Echo," Jan said.

Jan brought over the Polycom SoundStation conference phone and dialed a number. He waited as the phone rang on speaker. Echo had just left a coffee shop when he heard his cell phone ring. He did not recognize the number.

"Field office"

"This is Foxtrot, Authentication; x-ray delta tango."

"Echo acknowledges Foxtrot. Challenge code?"

"Bravo two, Mike."

"Go ahead, Foxtrot."

Echo let out a long breath of relief as he heard Jan begin to speak. "Echo, it's good to hear you," Jan said, "I have you on speaker with Dr. Turner, Victoria, and the Historian. Were you followed?"

"No, Captain," Echo said, "The enemy had no knowledge of my involvement, and I encountered no resistance. The equipment is already relocated and active."

Jan had new orders for Echo, "Head there now, Echo. I need you to start researching everything you can about Legion Services and their owner, Anton Drouin."

Jan said, "Specifically, I need to know if there's any connection between Drouin and the ISIS cell that we attacked last night." Echo thought at that. He was only a few minutes away from the sea container. "Echo acknowledges, Captain. I'll call you when I have something" Echo increased the pace of his walk as he made his way back to the sea container and his computer.

Victoria walked around the Historian's archive as they waited for Echo's phone call. The Historian called for tea and sandwiches to be brought down, as it was already past three in the afternoon. Victoria did not hear Dr. Turner come up beside her. "One does not need to be clairvoyant to see you've got questions, my dear," He gently told her in a quiet voice. "If you're ready, I'll answer them."

"I feel like I've fallen into a fairy tale," she said. "Yesterday, I was a student pursuing an economics degree; now I..." It happened. The feelings all hit Victoria at once, and her knees shook. If Dr. Turner were not there to catch her, she would have fallen onto the stone floor. Jan made it over to her in three large steps. Together, Jan and Dr. Turner lifted Victoria into a chair as she recovered. Dr. Turner looked at Jan and said, "She'll be all right, son. Give me a moment with her if you'd be so kind?" Jan reluctantly walked away as Dr. Turner looked back at Victoria.

"My dear," he said, "I'm not a psychiatrist, but it's clear that you're carrying something big."

She nodded, "Up until yesterday, I thought I'd get my degree, get married, and have children. Now I feel like I'm being hunted, and I don't know why!" She put her face in her hands and cried. The stress was too much, and the tears needed to come. Sobs shook her shoulders as tears streamed down her face. Through it all, Dr. Turner sat there patiently, not saying a word. When he saw that

Victoria was slowly beginning to recover, he handed her his white handkerchief.

She took it and said, "Thank you," through a final sob. "Look at me," she said, "I'm a mess." She forced a laugh, "You all must think I'm pretty silly, crying like this?"

"No, I think you're exactly the person you were created to be," he said.

"Remember that the outside culture teaches that men and women are the same, and pits them against one another in an eternal struggle to come out the victor. My culture, the culture of the Order, and our code of chivalry teach that men and women are separated pieces of the same whole, and we are meant to work together with Christ leading us spiritually to overcome impossible situations."

Victoria's eyes widened, "Why have I not heard that before? I've never heard that taught at mass!"

Dr. Turner was surprised. "You're Catholic?" he asked.

She nodded, "My mother took us, I was confirmed at sixteen, but I've never heard that before."

Dr. Turner smiled, "Are you so sure? The Bible talks about this in the book of Genesis. Do you remember that God caused a deep sleep to fall upon Adam, and he took the rib and formed the first woman?"

A look of understanding washed over her, "Part of the same whole..." she mouthed. Dr. Turner looked at her, his kind eyes. "And what happened after?" Dr. Turner went on, "After the expulsion from Eden, Adam and Eve needed each other to survive, and God was with them." Victoria was quiet, her mind working out what she had heard with new understanding. Dr. Turner continued, "You're here with us for a reason, Victoria. Right now, you need Jan to protect you and to do what he does best," His voice got quiet for a minute as he looked over at Jan and the Historian. "And trust me, Jan needs you too. More than he realizes."

MI-6 Headquarters, London

Archer had just ended a troubling phone call with Echo. Echo had told him about the hospital attack and the helicopter crash. Archer was terribly upset. Not only did he have confirmation of active ISIS cells operating on British soil, but he was now told that a well-armed and well-financed group of experienced operators were pulling security for the cells. After the Watford hospital incident and that request from the CIA to demand that special branch not look too deeply into what was clearly not an attack by a lone gunman, Archer started investigating on his own. It did not take long to discover that the CIA had hacked into the hospital record system and placed a false identity there of a "disgruntled employee" who was to carry out the attack. Archer phoned a few of his CIA friends, the older, more experienced field agents like himself who were nearing retirement.

All the men he talked to had the same sour response; there was a quiet operation going on in Britain, one they did not agree with. Some of these men had even been approached by the Deputy Director of Operations himself and turned him down. One had even retired in protest rather than take control of an operation that was going to end with an international incident. Archer then called colleagues in MI-5 and MI-6. He got the same answer; leadership had approached experienced field agents about a secretive operation, but none accepted. Once he got that troubling news, Archer thought for a minute, *"What do I know? I have the kidnapping and failed murder of an American college student. I have ISIS cells operating in Britain, certain to try a kidnapping and murder again. I have CIA involvement; they are running an op on British soil, and MI-5 and MI-6 are probably involved."*

Echo had given him something else, the one thing that could break this case open; a name – Anton Drouin. Archer picked up his desk phone and called one of his team members. "Will? It's John. Can you investigate Anton Drouin for me? He's from an aristocratic family and owns multiple companies and trusts. I need to see if there is a connection between a PMC called Legion Services and Drouin," He thought for a minute and added, "Also, see if Drouin has provided financial assistance to any MP or person in the MOD who oversees MI-6. Oh, and Will?"

"Yeah?" came the reply.

"Do so carefully."

The phone rang in the sea container an hour later. Echo picked up the phone, and it was Archer. "Echo, you won't believe this. Not only is there a connection between Anton Drouin and Legion Services, but we also found a financial connection between Drouin and the ISIS cell."

"That's the connection Jan suspected," thought Echo. "Furthermore," Archer continued, "Drouin was sloppy about hiding his financial connections. He either didn't know how to hide them or simply didn't care. Lastly, and perhaps most concerning, the weapons Legion Services are using definitely came through the CIA." Archer's eyes about popped out of his head when he discovered that little fact. The CIA was funneling bloody stinger missiles to this madman Drouin. The shipment of FIM-92 missiles stood out like a beacon in the FVEY intelligence-sharing system. The M-4 rifles would have gone unnoticed, but some fool at the CIA insisted on agency control of the entire shipment, where if they had done a routine weapons transfer between US Army units, the shipment of stingers would have been missed. Instead, they were lumped in together, and a name kept coming up; Jason Pogi.

Echo told Archer, "This is very useful information John. Thank you for looking."

Archer hesitated, "Echo, there's something more..." He knew he should not be volunteering this information, but it was important. "MI-6 is involved in allowing these ISIS cells to operate in Britain. I've uncovered financial connections between Drouin and many of our MPs and senior government officials. I've even found financial connections between Drouin and the CIA."

Echo gripped the phone a bit tighter as Archer relayed his suspicions. "Echo, understand that I cannot prove any of this in court, but it's very suspicious. These financial connections look like bribes."

Echo had to call Jan back and share this information. "John, again, thank you for sticking your neck out for us. What are we to do with this information?"

Echo was direct with his question. This was a deep rabbit hole, and the Order needed direction from their client on this extremely sensitive subject. "Just hold for now, Echo," Archer said, "This, as you know, must be handled delicately; MI-6 and a good portion of the British government just got caught in a nasty corruption scandal. I'll need time to get my house in order and ferret out who I can trust. I'll be in contact." Archer terminated the conversation.

Echo relayed the information to Jan, Victoria, Dr. Turner, and the Historian. All stood around the glow of the display table in silence as Echo spoke. "That's it," Jan said first, "Drouin is involved in all of this. Do we know where he is?"

"I'm working on that, Captain," Echo answered, "As soon as I find out, I'll call you. Captain, there is one other thing; MI-6 has ordered us to hold on any further operations. Given the circumstances, I agree. Conducting an op under these conditions is too risky."

Jan nodded; this made sense and explained why Legion Services were always one step behind his team. "I copy all, Echo," Jan said, "Call me back if anything changes."

A dark expression crept across Jan's face. He now knew the name of the man who was responsible for killing his team. Dr. Turner saw it first. An all too familiar expression on the faces of soldiers who had a chance to avenge a fallen comrade. If left unchecked, these feelings could brood over time into abject madness.

"Jan," Dr. Turner said. "JAN," he said once more, this time forcefully, "Look at me, son." Jan looked up at Dr. Turner. "Captain, I know," He consoled him, "I know you want nothing more than to hunt this jackal down and rip him apart, but you know this would be suicide without help. You need a team." Jan looked down; as much as he hated it, he knew Dr. Turner was right. "Besides," Dr. Turner said more gently, "You have the life of another in your charge. It's all right to remember the dead, but do not forget to protect the living."

Jan looked at Victoria, he knew Dr. Turner spoke the truth, and it bothered him terribly that he had a slip in character and allowed his thirst for vengeance to interfere with the oath he took years ago to uphold the code of the Order. Dr. Turner could see the tension; he had just the thing to break it. "It's getting on towards seven o'clock," He said, "I am eating dinner tonight with Father Matthew, the chaplain of our order. Will you and Victoria be so kind as to join me?"

Jan and Victoria were getting hungry, and dinner sounded like a good excuse to take a break from the heavy emotions being felt in the archive. The Historian declined, as he had an appointment later. Dr. Turner led on up the spiral staircase and out into the library of the medical school.

Late last year, an app took the world by storm. FrenFinder was an app that one could download to their phone and play for free. The app worked by having a user upload their picture, and then other people with the app would try to find that person. If the "Finder" found the "Fren," they would take a picture, and the app would compare the two with facial recognition software. If they matched, the "Finder" would get points that could be exchanged for background filters or even gift cards. The app also allowed users to wager money on not being found for a certain amount of time. If the user were not found, they would get a point bonus. If they were, they would lose a portion of the wagered funds, and the "Finder" would get a gift card. FrenFinder did not require proof of identity to create an account, and Victoria's image happened to appear in the database with a huge wager, the largest ever at £10,000. As Victoria walked through the library, she passed medical students working on assignments or finding books they needed. One student happened to have the FrenFinder app running and could not believe his luck. He quickly snapped a picture of Victoria discreetly and uploaded the picture to the app. The app buzzed on his phone and congratulated him on finding the "Fren." A gift card worth thousands of British Pounds was on its way to the overjoyed user.

On another phone, a notification from the FrenFinder app came up:

You've Been Found!

Major Aubert looked at the phone and smiled. "Gotcha!"

Chapter 10

Saint John School of Medicine

Dr. Turner had a private dining room reserved for his dinner appointment with Father Matthew. The medical school had a large dining room that served exceptionally good meals to the faculty and students. All the tables in this dining room had white tablecloths and silver flatware, and all the food the kitchen sent out was served on fine china. Along the perimeter of the room were alcoves that had tables set up and curtains that could be drawn closed in the event diners wished privacy. It was in one of these alcoves that a man in his forties greeted them. He had slightly greying hair and was dressed in a long sleeve clergy shirt with a white collar and a black jacket. Father Matthew greeted Dr. Turner warmly. "Good evening, Robert," he said as he shook Dr. Turner's hand.

Father Matthew looked over Dr. Turner's shoulder, "Will guests be joining us tonight?"

"Oh yes, excuse me. Where are my manners?" Dr. Turner apologized, "May I present Victoria King and Captain Jan Luczac?"

Father Matthew took Victoria's hand and introduced himself. He then took Jan's and said, "I'm glad to have you with us tonight, Captain. Dr. Turner has told me so much about you."

He gestured for all to sit and began to recite a blessing;

"Bless us, O Lord, for these, thy gifts, which we are about to receive from thy bounty, Through Christ, our Lord, Amen."

All made the sign of the cross, and Father Matthew took his seat at the table. He unfolded his napkin and glanced at the menu card that was on the table place. He nodded approvingly, "Three courses, and Rabbit as the main...delightful."

Father Matthew motioned to the steward, and the wine was served. It was a nice French white, a Pinot Gris. "It is a blessing that we have you here to join us," Father Matthew started, "I greatly value my friendship with Dr. Turner here, but I'm always looking for new friends." He had a magnetic personality.

"Thank you for letting us intrude on your dinner plans," Victoria said, "It's been a while since I've dined in such fine settings."

"Of course," he said. "The chefs here see what items are discounted for the week with the grocers and butchers. The menu is always in season, and it keeps the costs down while still allowing us to have fine meals."

"And the vow of poverty that the members of the Order take?" She asked.

"It depends," He began, "I have taken a vow of poverty. So has Jan here. Dr. Turner did until he went to medical school after serving as a Captain in the order himself; that's a bit of a tradition; many knights serve as soldiers and then serve as doctors. But to answer your question, knights and the clergy that serve them take the vow, but it is not required to serve the order." She looked at Dr. Turner, "You were a Captain of the order like Jan?"

"Long ago," he answered, "In Africa. I was wounded in combat and could not continue as a soldier, so I became a doctor. I've always maintained close ties to the order; I even taught Jan about chivalry and ethics when he was a squire."

"It's true," Jan said as he looked at Victoria, "Dr. Turner was a teacher with exacting standards, but he taught an important subject. A subject that taught me not to compromise or take shortcuts on missions, even when I thought I was going to die."

The salad course came out. It was field greens, potato, and grilled leek with a fine vinaigrette. Victoria took a bite, *"These chefs knew their business,"* she thought.

Father Matthew spoke next, "That is important. We have stressed the importance of a strong code dating back to the very founding of the Order of Saint John in Jerusalem during the crusades."

"There is something I don't understand," Victoria said. "How does a strong moral code keep a knight alive on a mission?"

"Mostly, it allows clarity of thought and awareness of right and wrong so that knights make morally correct decisions in situations where there's a grey area," Jan answered. "For example, what motivates a person to intervene and stop the abuse of a stranger while others film it on their phones? The person willing to stop the abuse has a strong moral code. They know the abuse is wrong, and they do not tolerate it in their presence." Victoria nodded, "You don't see a lot of that today. Most people don't want to get involved."

"And why do you think that is, young lady?" Dr. Turner asked with a smile.

"Robert, she isn't one of your students," objected Father Matthew.

"No, it's okay," said Victoria, "I'm grateful for the conversation. I think it's because most people are afraid of getting in trouble or getting hurt."

"Correct, my dear," Dr. Turner nodded and continued, "The difference between these two people is that one is willing to stop evil where he sees it. The other is willing to tolerate it. A strong moral code will guide a person in times of peril; a lack of a moral code will cause a person to flee evil rather than confront it." Father Matthew added, "It's a culture problem as well. The culture of the world abhors those with a strong moral code and will work to undermine it at every level."

Now it was Victoria's turn to ask a hard question, "Why do you think that is so, Father?"

He smiled at her and said, "Simple, my dear; the answer is because of fear." He expanded his reply, "Yes, the culture of the world is always afraid of those who have a strong moral code because immoral men cannot rule such people. Look at the way the culture of the world teaches the sexes to treat each other. It teaches women to disrespect men and to show the man in word and deed that he is unnecessary, a burden, not an asset. On the other hand, it teaches men that women exist solely for their pleasure. A thing to be conquered and possessed, a thing to be used and then to be discarded when something better comes along. The culture of the world teaches humanity these lessons because it fears the unified male and female relationship with Christ at the heart. Down deep, it knows it cannot oppose a unified family. If you view male and female as two parts of the same being, you get the best of separate qualities. You get the physical strength, the nobility of leadership, and the sense of justice from the male. You also get these abilities tempered and guided by the compassion and wisdom of the female. When unified with Christ at the center of a godly marriage, evil has a tough time existing in a culture occupied by such people, which is why evil uses every trick it can to drive men and women apart and cast them as enemies."

Victoria remembered the conversation she had with Dr. Turner in the archive. She replied, "That mirrors something Dr. Turner said earlier. He reminded me that Genesis taught us that men and women are two parts of the same whole, as God took a rib from Adam to make Eve."

"Dr. Turner has been paying attention to my theological ramblings," Father Matthew said. "But yes, that's correct. The reason God did this is because it was his intention for men and women to offer their strengths and depend upon one another to support their weaknesses. This causes the man and woman to work together to survive and thrive, depending on each other and God for their provision. The culture of the world opposes this and tries to drive men and women apart because if men and women cannot turn to one another for support, they often turn to sin or to the state to try to fill the hole in their lives. And sin, like the state, always tries to create dependency over prosperity."

The stewards came to remove the empty plates and wine glasses. The next wine glass was to be filled with 'La Vitoriana' 2013, a Spanish Mencia that was like a Pinot Noir. Father Matthew sampled the wine. Its flavor was deep and smooth; he could taste hints of black fruit, stone, and earth. He nodded to the steward, and the wine was served. The main course was Rabbit, served with wild rice and winter squash. The meat had a thick and glossy layer of mustard peppercorn sauce ladled over it. The aroma of rich food and wine filled the small room. The conversation turned into small talk as the four ate together. Father Matthew's knowledge of the Bible was nothing short of incredible. He could weave biblical stories and moral truths in and out of an everyday conversation like a tailor sliding a needle and thread through fabric. Victoria wished she knew the Bible like he did.

Father Matthew ended a conversation about the importance of daily reading. "... It's a funny thing, reading the bible," he said, "You learn all about the things you dislike most about yourself, and the realization causes you to run to the loving arms of Jesus, who was right all along."

Victoria had another question, "Jan told me that the order intervenes in world events. How does the order arrive at such a decision?"

"Simple," Father Matthew answered, "Sometimes we are asked by an intelligence service. That's what Jan and his team were doing when they rescued you. Other times, there are crimes against human dignity so appalling that the order is compelled to act Sua Sponte, or of our own accord. These latter cases involve the council of Grand Masters and the involvement of the clergy."

"What's the council of Grand Masters?" asked Victoria.

"They are the leaders of every priory around the world," Jan answered, "There are priories in Europe, Africa, Asia, North and South America. All are led by a single soldier who has risen through the ranks to lead the priory. These senior knights meet when a situation requires it. In fact, the one we are in may warrant such a meeting." Father Matthew nodded, "I concur. I've already sent word to Grand Master Petrov of the Priory of Saint Petersburg requesting such a meeting." That was Jan's Priory, and he smiled inwardly, *"Father Matthew was always three steps ahead,"* he thought. *"Lord help the man who challenges him to a game of chess."*

The Father's chess skills were legendary in the Order. Many knights have been bested over the years by Father Matthew in the ancient game of strategy. "Ah," Father Matthew said suddenly, "Dessert is on its way." The conversation again turned to less serious matters as the four enjoyed the Gran Mariner Crème Brulee. The custard was silky smooth, with strong flavors of orange and toffee. It was the finest that Victoria had ever tasted. Coffee was also served with dessert, but no Port or Brandy. Father Matthew explained that those spirits were served only on the Christmas Day feast when the order bestowed a knighthood on eligible squires. This was not a standing rule of the Order but a local tradition of the Priory that went back hundreds of years to a time when wine and brandy were in short supply and were served as a treat on high occasions. After the plates were removed by the stewards and everyone had another cup of coffee, Father Matthew said his goodbyes, always happy to have met new people. Dr. Turner offered an unused dormitory room at the Medical School for Victoria and Jan to spend the night. The hour was getting late, and both of them were getting tired.

Trafalgar Square, London

The black vans were on the move. In the front van, Major Aubert sat while Sargent Fontaine drove. Fontaine was steadfastly committed that he and he alone would drive the Major. Aubert was nearly moved to tears when Fontaine asked him for permission to drive. He would let Fontaine participate in this mission; the sergeant's wound was serious enough to take him out of combat for good. Aubert sat, watching the streetlights pass on his side of the vehicle as the convoy moved across

London. He had a distasteful mission briefing to give to his men. They were on a kill-and-capture mission. Drouin's orders were clear, take no chances, and shoot anyone who looks like a knight on sight. For some unknown reason, Drouin wanted the girl alive. Aubert did not understand why Drouin didn't just let them kill her. Taking a captive was much more dangerous, and Aubert thought his men had bled enough on this operation.

There were so many ways this could play out when they stormed the medical school, and he did not like any of them. He swore in his thoughts; this situation was bad. Still, he had done his best to stack the odds in his favor. He was hitting the medical school with fifty men once more, now that replacements for the dead and injured were flown in. The new men were upset, and they all wanted vengeance for their fallen comrades. Using FrenFinder was a particularly subtle piece of business. He was always looking for force multipliers, and one of London's 50,000 FrenFinder subscribers had unwittingly fed him critical intelligence and sealed the girl's fate by revealing her location via a geotag. The subscriber had a nice little gift card headed their way, and he and his team had a mission. *"Everybody is happy,"* he thought as the vans approached the medical school.

They had to be in the dormitory; it was the most likely place with many of the students still off for winter break. Still, Aubert would take no chance of missing them. A man would be dispatched to stand watch at every exit to the building. He had the men available, and he intended to use them. Half of the vans turned to go to the rear of the part of the building that housed the dormitory, and the rest went to the front. The Legion soldiers quickly fanned out once the vans came to a stop, running to their objectives. Aubert led his men to the front door, and Lieutenant Lapointe and his team went in the rear. The night desk manager looked up from his phone to see twenty heavily armed men dressed in black tactical clothing and body armor staring down at him. "There's been a terrorist threat against this building, you're going to wait outside," Aubert said to the desk manager's shocked face. When he refused to leave, Aubert yelled, "Right now! MOVE!!" The frightened man scurried out of his chair and tried to avoid the armed Legion soldiers as he ran for the door. One of Major Aubert's men opened the door that led to the hallway of the first-floor dormitory. The men entered the hallway and saw Lapointe's men at the other end. Aubert's men would search the first floor, Lapointe would go to the second floor and begin his search to avoid a crossfire situation if the targets suddenly stepped into the hallway. Four floors, two targets, fifty men for the assault; Major Aubert took a deep breath and thought, *"Okay, we're ready,"* as he waited for Lapointe. He did not have to wait long. "In position," Lapointe said over the radio. Aubert responded with a single word, "Begin."

The phone rang in the sea container. Echo picked it up and answered, it was Archer. "Echo, where's Jan and the hostage you rescued earlier?" He asked.

"They're keeping out of sight at our Medical School in London," Echo answered, "Exactly as ordered. Why do you ask?"

"Something strange is happening," Archer began, "I had a friend at GCHQ call me about a CIA tip that ISIS was looking at attacking a school."

"Did they say which one?" Echo asked.

"No," Archer said, "But the request was similar to the one we got when your team was attacked at Watford Hospital, only this time it came through signals intelligence at GCHQ instead of MI-6."

An alarm in the sea container went off, and Echo looked at the computer screen. It was the AI with a warning message:

<u>ORDER ASSET UNDER THREAT:</u>
SAINT JOHN OF JERUSALEM MEDICAL SCHOOL, LONDON UK
****
ISIS THREAT DETECTED, METROPOLITAN POLICE UNITS ARE RESPONDING
****
PROBABILITY OF ATTACK = 78.6%

Echo felt an icy ball in the pit of his stomach. He told Archer suddenly, "The AI is predicting an attack. I need to pull Jan and Victoria out of there now!"

Archer winced, "Let me know if I can help on the back end; Archer out."

Echo terminated the call and frantically tried to call Jan's cell phone number.

Jan and Victoria were alone in the dormitory room. There were two beds and a nightstand between them. On the nightstand was a single lamp. Victoria asked Jan, "What will we do now that we know who is involved in this? I can't go home, and I can't go back to school."

"You're right," Jan told her, "But Echo told us to lay low until he and our contact at MI-6 can figure out what to do. We should stay here in the dormitory as much as possible; we can't risk being discovered."

Jan felt his phone buzz in his pocket. He pulled it out and answered it. "Go ahead, Echo."

"Captain," Echo said, his voice full of tension, "Legion is attacking the medical school right now! GET OUT OF THERE!!"

Chapter 11

Saint John School of Medicine

Jan's hand tensed on the phone. He looked at Victoria. "They've found us," he told her, "We need to go now!" Jan saw the fear in Victoria's face return as she realized the Legion soldiers were here. He switched the phone call to a Bluetooth device that clipped to his ear and said, "Echo, I'm going to need you to feed me intel as we go. Get into the school's security system and bring up the surveillance feed. We are on the fourth floor of the dormitory, and I need a way out."

"Copy that, Captain," replied Echo, "Legion soldiers have taken positions on the first and second floors of the dormitory, and they control both stairwells. Go to the roof, and you will be able to access the rest of the structure from there." Jan and Victoria needed no further encouragement. They left the dormitory room and ran for the stairwell that had access to the roof. Jan opened the stairwell door carefully. He could hear the Legion soldiers on the floors below. He looked at Victoria and pressed his forefinger to his lips, and motioned for her to follow. Quiet and stealth were critical for survival. He and Victoria would die if a gunfight happened on the stairs.

They ascended the stairs together to the door at the top that gave access to the roof. Jan tried the handle; it was locked. He dropped to one knee and reached into his belt. Every knight carried a basic equipment kit on them, in an undergarment like a fabric fanny pack. Inside this unobtrusive pouch were basic items that would ensure survival on a mission if a knight were separated from his main kit. The contents of this pouch varied depending on personal preference and mission requirements. For missions taking place on urban terrain like this one, Jan stocked his basic kit with a pen light, a multi-tool, and a variety of lock-picking and entry tools. Before taking the time to pick the lock, Jan remembered his training from years earlier. *"Door fitment and installation are generally poor on most structures,"* the instructor had said, *"Before you invest the time to pick the lock, see if the door can be opened another, easier way."* With this door, the latch and strike plate did not fit properly. Jan extracted a short thin steel cable from the kit, slipped it around the latch, and pulled. The cable depressed the latch, and the door popped open. He quietly opened the door and led Victoria to the roof, quietly shutting the door behind them. The roof was not flat, and it had a steep hip covered with copper. The only place to walk was a narrow catwalk around the perimeter. Jan looked back at Victoria and said, "There will be ice, be very careful of where you step." She nodded back at him as he took her hand, and they made their way down the catwalk together.

Four stories below, two Legion soldiers were making their way to take up a blocking position at one of the building's exits. One of the soldiers motioned to the other to seek cover fifty meters away from the door, an easy shot for a man with a rifle. As they took up blocking positions, they heard a noise on the building above. It was a sound like someone's foot struck metal. Both soldiers looked up at the roofline, scanning for targets.

There. Motion.

It was too dark for target identification, but there was definitely something moving up there on the roof. The soldiers looked at each other and called it in.

Major Aubert's radio crackled in his earpiece, "Major, this is blocking team six, motion detected on the roof, University Street side."

The Major froze, "Roger, team six," he said, "Can you identify?"

"Negative, Major," the soldier said, "It's too dark up there, but we are sure there's someone moving...no, wait, two figures are moving up there." That was their quarry.

"Lapointe," the Major said into his radio, "Abandon search of the dormitory and converge on the main building. The targets have escaped through the roof." Aubert looked at his new sergeant, "Sergeant Garnier, take a team and go to the roof. Drive the target towards the capture team, but take no unnecessary risks, understood?"

"Oui, Major!" the man said as he ran off with his men towards the stairwell. Garnier ran up the steps. He was so excited he was not tired when he reached the top of the stars and the locked door. He nodded to the man carrying the entry tool kit. The man extracted a Halligan tool from his backpack and placed it in the gap between the door and the frame. He stretched the gap enough to place a wedge in the gap, flipped the tool around and pushed on the Halligan tool with all the force he could muster. The steel door groaned under the stress and popped open. The Halligan tool did its job, bending the door beyond repair. The Legion soldiers carefully stepped out onto the catwalk, one leaving the safety of the stairwell every two seconds. They moved ten meters down the catwalk and stopped, scanning for targets.

Major Aubert got on the radio as he jogged through the medical school. "Blocking team six, this is Major Aubert. Hold your fire. We have Legion soldiers on the roof."

He heard the reply in his ear, "Roger, Major. Team six copies. Be advised, movement has stopped."

Jan and Victoria paused at the door. As Jan suspected, it was locked. He knelt and extracted his pen light, it was too dark up here to see the lock, and Jan wanted a better look at the door fitment before he attacked the lock. The light had a red filter, so any illumination would not destroy his night vision. In the soft red glow of the light, Jan could see that the door fitment was as poor as the one they had come through minutes earlier. Jan removed a plastic card from his pouch, bent it to a shape that matched the contour of the door frame, and slid it along the gap between the door and the frame. The door opened easily and swung inward a few inches. Jan caught the door with his hand before it closed and motioned behind him at Victoria to cross the threshold. For a brief moment, Jan and Victoria's bodies were backlit by the light inside the doorway.

"Major, this is the rooftop team," Sergeant Garnier was looking through his ACOG 4x prismatic optic as he spoke into his radio, "I see a door open, and two figures are illuminated. I have visual confirmation of the female target."

Major Aubert stopped for a moment and consulted the map of the medical school. "Copy rooftop team," he replied, "Follow them, but keep your distance until I can head them off with a blocking force. I only need you to keep them from escaping back to the roof." Garnier nodded to his men and began to carefully move towards the door on the other end of the catwalk. Major Aubert called Lapointe on the radio, "Lieutenant, the targets are heading towards the library. How fast can you secure the first floor and librarian's station?" Lapointe was running as fast as he could with his men. He spoke into the radio between breaths, "Major, Lapointe here...Entering library mezzanine... first floor secure in three-zero seconds." Lapointe's men rushed to the Librarian's desk. It was long after hours, and the library had closed for the day. The normally well-lit space was now dark, with only the odd light left on by the custodial staff. Long shadows were cast by these few lights, leaving large areas of the library shrouded in darkness. Approaching the library collection, the Legion soldiers used the Insight M3X weapon lights mounted to the railed fore ends of their M-4 rifles sparingly, only using illumination when needed. As the soldiers moved through the dark space, they were careful not to get too far ahead of their teammates or to wander off into a spot that would get them into a crossfire if the target suddenly appeared. This was slow, careful work that required patience. They were able to be patient as they controlled the library's first floor, and it was only a matter of time before all avenues of escape were cut off.

Jan and Victoria entered the library's fourth floor from the stairs that led to the roof. Instead of a warm space bathed in the soft light of desk lamps, the library was full of ominous shadows. Jan took Victoria by the hand and ran with her to one of the staircases that led to the ground floor. Jan led the way with his HK USP 9 at low ready, pausing at each landing to stop, listen, and scan before motioning for Victoria to follow. This slow pattern of movement was repeated again until they were nearly on the second floor. Suddenly, Jan saw a flash of light below, odd and out of place. *"A weapon-mounted light,"* he thought.

Jan slowly backed away from the landing and returned up the stairs towards Victoria. He gently took her arm and led her to the library's third floor. Jan moved out of the light and along the wall, where the shadows were the darkest. He told Victoria, "The Legion soldiers are on the first floor and making their way up to us. If we don't do something, they will find us."

Victoria nodded and answered, "Jan, I'm with you no matter what. You've kept me alive this far." He smiled at her in the darkness, an unseen expression of tenderness. Jan cared for her deeply. His feelings for her were not romantic; instead, they sprung out of a sense of duty. Before the farmhouse raid, he and the rest of his team made a silent promise that they would rescue her or die trying. His teammates, men that he knew like brothers, had already made that sacrifice. Jan now understood the path before him was clear. He was going to exchange his life for hers and give her a chance at living a full life. "Victoria," he said, "There is a hallway on this floor that leads to laboratories and classrooms. It is to the Northwest, down that hallway." He pointed to the end of the library, where the hallway lights beckoned them with their warm glow.

Victoria nodded and took his hand. She was surprised when Jan held firm and would not move. "The hallway leads to several staircases," Jan continued. "Take one to the basement and keep heading Northeast. You will see large pipes that carry steam to the building from the utility corridor. Follow those, and they will lead you out of the building." He handed her a slip of paper and said, "Call this number when you get out and find a phone. It's Echo's cell number."

She looked at him in the darkness and asked, "But you're coming with me, right?"

Jan took her hand in his strong hands and said, "Victoria, I must stay behind and distract them so you can get away."

"No," she said. "NO. You're coming with me!"

Jan looked at her and said, "It's my time, Victoria. It's time for me to join my brothers. You will be safe, I promise."

Victoria shook her head in the dark, and tears welled in her eyes. If Jan was going to die here, she wanted to die here too. She could not imagine a life living with the guilt of knowing that he sacrificed his life for hers. As if he could sense her feelings, Jan said, "It will be okay, Victoria. I have lived a good life in the service of others, and I now have the privilege to serve you. I will soon be with my brothers, the only family I've ever known. Now...go, Victoria. GO." He watched her shadow as it ran towards the light of the hallway. He watched her as she raced away, towards life, towards safety.

Jan looked at the hallway for a moment after her form disappeared. *"Okay,"* he thought, *"It's time."* Jan reached into his pouch and extracted a handheld Surefire Z2 combat light and slipped the flashlight's lanyard around his left wrist. He braced his wrists together in the Harries shooting position, with the USP 9 in his right hand and the Z2 light in the other. Jan moved to a location in the shadows just beyond an overhead light. This position made him invisible due to an optical

233

property of light and shadow. From this position, Jan could see the staircase, and he had a warren of bookshelves behind him. Eternity and the restored fellowship with his brothers awaited him. He took a deep breath, got his excitement under control, and waited for the Legion soldiers to come. He could see the soft green glow of the USP's tritium night sights before him as he used his eyes to look for enemy movement.

As Victoria ran, the tears came. She could not bear to look back at Jan even though it was what she wanted most, one last look. However, she knew in her heart that if she did steal a gaze back at him, her legs would fail her, and she would return to die by his side. It was so unfair this knight, this good Christian man she had left behind, was going to die so she could live her imperfect life. She was ashamed, and she felt that she had not lived a life worthy of this man's sacrifice. Her thoughts tormented her as she ran down the hallway, her steps echoed, and her eyes burned. The staircase was just ahead. She ran to it and opened the door. The stairwell was illuminated with harsh light, and the walls were painted light grey. She could hear a faint noise echoing from below. *"Machinery noise,"* she thought. This stairwell would take her to the basement. *"Get there and follow the steam pipes,"* she thought.

Victoria began to follow the stairs down, deeper into the building. She had just passed the door that led to the second floor of the building when it suddenly opened. Adrenalin surged through her body at the sudden motion, and a large figure towered over her. She fell to the floor, curling into a fetal position, crushed that Jan was going to sacrifice himself for nothing. A voice gently said to her, "Victoria, my dear?" It was Dr. Turner. She flung her arms around him, her shock dissipating into relief. Dr. Turner asked, "Where is Jan?" She could not look at him as she answered, "Legion soldiers are here. He stayed behind so I could get away." Dr. Turner looked up at the ceiling where he had believed Jan to be for a long time. He then said, "Let's get you out of here. Please follow me." She nodded, so happy not to be alone at a time like this.

Blocking team four consisted of three men. All three were new to Legion Services, having just left the French Army. Legion paid better, and the work was not usually dangerous. This mission had changed that paradigm. These men were replacements for the men who died in the oxygen explosion at Watford Hospital. For the first time in their brief careers with Legion Services, all three men thought they were in mortal danger. All three were on edge, and as such they dispensed with certain firearms handling procedures that were in place for safety. Their mission was to block escape from this part of the building, the Northeast wing. They rounded the corner of a hallway, illuminating the space with their weapon-mounted lights, when they saw a shape moving towards them. The shape was a female form, and they could see her long blond hair in the light. There was also another figure behind the woman, still hidden in shadow. The lead soldier already had the selector switch on his M-4 carbine in the **AUTO** position, and in a panic, he mashed the trigger. The weapon roared in the hallway, sending a burst of six 5.56mm rounds screaming down the hall and into the target behind the woman. The report from the rifle echoed and faded as a shrill cry took its place.

Jan whirled around at the noise. *"Gunfire,"* he thought, *"No. Not in the direction of... OH NO."*

He began running towards the sound, his USP out in front of him. *"NO. NO. NO. NO..."* he thought as he ran towards the stairwell at the far end of the hallway.

The Major heard the gunfire echo deep in the building. "All teams report enemy contact," he said on his radio. There was no response for a while, and then a voice came on the radio channel. There was screaming in the background, a woman's voice. "Sir, this is blocking team four... I KNOW. KEEP PRESSURE ON IT! Sir, we had contact here, we have the female target in custody, but I also have a non-combatant with a gunshot wound to the chest. I need help..."

The Major swore. Team four were inexperienced soldiers, out of the Army, not from the Foreign Legion like he was. "HANDLE IT, Team Four! I'll send someone to you in a minute," Aubert barked into the radio. He had a situation that was spinning out of control, and he needed to stomp everyone back into line. "All teams, all teams, this is Major Aubert. Continue your search. There is a target still in the library. Blocking teams, hold your positions and CHECK YOUR TARGETS BEFORE YOU ENGAGE THE ENEMY!" He knew he could count on everyone else. Most of the soldiers he had deployed here were veterans and would keep their heads under fire.

"Sergeant Fontaine!" the Major shouted into the radio.

"Fontaine here, sir!" Aubert silently gave thanks that he had good men like Fontaine. He needed someone to get team four under control.

"Fontaine, drive to the Northeast wing and get to the second floor. Blocking team four needs your help; take command there and verify the capture of the female target!" Fontaine felt a surge of delight as he realized he was going to return to action one more time. He winced as he turned the steering wheel of the van to drive to the building entrance.

"Blocking team four, this is Sergeant Fontaine; report your position!" he said into his radio. "Sergeant, we are in the Northeast wing, second floor," came the response from team four.

Fontaine thought the man sounded frightened on the radio. *"As well he should,"* Fontaine thought, *"The man lost his nerve and shot a civilian – IDIOT!"* Fontaine pulled up to the entrance and ran up the stairs to the second floor and was greeted with the wailing cry he had heard on the radio earlier. He saw one member of team four trying to restrain the female captive while the other had broken open a first aid kit and was applying compression bandages to several gunshot wounds on an elderly male victim. The third man pointed his rifle down the hall, covering the other two men. Fontaine looked at the male victim who had been shot; at least two of the gunshot wounds were fatal, and the man was losing color in his face. His voice boomed in the hallway, "You two! Begin CPR on that casualty! You, bring the prisoner over here!" Victoria fought the Legion soldier with every ounce of strength she could muster. She twisted, kicked, and did everything she could to get away from the vise-like grip of the man holding her. Another Legion soldier approached her and quickly struck the side of her head with something dull and heavy. Her world went dark as the blow from Fontaine's sap made her black out.

Jan was down the hallway and made it to the staircase. He frantically ran down the stairs, looking for blood on the walls and floor. He had his USP in front of him, ready to fire if he saw the enemy. He imagined what he would do when he arrived at the scene of Victoria's murder; he promised himself that he would kill any Legion soldier that he saw. He continued to descend the staircase but saw nothing. He got to the basement door and could hear machinery on the other side. Jan yanked open the door and stepped through the threshold, his pistol and light at the ready. He could see no one. Jan pushed further into the machinery room, finding the insulated steam pipes. He followed them deeper into the basement, using his handheld flashlight to lead the way. Jan moved past hot boilers, noisy water pumps, and the monotonic buzz of electrical panels. After what seemed like an eternity, he saw the utility corridor that would lead him away from the medical school and towards safety. Jan froze; the gunshots he heard earlier could not have come from here. He was too deep inside the basement. He also was sure he had not seen blood or any rifle casings up to this point. With renewed hope, he moved deeper into the utility tunnel. *"Maybe she made it out!"* He thought as he ran.

Victoria's eyes slowly opened. She had a violent headache from Fontaine's sap. She tried to get up, but her arms could not move. She felt tension in her wrists, the cold bite of metal on her skin. She opened her eyes a bit more and saw the painted steel floor of the van. Victoria moved her head slightly, and she could see the boots of the Legion soldiers seated in the van. One of the soldiers must have seen her move, and he said, "Hey, she's waking up." Victoria felt a needle go into her arm, and her body lost consciousness again.

Fontaine brought the van to a gentle stop inside the aircraft hangar. Major Aubert stepped out of the vehicle and saw the bulletin boards of last night's costly engagement at Watford Hospital. He sighed, remembering the good men who fell in combat and would never return home. Still, he had led his men well, and they had recovered a prize for their employer. Despite a thorough search of the library and classrooms, they had failed to locate the enemy knight he believed had escaped the helicopter crash. *"Perhaps he never existed,"* the Major thought. He had an intense telephone call with Pogi on the short drive to the airport. Aubert needed cover for the operation and for the civilian that was killed in the assault. Pogi, being the weakling Aubert believed him to be, had blanched at the thought that a UK citizen had been killed in the operation. *"He probably had much to explain to his bosses,"* Aubert thought as he chuckled. Aubert failed to understand why Pogi was so worried. One call from Count Drouin would settle this problem, no matter who got involved from the American or British governments. No, this would be quickly forgotten, and Aubert and his men could get back to supporting Drouin's main operation of ISIS cells spreading fear through the European population. Aubert suddenly remembered how many letters he had to write. He had not lost this number of men since he was a young French officer in Africa. He shook the thought loose from his mind, and it was time to board the plane that would take him and the girl back to Germany.

Chapter 12

Schloss Drouin

Victoria awoke in a vast bedroom. Her eyelids were heavy, her consciousness – distant. She opened her eyes as far as she could, enough to let a bit of light and color in. She could feel the beginning of a roaring headache, and there was a dull ache on the left side of her head where Fontaine had hit her. She opened her eyes a bit further, her vision was blurry, and all she could see were shapes. Without warning, the memory of being taken by the Legion soldiers rushed back, and she bolted awake in a sudden panic. Her heart raced, and her breath was fast due to the surge of adrenaline. Victoria looked around the room now that she could see better. The moon let in just enough light through the windows for her to see around the room. She sat on a large bed with a satin bedsheet, and there was furniture in the room, but it was sparse. There was a table, two chairs and a bedside table; nothing else. Everything in the room was lavish. This was not customer-assembled furniture, these pieces looked as though they were made one at a time by master furacturemakers. The wall molding was ornate, and her eyes followed it up to the ceiling where the crown molding encircled a fresco painting on the ceiling.

The ceiling appeared to be painted by Michelangelo himself, it was so perfectly done. When one gazed at the fresco for an extended period, it felt as if they were transcending the cherubs and the clouds, soaring upward towards the heavens. Victoria swung her legs off the bed and placed them on the floor. As she looked down, she noticed that the clothes Mary had bought for her had disappeared, replaced by luxurious silk pajamas that could only be found in exclusive sections of the finest department stores. Feeling parched, Victoria stood up and began searching for a bathroom to quench her thirst. She crossed the room and entered an open door, stepping into the bathroom. To her surprise, the lights in the bathroom instantly turned on as she passed through the door, causing her to pause in astonishment. Something was amiss in the bathroom—the fixtures! The toilet lacked a seat and was made of painted steel, while the sink was positioned behind the toilet in a small basin that was separate yet connected to the toilet itself. *"It was like the toilets you saw in prison,"* she thought.

A closer look at the mirror hung above the toilet/sink revealed that the mirror was not glass but highly polished stainless steel. The bathroom had shower fixtures in the corner and a drain on the floor but no shower curtain or bathtub. The whole room was unlike the bedroom. Instead of being made of fine materials and lavishly appointed, the bathroom was sparse and institutional. Even the tile used to cover the floors and walls looked like it was chosen for utility rather than appearance. There was a fixture in the sink that looked like the spigot of a water fountain. She pressed the button, and mercifully, cold water came out of the fixture. She drank, feeling her body absorb the moisture. After another long sip, Victoria walked back out to the main bedroom. She looked around and realized things were off here too. All the furniture was bolted to the floor. The bed did not have sheets, and the satin fabric was stitched to the mattress with triple rows of stitching. She looked at the windows that had glass, but beyond them were bars. These bars could not be pushed out in the event of a fire, instead they were securely mounted to the building and designed to prevent escape. She looked at the door to the room, and a light could be seen beyond through the slim gap between the door and frame, like a hallway light. She walked to the door and tried the handle; it would not move. The whole door was solid in the frame, as if it were secured by more than the lock mechanism.

It dawned on Victoria that this room was indeed a prison, a nice one, but a prison nonetheless. She sat back on the bed, wondering what to do. Victoria did not have to wait long. The lights came on in the bedroom on their own, gently and softly increasing the light they gave. She heard an electronic buzzing noise at the door and a lock slam open with a metallic click. Two people, a man and a woman, walked into the room and shut the door behind them. Victoria heard the lock re-engage once more. The man was tall and thin, in his fifties and dressed in a morning suit. The woman was in her late thirties, sleek and with impeccable blond hair. Both people looked perfect, artificial even. The man spoke first. "Good evening," he said in perfect English, "My name is Andreas, the Butler for His Excellency Count Drouin. You have been taken as a prize by his Excellency's soldiers and will now serve him as a member of his Excellency's household."

"Who does this guy think he is?" thought Victoria.

"The house has many rules, and you will be required to learn them all, but for now, remember this; speak only when spoken to. Do you understand?"

Victoria slowly nodded, deciding to stay quiet because she was still unsure of these people. In her mind, she knew the Legion soldiers were nearby. "Very well," he said. "May I present Greta? She will explain your new role here as a servant of House Drouin." Andreas looked at Greta, who stepped forward. She was dressed in a sleek grey skirt and white blouse. Her blond hair was pulled back in a tight ponytail. The heels of Greta's shoes clicked on the hardwood floor as she walked over to the table.

Greta nodded at Andreas and said, "Thank you, Andreas. I will call if I need anything."

Andreas returned her nod, turned, and placed his hand on the door handle. After a second, the electronic buzz sounded, the lock clicked, and Andreas quickly let himself out. The lock clicked shut once more, and Greta looked at Victoria. "Come here," she said, "And we will talk."

Victoria hesitated, but she did get up and come over to where Greta was. "Sit," she said as she motioned to the chair opposite her.

Greta sat down in the other chair gracefully with perfect posture. She said, "You are now a servant in the Drouin household. Who you were before tonight does not matter. The only thing that matters is how well you follow instructions. If you disobey, the consequences will be severe. My name is Greta, and I am the head servant of his excellency Count Drouin."

This was difficult for Victoria to follow, *"Who was this nutty woman?"* she asked herself.

"There are many rules here, but we will start with the basics. You are to speak only when directly addressed. You will do anything asked of you by a senior servant or Count Drouin or his guests – and I mean anything they ask. You will dress in the clothing we give to you. You will maintain your physical appearance, and your grooming will be impeccable. You will always use formal English, and you will never use profanity. I will now ask you questions, and you will reply with a yes or no, nothing more."

"Are you ready to answer my questions?"

"Yes."

"Do you understand everything I have told you?"

"Yes."

"Do you require prescription medication?"

"No."

"Do you have any allergies?"

"No."

"Do you suffer from any disease?"

"No."

"Are you addicted to alcohol or any drugs?

"No."

"Do you smoke?"

"No."

"Are you sexually active?

Victoria refused to answer and glared at Greta. *"Who did this woman think she was, asking her all these intrusive questions?"*

Greta narrowed her eyes and asked again, this time more forcefully but while keeping her voice even, "I do not repeat myself to those under me; you WILL answer." Greta radiated power; the tone of her voice gave it away. Victoria had only met a handful of people like Greta in her life, mostly friends of her mother and father. She knew those friends of her parents had killed people in war or in the line of duty, and Greta spoke and carried herself the same. The realization scared Victoria more than anything she had heard or seen. Greta asked the question one more time,

"Are you sexually active?"

"No."

"Are you a virgin?"

"Yes."

Greta smiled, "That will give you some latitude, some. But I warn you, do not break the rules you have been told, or there will be dire consequences." Greta was softer, more motherly in her tone as she continued, "Now, you may ask me a question if you wish."

Victoria had but one, "You said I was a servant of House Drouin. What does that mean?"

Greta replied, "It means you have much to learn, my dear. Keep in mind the life you knew before, whatever it was, is gone. This is your home now. If you want to stay here, you will follow the rules."

Greta stood up. "I must leave now; the hour is late. We will begin your education tomorrow." She got up and crossed the bedroom to the door. She placed her hand on the door handle, paused, and was greeted with the electronic buzz and the lock deactivating. Victoria heard the lock slam shut once more, and she felt as though the noise of the lock was the sound of her future coming to a crashing end.

North London

Jan had reached the end of the utility tunnel. A brick wall faced him. The steam pipes he was following penetrated the wall and went underneath the street from there. A single light bulb in a wire cage provided light to the small utility vault. Jan looked to his right and saw a wall-mounted ladder that ascended to a cylindrical shaft in the vault's ceiling. *"A manhole,"* Jan thought, *"A way out."* Jan holstered his pistol and began to climb. When he reached the top of the shaft, he placed his hand against the iron manhole cover and pushed. The lid would not budge. He climbed up one more rung of the ladder and pressed his back against the lid, using the full strength of his legs to push it up. Finally, after much exertion, the lid moved, and he was able to slide it out of the frame and onto the street. He stuck his head out of the hole and looked around. The manhole exited into an alley, some distance away from the medical school.

Jan quickly climbed out of the hole and replaced the lid in the frame. Jan ran down the alley, and he could hear the wail of approaching sirens and emergency vehicles. *"Best to stay out of sight,"* he thought. Jan got near the end of the alley just as two BMW police cars carrying armed Metropolitan Police officers roared past. Jan's mind was embroiled in thought. *"There was no way that Victoria could have gotten that manhole lid off the frame,"* he thought, *"Could I have missed her in the utility tunnel?"* He realized that was not likely. Had she seen or heard him, she would have shown herself. If she was not on the street, and if he did not see her in the tunnel, that meant she was in medical school somewhere! He turned to go back to the manhole when he remembered the gunfire he had heard when he was in the library.

"That's right..." the accusing voice said to him, *"You sent her off by herself, and now she's DEAD."*

Jan stopped and sat down in the alley, his back to the wall. He tried to will the voice away, and he did not need to hear this right now. *"DEAD, Jan. Just like the rest of your team...But here YOU are, still breathing."*

"*Stop,*" he thought, "*That isn't true...if she had stayed with me, we would both be dead.*"

"*You can tell yourself that if it soothes your conscience, but I know better. All you had to do was stay there in the library and wait...*" the voice mocked. "*You can lie to yourself all you want, Jan, but you cannot lie to me. The reason you didn't stay in the library is you're scared of dying.*"

"*ENOUGH,*" Jan said in his mind forcefully.

"*We tried that once, Jan,*" the accuser went on, "*But as I said earlier, all you did was kill your team, and now you've killed her...and you were not brave enough to join them in eternity.*"

Jan broke. The voice was right. All he did was put that poor girl's life in danger, and he had the nagging suspicion that his brothers were ashamed of him. Victoria probably was too. Jan's train of self-destructive thought was interrupted by something vibrating in his jacket pocket. He reached inside his jacket to find his phone ringing. He did not recognize the number. Jan did not answer when the caller said, "Hello, Field office?"

When Jan did not answer, the caller repeated more forcefully, "Field office??"

Jan paused; he took a deep breath and wondered if he was cut out for this. He could disappear, find someplace warm and... NO. His sense of duty broke through, and he answered the caller properly, as a Knight of the Order should, "This is Foxtrot, authentication, please?"

"Golf-Mike acknowledges Foxtrot. Authentication; x-ray delta tango."

"Who is Golf-Mike?" he thought. "Challenge code, Golf-Mike?"

"Bravo two mike. Foxtrot, we need to talk. Meet me at North Weald Airfield. Golf-Mike out."

Jan looked at his phone, more confused than ever. North Weald Airport was a private field Northeast of London. Jan looked at the London Underground map on his phone and saw that the central line would take him within two miles of the airport and that the Metropolitan and Central lines would intersect at Liverpool Street station. *"Okay,"* he thought, *"Time to find out who is Golf-Mike."*

Schloss Drouin

Count Drouin had sent for Greta while he received an update from Major Aubert. He sat in his chair in the library while Aubert stood and delivered his report. "How long until we can resume operations, Major?"

"We are ready now, your Excellency," Aubert answered. "I have enough soldiers to replace the men we lost at Watford Hospital if we pull them out of Syria."

Drouin nodded, "The loss of your men is tragic, Major. Please convey my sympathies to their families."

Aubert thanked his employer, "I will, your Excellency."

Drouin had other matters to discuss, "And what of our operation in Britain? We lost one cell, but are the other two ready?"

"Yes, your Excellency," Aubert said, "The other two ISIS cells have their covers intact and can begin taking hostages for execution at any time. I recommend we move to the outlying residential areas of London rather than the city core; it will be more effective to scare the British voting population if we have the cells hunt those neighborhoods for victims, and there are far fewer cameras."

Drouin wondered how many victims it would take before British voters would demand that the government adopt harsh policies to deal with the threat. Several legislative proposals were waiting, one to curtail free movement, one to have MI-5 monitor every banking transaction, then another to cloister Britons in their homes - effectively putting the entire nation under house arrest. The plan was simple. First, pump fear into Britain. Once fear is permitted to simmer a bit, a proposal that exchanges freedom for security will be introduced, followed by another, and another. Together, these proposals would make everyday life so intolerable that UK subjects would soon be begging for a solution that would deal with the ISIS threat but allow life to return to normal. Such a fix was already drafted in the form of a proposal, one that would make the Triumvirate wealthy beyond imagination. The final proposal was the universal adoption of a digital currency. This new monetary policy would force every Briton to adopt the E£B or the "E-pound" digital currency.

The digital currency would promise to eliminate ISIS's funding mechanism, or if they tried to use the E£B, the financial network would be able to detect suspicious purchases and funnel that intelligence to MI-5 for action. The E£B would promise an end to the terror of being snatched off the street by religious fanatics and allow the harsh restrictions on everyday life to cease. In practice, the E£B would allow the Triumvirate to fleece the British population for every shilling they would ever earn. Saving would be punished, while consumption would be rewarded. Under a promise of security, the E£B would allow the implementation of a rationing system like the one the United Kingdom adopted during World War two, but with one critical difference. Instead of ration stamps that would vanish at the end of the month, the actual currency would vanish instead. Different people would earn more or earn less depending on their profession, but everyone's currency would hit zero on the last day of each month. Most people would not notice a difference, as they lived paycheck to paycheck anyway.

Businesses and Corporations would be under a different rationing system, with their E£B rations turning over every calendar year.

Drouin was sure there would be a few Britons who would object, but there were not enough savers to overcome the will of the majority. Besides, the best part about a digital currency was that it could be turned off at any time, such as when faced with a particularly vocal dissenter. How vocal would such a person be once the money they earned for the month was simply unavailable? And if a politician or the crown had second thoughts, a few more kidnappings and beheadings could always be arranged.

The brilliant part of this plan was that the Triumvirate owned the crypto company that would mint the E£B, and they also owned the company that would be responsible for all banking and point-of-sale transfers for the E£B. The British government would love it; tax evasion would be impossible, as would illegal commerce. Crime would be reduced drastically, and the ISIS threat would conveniently end. The truth, of course, was that the end of the ISIS threat would be arranged, and the ISIS cells would then be moved to a new area of operations to be joined by other ISIS cells flooding in alongside refugees from Syria. The operation in Britain was just a trial run, and the Triumvirate planned to repeat this operation across Europe. Britain was critical to the plan, not only to iron out problems with managing the terror cells and passing legislation but as a model of peace they could later point towards once the fear was unleashed in other European nations.

Drouin leaned back in his chair, full of confidence. "Major, is there anything further?" Drouin asked.

Aubert cleared his throat, "Your Excellency, there is one item where we will need your help. In the operation to capture the female you wished; a UK citizen was shot by Legion personnel. I've spoken with Jason Pogi about the incident, and he was not sure he could contain the situation. I respectfully ask that a phone call be placed to senior officials in both the British and American governments."

Drouin smiled; he loved calling these sniveling officials. They were obsessed with status and title; oh, how they quaked with fear at the mere suggestion of revoking their privilege! "Of course, Major," Drouin said, "This issue will soon be forgotten. You are dismissed, Major."

Aubert bowed and left the library. The great doors of the room opened for him as Andreas and Greta walked inside. Andreas crossed the room, bowed to Drouin, and said, "Your Excellency, may I present Greta?" Drouin nodded and waved Andreas away. He wished for privacy with Greta. She walked in front of him and performed a low and subservient curtsy. "M'lord Drouin calls," she said.

Drouin looked at her for a moment, *"She really was stunning,"* he thought. *"And is as ruthless as I,"* he added with a smile.

Drouin held out his hand, which she took and kissed. "Please tell me how our new guest is fairing," Drouin asked.

"It would be my pleasure, M'lord," Greta replied. "I have met with your Excellency's newest servant. She is frightened, but she poses more of a challenge to break than your other servants. She did not come into your Excellency's household through the normal channels, where much of that work has already been done. Still, I am confident that our methods will work on her. They always do."

"How long will it take?" Drouin asked.

"The answer to your Excellency's question is psychological in nature," Greta answered. "We must convince her of our total power over her and make her fear the consequences. All the while, we gaslight her with responses carefully structured to make her question reality. We make her believe that wrong is right, down is up, and black is white. So long as we keep the psychological pressure constant, she will begin to choose the actions we wish her to perform. Once that happens, she will break like all the others."

Drouin considered that for a while. It was obvious Greta was unsure how long this process was going to take, and she was incredibly careful with her words. Drouin's anger was a force not to be taken lightly. He was always impressed by Greta. Not only was she ruthless, but she was also cunning and intelligent.

"I want her broken," Drouin ordered, "See to it personally."

He saw this girl he ordered Aubert to take as a prize, a trophy of war he had seized from the Order of Saint John. The order had prevented his family from ruling Europe over two hundred years ago by provoking his ancestor's anger. Now, he was poised to finish what Napoleon started without firing a shot. The girl began as a simple loose end in operation, but now he would keep her here at his Schloss, like a jewel on his crown. And she was lovely like all the other Jewels Drouin kept in his household.

"I shall, M'lord," Greta replied. "May I be of any further service to Your Excellency?"

Drouin stood and said, "You may, my dear." Drouin took a step closer to her, and he could smell the fragrance from her perfume; citrus blossom. Drouin would take Greta into his bed that night, but his thoughts would not be on Greta but on his newest servant.

Chapter 13

Epping, UK

The London Underground sign for Epping Station slid into view out of the window as the train came to a gentle stop. End of the line. Jan stood and walked onto the cold concrete tiles of the station platform. It was late, and the fog had begun to set in. The station lights cast an eerie yellow glow onto the platform as Jan walked towards the exit. He had been alone on the train, lost in thought. *"Who was the caller, and where was Echo?"* Those two questions occupied Jan's mind for the entire trip out of London.

Jan had tried calling and texting Echo to no avail. Where was Echo? It was unlike him to go radio silent like that unless ordered; did Legion get to him too? *"We both know the answer to that, Jan,"* the accuser had returned.

Jan tried to will the voice away once more. He did not need the distraction, not now. *"Oh, you won't get rid of me that easily,"* the voice taunted. *"You have a two-mile walk to the airfield, and I'm going to take advantage of it. I so do enjoy our time together."*

Jan increased his pace to the 120 steps per minute pace known to all militaries throughout the world. His steps echoed on the wet concrete of the sidewalk, and the damp, cold air tried to steal away his body heat as he moved. The lights of buildings gave a luminous quality to the fog. Long, angry shadows cut shapes into the street, where the light shone through the bare trees. *"Aleksy, Lew, Kuba, Anatol, Olek, Stefan, Filip, Igor, Victoria, and now Echo. Racked up quite the score, haven't we, Jan?"*

Jan's thoughts were dark and angry. All he wanted was for the voice to go away. More than that, he wanted answers; who was the voice on the other end of the phone, this Golf-Mike? That was not a standard radio designator used by the Order. Come to think of it, Jan had never heard that designator used on a mission, not ever. Jan rounded a corner near a church and kept walking; his steps landed heavier and heavier as he went. Ahead and on the opposite side of the street, three figures stepped into the light, young lads on their way to a public house for a pint. The three saw Jan and pointed. Jan did not stare, but he didn't look away either; one did not show weakness out on the street. This was not working; the young men stopped and turned to follow him. Jan stopped and turned. He looked at the one he thought was the leader of the group and glared. The young man stopped, looked at his mates, and continued his advance. *"Great,"* Jan thought, *"They want to fight."*

These were not criminals; an experienced hold-up crew would take one look at Jan, massive and very fit, and decide that whatever he had was not worth the risk. These three were idiots that just wanted to hurt someone. "Hey, you," the leader said, "We wanna talk." Jan did not answer but glared back at the young man. Jan unconsciously took a step back and slid his hand inside his coat, ready to draw his USP 9.

The leader spoke again, this time forcefully, his voice full of anger, "What's the matter, pops? You deaf or somethin'?"

The three young men kept coming, and the two men flanking the leader fanned out, trying to circle around Jan. Jan finally spoke, his voice icy, "I heard you fine, lad. Why don't you have the first pint on me?"

Jan held up a 20£ note in his hand, hoping the peace offering would work.

"Yeah?" the leader said, taking a step forward, "How 'bout we take it all?" This was not working, and Jan did not have time for this distraction. Before the young men encircled him, Jan took two fast steps toward the leader.

Jan's hand had already gone to his hip, smoothly drawing the USP. His left hand shot out like a rocket, grabbing the leader by the jacket. His right leveled the big H&K pistol against the leader's head. "How about your friends tell me which one of them is going to clean up the mess?"

Jan's thumb disengaged the safety, and the pistol made an audible click as the mechanism was set to **FIRE**. The leader looked to his friends; all he could see was their figures departing into the mist, traveling as fast as their feet could carry them. The leader then looked back to Jan as he began to feel a feral, animal fear as he had never felt. "Friends are hard to come by," Jan said to the shaking kid, "So are second chances."

Jan released his grip and re-engaged the USP's safety. Jan gestured with his thumb and said, "Beat it." The youth needed no encouragement; he ran for his life in a panic, and a dark wet spot began to appear on the fly of his trousers.

Jan watched the men run in terror and re-holstered the pistol. *"So why didn't you kill that little punk? You certainly had a reason. It doesn't take much for people to die around you, Jan."*

Jan turned and kept walking. He did not have time for lies. *"Lies? Come on, Jan., I have NEVER lied to you. I have always told you the truth."* He took a route that left the street and went into the bush. It was faster and more direct to hike cross-country to the airfield.

"It's more private, too; I like that. No distractions." Jan tried to focus on the principles of land navigation. The fog had lifted out here in the fields. Jan counted his steps, oriented his direction using landmarks, and did everything he could to keep his mind off the accusing voice in his head. Before long, Jan had entered the town of Coopersale. There was a pub ahead, on his right. Jan hoped that he could sneak by and avoid attention. The altercation with the three young men still hung in his mind. *"Start something, Jan,"* the accuser suggested, *"I promise you'll feel better after you draw some blood."*

Jan was not going to take the bait. He turned down an alley, avoiding the pub altogether. *"Look, Jan, I'm not here to abuse you. I'm here to tell you things you need to hear, and right now, you need to hear that your actions got the people you care about killed. I cannot make this easier, but you must accept it. The sooner you do, the sooner this will end."*

Maybe the voice was right. Perhaps he was a liability. Did Jan not owe it to himself and the Order to entertain this possibility? Jan left the town of Coopersale and walked into the Gernon Bushes nature preserve. Once he passed these woods, he could emerge on Epping Road and take a short walk to the airfield. The woods in the preserve were dark. The hornbeam trees were free of leaves but tangled their branches above to form a thick canopy that blocked out most of the light. The light that did penetrate the forest floor made the woods look like a scene out of a fairy tale. *"Jan, listen to me,"* the voice said to Jan. *"I have always had your best interests at heart. Just find someplace to disappear. Learn a trade, raise a family, just put all this pain behind you. Nobody has to know."* But Jan would know, and somehow, he knew his fallen brothers would know too. Jan decided to answer his accuser for the first time since he got off the train.

"What's stopping you, Jan?" the accuser asked.

"My oath to serve the Order, my duty to the sick and helpless, and the blood of my fallen brothers; THAT'S what stops me," he replied. The fog cleared from the street and with it, his accuser. Jan had reached North Weald Airfield.

"Okay," Jan said to himself, *"I'm here, where am I supposed to go?"* Standing on the side of the road and peering into the airfield would look suspicious. Jan looked at the perimeter fencing. Like most chain link fences, the fencing was poorly installed and provided no barrier to someone who knew what they were doing. Jan removed the clip that held the fence to the post and lifted the bottom of the chain link fence enough to roll under. He quickly moved to a patch of tall grass that overlooked the airfield and sat down. He extracted a small monocular from his personal kit and performed a slow scan of the airfield. He saw the control tower, a few scattered businesses, hangars, and... there. A Gulfstream III private jet, all by itself, parked on the ramp two hundred yards away from his position. The G-3 was out of place here; this was a field from where small, single-engine private aircraft flew. Jan could see the port side of the aircraft, its interior lights were on, and the pilots were visible operating the aircraft.

The main engines were not running, but Jan could hear the whine of an APU. Suddenly Jan focused on the G-3's tail. The tail background was black, but there was the unmistakable shape of a white Maltese Cross painted on the tail. Jan rose slowly from his observation position. Only select men in the Order flew around on large jets like these, a Grand Master of a Priory. *"Now I know what Golf-Mike means,"* Jan thought as he began to approach the aircraft.

CIA Headquarters, Virginia

James Carver had stayed late at the office after calling his wife hours ago. That conversation had gone poorly and spoiled the man's mood for the rest of the evening. The situation in London was so far off the rails he was not sure it would ever be fixed. Somewhere during the day, the operation had transformed from a minor disagreement between allies to a full-blown international incident. He was shouting at Randy Campbell on his secure desk phone. "Randy, I've had enough. Pull Pogi out of the field, NOW."

Campbell had been scolded for the past twenty minutes, and his patience was gone. "Jim, if you pull him out of the field now, we lose the ability to manage this situation entirely. Yes, I know he's over his head, but Pogi is also the only one behind the wheel of this op. You WANTED it small, remember?" Carver knew Campbell was right, but that did not mean he had to like it.

"At least get the Stingers back, they shot down a helicopter yesterday, who knows what they're going to do tomorrow!" the senior man whined.

"Jim, I've already talked to Major Aubert," Campbell said. He had never seen the director so agitated. "He said he didn't need them anymore and we've got them. All units one hundred percent accounted for minus the two missiles fired."

Carver looked at the ceiling of his office and let out a slow breath. *"Thank God,"* he thought.

"Randy, there's another issue. I am hearing from MI-5 that there was a civilian killed in this assault on the medical school. The Brits aren't going to let that one go, Randy. If a foreign intelligence service did something like that at Harvard, would we let it go?"

Campbell did not have a satisfactory answer to that. He knew the director was right; this kind of incident simply did not happen among professional intelligence agencies. It was one thing to keep the host nation in the dark. Losing control of an operation and getting civilians killed was something else entirely. Carver interrupted Campbell's train of thought. "Hang on a minute, Randy. My secretary is buzzing me on the other line."

Carver put the call on hold and picked up the line. "What is it, Tina?" he asked.

"Sir, my apologies, but Mr. Wright is on line two," she answered.

"Lovely," Carver thought.

It was only a matter of time before MI-6 figured out what was going on. Now he was getting a call from the Chief of MI-6. Carver sighed and told Tina to put Wright through, "Cecil?"

"Yes, James. Good to hear you," Wright said.

Carver decided to play dumb. Maybe he could bluster his way through the call if he feigned ignorance. "James," Cecil continued, "It's late here so I won't waste our time. I know about the CIA operation in London."

"Oh?" Carver said.

"James, don't play coy with me. I've seen your field agent's requests for MI-6 to assist with that little fiasco over in Watford. He was rather insistent with one of our analysts here."

Carver winced. He knew that Pogi's mistake was eventually going to come around and bite the

CIA, and here it was. Pogi didn't have the experience to make these requests quietly, much less not let people like Drouin call the shots out in the field. "All right Cecil, I won't. Yes, there is a CIA op in London. Yes, the op was mismanaged and one of your citizens was tragically killed in an accident. I can assure you we are doing everything we can to abandon this op and hold those who were negligent accountable." Cecil did not respond at first, and Carver worried he might have given too much information away.

What Carver heard next shocked him. "James, don't bother," Cecil said. "I've been ordered to ignore this."

"What does that mean, Cecil?" Carver asked. He instantly thought about how he would react if the situation were reversed. The FBI would never leave him alone over something like this. They would want to know who was responsible. The U.S. State Department would kick out the ambassador of the responsible nation... Yes, this would be an international mess.

Cecil continued, "It means the Chief of MI-6 got a call from the Foreign Secretary and we were told to drop the matter. MI-5 got the same orders. James, whatever is happening, my government wants it to continue."

Carver thought for a minute and said, "Cecil, we've both been kept in the dark on this, and I don't like it."

"Nor do I," Cecil replied.

"James, if there's anything you can tell me, now is the time." Carver agreed. He told Cecil what he could, that orders came down from the EOP to start the operation in London and that Legion Services was involved. Carver also told him about how Anton Drouin also had a say on the management decisions. Carver commented that the extreme violence and unprofessionalism on display was probably due to his involvement.

"So, you've been stuck with an intrepid billionaire and garbage orders from your civilian leadership? Not an enviable position, James," Cecil was enjoying this conversation wholeheartedly. It was rare one got an opportunity to rub the DDO's face in it, and he was savoring the moment. Cecil knew the intelligence game was a European thing. Most of the European intelligence services went back centuries; The CIA was just a new kid on the block with all the shiny toys. Privately, Cecil could not stand Carver. He was one of those career civil servants who would be just as happy running the Department of Agriculture. Carver did not have one ounce of patriotism in his body, which was an insult to Cecil and the whole spy craft profession. *"The man wouldn't have lasted a day during the cold war,"* Cecil thought.

Carver had already lied to him once; it was time to kick the CIA off its high horse. "I think it might be time to end any amateur involvement with this operation, don't you?" Cecil said.

Carver's eyebrows rose, "Cecil, we both know I'd love to cut Drouin loose, but I've got orders to keep him involved."

"Exactly, my dear fellow, you have orders, I don't," Cecil said. "Can you confirm that Drouin no longer has the Stinger missiles?"

Carver was quick to answer, "THAT I can confirm, Cecil."

"That's splendid James. I tell you what, I'm feeling generous. I'll clean up this whole mess in London and get Drouin off your back. Nobody will know the CIA was involved."

Carver could not believe his luck, "But what about your citizen? Surely you want some formal apology or..." Carver wondered what kind of concession Cecil might request.

"Good heavens, James!" Cecil exclaimed. "I have the image of my agency to maintain. I will not have that image tarnished by drawing any attention to the possibility this operation ever existed. If this became known, it would only encourage our enemies to carry out operations in the United Kingdom. No James, mum's the word here; isn't it always?"

Carver nearly leaped for joy. This situation could not be better. Cecil had given him a way out, and he was going to take it. "All right, Cecil. Call me when it's done," Carver said through a smile.

"Will do, James," Cecil terminated the call and thought for a bit in his office. Cecil did not like what he had just heard from the CIA's DDO. Not only was this operation wildly unprofessional, his suspicions about the Executive Branch of the United States being involved in this mess were confirmed. Adding that information to his strange orders from the Foreign Secretary telling MI-5 and MI-6 to ignore the facts that a British subject was murdered, and a foreign paramilitary squad was running amok in London. These two things told Cecil that the politicians were trying to run their own operation on British soil, and European aristocracy was involved.

Cecil scoffed, *"I should show these clowns who they're dealing with,"* he thought. Cecil already knew who he needed to call. Cecil picked up his phone and began to dial John Archer's number.

North Weald Airfield, U.K.

Two men stood guard at the G-3's folding staircase. They were dressed in MultiCam combat uniforms and wore the Maltese Cross of the Order on their Left sleeve. When Jan got close, they snapped to attention and gave Jan a crisp salute. Jan stopped and returned the ancient gesture. One of the guards spoke, "Captain Luczac, his Excellency the Grand Master of the Priory of Saint Petersburg is expecting you."

Jan took a deep breath and ascended the stairs. Inside the soft light of the jet's cream-colored interior sat an older man with an intense look. He looked to be about sixty but trim and fit for his age. He had a mustache, and his hair was silver and perfectly styled. He was dressed in the black dress uniform of the Order. Grand Master Petrov stood when he saw Jan enter the aircraft cabin. Jan walked over to him and saluted, "Captain Luczac reporting as ordered, sir."

Petrov returned the salute and offered his hand, "Good to see you again, Captain." He gestured to an empty seat, one of four that surrounded a table in the aircraft cabin. Jan saw that Echo and Father Matthew were there as well.

Jan sat and tried to start, "Sir, I..." Petrov held up his hand and gently stopped him from continuing. "Captain," He began, "I am pleased. Your conduct has kept the expectations for a soldier of the Order. You have continued with the mission despite impossible opposition; no one could have done better."

Jan could not look at his senior officer. He felt he did not deserve praise for what happened; He was the captain of his team. He alone was responsible for the mission and for the team's safety. Worst of all, Victoria had been lost, and she was probably dead. "Sir, permission to speak frankly?"

Granted," Petrov said.

"Sir, that may be your understanding, but the truth of the matter is that my team is dead, and the young woman we rescued is dead too. In fact, it is time I resigned my commission as an officer of the Order."

Petrov looked at him for a long moment. No one at the table spoke. After an eternity in the plush interior of the cabin, Petrov said, "Jan, I'd like you to turn around and meet a friend of mine."

Jan looked and saw another figure standing in the cabin, "Hello, Captain." It was Stefan. Nothing could have prepared Jan for the shock of seeing his old friend. He stood and embraced Stefan in a great bear hug. Tears came for both men as they were reunited.

After a long moment, Jan had nothing but questions, "Stefan, I thought you were dead! How? I saw the missile hit the helicopter!"

Stefan gestured for both men to sit, and he sat opposite the table on a bench. "We took a hit to the starboard engine, Captain," Stefan told him. "I moved the aircraft away from the missile fire, and we looked for an emergency LZ. We saw one a few hundred meters to the Northeast, and I tried to get the airspeed up in case we had to autorotate. Filip and I felt vibrations through the controls, and when I flared the aircraft for a hard landing, something on the swashplate broke. I lost cyclic and collective control, and we hit hard."

Jan was still amazed he had not lost his team in the crash. There was only one other thing Jan wanted to know, "Stefan, who else made it out?"

The pilot took a deep breath and said, "Kola took a hit before we got off the ground. It wasn't bad - Kuba pulled him into the cabin and started working on him. Aleksy, Lew, and Anatol made it out without injuries. The helicopter hit hard and rolled to the Port side; Filip was injured badly; I don't know if he will ever fly again. Kuba broke both his legs and shattered his collarbone. We lost Igor and Kola in the crash. Jan, I promise you I did everything I could."

Jan let out a slow breath. He buried his face in his hands and sat there for a long time. When he spoke again, he said, "Stefan, thank you. Thank you for saving them."

Stefan remarked, "It wasn't me, Captain. I head-butted the instrument panel and passed out. Aleksy pulled me from the wreckage. Aleksy, Lew, and Anatol saved us."

It was Echo's turn to speak, "Captain John Archer helped us too. GCHQ intercepted a radio call from the police and told Archer about the helicopter crash. He was able to step in for us and secret our team away before the Legion soldiers could find them."

"God bless him," said Jan. "Echo, do we know if Victoria was killed in the assault on the medical school?"

Echo looked at Petrov, and then back at Jan, "Captain, about that..."

"They took her son," Father Matthew interrupted. "When the two of you were separated, she ran into Robert by chance. He was looking for you to try to get you out of the school when the Legion solders came. He tried to get her out, but they ran into an enemy patrol." Father Matthew was quiet for a while and said, "Dr. Turner was killed, Jan. I'm sorry, son, I know the two of you were close."

Jan's hands were in his lap. If the others could have seen them, they would have noticed the skin on his knuckles went white as he made a fist. "Where did they take Victoria?" Jan asked in a quiet voice that showed no emotion.

Echo answered him, "We have traced Anton Drouin to his ancestral home in Germany. We believe that Victoria is there as well."

Jan leaned back in his seat. "Good," he answered icily.

Echo and Petrov shared a look. "Captain," Petrov began, "The Order is massing an operation to take Drouin down and rescue Victoria. Archer's division over at MI-6 was worried about the ISIS cells, but things have escalated. Legion is running all over London and Watford and now they've killed a U.K. citizen. Let's just say that Archer is quite angry and has given the Order a free hand. He has also opened the MOD inventory for the operation in Germany and will lend us drone support."

"When does the mission start?" asked Jan. "One week from today," Petrov answered. "Your team will be training with the new weapons tomorrow at a forward staging area in Germany. We are flying in soldiers of the Order from all over Europe and North Africa. This is going to be the largest direct-action mission we have ever undertaken."

Jan had only one final thing he wanted to say, "I want to go, sir. I want a chance to settle this." Petrov looked at his young captain. Jan had led his men with distinction and was fearless in battle. Nonetheless, Petrov had a feeling he could not shake. A lifetime of leading combat operations had taught him to pay attention to such whispers from his psyche. Even though the captain didn't show it, something was off with Jan. Petrov looked at Stefan and said to him, "Tell the pilots we are ready to depart for Germany," Petrov then looked at Jan and smiled, "Welcome to the team, son."

THE CODE OF THE ORDER

DAY ONE

Chapter 14

Karlsruhe Airport, Federal Republic of Germany

The Gulfstream III descended through the early morning air. It would be dawn soon, and Jan wanted to be on the ground, reunited with his team. The lights of rural Germany spread out underneath the aircraft like distant constellations of stars. The pilots were entering the final approach to Karlsruhe and were speaking with the tower. "Gulfstream N6117Q, Karlsrhue tower, winds zero-six-zero at five knots, Runway two-one, cleared to land," a voice said over the radio with a mild German accent. The pilot of the Grand Master's jet fought through some minor turbulence and responded, "Roger, Runway two-one, cleared to land, November six one one seven quebec."

Jan could hear the landing gear unfold into its deployed and locked position. The ground zipped by as the Gulfstream came in over the airfield, floated over the runway, and the passengers bumped in their seats as the aircraft landed. The Gulfstream III quickly left the runway and taxied to a stop on the tarmac at the Southern end of the airfield. Karlsruhe was an old West German Air Force base during the cold war. Hardened aircraft shelters and other relics of the past could be seen scattered about. The flight crew unfolded the airstair and began securing the aircraft. Jan and the other passengers descended the airstair and waited on the tarmac. Jan filled his lungs with the cold morning air. It felt good to be focused on the mission, and much needed to be done to prepare for the assault. The Gulfstream pilot came up and addressed the group, "The transport helicopter is on its way; it should be here in a few minutes. You are welcome to wait inside the aircraft cabin until then, it's chilly out here on the tarmac."

Every man in the group declined; they wanted to be outside and preferred the fresh morning air to the artificial environment of the Gulfstream's cabin. Petrov told the others, "There is a staging area we have set up near Drouin's estate. We will be able to fly there direct, as we have set up a heliport there. Ah, here comes one of the transport helicopters." The shadow of a large transport helicopter came into view. The pilot brought the large aircraft into a graceful hover and gently set the aircraft down on the concrete. As the helicopter taxied to their position, Jan saw that it was a Eurocopter H215 Super Puma. These aircraft were bigger than anything he had ever used on a mission. An H215 could carry twenty-two soldiers with their combat load. How many soldiers were they using for this?

The H215 came to a halt near the group. The five men walked single file towards the open door of the helicopter, where a crew chief stowed their bags and gave them places to sit. The seats were basic fabric jump seats that faced away from each other along the centerline of the helicopter cabin. As the passengers sat down, they were greeted with the familiar smell of old canvas and jet fuel. The scent brought back a flood of memories for the passengers, the smell of the calm moments before combat. The pilot pulled up on the collective, and the rotor blades clawed at the air. The Super Puma rose into the breaking dawn, leaving the tarmac behind.

Schloss Drouin

Victoria awoke after a restless sleep. She hoped the whole experience had been a nightmare, but the gilded environment of the prison cell brought her back to reality. The lights in the room came on, and she heard the electronic buzz of the door lock. Victoria looked over as her bedroom door opened, and a short motherly woman walked in. She had dark hair and was dressed in a red Chanel suit. "Good morning," the woman said, "My name is

Marisella, and I am your etiquette teacher. I will spend the day with you." Victoria did not say a word, choosing instead to play along with the "house rules" as Greta had described last night. Victoria's decision was not lost on Marisella. "Do not speak unless spoken to," she recited. "Very good. You will find your life here easier if you listen, learn, and remember. I am here to help you with that."

Sometime during the night, Victoria decided she needed to be exceedingly cautious. There were many things going on in this place that she did not know or understand. *"Be as wise as a serpent and gentle as a dove,"* she remembered from Mass a world away and a lifetime ago. The words from the gospel of Matthew echoed in her mind as she listened to Marisella speak.

"It has been a while since you've eaten," Marisella said. "Breakfast is coming soon. Until it arrives, I want you to come and talk with me." Marisella gestured towards the table and chairs as Victoria put her feet on the floor and got out of bed. As they sat down together, Marisella told Victoria that she had permission to speak freely during their time together. "It makes conversation easier if you do not have to request permission each time you speak," Marisella said.

"This is a time for learning, my dear. You may make mistakes here with me, it's better you make them now than make them later, when there are consequences."

"Wise as a serpent," Victoria thought. She needed more information, and she decided she would ask questions very carefully. "Marisella, Greta said, 'I am a servant of House Drouin' what does that mean?"

Marisella paused and replied, "That title can take many forms. I am a servant of House Drouin. Greta is a servant of House Drouin. The Lord of the house, his Excellency Count Drouin takes care of us all." The delicate and evasive way Marisella answered that question was not lost on Victoria.

"What will my service to House Drouin be?" she asked.

There was a knock at the door. "Breakfast," Marisella explained. "Just a moment."

Marisella walked over to the bedroom door and placed her hand on the door handle. The door buzzed and unlocked to let a steward dressed in a white shirt into the room. He pushed a meal trolley that had service for two. The steward quickly set the table with a white tablecloth and sterling silver flatware. A silver charger was placed at each setting, then a plate covered with a silver cloche was set on the charger. Balled melon in a chilled crystal glass bowl was added, and a china cup was placed for breakfast tea. Finally, a small silver vase with fresh cala lilies was set between the two plates. The steward brought out a china teapot and placed a silver bowl of sugar cubes and a china creamer next to the pot. The placement was off, and the steward quickly corrected the error. The steward removed the silver cloches, and a puff of steam wafted up toward the ceiling. A crepe stuffed with brie cheese and roasted red peppers was on the plate.

Victoria was hungry, and the smell of food was intoxicating. The steward bowed and pushed the meal cart out of the bedroom. Victoria realized that he had not said a word, not one. *"Do not speak unless spoken to…"* She thought.

Marisella looked at Victoria and said, "That was an example of service. Did you notice how the steward did his work quickly, silently, and perfectly? That is the level of service we strive for, and one you must emulate if you wish to stay, my dear."

This opened another opportunity for a question, "You said, 'if I wish to stay.' Does that mean I can leave if I want?"

Marisella thought for a minute and was careful with her words. "That is the incorrect way to talk about one's service here. The correct way to think about one's conduct is that each action is a choice to stay."

Victoria was getting frustrated. This manner of speaking was getting on her nerves, but she remembered she was inside a prison with armed guards outside. "Marisella, I don't understand, can you please help me?"

Marisella was so unlike the others. She was not cold; she was tender, motherly even. She seemed genuinely concerned for Victoria and her well-being. Marisella took a deep breath and said, "My dear, it will be easier once you understand that we all have been saved from the world by our patron, the Lord of this house. For example, do you think you are a prisoner here?"

Victoria was silent, worried she might have said too much. Marisella noticed the concern, "My dear, you may answer truthfully. You have nothing to fear from me."

Victoria responded with a quiet "yes."

"I understand," Marisella said, "most servants feel that way at first. Look around you, you see a cage, yes? But believe me when I tell you that this is not a cage, it is instead a place of solitude to give you time to think, and time to adjust to your new life. Look at the meal you have set before you, this is how you will dine each day as a member of House Drouin. The quarters you see here? Temporary. Once you decide to stay, you will be assigned a room. There are gymnasium and pool facilities here to maintain your health, recreational facilities to fight boredom, and a palace in which to live. Moreover, this wonderful home is just the beginning; you will travel the world with our Lord, with other women your age. Together, you will live a life that most people could never dream about. THIS is the life of a fairy tale."

Victoria looked around the room and at the half-eaten plate of food. The breakfast crepe was delicious, the best she had ever tasted. The melon was sweet and perfect, served chilled in its fine glass. Everything here, everything about this place, screamed luxury and exclusiveness. *"Would it be so bad to disappear and live here?"* She thought.

Marisella had a question, "Do you want to stay here with us?"

Victoria realized that saying yes was the easy answer; in fact, everything about her experience so far made saying yes one of the easiest choices she had ever made. Was that intentional? Victoria heard herself answering. "Yes," she said, without even considering her answer.

Marisella smiled, "Splendid. We are all so happy you have chosen to stay. That also brings me to my next question; would you like some new clothes?"

Victoria nodded. The silk pajamas were nice, better than any set she owned, but she would like more suitable daytime clothing.

"I thought so," Marisella said. "The tailor is on his way; we will get you measured for some new clothes." It was just what Victoria wanted to hear. "I can give you my dress size," Victoria said. It would be so nice to have proper clothing. The room was heated, but it was an old structure, and modern heating systems could not fully drive away the chilly air. Dawn had broken, and the morning sunlight was streaming in through the windows. Victoria and Marisella heard a knock at the door once more. The electronic lock disengaged with its signature buzz, and the door opened to let in a diminutive man dressed in pinstripe trousers and a vest. He also wore a blue shirt and pink tie. He also had a measuring tape draped around his neck. He walked to the center of the room, followed by a man in a doorman's uniform carrying a small stool upholstered in green velvet. The tailor waited for the doorman to leave and looked at Marisella, waiting for instructions. Marisella rose and addressed the tailor, "Hans, thank you for coming. Please take the measurements of the young lady."

"It would be my pleasure to do so," Hans said.

"My dear, I have several styles of garments for you to review, may I?"

He came over to her with a leather portfolio. There were three garment options. One was a sleek skirt and blouse, the other was a cocktail dress, and the last garment was a white ball gown, long and elegant. All three were very nice and were cut in the latest style. Victoria noticed that these images were not pictures; they were hand-drawn sketches like the top designers made when creating a collection for their line. "They're all beautiful," Victoria said. "Do I choose one of them?"

Hans looked aghast, "No, my dear. You will need all three. If you please, the skirt and blouse for everyday wear, the cocktail dress for routine evening engagements, and the ball gown for formal events. Those will come later, but I can have the cocktail dress, skirt, and blouse ready for final fitting this afternoon."

Victoria was taken aback by this. Custom-tailored clothing ready for final fitting in less than a day? "How can it be ready so soon?" Victoria asked.

"I am the tailor to his Excellency Count Drouin, and he is my only customer," Hans explained.

"We have a staff of seamstresses here who can expertly sew garments together, all I need to do is ask."

Who has a tailor on staff? Victoria thought. Count Drouin had waiters, butlers, an etiquette coach, master chefs, household management, a private army, and now a tailor. The wealth required for a serving staff like this was staggering.

Hans gestured for Victoria to come over to the green stool. "Now," he said, "I will need to take your exact measurements for the final alterations to your clothing. Undress please."

Victoria froze. This was unlike any "fitting" she had ever done. The last one was for her high school prom, which did not require anything invasive. "Is something wrong?" Hans asked.

Marisella answered, "Hans, she is new here. She doesn't know that his Excellency requires such a close fit to all clothing."

She looked at Victoria, "Don't worry, my dear. Hans is very professional; but being fitted for clothing is a requirement to stay. Do you want to stay with us?"

This was all very awkward, Victoria knew what Marisella was saying was not true, but she was convincing. She again found herself agreeing without really thinking. She stood there on the green stool in a state of nature, willing herself not to be embarrassed. Hans took the necessary measurements expertly, asking her to move when needed. Marisella gave Victoria no privacy, calling for the steward to remove the breakfast settings. When the steward came, he did not look at Victoria once; it was as if she were invisible, not a naked twenty-two-year-old woman getting measured. When complete, Hans opened a clothing box he brought with him. He unfolded the tissue paper inside and removed a soft terrycloth robe. He asked Victoria to come down and gently draped the robe over her shoulders and helped her put it on. "Thank you, my dear. I will be back this afternoon."

Victoria nodded awkwardly, still unsettled from having her measurements taken. He smiled and left the room, the door once again buzzing to let him out. "Now that Hans has your measurements, why don't you take a nice hot shower, and we can begin? Soap and shampoo are in the bathroom," Marisella said.

A hot shower sounded good to Victoria, too, as she walked over to the bathroom. As the hot water rained down and warmed her skin, she felt as if she was washing something else away, too, a part of the person she used to be.

Staging Area "Snake One"

The H215 Super Puma came in low over the countryside. The pilot was taking the opportunity to practice his nap of the earth flying skills. All the pilots would need those skills for the coming mission. As the pilot pulled back on the cyclic and collective to fly over a row of trees, he hit the PTT button on the control stick. "Snake One traffic, this is Viper three, over the farm, request traffic advisories, over."

A few seconds passed, and a voice came back in response over the radio, "Viper three, no traffic in airspace, wind heading one five zero at three knots, cleared to land on pad zero three."

"Roger," the pilot said into the radio, "Viper three cleared to land pad zero three." The big transport helicopter climbed a bit to come into the staging area to land. The pilot slowed and flared the aircraft as he brought it into a hover and gently set it down on pad three. The pilots followed their engine shutdown checklists as the crew chief helped the passengers out of the cabin.

Petrov led the group to the main tent. Stefan held the flap open as the group walked in. "Captain!" Lew exclaimed as he saw his commander. Aleksy and Anatol were there too. The men greeted each other warmly as the team was reunited. A dozen questions flew about the tent, "How was Kuba doing, what happened to Victoria, how was everyone holding up?"

After about five minutes of joyous fellowship, Petrov called for his soldiers' attention. "We have a mission briefing in three hours. Get some rest."

Jan and the others needed no encouragement as they found empty cots.

Two hours and fifty-five minutes later, Jan led his men into the command tent. He saw that sand tables had been set up in the front of the tent, and there were rows of folding chairs. Soldiers of the Order were everywhere; there had to be one hundred men assembled in this space. Jan and his team were dressed like the others; they had drawn fresh MultiCam combat uniforms from the supply tent. They chose seats, and Jan joined the other captains in the front row. The assembled soldiers did not have to wait long, Grand Master Petrov walked into the command tent, and the soldiers stood as one and came to attention. Petrov took his position in front of his men and said, "At ease, soldiers. You may be seated."

Petrov pointed to the bulletin boards behind him and said, "Gentlemen, this is Operation Green Tower. There are two objectives; One, we will rescue a kidnapped twenty-two-year-old female who was under the Order's protection. Two, we are after information about additional ISIS attacks in the United Kingdom and the European Union. This information and the location of the ISIS cells is on the computer network inside the home."

Jan's attention was immovable, just like the rest of the soldiers. Petrov continued, "One day before the assault, four sniper teams will insert by helicopter here, and here." He pointed to locations on the map that flanked either side of the Schloss. The LZ points on the map were inside the estate yet were far enough away from the home that the noise from the helicopter would not be heard. "You will notice that the insertion points for all sniper teams are ten kilometers away from the structure. Teams will hike to the structure through the forest and set up observation points at these four locations."

Petrov pointed to the map of the Schloss and the grounds that surrounded the house. The Schloss looked like a capital "I" on its side, with one wing to the East and one to the West. The home entrance faced south, and the back of the home faced north. There was a swimming pool and botanical gardens to the North of the property. "These locations will allow sniper teams to remain undetected, but still allow easy engagement of any enemy personnel. We have arranged engagement zones to cover the LZ and prevent enemy flanking maneuvers. Teams November one and November two will be at the North of the LZ, and Sierra one and Sierra two will be positioned at the South. November and Sierra two will overlook the LZ, November and Sierra team one will be to the West. There is a bit of flexibility in the final positions. Choose a location that will allow unobstructed observation of the target zones. Distance to the schloss will be between one thousand and one thousand three hundred meters."

Petrov turned his attention to the flight crew. "Air crews, we have four H215 Super Puma transport helicopters and two EC155 helicopters that we will be configuring as gunships. The Super Pumas will come in low from the East, and land here on the grass yard by the East wing of the schloss." The word "yard" did not do justice to the terrain feature. This area was the size of two football fields, perfectly flat with a manicured lawn. It was the ideal landing zone for a helicopter assault.

"Let me introduce Viktor Fedorov," Petrov pointed to a short man with a close-trimmed beard and a barrel-shaped chest. Fedorov had icy blue eyes that had seen dozens of close air support missions. "Viktor is our combat air controller. As helicopter crews approach the target area, call for Copperhead Actual on the ATC frequency. He will insert with Sniper teams November one and two. Once the Pumas land and offload their troops, they will take off and orbit the area providing support for the troops on the ground. The gunships will go in first and attack any enemy personnel on the ground in the immediate area of the LZ The gunships will also cover the Pumas on the ground once they land."

Petrov pointed to the aerial photo of the Schloss. "Gunship pilots, be on the lookout for heat signatures on the roof of the schloss and the woods. If any aircraft come into the airspace of the estate, they are to be considered hostile and engaged. We will have overhead drone support from a Royal Air Force Watchkeeper WK450. The drone will orbit at 15,000 feet above the battlefield and provide real time recon of the killbox."

A pair of soldiers behind Petrov turned one of the bulletin boards over to reveal a floorplan drawing of the first and second floors of the East wing of the Schloss. "Blocking teams, you will be divided into one of three groups. Group one and two will be the blocking force. Their job is to occupy and hold the staircase that leads up to the second floor, and the gallery that connects the East wing with the rest of the schloss. Group three will enter the building first to secure the area and then provide security for the search, I.T., and blocking teams. Two more teams will insert on

Viper four right behind the main blocking element. One team will search for the kidnapped female. The second floor of this wing of the schloss is all bedrooms, and that is where we expect to find her. Be on the lookout for locked or fortified bedrooms. The other team will be the I.T. team. Their job is to force entry to this room here. This room is an office, and we expect to find a network connection inside. The I.T. team will connect a laptop, force their way onto the LAN, and copy every hard drive connected to the LAN. The target network is isolated from the internet. We expect that the information we want will be located on that network. Once the objectives are complete, the blocking teams will fall back and cover the extraction all the way to the LZ. Mission time will be 01:00, total mission time is expected to be three zero minutes."

Petrov closed the meeting by pointing to a series of thin binders on one of the tables. "Captains, come up to this table to get your mission assignments and to dispatch your team members appropriately. There will be a final mission briefing in three days. All captains will see the quartermaster to draw equipment and weapons."

Petrov looked around the room. There were no questions, but those would come later as he and the teams planned the assault. Having nothing further to add, he said, "Dismissed."

Chapter 15

Schloss Drouin

It was time for a light lunch. The steward brought Marisella and Victoria seared salmon with roasted tomatoes, white beans, and grilled eggplant. The dish was expertly plated with a medallion of eggplant underneath a portion of perfectly cooked salmon, topped with beans and tomatoes. Marisella explained that most of the food served here at Schloss Drouin was lighter in fare because eating rich food all the time tended to upset the stomach. As the two women ate, Marisella critiqued Victoria's manners. Marisella commented on how Victoria held her fork, how large of a bite she took, and how she used her napkin. When Victoria became frustrated, Marisella was quick to offer soothing words. "I know this makes little sense, but perfect manners are required if you want to stay with us," Marisella said.

"Do you wish to stay?" There was that peculiar question again. Marisella always asked it with a tinge of sorrow in her voice. There was no other real option other than to say yes. Victoria was not in a hurry to discover what Greta meant when she said, "severe consequences."

"I'm so glad you want to stay," Marisella said again. The choices were frequent, once every other hour. Every choice reinforced the idea in Victoria's mind that to stay here, a person needed to constantly agree to say yes. The two finished their lunch, and Marisella called for the plates and flatware to be removed. Marisella praised Victoria for her attention and willingness to try. "I know this is a foreign way of life to you," Marisella said, "but I'm pleased that you're making such an effort."

"Thank you," Victoria said, playing along. "Thank you for helping me, Marisella."

Marisella seemed pleased at this, and Victoria made the decision to keep playing along with this charade. A knock was heard at the bedroom door, and it opened with a buzz. It was Hans with the clothing he made from the measurements he took on Victoria earlier. Hans was pushing a rolling clothing rack with several garments in various stages of construction. Hans smiled and said, "Good afternoon, my dear. I'm here for your final fitting. Please remove your robe and put these on." He held up a set of women's undergarments and a pair of shoes with stiletto heels. "You are required to wear shoes at all times in the house," he said. "It accentuates a woman's loveliness."

Victoria was a little uncomfortable with undressing in front of these strangers, but she had done once before, and she knew the inevitable question that would come if she resisted, *"Do you wish to stay?"* Victoria found herself doing something she would never have done a week ago. She did as she was told and disrobed to put the undergarments on. She put on the shoes, noticing the **CHRISTIAN LOUBOUTIN** label printed on the insole. One by one, Hans handed Victoria garments to put on, and she stood on the green stool. Hans quickly took the supplemental measurements he needed, marking the garment with a knife-like sliver of soap. The ballroom gown was the last garment she tried on and took the longest to prepare for alterations. The garment fit like a fine glove; it was nearly perfectly altered. The gown was made of satin and was cream white. Victoria knew the gown would be beautiful and that she would look stunning wearing it.

Hans finished his work and took the garments back as Victoria put the robe back on. "Thank you, my dear," Hans said, "I will be back tomorrow with the finished garments. Please keep the undergarments and shoes with you, I will return with additional pairs when the garments are done." He bowed to Marisella, "Good afternoon," he said as he rolled the clothing rack towards the door.

Marisella waited until he left the room before speaking. "I think we are done for today," Marisella said. "Tomorrow, you will meet your athletic coach and Hans will be back here with your clothes. You will also meet with the physician for House Drouin, and he will evaluate if there is any special medical accommodation we need to furnish. Please remember your manners you practiced with me today, tomorrow you will need to use them for real."

"Everyone here was extremely polite," Victoria thought, *"that was for sure."* Humans were social creatures, and it was easy to emulate behavior that one saw from others every day.

Staging Area "Snake One"

Jan sat with his team as he looked at the binder he took from the mission briefing. "Anatol, you're going to be on sniper team Sierra two. Have you drawn a rifle from the armory?"

Anatol's face broke out into a wide grin. "I have, Captain," he said. "It's beautiful, they gave me a brand-new Accuracy International L-115A3 in .338 Lapua Mag. We got the best optics to go with it too, Schmidt & Bender PM scopes and clip on thermals. My spotter is getting an H&K 417 with a Trijicon ACOG. Captain, this is the absolute best equipment."

It was good to be with the team again, planning missions. Jan tried to be professional, but part of this mission was personal. He made Victoria a promise, one he had failed to keep, and he was determined not to fail again. "That's good to hear, Anatol," Jan said. "Better get over to the range tomorrow and start getting a DOPE card together."

Anatol nodded, "I've already met my spotter, Dimitri. He is good, really good."

Jan turned to Stefan next. "Stefan, you will fly one of the gunships. Looks like we are using snake names, so your callsign, 'Rattler One' will be easy to remember."

Stefan smiled; he had always liked the name "Rattler." He had earned it on a mission in Africa twenty years earlier. "Aleksy and Lew, you will be with me on search team one," Jan read. "We will insert on Viper four, the I.T. team will be right behind us on the same bird. Viper one through three will carry the three blocking teams and they will deploy and breach the structure first. We follow right behind and start searching room by room. I've been to the quartermaster, and we will be drawing Heckler & Koch G36C rifles and USP pistols in .45 Auto."

The G36C was the short-barreled version of the German infantry rifle, perfect for CQB operations, and the 5.56 NATO round hit harder than the 9mm MP-5SDs they had used at the farmhouse. "Blocking teams will be armed with the same weapons, but each squad will also have H&K's belt-fed squad automatic weapon, the MG-4 in 5.56 NATO. MI-6 really came through for us on the kit. In addition to the H&K small arms, we're going in with Harris PVS-18 panoramic NV sets." Normal night vision tubes or binoculars had an extremely limited field of view. The PVS-18 solved this problem with four separate night vision tubes and made the operator look like he had the head of a spider with multiple eyes. In practice, the panoramic night vision goggle sets allowed the operator to have near-normal vision and depth perception, but he could also see in complete darkness.

Aleksy had a question, "Captain, what kind of resistance are we expecting?"

Jan had a quick answer, "Well, the entire force of Legion Services will be there, plus whatever reinforcements they've managed to bring in. Resistance is expected to be heavy, why?"

The response came across harsher than Jan intended, but it hung in the air like a storm cloud. Aleksy gave Jan the benefit of the doubt and said, "Captain, I just want to know how big of a fight we are going to pick, I hope it's a big one." Aleksy gave Jan a wicked grin.

"Well, I hope you're ready, Aleksy. It's going to be a nasty one. Some of us probably won't come back, so I hope you've got your affairs in order." Jan thought for a minute and added, "Aleksy, if you're worried about getting killed you better tell me now; that goes for all of you. This mission will be dangerous." It was suddenly noticeably quiet in the tent. Lew's face was flushed with rage. The captain had changed somehow; he would never have spoken to his men like this – had Jan lost his nerve?

Anatol looked like he was ready to rip Jan's head clean off his shoulders. Anatol had lost his spotter two days ago, and the emotion from the loss was still fresh. Aleksy wondered if Jan's attachment to Victoria might be clouding his judgement. Stefan, at forty-five years of age, was the oldest member of the team by far. He had seen the most combat and had grown wise over countless operations. He decided to speak before one of the young men said something they would soon regret. "I think we all feel the same way, Captain," Stefan offered, "We know this mission will be dangerous. But remember that day in Flamstead when you gave the order to move up the Farmhouse assault? We went with you then; we will follow you now."

The young men calmed down, recognizing what the older man was trying to do. Jan nodded and said, "I'm sorry, lads. I shouldn't have put it that way. We've been together a while now, and I know you will all do what it takes to accomplish the mission. I apologize if you thought I felt otherwise."

The soldiers relaxed a bit. "Perhaps we are tired, Captain," Aleksy offered. "If there's nothing further, we should get some rack time and transition our sleep cycle to night operations."

Jan took a breath; he was going to suggest this to the group. "Right, Aleksy. Unless anyone has any further questions, get some rest, that's an order," Jan said with a friendly smile, feeling like his old self again. All the team members chose a cot and got inside the warm green sleeping bags. All quickly drifted off to sleep except Stefan. Instead, he stared at the canvas ceiling overhead, lost in thought. He did not like that his commander had snapped at a simple question. Questioning Aleksy's resolve was out of bounds, and that comment told Stefan that Jan was under a significant amount of stress. As he closed his eyes, Stefan promised himself that he would keep an eye on Jan.

Schloss Drouin

It was dinnertime. The steward announced his presence with a buzz from the door. Victoria hated the electronic lock; it was a constant reminder that she was in prison. She had taken a nap earlier in bed. There was nothing else to do in the room. There was no clock, and Victoria could tell time only by the light outside and the meals she was served. *"Dinner o'clock,"* she thought dryly. The steward was fast, setting the table with fine china and sterling silver flatware. He placed a vase with flowers and a candlestick.

When the steward revealed what was for dinner when he removed the cloche, Victoria saw that it was poached Dover sole with beurre blanc shallot sauce and spinach. Victoria noticed that the dinner service was for one. The steward left, pushing the dinner cart out of the bedroom without saying a word. When the door opened to let the steward out, Victoria began to eat. The fish was perfectly cooked, delicate, and light. The sauce was the perfect accompaniment to the fish and the spinach. A dish like this would fetch fifty pounds or more if it were served in the Savoy Hotel. Victoria was almost finished when she heard the door lock buzz once more. It was Greta. Victoria remembered the unpleasant and invasive conversation they had shared last night. She reminded herself to be cautious with her words and to remember her manners. "How are we this evening, my dear?"

"I am well, thank you," Victoria answered. Victoria realized that no one had used her name. Instead of saying, "*Victoria,*" they addressed her as "*my dear,*" or "*darling.*" This was another one of those odd things about this place. Come to think of it, no one here had even asked her name.

"I'm glad to hear that, my dear. Tomorrow, you will meet the athletic coach we have on staff here. He will come to your room at seven in the morning and escort you to the gymnasium. In the afternoon, you have an appointment with the physician," Greta said. "Breakfast will be served at six, we will have an early start to the day."

Victoria was careful to stay silent, as Greta did not ask a question. It was as if there was a continuous test going on, and the household staff were watching her, seeing if she was obeying the "house rules." Greta looked at Victoria for a full minute. Thinking this was some kind of test or game, Victoria did not answer, careful to keep her body language passive. Greta spoke first, breaking the silence. "Very good, my dear. You're learning the house rules quickly, and that pleases me. Marisella tells me you are a quick learner, and that you're choosing to stay with us. I can tell you that the life you live here will be much better than anything you'll manage on your own. Look around you, a normal person, even a person of privilege could not amass such wealth in two lifetimes. The Lord of the house, Count Drouin hopes you will stay with us, but that is your decision. Do you want to stay?"

Victoria looked at her. Greta's eyes betrayed nothing; she had the stare of a gambler. Victoria was intelligent; she figured out a while ago that she would tell these people exactly what they wanted to hear, *"I want to stay," "It would be my pleasure," "I will speak when spoken to."* People who were expecting an answer were easy to fool. *"Be as wise as a serpent and harmless as a dove,"* she thought. Victoria told Greta the answer she wanted, "Yes, I would like to stay."

"Splendid," Greta said. "In that case, I will see you tomorrow. Please go to bed early, tomorrow will be here soon." Greta left the room and left Victoria alone. She walked over to her bed and put on her silk pajamas. The fabric felt wonderful against her skin. She wondered what tomorrow would bring in this twisted finishing school.

Staging Area "Snake One": KD Range

Anatol pressed his body against the butt of the rifle. He had spent time positioning his body behind the rifle, so each breath raised the crosshair slightly. When he exhaled, the crosshairs settled back to their natural point of aim, the target perfectly centered on the target over a kilometer away. The sniper teams were using the Qioptiq SVIPIR-2+ Thermal optic mounted to a canted rail on the L-115A3 sniper rifle. This Infra-red device was positioned in front of the Schmidt & Bender PM 5-25 x 56mm riflescope.

Anatol could see the steel silhouette target clearly in black and white, even in the dead of night at 1,200 meters away from his position. He and Dimitri had taken four shots at this target already, working to build up a hasty Data On Previous Engagements or "DOPE" card. The other sniper teams were shooting at similar targets at the 1,200-meter line; this was the longest calculated shot any of the snipers would have to take. Dimitri was amazing. He was a human-ballistic computer and made Anatol's job as the shooter a piece of cake. Dimitri was watching the silhouette target through his spotting scope, reading the wind. Anatol was ready to shoot. He took a breath and let half of it out. "Ready," Anatol said to Dimitri. "Sniper, target area still clear, hold one mil left for wind, send it."

Anatol increased the pressure on the rifle trigger. He felt the trigger's first stage swing to the second stage, where he felt the wall. He kept applying pressure until the trigger broke. The rifle surged rearward as it launched a 250-grain projectile downrange. Dimitri watched the target closely. The bullet would take two seconds to travel the 1,200 meter distance, and under these conditions, he could actually see the bullet travel down range. In the IR spotting scope, he could see the heat coming off the bullet as it streaked towards the target, white-hot against the grey background. The bullet landed within ten inches of the other four shots and smacked the steel plate with authority. Even after traveling over a kilometer, the 338 Lapua Mag still hit the plate harder than a 5.56 NATO would at point-blank range.

"Impact," Dimitri said to Anatol. The sound of the plate being struck arrived three and a half seconds after the bullet hit. This rifle was amazing, and Anatol had fallen in love with it. He and Dimitri had another night of range practice, but the truth was they did not need it. They were ready. Anatol said a silent prayer for any enemy unlucky enough to walk in front of his rifle.

DAY TWO

Chapter 16

Schloss Drouin

The door to Victoria's bedroom buzzed promptly at six o'clock. She sat up on the bed as a very fit man in a tracksuit walked in with the steward pushing his serving cart. The steward got to work setting the table as the man in the tracksuit walked to the bed. He had olive skin, and his parted hair was black. He had a mustache and an intense look. His hands were strong, and bulging veins were easily visible through his skin. "Good morning, darling," he said in a Castilian accent. "My name is Julio. I am the athletic coach for House Drouin."

Marisella's words hung in Victoria's mind as she listened to Julio. This was a test of her manners and how well she remembered the house rules. Julio went on, "I will take you to the gymnasium after breakfast; please sit and eat."

Victoria walked over to the table and sat down. She saw that hot oatmeal was being served with a side dish of chilled fruit: blackberries, raspberries, and blueberries. Victoria poured a cup of breakfast tea and began to eat. She was careful to use her table manners and not finish the entire meal.

Victoria knew she was going to be exercising soon, and a full stomach made her sick when she ran. The whole time Victoria ate, Julio was standing there, watching her. Julio made Victoria very nervous. He was not harsh with his words; he did not say anything at all. Still, Victoria found him threatening. When Victoria finished, she stood, pushing her chair and leaving her napkin on the table.

"I brought you suitable exercise attire," Julio said. "Please remove your pajamas and put these on." Julio held up a set of athletic leggings and a sports bra.

Victoria hesitated; she did not feel safe around Julio. Of course, he noticed her hesitation right away and was quick with the expected question. "Athletic attire is required in the gymnasium, I'm afraid," he said. "Do you wish to stay with us?"

"I can change quickly," she thought. *"Just slip out of the pajamas and into the sportswear. Ten seconds at most."* Without thinking about it, Victoria compromised her values once more and told Julio, "Yes." She removed her pajamas, once again baring her body in front of a total stranger. She took the offered clothes and slipped them on. Julio also had a pair of running shoes and socks that came just above the heel.

Julio held out his hand and pointed it at the door. Victoria walked towards the door with a flurry of thoughts racing through her head. It was not lost on her that she was being let out of her prison cell for the first time since she arrived here. A thought occurred to her that she might be able to make a run for it. Victoria could move pretty fast, and she thought that on a good day, she could outrun most people. One glance at Julio stifled this thought. Julio had the body of a sprinter or swimmer. Victoria was not only convinced that Julio could outrun her, but she was also sure that once he caught her, he was strong enough to force her to do whatever he wanted. *"Be as wise as a serpent..."* she thought.

Running with no idea where she would run was not wise. She reconsidered her plan. She would instead go with Julio and do what he wanted. The trip to the gymnasium would allow her to observe different parts of the house and collect information that she could use to escape later. If an opportunity arose, she promised herself she would take it. As she approached the door, she heard the lock buzz, and the door was opened for her by an armed Legion soldier. He had a rifle slung over his chest and body armor. *"Good idea; I didn't try to run,"* she thought.

She now knew her room was secured with more than just a lock; there was an armed guard outside as well. As they walked down the hallway, Victoria saw that there was another Legion soldier on the floor; he was patrolling the hallway. *"So, there are at least two soldiers on this floor,"* Victoria thought. That was useful information. She looked around the hallway. There were other bedroom doors here, some had locks like her bedroom, and some did not. Tall doors opened to lead them out of the bedroom hallway and into another long gallery. There was an ornate red carpet, and the walls were granite and carved marble. Large oil paintings lined the walls; some looked to be the work of Renaissance masters.

Victoria recognized the style but not the pieces themselves. When they got to the end of the hallway, Julio said, "We will go through this door."

Behind the door was a staircase that lacked any decoration. It was out of place for the style of the home, but it was centrally located. It occurred to Victoria that stairwells like these were probably scattered throughout the home and allowed servants to move about unseen. They took this staircase down three levels. This would put them on the first level of the house. There was another hallway down here in the basement, well-lit with overhead fluorescent lights. Victoria saw activity here. Stewards and doormen moved about, maids were pushing cleaning carts, and soldiers were moving as well. Julio said, "First door on the right."

Just beyond that door was an expansive gymnasium. An indoor racetrack was on the outside of the facility, separated by two glass walls and a ceiling. Inside the racetrack were dozens of weight machines, free weights, and exercise machines. The exercise machine floor had a high ceiling, and there were observation windows set in the second-story wall above the room. These observation rooms were just above the racetrack. The machines looked new; this room would have been the envy of any Division 1 college sports team back in the United States. Being private, the machines and weights were available, as was the racetrack. Julio led her to the racetrack and said, "We will warm up, and then we will jog for a bit. Later, we will do a series of exercises to tone muscles."

He had a question for her, "Do you have a medical condition that prevents you from exercising?"

"No," she said.

"Do you have any sports injuries?" he asked.

"No," Victoria answered again.

"Bueno," he said, "You will do as I do. Ready? Begin."

On the racetrack, Julio did a few sets of jumping jacks to get his blood flowing and his muscles warmed up. He also did a series of stretches for his legs and to his core and shoulders. Victoria watched what Julio did and followed along. Once they were warmed up, he said, "Now we run. I will set the pace, and you will follow me. Let's go."

Julio took off, jogging down the track with Victoria right behind him. Victoria was determined to show Julio what kind of athlete she was and matched his pace. The track covered a 200-meter oval, and they ran two kilometers together. Julio looked at Victoria and asked, "How are you feeling?"

Victoria decided to take a risk with her response, "I'm doing well, is this all you got, Julio?"

He flashed her a wicked grin and increased the pace. "Okay," she thought. "*Athletic trainers are all the same; a bit sadistic and playful. If you challenged them a bit, they always loved it."*

Victoria made the decision to flirt with Julio a bit in hopes that he would give her more information about this place and what her "service" would entail. She easily kept Julio's pace. Victoria competed in track and field events when she was in High School, and she kept up the habit of running. Even this faster pace was easy for her to maintain. Julio kept running for three more kilometers and then began to slow their pace. Both she and Julio were perspiring from the run. Julio stepped through an opening in the wall that led to the interior of the racetrack, where the weight machines were located. Julio walked to a table in the center of the room that had towels stacked on one side. He pulled out two towels and opened a cabinet door underneath. He pulled two chilled bottles of water from a refrigerator concealed in the cabinet and threw one to Victoria. She caught it mid-air and twisted off the cap. She gratefully drank the cool water, and although she was not tired from the run, she was thirsty. "You did well on the run," Julio praised her. "Most girls who come here to me are not in your physical condition. It will make things easier."

That remark caught Victoria's attention. *"Most girls who come here? What does that mean?"* She thought. Julio pointed at one of the machines. "Incline press," He explained. "We will start you at ten kilos per side. Please sit down on the machine."

Victoria sat down and began the exercise. The machine targeted her chest and shoulder muscles. She easily pushed the weight away from her chest. Julio coached her as she lifted the weight. He critiqued her form, asked for one more rep here and there, and spotted her when necessary. The coaching repeated as Julio asked Victoria to do weight exercises on the lat pulldown, bicep curl, and push-down station. The exercises ended, and Julio was impressed. "My dear, you did very well today. At this rate, you'll be teaching me a thing or two about strength training."

"Now was the time," Victoria thought. She was going to push the charm with Julio as hard as she dared and try to learn as much as she could about this place. "Stop," Victoria said, biting her lower lip, and continued, "A big, strong man like you?" Her eyes sparkled, and she unsuccessfully suppressed a giggle. Suddenly, she turned serious and spoke in a whisper. "Julio, I've been scared. I know this is against the rules, but..."

Julio looked at her with an impassive look. "I don't know what I'm supposed to do here." Victoria said. "What do I need to do to stay?"

Julio looked at her. "Do you want to stay?" he asked.

"Yes," She lied. "It's beautiful here. It's like something out of a fairy tale, and I don't want it to end."

Julio responded in a quiet voice, "In that case, I'd recommend that you do exactly as you are told. And make sure you take care to follow any orders Greta might give you."

Victoria pressed him further, going as far as she dared. "Is there anything you can tell me about what my service here will be? Greta mentioned that I would be serving, but she didn't say how."

Julio hesitated as if he were trying to avoid disobeying direct orders.

"Julio," Victoria cooed, giving her best *"come hither"* look, "If you tell me, I can stay. We can spend more time here at the gym. I liked this morning, the exercise... And I like spending time with you."

Julio's head looked up quickly. She had sunk that last hook deep, hoping the flirting was working. Julio looked at her for a long time before he spoke again. "Those are questions for Greta," he said. "I cannot answer them. Come, it's nearly lunchtime, and Hans will have delivered your new clothing by now."

Staging Area "Snake One"

Stefan woke early. Transitioning to a daytime sleeping schedule for night work was not easy, and the first day was met with broken sleep. There was something pressing on Stefan's mind anyway. He went into the command tent to see Petrov. He walked right up to his commander and came to attention. Petrov returned the salute and said, "At ease, Stefan. What brings you here?"

"Here goes nothing," Stefan thought. It was a serious breach of protocol to do something like this, but the situation was so serious that he felt compelled to act.

"Sir, I'm worried about Captain Luczac," he said.

Petrov looked at the pilot hard for ten long seconds before saying, "Clear the room. I want a moment with Stefan alone."

When the other battle captains had left, Petrov continued. "What is your concern, Stefan?"

Stefan took a deep breath and said, "Jan is not himself, Sir. Yesterday, he came dangerously close to calling out one of our team members for an act of cowardice. He seems to be carrying around a lot of combat-related stress, and if it's not dealt with, he will be putting the mission at risk." There it was. Stefan could not pull back his words, not now. He had just made the accusation that his commanding officer was not fit for duty. He did not have any specific evidence, just a hunch that came from a lifetime of combat experience and working with many Captains of the order over the years. He knew the other boys on the team were too young to see the danger; they were all young like Jan and had not known defeat on the field of battle. Stefan had seen it; he had seen a mission completely unravel, and that memory compelled him to act.

Petrov had seen failure, too, and knew what Stefan was doing. He respected the pilot for coming in here and speaking his mind; most young knights would never dream of doing so. "I've seen it too, Stefan. I saw it on the plane. To be honest, I've considered pulling Jan from front-line service on this mission; what you have just told me only confirms my feelings on this."

Stefan became nervous. Getting Jan pulled from combat duty was not what he had in mind.

"Sir, If I may offer a suggestion?" Stefan said.

"Please do," Petrov answered, "I don't have many options, and one more would be welcome."

Stefan thanked the Lord that Petrov was a commander who was willing to listen.

"Sir, the way I see it is this; If you replace Captain Luczac, who do you choose to replace him on the mission? The other experienced captains are leading their own teams, and if you bring someone forward who isn't ready, we have exchanged one set of problems for another. I propose we have Father Matthew talk to him. Father Matthew has been on combat operations before, supporting the order as a chaplain. He knows how to combat stress and can evaluate if Jan's troubles can be fixed right here and now or if it's something more serious that needs treatment. If it's the latter, you can pull him from the mission. Involving Father Matthew gives you more information and allows you to make a better decision as a commander, Sir."

Petrov smiled. This pilot was wise beyond his years. If he were more experienced with CQB, Petrov would have replaced Jan with Stefan on the spot. Still, the pilot mentioned some excellent points, and Petrov thought the idea of involving Father Matthew was brilliant. "Well done, Stefan," Petrov said. "I'll talk to Father Matthew right away. Is there anything further?"

Stefan came to attention and saluted his commander. "No, sir."

Petrov once again returned the salute and dismissed him. As Stefan left the command tent, he felt relief. It was regrettable that he had to bring this problem to Petrov's attention, but it had to be done. He was careful to keep the focus on the mission and off Jan. The Captain needed to talk to someone, and this was a way to get Jan the help he needed and preserve the integrity of his command. Stefan silently prayed that Jan would have the sense to listen to Father Matthew and not squander the second chance. There came a time in every captain's career when he either rose to the occasion or was crushed by the burden of command. Combat operations were a harsh school with painful lessons, and while some men excelled in such an environment, some did not. Stefan had seen enough commanders to know that Jan was among the former, but the problem was that Jan needed to believe that too. As Stefan pulled open the flap of the tent to return to his cot, he was satisfied with how the conversation with Petrov went, and he trusted Father Matthew to take care of the rest.

Chapter 17

Schloss Drouin

The door to the bedroom buzzed again. Victoria and Julio had returned to the bedroom, where she found two of the garments that Hans had made, with a personal note thanking her for the opportunity to apply his craft and a promise to return later that day with the gown. Victoria had a chance to take a hot, relaxing shower. She felt refreshed after the strenuous workout, and the hot water soothed her aching muscles. She found some basic cosmetics and hair care items in the bathroom, and she took advantage of them. Her lunch came promptly at noon, served by the same steward and in the same luxury that the house prided itself on delivering. Victoria chose the skirt and blouse, as well as the Christian Louboutin shoes Hans had her try on yesterday. Victoria regarded herself in the mirror. She looked stunning in form-fitting clothing, perfectly and expertly tailored to fit her body.

The clothing accentuated her natural physique, but at the same time was comfortable. In truth, the clothing fit like a glove, allowing a full range of motion, and was not restrictive or tight in any spot. *"Hans really knew his business,"* she thought as she admired the clothing once more in the mirror.

The buzz interrupted her thoughts, and Marisella walked in. "Good afternoon, dear," she said. "The doctor is ready for your appointment."

Victoria followed Marisella out of the room; instead of leaving the wing and walking down the gallery, Marisella led her to a room tucked around a corner in the East wing. One of the Legion soldiers opened the door, and Marisella and Victoria walked in together. Inside, Victoria was greeted by a well-lit exam room with pastel green cabinets stocked with medical supplies along one wall. In the center of the white tiled floor was an exam table. A dark-haired man with horn-rim glasses and a white lab coat was reading a chart by the window. "Good afternoon, my dear," he said. "I am Doctor Costa, physician to House Drouin. I will give you a full physical check-up, as I do with all servants here. Marisella, please be seated and make yourself comfortable."

Marisella followed Dr. Costa's advice and took one of the comfortable chairs that were lined up against the wall opposite the cabinets. The whole room had a strange layout. It was as if the waiting room and exam room merged into one lavish medical facility. Victoria noticed the oddities, but there were already so many things out of place in this home it got lost in the noise. Dr. Costa turned to Victoria after making sure Marisella was settled. "My dear, please remove your clothing, and we can begin."

Victoria hesitated again. This was a doctor, and this was a medical exam, but a physical in the nude? Everything about this house was wrong. Marisella sensed her trepidation. "It's all right, my dear. I know things seem different here, but we only want what's best for you. Dr. Costa here is very kind and gentle, and a physical is a requirement of service. We all get one once per year, myself included."

Marisella hesitated for a moment and added, "Do you want to stay? Please say yes. You are fitting in so well here, and I like you. Hans likes you, Julio can't wait to train with you again, and even Greta is happy with your progress. I know she can be a little abrasive at first, but you'll soon see she's kind and welcoming."

Victoria was shocked to learn this. She thought Greta hated her. Everyone here was so nice and welcoming, she had beautiful, custom-made clothing, and she dined like royalty. Was this place really that bad? She found herself agreeing to

Marisella's plea and removing her clothes without really giving it a second thought. The physical was uneventful. Dr. Costa did a thorough and professional examination and pronounced Victoria in excellent health. He asked her the usual questions, "Was she taking any medication?" and "Were there any pre-existing medical conditions?" Everything one would expect a doctor to ask a new patient coming into their practice. After Dr. Costa marked his chart and made a few notes, he told Victoria that she could go back to her room, and he thanked her for stopping by so he could complete his work. Dr. Costa also told her that if she had any health trouble to call him at once. Once Victoria and Marisella got back to the bedroom, a surprise was waiting. Hans was there with the ball gown. Hans greeted her warmly. "My dear, so good to see you!" he said. "Let me look at you! Oh, my clothing fits you so well! I've always loved dressing people to look their finest, but you make my work too easy."

Victoria blushed at the flattery. "I now have one more thing for you to try on, something pretty. Please get undressed, and we will begin." Victoria pulled her blouse off once more. She could not wait to see how she looked in the beautiful gown Hans had made for her.

Airspace South of Staging Area "Snake One"

The helicopters flew low over the countryside, faster this time now that the pilots were familiar with the terrain. The hulking Eurocopter H215 transport helicopters were flying in a diamond formation, while the EC155 gunships were one minute ahead. Stefan rolled his aircraft right to clear a tree as he flew his helicopter as fast as it would go. The terrain and vegetation streaked past in a blur of green through his night vision binoculars mounted to his flight helmet. The EC155 helicopters had been outfitted with two M134 Gatling guns and two Hydra-70 rocket system pods that held nineteen rockets each. More than enough firepower to chew up enemy infantry and unarmored vehicles. He called the combat air controller on the radio. "Copperhead Actual, this is Rattler one and two, two miles out from the station; request threat advisories in kill box delta; how to copy over," Stefan said into his radio.

He was calling for both gunships; Rattler two was listening in on the air control frequency. "Rattler one and two, this is Copperhead actual; I read you five by five," Viktor Fedorov said into his backpack radio.

Fedorov had chosen a spot on a hill overlooking the LZ. He had a MilDef DS11 ruggedized tablet that was displaying the IR feed from the Watchkeeper WK450 drone that orbited the battlespace 15,000 feet above. Fedorov continued with his report to the gunships, "Kill box delta clear of threats and traffic, orbit West end of structure when you get on station, over."

Stefan pushed the gunship as low as he dared; the forest line was just ahead. As the helicopter approached the tree line, Stefan pulled gently back on the cyclic, and the helicopter rose to clear the treetops. Rattler-2 matched Stefan's maneuver five hundred meters to Stefan's port side. The two helicopters streaked in towards the target just above the trees. *"There,"* Stefan thought.

"Rattler Two, break now," Stefan said into his radio microphone.

"Copperhead Actual, Rattlers on the station." Rattler two broke off from the formation, and both helicopters began to orbit the practice target area, nose down towards the field where IR glowsticks had been placed to simulate the exterior structure of Schloss Drouin.

"Copy Rattler one and two, weapons free on any enemy personnel West of the target structure," Fedorov told the gunship pilots.

The gunships had to hold their fire on the East end of the structure, but they were weapons-free anywhere else. The practice run did not call for live ammunition, but Stefan could imagine the utter carnage this gunship could rain down on the Schloss when they did this for real. After two orbits, Stefan called Rattler two. "Enemy forces neutralized, orbit target area, and provide fire support," he said into his mic.

As Stefan began his orbit, he could see a disturbance above the trees to the East. That would be Viper one through three. Viper four was one minute behind them; The blocking teams would land first, breach the Schloss, and then secure the stairwells to the second floor of the East wing. Viper four held the search and IT teams, who would then hack and download every hard drive on the Schloss's LAN and look for Victoria. Once the troops were offloaded, the EC215 transport helicopters would take off and orbit two kilometers away from the LZ. "Copperhead Actual, this is Viper lead, inbound to LZ, ETA three-zero seconds, over,"

Viper One's pilot called Fedorov over the ATC channel. Fedorov was quick to reply, "Viper lead, this is Copperhead Actual, winds two one zero at five knots, cleared to land LZ delta."

Stefan saw Vipers one, two, and three come in fast, flare, and land on the grass one hundred meters East of the East wing. Aerial photographs showed that this area was a large grassy field, a perfect LZ. Stefan could see figures running away from the landed EC215s, their IR strobes blinking brightly through his night vision goggles. The teams fanned out from the transport helicopters to their objectives, running as fast as they could on the grass. The blocking teams breached the plane of the structure as Viper four became visible, flying low over the trees. "Copperhead Actual, this is Viper One, drop off complete, request permission to depart, over," the Viper One pilot said over the ATC frequency.

Fedorov replied, "Copy Viper one, Rattler one and two, stay clear of LZ Delta. Viper one, proceed to pattern area heading three-three-zero after dust off, Rattler one and two, continue to orbit kill box delta and provide fire support."

Vipers one through three lifted off from the LZ as Viper four landed quickly and offloaded the IT and search teams. Stefan saw Vipers one, two, and three fly North and begin their orbit as he held the position on the North side of the LZ, still providing cover. A one hundred and twenty pound sack of sand was waiting for the search teams. Petrov suggested this to simulate the possibility of a wounded comrade or if Victoria was non-ambulatory. Jan's team found the bag, and a figure struggled to lift the bag onto his shoulders. The IT and rescue teams ran to the North side of the Schloss, delineated by the IR glow sticks. Jan knelt by the "door" and called Fedorov on the ATC channel. "Copperhead Actual, this is search and IT teams, objective complete, we have one non-ambulatory hostage, request immediate dust off, over."

Fedorov looked at his tablet for threats and called the transport helicopters. "Copperhead Actual copies, Search team. Vipers one through four, immediate dust off requested, proceed to LZ, land echelon left formation, winds still two zero at five knots, clear to land. Rattler one and two, Viper flight inbound kill box delta, monitor the area for enemy activity, check fire to the East."

One by one, the Viper and Rattler pilots checked in and acknowledged Fedorov. The EC215 transport helicopters beat the air with their rotor blades as they flared in hard one by one to the LZ. The four big helicopters landed on the grass lawn and waited for their passengers, their main rotors spinning furiously above the aircraft. The teams ran for their aircraft as the turbine engines of the helicopters screamed and filled the field with the stink of jet exhaust. The EC215 crew chiefs had the sliding doors open and were waiting for their passengers, counting the men as they ran past to find a seat. One by one, the Super Puma pilots lifted off as they got confirmation from their crew chiefs that everyone was on board. Fedorov abandoned his position and sprinted all the way towards Viper four.

Once all the Super Pumas were airborne, Viper One and Two flew towards clearings identified to the North and South of the Schloss. These locations were the exfiltration locations for the November and Sierra sniper teams. Rattler one went North, while Rattler two went South to cover the secondary LZ's. The gunships orbited above while the sniper teams ran onboard the waiting helicopters. Once Viper One and Viper Two had taken off a second time, the training exercise was called by the TOC. It was a successful second dress rehearsal of the real assault that would take place two nights from now. Father Matthew was waiting inside Viper four, having decided to come along for the ride. This was not his first ride on a military helicopter. He had seen his share of blood, and he had provided comfort to the souls of dying men as they departed this world for eternity.

There was one soul on board this helicopter he was concerned about; Petrov had asked him to ride along for the final assault rehearsal. Father Matthew made his way to the back of the helicopter and sat down next to Jan. One look at the other men seated there was enough to request privacy. The two troopers shuffled forward into the front of the cabin, leaving Jan and Father Matthew alone. Father Matthew picked up a headset and gestured for Jan to do the same. They picked a private channel so they could talk privately. "How are you, son?" Father Matthew began.

"We are well prepared, Father. The team is ready," Jan said in response.

"It looked like it from up here, son," Father Matthew said. "Although I don't have a trained eye for such things," he added. Jan smiled back; Father Matthew was particularly good at getting people to talk; he was a priest. "Jan, when I asked, 'How are you' the mission is not the topic I was asking about. How are YOU, son?"

Jan took a breath. The uncertainty and doubt he felt gnawed away at his confidence ever since that awful night when he thought he had lost his team. "Father, I've been through a hard time.

There's no hiding that. But I'm okay; truly, I'm fine."

There was an emotional wall around the young captain's heart, Father Matthew saw. So common in these young field commanders. They shut everything and everyone out and internalized the emotional stress of combat. Jan had to learn to let this out in a productive way, or the pain and guilt would eat a man alive from the inside. "Son, I've been on many combat missions, and I've spent time with many captains of the order," Father Matthew probed further. "I know the difference when a man is fine and when he's not. You need to talk about this, Jan. There's no shame in it."

Jan looked at Father Matthew for a long time. Eventually, Jan spoke first, "Okay, Father. When I thought my team was dead, it hit me harder than I realized. Once Victoria and I were safe, I needed some time alone in prayer."

"Thank God for that," Father Matthew thought. The fact Jan was turning to the LORD in time of despair made his job easier. "Can you share what you said, son?" Jan nodded. "I had a bible, and I did some reading. Samuel II Chapter twenty-two."

Father Matthew considered that for a moment. The tail end of that chapter dealt with the guilt of King David when he had a chance to stop a massacre and did not. Perhaps the young captain felt guilty about the loss of his men and the loss of the woman he was protecting. "I felt better after reading the chapter," Jan went on, "but thinking that I led Victoria into danger and that mistake got her killed was too much. Father, something inside me broke at that moment, and I lost all confidence in my ability to lead men into combat." Father Matthew said nothing; the young captain needed to get this out if he had any hope of returning to duty. "I'm still upset about Dr. Turner paying the price for that mistake, but at the same time, I'm relieved that Victoria is alive and that we are going in to get her. I don't think I have had time to process these feelings."

After a quiet moment, Father Matthew said, "Process them now, son. You must find a way to manage these feelings and conquer this self-doubt." He pointed towards the front of the helicopter cabin, "Those boys there are depending on you to lead them in and out of danger. May I speak frankly?"

Jan nodded, he was not sure what Father Matthew was going to say, but an inner voice told him he needed to hear this. Father Matthew took a deep breath and began, "Son, I love you as a brother in Christ and as one of the soldiers in my spiritual care. What is ailing you is common to young captains when they meet their first defeat. They all doubt themselves, and they all start to hear an accusing voice that second guesses their every move." Jan sat rigid in his seat. How could Father Matthew know about that voice that tormented him day and night? "I'll speak plainly, son," Father Matthew continued, "your confidence problem stems from the fact you feel responsible for everything that has happened, and that's simply not an accurate assessment." Father Matthew was being as gentle with Jan as he could. "What is an accurate assessment is this; you are blaming yourself when you should be blaming the enemy, son."

Jan could not look Father Matthew in the eye. Inwardly, Jan knew he was right, but the sense of responsibility was difficult to overcome. "As I said earlier, most young captains have difficulty separating events that invariably occur on missions," Father Matthew went on, "Some of those occurrences are things they should hold themselves accountable for, and others are simply bad luck. We live in a fallen world, and this is a risky profession. As a captain of the order, you must learn the difference between things that are your fault and things that are the fault of the enemy."

Father Matthew paused to gauge how well his message was coming across to Jan. This was always a delicate and critical part of any counseling session. Jan hung his head, knowing the priest was right. Jan felt like a fool for doubting himself and for listening to the damnable voice inside his head. Jan looked up. To him, the decision was now very clear; he would rise to the challenge and conduct himself like a captain of the order, or he would not and let someone else take his team into danger. Inwardly, Jan knew what his answer would be. Living with himself knowing he failed this test of leadership and character would be impossible. Jan looked Father Matthew directly in the eye and said, "Father, I'm happy you came to talk to me. I assure you I will lead my men as a captain of the order should, and I will put the lives of my men and the woman we are rescuing before my own. We defend civilization..."

Father Matthew regarded the young man in front of him. He remembered how Jan came to the order as an orphan, how scared he was, and how he grew to be a fine squire and later an impressive knight. He remembered the council of Grand

Masters when they discussed promoting young knights to the rank of Captain; Jan was on that short list. It was always a risk promoting one so young; in ages past, the order would only promote older knights, those who had earned the respect of their men through battle and had the intelligence and experience to shape world events for the force of good.

In Jan's case, some had seen incredible potential, a young captain with the ability to grow into a Grand Master one day. Father Matthew knew this to be true, and he tipped the scales in Jan's favor at that council meeting. Today, many years later, Father Matthew felt only confidence. He had successfully reached the young man and averted the captain's career being cut short. He had that pilot, Stefan, to thank. Jan was lucky to have the support of such good and loyal men. The priest's decision was an easy one. The order would keep Jan where he was, leading his troops into battle. When Father Matthew finished the line, he sealed Jan's position as a captain, "...and we care for the afflicted."

DAY THREE

Chapter 18

Schloss Drouin

Anton Drouin sat in his office, where he had ordered his servants to bring him breakfast. The steward appeared promptly and set a table fit for a king. Count Drouin shifted his attention between his German newspaper and the snow-covered Alps in the distance while the steward went about his work. Drouin was not even aware of the other person in the room; all his staff conducted themselves as such. He glanced at his watch and thought, *"Greta will be here soon."*

The steward lifted the silver cloche, and the aroma of the dish hit Drouin's nostrils. The delicious scent of meat and cheese wafted up from the Croque Madame on the warmed plate. The steward refilled Drouin's coffee cup, bowed, and left his master. Drouin took his sterling flatware in his hands and began to eat slowly, savoring the mastery of the executive chef who prepared his meals. Halfway through his meal, he heard the office door open. Greta walked into the room and stood in front of Drouin's breakfast table, waiting to be addressed. He let her stand there for a good while; Drouin was not ready to speak yet, and he was finishing his coffee. He poured himself another cup of the steaming Italian roast when he looked at Greta. "How is our guest?" Drouin finally asked.

"Physically, she is in excellent condition," Greta began. "Stamina, strength, and muscle tone are all exceptional. She will make a fine prize for your bedchambers, M'Lord."

Count Drouin regarded this for a moment; he appreciated fine things, especially women. "Ah, and what of her psychological condition?" Greta swallowed. Count Drouin was very particular about the personalities of the women he kept. He expected these women to have no opinions or ambition; they existed to serve him, nothing more. Once, in his youth, he tried courting a woman at university, and the experience left him emotionally traumatized. That woman toyed with him and was never serious about her romantic cues. Drouin vowed to never again let a woman that close to his heart. From that moment on, he used his social status, power, and money to ensure he would not just dominate a romantic encounter but rule it. That is what he did here at the schloss. The women he employed were less than slaves; they were human drones. They had no ambition, opinions, or objections to their lives. These women had been psychologically broken down to the point where they were not human anymore.

Greta answered him carefully. "She's not like the others, M'Lord. She has not suffered an emotional shock prior to coming here; we find that makes the girls more psychologically malleable for programming. With our new guest, we will have to induce a shock."

Drouin put down his newspaper, instantly curious. "Please go on, Greta."

Greta swallowed and said, "M'Lord, we have been forcing her to make a choice to stay here at the Schloss. We have shown her the many luxuries and benefits of living here. We have also forced her to choose to disrobe in front of strangers, baring her body in ways she would not have done prior. Tomorrow evening, I will induce a psychological shock. I will reveal to her what her purpose here will be. I will take Anna and Marie to her room, and they will demonstrate what service is like. I will then show her what the consequences of saying "no" will be. I expect an objection, which I will counter by reminding her that she has already compromised who she is and that she has chosen to parade naked in front of the staff."

A large grin crept across Drouin's face. Greta was a master manipulator, psychopathic even. She was a grandmaster chess player, always five moves ahead of her prey. It amazed Drouin that instead of chess pieces, Greta moved people. "Please continue with your work, Greta," Drouin ordered. "If there's anything you need, anything at all, just ask."

Greta smiled at her master and asked, "Yes, M'Lord. Is there anything else I can do for you?"

Count Drouin thought for a moment as he took a sip of coffee. All this talk of breaking a new servant had awoken his more animal desires. "There is indeed. Have Anna brought to my bedchamber."

The door buzzed to Victoria's room. In walked a short, thin man with tight black pants and a silk shirt. He had flowing jet-black hair and dark eyes. He also wore dancing shoes and seemed to walk on air as he moved across the room. He walked up to Victoria and offered his hand with a flourish. Victoria cautiously placed her hand in his, and he put one foot behind the other, using one leg to bow as he brought her hand up to his lips. The man then spoke with an Italian accent, "Good morning, my dear. My name is Marco, and I am the dance instructor for House Drouin. Today you will come with me to the ballroom."

Marco was carrying a shoebox. Inside was a pair of women's dance shoes in Victoria's size. "I see you have eaten and bathed. Please change into your ballgown; I will wait." Victoria walked over to the wardrobe in her bathrobe. She had showered, styled her hair, and put on makeup right before Marco entered her room. Victoria hesitated again, an echo of her former moral compass raising its objection to baring herself in front of a man she had known for less than two minutes. Marco noticed her hesitation. "All servants here are required to learn classical dance. Do you wish to stay with us?" The question again.

It appeared that whenever Victoria was about to do something, she would resist under other circumstances. Fear also crept into her mind. She was in no hurry to find out what would happen if she wanted to leave. Although unsaid, it was clear from every conversation that leaving this palace was extremely unpleasant. "Yes," she said as she removed her bathrobe and began to put on her ball gown.

Five minutes later, Victoria and Marco were outside her room and made their way down the hallway of the second floor. Victoria glided across the carpet of the hallway. Hans had once again shown off his skill as a tailor. Victoria looked stunning in the white gown, and it moved with her as she walked. Most formal wear was tight and restricting, uncomfortable even. Not this gown; it fit her like a second skin. In the middle of the East wing of the house, there was a great marble staircase that allowed access to the first and third floors of the wing. The staircase was in a large room, with the center part of the stairs leading to the first floor and the edges of the stairs leading to the third floor above. It was a space that was so big that it looked like it belonged in a luxury hotel in Las Vegas rather than in a private residence. She followed Marco downstairs to the first floor, and the heels of her dancing shoes made clicking noises that echoed off the walls. Marco's feet made no sound at all as he walked. He led her to a pair of large doors on one side of the room that held the staircase. A pair of servants dressed in blue jackets opened the doors; they swung open to reveal a ballroom that had a dance floor the size of a basketball court. The floor was made of polished hardwood with walnut inlays around the perimeter. The walls were crammed with ornate molding, and one side of the room had floor-to-ceiling windows that let in plenty of natural light. Above, the ceiling was painted with a fresco, and four large crystal chandeliers hung from massive beam supports.

In the corner of the ballroom, a quartet of musicians with stringed instruments waited. They were also dressed in the blue jackets that the servants outside wore. The home had a uniform system; waiters and stewards were dressed in white, musicians, doormen, and porters wore blue, and soldiers wore black. People with specific jobs or teachers seemed to wear whatever they wished, but all of it was fashionable and stylish; everyone here dressed impeccably.

Marco addressed Victoria formally: "How much formal dance experience have you had, my dear? Any formal lessons?"

"No," Victoria said, "nothing like this."

Marco clicked his tongue and said, "Nobody dances like civilized people anymore; a pity. We begin with the waltz, my dear. Come over to me and place your hand on my shoulder."

Marco slid his arm around Victoria's slim waist. His hand slid across the satin of her gown. Marco nodded to the musicians, and they began to play "Waltz of the Flowers" by Pyotr Tchaikovsky. Marco looked into Victoria's eyes and said,

"Listen to the music for a moment, my dear. Move with it; let the music guide you around the ballroom. Now I will show you the steps. Take a step backward and..."

Marco knew how to lead as a dance partner. Victoria felt his arm guide her; it gripped her hips and back, leading her as they moved together. Marco moved in perfect choreography with the music, pacing his steps with every crescendo and catching every note with movement. Victoria stumbled a few times, occasionally missing a step and drawing a scowl from Marco. After a while, he stopped and said, "Good. Now watch my feet."

He released her and took a step back. Marco moved his feet in a box-like pattern; he took a forward step with his left foot, then slid the right across the floor so his feet were shoulder width apart. He shifted his weight to the left foot and brought his feet together. He then took one step back and slid his left foot to the starting position, finally shifting his weight once more and sliding his right foot to the position where he started. This made his body rise and fall in the characteristic movement of the waltz. "We move together in a box, you see? Then, once we finish the steps, we turn towards the center of the floor and repeat the box."

He motioned to the musicians. They stopped playing and went back to the beginning of the musical piece. "We begin again. Take a step back with your right foot...now."

Victoria and Marco danced all morning. They waltzed, tangoed, and all the classical dances; Marco simplified them for a beginning partner. In her white dress, Victoria looked like an angel gliding across the dance floor. If the room were crowded with ladies and gentlemen attending a party, she would have had a dozen suitors at the end of the waltz. Marco's face softened as he could see that she was trying her best to listen and learn the steps. This type of dancing agreed with her, and she found herself enjoying the activity. She felt a twitch of sadness when Marco called for the musicians to stop. "That's all for today, my dear. You have done very well, and I look forward to our next lesson. We will see each other once a week, I think."

She looked at Marco and said, "I would like that. Thank you for spending time with me; the house can get a little lonely at times."

He motioned with his hand for her to follow him as he walked towards the door. "Do not worry; tonight, you will attend a cocktail party. Count Drouin may even attend, and you might get to meet him." They came to the top of the stairs, and Marco turned left to take her back to her room. "Tomorrow, Greta will come and explain your service. You've been doing so well here, my dear. All the staff adores you, and we look forward to you joining us."

That was nice to hear. Victoria was still very unsure of what her "service" would entail, but she liked the staff. They seemed harsh at first, but they welcomed her warmly when they saw she was trying to fit in and do what was asked of her. She and Marco returned to her room. "Lunch will be up soon, my dear," he said. "I know you're trying. One more day, and everything will be clear.

Lunch arrived promptly at noon. The steward came with his cart and quickly set the table in Victoria's room. Without saying a word, he placed the white tablecloth, sterling silver flatware, and coaster. He placed the entrée and used a small set of tongs to place a piece of bread on the correct plate. When he lifted the cloche, a Belgian endive salad with seared tuna, citrus, walnuts, and shaved parmesan cheese was revealed. The steward held Victoria's chair for her and helped her to sit. Marco had asked her to eat the meal in her gown, but she must be careful not to stain the garment. "Good practice, as you will be dining in fine clothing often," he said.

Victoria was nervous. She did not want to spoil Hans' work with a carelessly dropped bite of food, so she was incredibly careful with her utensils, making sure that she did not lift any food off her plate unless she was sure she had control of it with her fork. The salad had a light champagne vinaigrette and was the best salad Victoria had ever tasted. She could count the expertly layered flavors as they stimulated the surface of her tongue. Concern about staining her gown forced Victoria to slow down as she ate. Living here in this house disconnected her from the life she had known. The practice of eating on the go and constantly rushing to a meeting or lecture was unknown here. The privilege of extreme wealth allowed her to slow down and think. Time even seemed to crawl along at a snail's pace. This must have been how the kings and queens of antiquity lived. Freedom from concern was the best way to put it. Here, she did not have to worry about a schedule, tedious work, or even earning a living. Instead, every need and every desire were anticipated and met with peerless service in this strange house. A memory of Jan interrupted her thoughts, and the start of a cry began to assault her sinuses.

Victoria felt guilty; here she was, sitting in the lap of luxury while Jan was lost; he probably gave his life to save hers. And poor Dr. Turner was needlessly shot in the hall of the medical school and left to die by those cruel soldiers. Victoria's eyes watered at the thought. So much had changed in her life over the past few days, and the shock of it was taking its toll on her. Victoria's thoughts then drifted to her parents and family back in Idaho. Would she ever see them again? Did she want her old life back? Living in this house, even with the oddities, was something out of a fairy tale. A real castle, with servants and grand parties. She felt like she had stepped out of time and fallen backward two hundred years when Europe was ruled by kings and royal dynasties.

The door buzzed once more, interrupting her thoughts. Marisella walked into the bedroom. "I'm sorry to have interrupted your lunch, my dear," she offered as an apology for the intrusion.

"It's no bother, Marisella," she said, then added, "I'm happy to see you."

Marisella beamed, "I'm happy to see you too, my dear. Tonight, we have a cocktail party planned, and we want you to come."

A cocktail party sounded nice, something to take her mind off the sad thoughts she felt a minute ago. Victoria looked up at Marisella. "I'd like to go," she said.

"In truth, I was thinking of my old life, and I'd like a diversion."

"Excellent," Marisella thought. *"She's accepting her life here, and that will make Greta's job that much easier tomorrow night."*

Marisella spoke again, her voice and face betraying nothing of her true thoughts, *"I am so glad you have decided to stay, my dear. You'll like the party, I promise."*

CIA Headquarters, Virginia

Director Carver arrived early at the office that Friday morning. His driver stopped the government issued Buick in the executive section of the underground parking garage. Carver's driver opened the door for him and handed over his briefcase. The Director of operations walked the short distance to the security checkpoint and handed the guard his credentials. "Good morning, Director Carver," the guard said, as he made sure the man in front of him was the same as the picture on the ID. Sure of his identity, the guard waved Carver through the checkpoint as the armed guards relaxed a bit. One adjusted the sling on his MP-5, making carrying the weight of the weapon more comfortable. The director of security arranged a test for the executive guards last month, trying to sneak a double through the checkpoint. The guard checking the ID missed it, but one of the armed guards spotted something off and held the false executive for further scrutiny. The quick thinking of the guard saved everyone on that shift from getting into the deepest of trouble, and everyone was still on edge.

Carver thought this was hilarious enough to tolerate the delay. Carver boarded the elevator at the end of the checkpoint; this elevator car had only two stops; this one at the checkpoint and the seventh-floor office wing of the George H. W. Bush Center for Intelligence. Carver entered his office and saw that Tina had already laid out his copy of the President's Daily Brief and started the coffee pot. He began to fix himself a cup of coffee when he heard his office phone ring. It was the STE-encrypted phone, and he walked over to his desk to answer the call. "Carver," he said when he pressed the speakerphone button.

"James, It's Randy Campbell," the Paris station chief said into his STE phone 3,800 miles away.

"Sir, I don't know how it happened, but the American Citizen that ISIS picked up is alive, James."

Carver sat down in his office chair. "That's a loose end, Randy," he said. Carver swore: Who knows what that young lady knew? Campbell went on, "Pogi saw her today and called me. Apparently, she was picked up by the assault team that hit the farmhouse. Up until now, we thought that was the 22nd SAS acting on a tip from MI-6, but get this, James, it's a paramilitary wing of an ancient order of knights."

Carver thought his station chief had gone crazy. "I think you need to say that again," Carver said quietly into his phone.

"James, I didn't want to believe it either," Cunningham said. "But Pogi heard this directly from Major Aubert. There's an ancient order of soldiers that traces its origins back to the eleventh century. Now most ancient orders of knights, like the Templars, were wiped out or became charities, but one order survived to this day with its paramilitary wing intact."

Carver sat wide-eyed in his office, staring at the STE phone. "Furthermore, this order had a run-in with Drouin's ancestors two hundred years ago," Campbell went on, "and now there's some kind of blood feud."

Carver took a sip of his coffee and asked, "Randy, have we confirmed any of this?"

Cunningham was quick to answer, "No, the analysts are going to have to run this one down. But I also think that it's very telling that Drouin ordered Legion Services to shoot up a hospital and a medical school. No matter what we think, Drouin believes this order exists."

Carver leaned back in his office chair, still shocked by this information. How could the CIA spend so much time monitoring Europe during the decades of the Cold War and miss this? "Randy," Carver said into his phone, "are we sure that Legion eliminated these knights at the hospital and the medical school?"

"That's why I'm calling," Cunningham said. "I need your help to order the analysts to look at this organization and discover how big the paramilitary order actually is."

Carver picked up a pen. "That I can do, Randy. What is the order called?"

Carver wrote as Cunningham spoke. "The order used to be called the Knights Hospitaller, but today it goes by The Order of Saint John."

Chapter 19

Staging Area "Snake One"

The soldiers of the order filed into the command tent, their faces stern and their minds on task. As before, the captains of the individual teams sat up front. Soon, Petrov walked in with his battle captains and called the mission briefing to order. "Good evening, gentlemen," Petrov began. "Our assault begins in twenty-nine hours. After this briefing, the sniper teams will insert ten clicks from the target area. Viktor will also insert with the November teams. Sniper teams will establish their overwatch positions and begin to report enemy activity. Snipers will engage the enemy once the helicopters arrive and provide overwatch for the assault teams. Blocking teams will arrive on Vipers one through three. You will enter the building's West wing and proceed to the second floor of the structure. You will need to hold this staircase and the hall leading to the rest of the Schloss."

Petrov pointed to architectural drawings that showed the grand staircase that Victoria had climbed with Marco that morning. Andrei and

Ivan, the blocking team captains, could tell from the drawings that the space was immense. "As we discussed earlier on the sand table," Petrov went on, "We want to hold these locations. If the enemy wants to come to you, fine. You will be fighting from a fortified position and should have the advantage."

Andrei and Ivan nodded. The blocking teams would bring portable ballistic shields with them. The shields had a firing port that could slide open and allow the light machine gun to attack the enemy while the operator was safely behind the shield. "The enemy will have to ascend the staircase from the first floor to get to team two, and in the case of team one, the enemy will have to navigate a long hallway with no cover. If the enemy tries to flank your positions outside, they will be engaged by the sniper teams and the attack helicopters."

Stefan nodded and looked at the other attack helicopter pilot. Together, they would make sure that the enemy would pay dearly if they tried to flank the blocking teams' positions. "Blocking teams, remember that we only need to be guests at the wing long enough to find the hostage and clone the hard drives on the LAN. We don't intend to move in and stay." A slight chuckle made its way around the room among the seated men.

"Blocking team three," Petrov addressed Diego, the final blocking team captain, "There are multiple rooms on the second floor. Your job is security for blocking teams one and two, as well as the IT team and search team. You will be out front, engaging any enemy soldiers on the second floor while blocking teams one and two set up behind you. Once the blocking teams are in place, you will hold and defend a path from the LZ to the second floor of the structure. The IT and search teams will be right behind you on Viper four. We expect enemy resistance in the East wing to be light, followed by a heavy counterattack."

Petrov turned to Jan and Echo. "Captain Luczac, you will lead the search team. The East wing is a long, rectangular structure that has a row of bedrooms facing the East. We expect to find the hostage in one of these rooms. Architectural drawings show that these rooms have been fortified; they look like large prison cells. Use the fiber optic camera to look under the door, and once you find the hostage, have your combat engineer explosively breach the room for you."

Lew sat with the rest of his team, staring ahead. He would make sure to pack plenty of "bang" with him on the mission. He also planned to bring a few M18 Claymore mines with him to prevent the enemy from flanking the teams and to cover their escape if they had to abort. "The physical condition of the hostage is currently unknown," Petrov said, "If she is non-ambulatory, we will have to carry her out. Be ready for that possibility, search team."

Jan nodded. He would carry Victoria across Europe if he had to; nothing would stop him from rescuing her. "Echo, you will go with the IT team," Petrov said.

"Two soldiers will escort you to this room," he said, pointing to a small alcove on the architectural drawing. "This room has a small server rack and a terminal. From here, you will access the LAN and clone all information from every device connected to the LAN. I want you to download computer hard drives, smartphone data, tablet memory, everything you can find. This information is critical to our hosts at MI-6, and the order will deliver it for them."

Echo nodded. He had yet to encounter a firewall or password he could not crack. So long as the soldiers could keep the enemy away from him and give him time to do his work, Echo would penetrate the server's security and force it to give up its secrets. Echo usually served as a battle captain on missions. From the safety of a TOC, he would pass along intelligence information and assist the assault team with the completion of their mission objectives. This time, he was going in with the team. This filled him with excitement; he remembered the unspoken oath that was made amongst the team back at the abandoned factory in Flamstead. He and the team had pledged their lives to defend Victoria from the ISIS cell, and as far as he was concerned, nothing had changed. "From Echo's calculations, we expect the total data size to be about twenty gigabytes. Fortunately, the Schloss has modern LAN wiring and routers. That will limit the download time to approximately eight minutes. Blocking teams will need to hold their positions until the IT team completes its task. Can I count on you, soldiers?"

The assembled knights responded as one. Their unified voices boomed in the command tent. "YES, SIR!"

Petrov was ready to adjourn. "Well then, soldiers, may almighty God be with us all. Father Matthew, will you offer a blessing, please?"

Petrov stood aside as the priest came forward. He made the sign of the cross and began to speak: "Soldiers, please stand."

"God of power and mercy, you are the giver of life. On this day before we march to fight the forces of evil, give us peace in our hearts. Let our courage be strong, and let our aim be true. If we are to fall in battle, let us find ourselves in your loving presence, surrounded by your heavenly host. Give us success on this mission, so we may rescue your child Victoria from the torments of evil men. We ask your spirit to be with us as we fearlessly confront the works of the devil. In the name of Jesus Christ, we pray, Amen."

The assembled knights repeated the *"amen"* in a low murmur as Petrov came forward. "Viktor, sniper teams November and Sierra," he said, "Be ready to board your helicopter in one hour...Soldiers of the order!"

All the men assembled came to rigid attention. Petrov looked at them, *"This is what it means to be a knight of our order,"* he thought, *"we stand in the breach and step into danger because we refuse to stand by and let evil reign without a fight. We will defend civilization, or we will die trying; because it is right for good men to violently resist evil when it comes calling."*

Petrov was emotionally moved when he gave the final order, "Dismissed."

Schloss Drouin

Victoria had finished getting dressed when the door to her room made the familiar buzz. Marisella walked in through the bedroom door and said, "Good evening, my dear. Are you ready to come with me to the party?"

Victoria took one last look at her appearance in the full-length mirror that was set inside a gilded picture frame. The cocktail dress hugged her body and was shorter than usual. Even so, it fit her like a glove, thanks to Hans' expert tailoring. "Yes," she said, "I've been looking forward to going."

Marisella smiled; remember, this is a bit of a test," she said. "Remember the rules, and you will do fine. Now, come walk with me, and I'll let you know a bit more about your service here."

"Finally," Victoria thought.

She followed Marisella out of the bedroom, noticing the armed guards in the hallway outside her room again. It was as if the soldiers were there all hours of the day. Instead of taking the staircase to the first level of the building, Marisella led her down the hall of the gallery. Victoria thought it must be as long as a football field. As the two women walked past the large paintings of the Renaissance masters, Marisella shared additional information with Victoria. "This is a social affair,"

Marisella began, "but remember that the house rules apply; here more than ever, never forget that you are a representative of House Drouin now and that you are serving the master of this house, even though you are still learning. Conduct your behavior as though this were an office party. Be respectful; you will not know the rank and status of the people you meet. Never speak unless you are spoken to first, and be mindful of how much you have to drink. The people at the party know you are new to service here, but step over the line too far, and the master of the house will dismiss you."

The two women continued down the gallery. Victoria had questions but forced herself to remain silent. *"Be as gentle as a dove..."* she thought.

Marisella must have noticed the quiet conflict because she asked Victoria, "Do you have any questions, my dear?"

Victoria took a deep breath before she responded. "Marisella," Victoria said, "you mention that I am serving House Drouin. I know that I will be expected to travel with Count Drouin, but I am not sure what I will be doing for him."

Marisella paused before answering, her mind searching for the right words. "Greta will explain more of this tomorrow, but for now, think of service as a personal assistant. You will take notes at meetings, plan evenings, make reservations at the finest restaurants, and arrange transportation. An army of assistants will help you with this task, but you will be the point of contact, relaying Count Drouin's orders and wishes to this larger staff."

Victoria listened to Marisella's every word. *"She's holding something back,"* Victoria thought. "She is clearly uncomfortable talking about this subject and is trying to choose her words with care."

Marisella and Victoria came to a large door at the end of the hall. There were two servants standing at the door, wearing their signature blue jackets. Before continuing, Marisella said to Victoria, "Beyond this door lies Count Drouin's private apartments. You must never enter here unless someone calls for you. Remember what I've taught you."

She stepped in front of Victoria, looking at her appearance one more time before entering the West wing of the Schloss. "You are so very lovely, my dear," Marisella said. "I want you to relax; I know you will do well, and above all else, SMILE." Victoria took a deep breath as Marisella ordered the servants to open the door with a wave of her hand.

Viper Four, En Route to LZ Sierra

The H215 transport helicopter's rotor blades beat at the still air of the German countryside as they raced to the landing zone. In the cabin, four two-man sniper teams sat on plastic seats that faced outward from the centerline of the aircraft. Viktor sat next to the crew chief, watching the farmland race by. Off to the right of the H215, Stefan was escorting the transport helicopter in his dark grey EC155 gunship. This time, his helicopter was armed with 7.62 NATO ammunition for the M-134 miniguns and had its launcher pods loaded with 70mm Hydra rockets. Stefan watched the terrain from an altitude slightly higher than the transport helicopter, scanning for obstacles and threats. Stefan saw the forest below zip by in the green hue of the night vision goggles mounted to his flight helmet. "One minute out," he said into his intercom.

Nikolai nodded to Stefan. His co-pilot was a replacement, but just as good as Filip. Stefan raced ahead of the transport helicopter and began to orbit the landing zone area, letting Nikolai scan the area with his FLIR pod. "Pilot, LZ clear, no enemy activity," he said into the intercom.

"Roger," Stefan said as he hit the PTT button on his control stick to talk to the H215 pilots, "Viper four, this is Rattler. LZ clear, no obstacles or traffic."

The pilot of Viper four acknowledged as he flared the aircraft and gently set it down in a forest meadow. The aircraft was deep inside the Drouin estate, which consisted of the manicured grounds of the Schloss surrounded by tens of thousands of acres of pine forest. This meadow was the LZ for the Sierra sniper teams. Once the drop-off was complete, the helicopters would take the long way around the estate to the north and offload the two November teams, along with Viktor, the forward air controller. Stefan orbited the LZ and watched four figures jogging away from the helicopter and into the safety of the tree line. "Rattler, this is Viper four, drop-off complete, ready to lift off."

The voice of the transport helicopter's pilot came through the headset built into Stefan's helmet. Stefan radioed back, "Roger Viper four, follow me heading one, three, zero." The two helicopters flew low over the treetops on a course that would take them out of the estate. One forgiving thing about this area of operations was that the estate was so large that the order could insert its sniper teams without fear of detection.

The drone footage had not shown any sign of aerial search radars or evidence of modern air defenses. *"The enemy simply wasn't expecting an aerial assault,"* Stefan thought.

"Pilot, turn coming up in two thousand meters, turn left heading zero one zero on my mark," Nikolai said over the intercom.

He watched the moving map on his multi-function display; they were coming up on a waypoint on their flight plan. "Mark. Turn left, heading zero one zero."

Stefan gently pushed the cyclic over and gave the aircraft a bit of left rudder through the pedals. He watched the heading indicator numbers swing from left to right on his heads-up display. He eased out of the turn when he saw the aircraft was on the proper heading. *"Fifteen minutes on this course, then we turn left again,"* Stefan thought, remembering the flight plan.

He looked back over his shoulder, seeing Viper four keeping pace. Stefan's hands relaxed on the controls. The flight plan called for a level flight over the forest until the turn. The easy flight gave him time to think. He mourned the loss of his flight crew. Filip would never fly again, and Igor's death left a gaping wound in Stefan's heart. *"You never did forget about them,"* he thought to himself. *"Try as you might; they will stay with you forever. How many funerals have I attended? How many crying family members have I comforted? Too many."*

Through years of practice, Stefan had learned how to compartmentalize and rationalize the inevitable loss of soldiers in combat. He focused on the things over which he had control. After the missile hit, Stefan flew the crippled helicopter better than anyone could have; the control linkage failed, not his flying skill. He turned the helicopter to avoid the incoming missiles. That maneuver had saved the aircraft from getting hit twice, instead suffering a glancing strike. No, when he added up the calculus of the incident, he was not to blame. Instead, his actions were to be commended. His flying skills saved the lives of the people on board his aircraft. Therefore, Stefan could place the blame for the deaths of his crew and passengers at the feet of the enemy, where it belonged. As fate would have it, Stefan had a rare chance to get even. Even though his aircraft crashed days ago, He put a pilot in command of Rattler One. Petrov would have never let him fly if the Grand Master felt the slightest doubt.

Nikolai's voice broke the silence, interrupting Stefan's thoughts. *"Pilot, turn approaching, turn left heading two eight zero...Mark."* Stefan banked the EC155 into a gentle turn, pointing the nose of the aircraft in a direction that would bring them to the final drop-off location. One minute later, the helicopters crossed back inside the Schloss estate. The North, or "November" LZ, was just ahead. As before, Stefan raced the EC155 gunship ahead of the transport helicopter to scan the LZ for threats with the FLIR pod. Finding none, Stefan radioed to Viper four that the LZ was clear. The big transport helicopter flared and gently set down on the wide gravel bank of a river that flowed through part of the estate. The two November sniper teams were ready.

The instant the crew chief said "go" and slapped each man on the shoulder, the teams jumped out of the open helicopter door and ran for the tree line, followed by Viktor. The soldiers ran fifty yards into the concealed safety of the woods, where they stopped and dropped to one knee. They could hear the helicopter increase power and fly away from the LZ. As they let the sound fade into the distance, the forest became quiet again, and the men waited, listening for any noise that did not belong. Hearing none, they flipped down their AN-PVS 31 goggles and began to walk towards the objective in a single file line, spaced about twenty meters apart. Anatol was on point, with Dimitry next in line. He watched the forest slowly creep by through the green-tinted hue of his night vision goggles. Unlike the wilds of North America, most European forests were carefully managed by professional foresters, and the Schloss estate was no exception. This made for excellent visibility with no obstacles, and the team was able to maintain a good pace. *"As easy as walking along a trail in a park,"* Anatol thought.

The men of November one and two had all night to cover the ten kilometers to their respective hides. Even though every single one of these men could hike a kilometer in just under ten minutes over difficult terrain, they would take their time to avoid detection. Anatol moved the beads on his pace counter to measure the distance he traveled. Ordinarily, one would stop every so often and check a compass, but the PVS-31 had one built-in, which made land navigation easy. The forest canopy closed in overhead, blocking the starlight and reducing the effectiveness of the soldier's night vision goggles. Anatol put up his fist, bringing the column to a halt. All the men took a knee and covered their sectors, scanning for threats. He pulled out a dim infrared illuminator, only visible to night vision equipment, and used it to check his map. The team was at the point where they would separate and perform the final stalk on the sniper hides.

The stalk was only one thousand meters, but it would take a long time to complete. The risk of enemy patrols increased with every step they took. The enemy was a private security company made up of elite former soldiers, and the team could expect the enemy to be patrolling the area around the schloss. Anatol made a hand signal that ordered the team to come together from their twenty-meter spacing. Once assembled, Anatol signaled to the team that it was time to split up and begin their stalks. Dimitri and Anatol shook hands with the other team and Viktor, silently wishing the other soldiers good luck. The two teams rose to their feet and parted ways; they would not see one another again until tomorrow night.

Schloss Drouin

The doors to the library parted, and Victoria saw the most beautiful repository of books in the world. Oaken bookshelves holding the rarest of volumes and the most valuable of first editions stretched from floor to ceiling. Every square inch of the walls was covered with rich wood, assembled and fitted by expert carpenters. A well-stocked bar was in the corner, built into the wall, so guests that visited this room could enjoy a drink from a proper bar and not from something so pedestrian as a beverage cart. Waiters milled about, carrying drinks and hours d'oeuvres on gleaming silver serving trays. Guests were dressed in cocktail dresses or tuxedoes, sipping beverages from hand-cut crystal glasses. The entire floor of the room was covered in a massive oriental carpet; Victoria lost herself in the swirling tans, golds, and greens of the pattern woven into the pile. Marisella guided Victoria to a quiet corner of the room. "Don't worry, dear," Marisella said. "I'll stay here with you, and no one is expecting you to work tonight. Look around you; this is the type of environment in which you will find yourself. Richly appointed rooms inside mansions, surrounded by important and wealthy people."

Victoria took a moment to cast her gaze around the room. She saw a man in a blue military dress uniform speaking with another younger man in a black tuxedo. She saw Greta standing in front of a fireplace, speaking to an older man seated in a high-backed chair. The older man caught her attention; he was dressed in much more formal attire than a mere tuxedo. He wore white gloves and a silk cobalt riband finely embroidered with gold thread. In fact, this man commanded the attention of everyone in the room. Victoria could see every servant turning their eyes in his direction every so often.

"In fact," Marisella went on, "one important aspect of your service is to listen, watch, and discover important things. This is why one of the house rules is to speak only when spoken to; it is hard to listen when you are talking."

Victoria nodded. *"It's like being a spy,"* she thought. *"This whole room is something out of an Ian Fleming novel."*

Marisella continued with a question. "For example, my dear," she said as she waved one of the waiters over, "can you tell me who is the most important man in the room?"

Victoria swallowed, "That's easy, the man with the blue riband."

Marisella beamed. "Very good, my dear!"

The waiter approached, breaking the conversation. "I'll take an old-fashioned," she said to the waiter. "My companion here will have an orange blossom."

The waiter nodded, walking towards the bar to relay the order. "You were correct in your choice, my dear," Marisella continued, now that the waiter was gone. "But can you tell me why?"

Victoria looked away from the man and said to Marisella, "It's his attire, for one; he is much better dressed than anyone else. That is difficult to do at a black-tie affair, but he pulls it off. Another reason is that the servers glance in that man's direction every so often, and they aren't doing that with the other guests."

Marisella smiled, "very good, my dear. It's one thing to notice something out of place. It's quite another to understand why a thing is out of place. This aspect of service to Count Drouin is so important that you will receive additional instruction on exactly how to articulate natural intuition, a master's course on 'how to read the room.' In time, you will learn how important this skill is to serving House Drouin. You could say that our House's very survival depends on it. Look around you. Look at the servers."

The waiter was approaching with the woman's drink order. Marisella abruptly cut off the conversation as she thanked the man for bringing the cocktails. She waited until the man departed before continuing, "The servers and waiters here, every single servant who works for House Drouin has had instruction on intelligence gathering.

Count Drouin wants to know what occurs with guests here at the Schloss. That is why I warned you to remember the house rules and to be very cautious of what you say. Everyone here has ears, and everyone makes reports. How is that orange blossom?"

Victoria swallowed before she answered, her mind racing with thoughts, "It's good. I've never had this cocktail, but I like it."

Inwardly, Victoria was stunned. She had no idea how deep this web of intrigue penetrated. Everyone she had seen or met had given a report on her performance. Marisella took another sip of her old-fashioned; it had a wonderful taste. Flavors of citrus, smoke, and cherry fused with the craft American bourbon to produce magic on the palate. The drink slid down her throat with no harsh aftereffects. The skill of House Drouin's bartenders was world-class. Marisella took another sip and said, "You have a natural ability for this work, my dear. If you decide to stay with us, you may grow to be one of House Drouin's finest assets. Do you wish to stay?"

The question was so different this time. Instead of a threat, it sounded like a gilded invitation to a new life, one of intrigue, wealth, and power. This was the first time anyone had courted her professionally. Her life before college had been one of polite smiles in deference to her wealthy parents. As a teenager, she earned some respect for her marks, but most teachers passed her through their classes as just another student to grade and pass along to the next grade level. Here, in this strange house, surrounded by these strange people, an epiphany occurred to her. This was the first time in her life that a powerful organization wanted her. It wanted her skills; what she brought to the table.

They valued what she and she alone could contribute. The realization of House Drouin's desire was more intoxicating than anything she would taste in her glass. Her answer this time was not forced, and it concealed nothing. Victoria wanted to be part of this House. "Yes," she said, "If House Drouin will have me, it would be my pleasure to serve."

DAY FOUR

Chapter 20

November One

Dawn would break soon. Although Anatol and Dimitri had arrived at the location hours ago, much work was needed to prepare the sniper hide. The hide not only had to be invisible from observation, but it also had to be comfortable enough to live in for at least one day, possibly more. To accomplish this goal, Anatol had spent one hour carefully removing and saving the ground cover of leaves and pine needles. Once the ground was clear, Anatol spread out a rain poncho to act as a moisture barrier. On top of the poncho, he placed wool blankets and the rifle's drag bag to make a padded, warm place for the men to lay. Dimitri had gone back into the forest to find suitable sticks to construct the hide. When he returned, he had two dozen green sticks about two feet in length in his arms. The two men then had to drive these sticks into the cleared ground.

Usually, they would use a small sledgehammer or the end of an entrenching tool, but the ground here was frozen. Anatol shared a solution to this problem with the other teams. He brought a small, battery-powered electric drill with a masonry bit attached to the drill chuck. He then drilled into the frozen ground making a perfect ¾" hole. The sticks went into these holes, and Dimitri strung a fine mesh net over the sticks protruding from the earth. On the mesh net, Anatol and Dimitri carefully placed the ground cover of leaves and pine needles. When the two men had completed their work, the hide looked like a small mound or pile of leaves. Anatol grasped the L115A3 sniper rifle by the bipod mount and crawled into the hide, dragging the rifle in with him. He flipped the bipod down and mounted the rifle. A moment later, he could feel Dimitri crawling up beside him with the spotting scope. The two soldiers settled in for a long wait.

Dimitri had pulled Parkas in with him, he covered Anatol with one, and he pulled the other over his back. With no physical activity, lying on the frozen ground would get cold, and the two men needed to take measures to prevent hypothermia. Anatol settled into the rifle and peered through the Schmidt & Bender 5-25x scope. At this distance, Anatol dialed the power ring to 15x to strike a good balance between detail and field of view of the target. Dimitri had his H&K 417 designated marksman's rifle next to him while he worked to set up the Leupold MK 4 12-

40x60 spotting scope. He also had a Command Launch Unit from a Javelin anti-tank missile. This was a sophisticated thermal imager and laser range-finding system that easily cut through smoke on the battlefield and could be used to spot enemy troops. The two men settled in and began building a range card for their target area. This work was repeated at three other hide sites. Together, the four sniper hides formed a kill box from which nothing could escape.

CIA Headquarters, Virginia

Director Carver was in a foul mood. His third marriage was already on the rocks, and being called into the office on a Saturday did not help matters. The trip to his office was like any other day; the CIA had operations underway throughout the world, and the headquarters building was never empty. Carver checked his watch. It was ten in the morning in D.C., which meant it was four in the afternoon in London. "Why couldn't this wait until Monday?" he asked aloud in the quiet privacy of his office.

Carver had received an urgent message from Cecil Wright regarding an "unapproved operation." How infuriating. Carver knew that this call was eventually coming; by admitting to Cecil that there was a CIA operation on British soil without his knowledge, he had also given Cecil professional leverage. *"This is how the game of intelligence operations and geopolitics is played,"* he thought.

Even though that may be true, it did not mean that Carver had to like it. He came up through the civil service ranks by playing the political game, and finding oneself in a situation where another person had this kind of leverage was a career-ending hazard. Carver swore; he had to find a way to get out of this. He would even up with Cecil and bury this operation under the security of a special-access program. *"Nothing like using the government's national security apparatus to bury embarrassing information,"* Carver thought.

The classification system had been used by civil servants for decades to bury mistakes and avoid accountability; he was simply continuing that tradition. Carver walked over and poured himself a cup of coffee. *"Enough procrastinating,"* he thought. It was time to call Cecil and end this. He pressed the speakerphone button on the STE and dialed the number to Cecil's office. The phone rang once. "Cecil Wright's office," an accented voice answered. "Director Carver returning Mr. Wright's telephone call; I will hold," Carver said.

He did not have to wait long; Cecil's secretary completed the call in less than thirty seconds. "C here," The Chief of MI-6 said into his secure telephone.

Cecil used the name given to every Chief of the British Secret Intelligence Service going back to the first Chief of Intelligence. Captain Sir Mansfield Smith-Cumming was the first leader of SIS and had a custom of signing official documents with a single "C" in green ink. The custom stuck, and every Chief of SIS succeeding

Cumming signed his documents with that green "C." The fact that this official name also shared the first letter of his given name pleased Cecil to no end. "Cecil, It's Jim Carver."

Cecil smiled in his office. *"Okay,"* he thought. *"Time to give this man a real shock."* Cecil leaned forward in his office chair as he spoke, "Jim, do you remember that I told you I was going to handle this situation with Drouin?"

Carver remembered; at the time, he had been relieved that MI-6 was not interested in throwing an official fit, but now he felt only dread. "Yes, Cecil, I remember," Carver said.

"I understand you have a man inside House Drouin?" Cecil asked.

Carver swore under his breath. Pogi was more trouble than he was worth, *"The arrogance of new field agents knows no bounds,"* he thought.

"Jim," Cecil said very quietly, in a voice full of foreboding, "Pull him out; NOW."

Cecil disconnected the call, and the line went dead. In the DDO's office, a bewildered senior civil servant looked dumbly into his phone.

November One

Anatol peered through the Schmidt & Bender riflescope. Even at 1,150 meters away, the target image was perfectly clear in the still January air. The sun would be setting soon, and he would switch to the Qoptiq SVIPIR-2+ clip-on thermal imager. For now, he watched the Legion sentries patrol the Schloss grounds. Dimitri and Anatol had watched them all day, alternating watches so the other could sleep. Earlier in the day, they had built a range card. The range card was a simple sketch of the target area that broke the Schloss up into different sectors for easy target identification. Sector One was the building face of the East Wing that faced them. Sector two was the corner of the East wing and the long part of the building that connected the East wing with the West wing. Sector three was the long part of the building itself; sector four was the opposite corner of the West wing; and finally, sector five was the West wing itself. The roof was named Sector Romeo, and the ground in front of the schloss that held the gardens was Sector Golf.

Every sector was sketched out on the range card, and ranges were assigned. One happenstance of the target area was that the Schloss itself blocked much of the wind, making for less correction but not an easier shot. They had watched the area for hours, and the wind blew consistently left to right at a ¾ value. For Anatol, that meant the wind was coming at their firing position at a 45-degree angle at 5mph. Under these conditions, the snipers calculated they would have to hold ½ of a milliradian into the wind so the bullet would fly true. The bullet drop was easy; they had worked out the drop at the known distance (KD) range earlier that week and had already dialed the scope to hit dead on at 1,150 meters. For a shot that was further or closer than this baseline, all Anatol had to do was hold over or under with the crosshair. Having completed the ballistic solution for the shot, the snipers resigned themselves to watching the target. They had identified the patrol patterns of the sentries, and they knew that there was a shift change every four hours. Their orders were to check in and report only if there was an indication that the enemy knew an attack was imminent or if a threat to the helicopters appeared. Otherwise, radio silence meant the attack was clear to proceed.

Anatol clutched his rifle as he felt the breeze gently blow through the pine forest. He could smell the pine sap and the earth. The air was cold as the breeze blew the chill against his face. He loved the feeling; it was like sitting in a hunting blind waiting for a deer to wander in front of his rifle. He watched one of the sentries walk along the schloss; the crosshairs of the rifle scope tracked the enemy soldier as he moved. With the quality of glass that was used in the German-made scope, a high level of detail could be seen. Anatol could see that the man had not shaved today, and he could see that he wore a wedding ring. Snipers did not have the luxury of dehumanizing the enemy. Instead, through the scope of a rifle, there could be no mistake that Anatol and the other three snipers would soon be taking the lives of human beings. This was a heavy burden of combat, and it drove some men mad.

For Anatol, he rationalized it as the terrible cost of necessity. If he failed to act, his brothers would die; the young woman who trusted the order for protection would die. Fortunately, when the time came, Anatol would be spared the high-definition brutality if he took the shot through glass. Instead, he would view the world through the artificial eye of the clip-on thermal imager. Rather than seeing an enemy fall in real life, Anatol would see it happen on a screen, in black and white. The knowledge of this somehow made his duty easier. When the time came, he would not fail, and his shot would fly true.

Schloss Drouin

The sun had just set, and the light of day began to fall outside Victoria's room. Greta was on her way. During the cocktail party last night, Marisella said that Greta would come to see her and ask if Victoria was ready to serve House Drouin. She felt that her answer was merely a formality; she had made her decision the previous night in the library. The door made its familiar buzz, and she hoped that this would be the last time she heard such a sound. Greta walked in confidently; she was dressed in a pair of riding boots, tan riding pants that hugged her figure, and a white blouse that revealed her toned arms and shoulders. Her blond hair was drawn up in a tight braided ponytail. Greta's boots clicked on the wooden floor as she walked towards Victoria. "Good afternoon, my dear. It's so good to see you once more."

Victoria smiled; she was genuinely happy to see Greta this time. Instead of viewing Greta as a jailor, Victoria now saw her as someone who could help her; help her to stay.

Victoria said nothing, remembering the rules of the house. She now understood the practical side of this rule as well. If one is speaking, they are not listening. "You know I am here to ask you a question," Greta went on. "Do you wish to stay with us?"

Victoria began to answer but was interrupted by Greta. "Oh, my dear, I just realized something! No one has told you what your service here will be."

Victoria was confused. *"That was not true,"* she thought. *"Marisella had explained this last night, didn't she?"*

Anticipating the question, Greta continued. "It's true that Marisella told you about part of your service: to watch and listen to the associates of Count Drouin. But she did not tell you about the other part, your routine duties."

Seeing the confused look on Victoria's face, Greta sat down and said, "Please come and sit; it's easier to show you than to explain."

The door buzzed once more, and two young women walked in. They were dressed in silk robes that were very short. So short that these women would have to walk rigidly erect; otherwise, they would reveal themselves for all to see. The two women walked into the room and stood in front of Greta, saying nothing, eyes fixed straight ahead. "My dear, meet Anna and Marie," Greta said.

"They will show you what your service here at House Drouin will be. Anna, Marie, you will disrobe."

On Greta's command, Anna and Marie removed their robes and stepped out of their shoes. Victoria's suspicions were proven correct; the women wore no undergarments and were standing in front of Greta in a state of nature. Victoria immediately noticed their eyes. There was no emotion; no shame, fear, anticipation, nothing at all. Greta spoke, and Anna and Marie obeyed. *"They were like robots,"* Victoria thought. *"No humanity at all."*

The thought sent a chill up her spine. Greta issued another command, "Anna, you will sit on the bed. Marie, kneel here next to me." The young women obeyed. For the next twenty minutes, Greta sat in the chair and issued command after command. Anna and Marie obeyed her without speaking a word or hesitating. The two women performed the most lurid sexual acts on one another; they responded in action to whatever perversion Greta's mind could produce. Throughout the ordeal, their faces were rigid. There was no pleasure or expression; the women simply stared ahead like living dolls. Victoria was forced to watch it all. What began as disgust grew into horror, and horror eventually slipped into fear. This was not what Victoria had in mind. Instead of living a life of intrigue and mystery, she realized she would live out her days as a sexual plaything. A white-hot flash of anger arced inside her mind, and she stood up, glaring at Greta. "I WON'T DO IT," she said defiantly. "I won't be one of your playthings. You people are SICK."

Greta leaned forward in her chair menacingly. "Really, my dear?" she said, her voice full of hatred. "Let's not forget your behavior. Ever since you got here, you've been prancing around naked. You showed yourself to be completely indecorous with Marisella, Hans, Dr. Costa, Marco... and don't even get me started with Julio. I saw you two in the gym. You were ready to jump into bed with that man like a whore."

Victoria's jaw dropped, "That wasn't the way it was! I only did that because they said I had to in order to stay!"

She was nearly shouting now; she had lost control of her emotions, and her hands were shaking with rage. "I don't believe you," Greta countered, her voice calm and even. "I think part of you liked being the center of attention. You might be able to fool some boys in college, but you can't fool me, my dear. I have seen dozens of girls come through here, and they are all like you at first. Once the hesitation passes though, they are no different than Anna or Marie here."

Victoria could not stand to look at this insufferable woman any longer. "I'm not like them," she said. "I have feelings, I'm a person."

Greta laughed at her. "I can see your resistance to this; you think you can just... leave? Well, you can. But you don't get to choose where you will go." Greta stood and walked over to look at Victoria's angry face. She bent down slightly to look Victoria in the eye. "If you no longer wish to stay, fine. But there's only one place you'll go. In the city of Mumbai, there is a brothel that caters to high-paying but sexually deviant clients. The girls we send there don't last a month. Be it sepsis or death at the hands of a client, going to Mumbai is a death sentence. The choice is simple, my dear; serve here and live, or serve the brothel and die."

Victoria looked at Greta, and a tears began to form in her eyes. Inwardly, Victoria knew this was the end. Leave and die in agony, or stay and have a part of her soul die each day until there is nothing left. This time, no one was coming to save her, and she was truly alone. Greta ignored the mental anguish of Victoria, walked to the barred window, and looked out into the twilight, confident of her work. While still looking into the fading light, Greta began to speak once more. "I only have one more thing to ask, my dear."

Greta turned and stared right at Victoria. "Do you wish to stay?"

Chapter 21

Paris

Randy Campbell returned home from dinner with his wife to find his STE phone ringing. He walked into his study and closed the door before answering. "Campbell," he said into the phone.

"Where on earth have you been?" came the reply. "I've been calling you for the last thirty minutes!"

Campbell winced; he was not expecting a call from the DDO. "I'm sorry, Jim. I was at dinner. What can I do for you?" he offered as a way of apology.

Carver took a deep breath and said, "Okay, Randy. It's Saturday; I suppose you're entitled to a night off. But look; I need to discuss something with you."

Campbell's ears peaked. "I'm listening, Jim." Carver described the odd call from Cecil Wright, his cryptic warning to pull Pogi out of the field. Campbell's knuckles went white around the phone as he listened. When Carver finished speaking, he asked, "What do you think, Randy?"

Campbell took a moment to get his breathing under control. "We need to get Pogi out of there, NOW. If I am hearing you correctly, you've just told me that MI-6 is going to strike House Drouin in a direct-action mission. That means SAS, James. The Brits do not have the same laws we do in America, and MI-6 is sending the boys from Hereford on a straight up assassination mission."

Across a great ocean, the DDO went bone pale. "You don't really think... They can't," Carver stammered.

Campbell shook his head in frustration. "Jim, listen to me like you've never listened before. This isn't some academic exercise. The Brits are out for blood, and Cecil gave you the courtesy of a warning so we can pull our man out of there before the fury of heaven rains down."

Campbell paused. A realization hit his synapses like a lightning bolt to the brain. "Jim," he started, "MI-6 is going to use the order to do this."

Carver set his coffee mug down on his desk. "The knights?" he asked.

"Yes," Campbell answered.

"I got the report from our analysts. The team that took out the ISIS cell and annihilated a Legion Services QRF was only six men. The report you gave me indicates the order has hundreds of soldiers, Jim – HUNDREDS. The order is going to attack House Drouin with a company-size force of soldiers that rivals the skill of our SFOD-Delta operators. They're going to have air support too, James. Imagine the carnage they can inflict!"

Carver was shocked, but he had heard enough to realize he needed to get Pogi out of there as soon as possible. "Okay, Randy. I'm convinced; pull Pogi out of there. How fast can you send word?"

Campbell replied, "I sent the recall code out a minute ago, James. Let's just hope it reaches Pogi in time."

Schloss Drouin

Victoria had been crying since Greta left with her "playthings." Any desire to help these awful people evaporated during that horrible display of service. *"They want me to be a whore,"* she thought.

The realization saddened her; she thought one day she would give herself to a good Christian man. That was not going to happen now. Now she would be passed around as a living doll for men to inflict their sinful urges on her body. Everything about this place suddenly made sense. The door locks, the armed guards, the control, the watchers, everything. The house was truly a gilded cage, but it was more than that. Fear of being sent to an awful place where cruel men would pay to inflict pain on her created a prison in her mind. The moments went by, and she was deathly afraid that she would hear the door buzz once more and be dragged off to a bedroom. Victoria prayed; she knew no one was coming to help. Jan was probably dead, and the order did not know where she had been taken. With nowhere else to turn, she begged Jesus for help.

"Lord, I'm not perfect, but you said you love me, you said you would never leave me. I need you now. Please know what is going to happen to me is not of my doing. It is my wish to be saved from these evil people. If there is a way, please send me a rescuer. If that isn't possible, then please end my life quickly.

Amen."

Victoria felt a small bit of comfort from her prayers. She tried to remember her feelings when she was at the farmhouse—how she felt unafraid to pass from this earth into eternity. Her memory of that experience strengthened her for this current ordeal. *"I will act as a Christian should no matter what happens from this day forth,"* she thought. *"Jesus didn't forget me back at the farmhouse; he intervened and sent me a Christian knight. He will provide for me."*

Suddenly, Victoria remembered a passage of scripture from her time in Idaho. There was a passage in the gospel of Matthew that spoke about God caring for the creatures in creation and Jesus telling the disciples not to worry, saying that God would provide as he does for the birds of the air. *"I am more valuable to God than a bird,"* she thought. *"He will take care of me the way he did in the farmhouse."* The fear melted away from her heart. As before, God was with Victoria, and he would be with her until the end, whatever form that end might take. A final thought occurred to Victoria as she felt the peace of sleep begin to wash over her mind. *"In the coming days, Lord, help me not to do my will but yours. And give me the wisdom to know the difference."* Victoria's mind succumbed to the call to sleep. She felt herself drifting off to a place that knew nothing of fear.

Sunday, February 1, 2015:

Staging Area "Snake One"

It was just after midnight. Jan and his team were stuffing magazines into pouches mounted to their MultiCam plate carriers. Every man had the Harris PVS-18 panoramic NVD mounted to their ballistic helmets. The night vision unit was heavy but allowed an unequaled field of view in a CQB environment. Jan loaded his USP 45 and decocked the pistol, making sure the safety was engaged before placing it in a Safariland ALS holster. He checked again to make sure all his magazine pouches were full. Jan looked over at his team. Aleksy was topping off a G36 magazine with ammunition. The team had loaded these with a few rounds of M196 ammunition first, so the last three rounds fired from the magazine would be tracer ammunition. This was an easy way to let the operator know their primary weapon was running dry and it was time to reload. Jan put his helmet on and tightened the chin strap. The panoramic night vision unit, or "panos" were heavy, and although an external battery was mounted to the back of the helmet to balance out the weight, it was still front-heavy. Jan looked over at his team; Aleksy and Lew were putting the final pieces of their kit together. Lew remembered the awful feeling of having nothing to offer his Captain at Watford Hospital. He had promised himself that he would never again be caught without explosives and had brought enough "bang" to level the building.

Lew kept the explosives organized in a backpack, everything he would need on the mission was easily and quickly extracted. Aleksy was inserting a magazine into his G36C. The rifle the team was using was the compact version of the German Army's standard service rifle. Instead of a full-length rifle, the G36C had a barrel that was only seven inches long. The short barrel length allowed it to be used in close quarters like a submachine gun but also gave the operator the option of engaging an enemy out to three hundred meters. The rifle's 5.56mm NATO cartridge was also far more powerful than a submachine gun's pistol-sized 9mm. Aleksy put the rifle's sling over his shoulder and brought the weapon tight across the front of his body.

Having finished their tasks, Lew and Aleksy looked up at Jan. The three men were ready. The other knights in the supply tent were making their way outside to board the helicopters. Jan led his team outside, where they could hear the scream of the turbines and smell the oily stink of jet exhaust. The crew chiefs had placed small chalkboards in front of each helicopter pad. On each, a number was written that signifies which "viper" flight was which. Jan and his team made their way to the chalkboard that had "4" written on it and lined up in front of the helicopter crew chief.

The IT team arrived less than a minute later. Jan looked over at Echo and nodded. Echo was usually buried inside a TOC or cargo container, playing the role of "battle captain" on missions; this time he got to go with the team, and he was excited; finally getting a chance to participate in a direct-action mission. Although it was not expected that Echo would fire a shot, he was still going into a combat zone and was armed with a Heckler & Koch MP-7. Originally developed for a NATO personal defense weapon, or PDW trial, the MP-7 was a small weapon that used a 4.6x30mm cartridge that had the appearance of a micro-rifle round.

The small overall size of the ammunition allowed the rounds to be fed through the grip of the MP-7, permitting a very compact weapon. These weapons were originally intended for drivers, artillery troops, and officers; soldiers who needed something more than a pistol but would have their jobs encumbered by carrying a rifle. For Echo, the computer specialist, it was the perfect weapon. Jan looked over at the EC155 gunships. Their main rotors were already turning as the crews readied the helicopters for liftoff. Stefan noticed Jan and gave him a wave. The connection between the two men was broken by the booming voice of the crew chief. "Viper four passengers present and accounted for!" he shouted. "Teams board your helicopters! Go, GO, GO, GO!"

The search and IT teams jogged to the open door of the big H215 transport helicopter, quickly boarding and finding a seat. Down the line on the pads, the blocking teams were boarding their transports as well. Inside the EC-155, Stefan had completed his pre-takeoff checklist and they were ready to depart.

Stefan pressed the PTT button on his control stick to talk to the pad controller. "Pad control, this is Rattler One, ready for departure. Request clearance for takeoff."

The pad controller was quick with the reply. "Roger Rattler One, this is pad control, winds zero-six-zero at five knots, cleared to depart, proceed North to rally point one."

Stefan acknowledged permission to leave as he gently raised the collective and moved the cyclic as the helicopter lifted off the pad into a hover.

Clear of the ground, Stefan continued to raise the collective and gently move the pedals to come about and point the aircraft's nose in the direction of the rally point. The helicopters would get into formation at that point and then proceed to the target area. Rattler Two lifted off the pad a few seconds later, following Stefan into the night sky.

Schloss Drouin

Jason Pogi furiously packed his attaché case as he called down the valet for his automobile. Rushing out into the night at this ungodly hour is not how he wanted to spend his Sunday. Campbell called him with a seemingly innocuous call, but hidden within the verbiage Randy used was an emergency recall code. Pogi remembered this lesson from his term at the farm: when an emergency code is issued, it means just that. No matter what the field officer is doing, the emergency orders take precedence, and they are to be obeyed immediately without question.

"Leaving us so soon?" a voice asked from Pogi's doorway.

He turned to see Major Aubert leaning on the door frame. *"Think fast, Jason..."* Pogi thought. "Tell me about it, Major. The boss wants me in the office at 03:00." Pogi leaned in a conspiratorial way and whispered so Aubert could hear him. "I shouldn't tell you this," Pogi started, "but something is about to break loose in Turkey, and they've called me back to Paris at once. I'm not the only one; they're going to set up a crisis center." Pogi put the last item in his overnight bag. He looked longingly over at Marie's sleeping form, wishing they could have another go. As he walked out the door past the Major, he said, "I'm sorry I can't be more specific, but I will be gone for the next two weeks." To keep up the subterfuge, Pogi added, "You didn't hear this from me, but I would stay off any Lufthansa flight if I were you. Good night, Major."

Major Aubert chuckled as he watched Pogi head down the hall towards the home's grand entrance. It was late, and Aubert wanted one last glass of Cognac before he turned in for the night.

Pogi walked with purpose towards the home's exit, his porter struggling to keep up with him. A steward held open the door as he walked outside; he could see his Mercedes-Benz sedan pulling up. The valet had just enough time to exit the vehicle and hold the door open before Pogi covered the ground from the front door to the waiting car. The porter placed Pogi's bags in the trunk and closed the trunk lid. It took every ounce of self-control

Pogi had not to floor the accelerator. He knew enough about clandestine operations that something very bad was coming; Randy's call was an urgent warning to get out of there before it happened.

It took two agonizingly long minutes to drive out the gate gently and slowly and past the guardhouse. The exterior lighting blazed a path before him with light. At the end of that light was a sharp turn and safety. Another minute, and he had made the turn. Out of sight of the guardhouse, Pogi buried the E500's throttle, and the car rocketed forward, quickly accelerating past 90 mph. There were deer on the property, and it was risky to travel the forest road at this speed, but Pogi did not care. He would rather risk a fatal collision than spend one more minute on this property. As he accelerated down a straightaway, his peripheral vision detected movement above him. He looked just in time to see two dark objects pass over the top of his car. He didn't know what they were, but they were large and they were fast. In the darkness, Pogi imagined that they were avenging spirits, racing to unleash hell upon House Drouin. Jason Pogi felt an icy pit of fear grow deep inside his stomach as he pushed the car past 120 mph.

November One

It was time. Dimitri looked at the tritium glowing on his watch and nodded to Anatol. The Helicopters would be here in three minutes. Anatol was already watching his target walk his patrol pattern. He moved with the sentry, the scope reticle following the man's each move. "Sniper, target, sector two, twenty meters right from the building corner, range 1,129 meters," Dimitri called out.

"Copy," Anatol replied. "Sniper has an enemy sentry armed with an M4 rifle, dressed in tactical clothing, passing a lamppost now."

Dimitri made an adjustment to the Command Launch Unit he was using as a thermal spotting scope. Dimitri said quietly, "Roger sniper, that's your target. Set parallax and mils."

Under the soft blue glow of a chem light, taped over to allow the minimum amount of light needed for the task, Anatol adjusted the elevation turret on the riflescope for the range of 1,130 meters. He felt and counted out the 1/10 mil graduations on the turret as the scope clicked to the proper elevation. A difference of one meter would not affect the shot. Anatol also adjusted the parallax knob on the scope to give a sharp image of the crosshair and the target. The dim blue light was invisible to night vision devices and made scope adjustments possible. Anatol flicked the rifle's safety off, looked back through the scope, found his target once more, and took a deep breath, letting half of it out of his lungs. His finger hovered over the trigger as he said "ready" to his spotter. Anatol's voice was barely audible. Dimitri was quick with his final instruction, not wanting Anatol to lose his breath. "Sniper, hold ½ mil left for wind; send it."

Anatol gently put his finger on the rifle trigger and began to apply pressure. The trigger easily swung through its first stage and then hit the wall of the second stage. Anatol continued to apply pressure as the trigger broke cleanly. The rifle bucked hard, and the sound suppressor snapped as the round in the chamber went off. The L115A3 settled quickly, and Anatol was able to see the white-hot bullet travel downrange. The bullet hit the sentry's shoulder, severing his right arm as it entered the man's chest cavity, shredding his heart and lungs before exiting. The man was dead before his body collapsed on the stone patio.

Dimitri could hear the sniper team at November 2 taking their shot through his tactical hearing protection, which blocked the harmful report of the suppressed rifle but also amplified ambient noise so the team could hear anyone trying to flank their position. Anatol gently worked the bolt of the L115A3, careful not to make excessive movement. Dimitri could see another sentry walking towards the location where the first man fell. The man's movements were casual, it was as if he were walking over to chide his comrade for falling. That would change in a few seconds when the second enemy sentry got close enough to see the mess. "Sniper, target, sector three, one hundred meters to the right of the previous target, on the walk."

Anatol pivoted the rifle slightly to line up for the next shot, quickly falling back to his natural point of aim. "Got him, enemy sentry armed with an M4 rifle walking East," Anatol whispered to his spotter.

"That's your target, sniper," Dimitri confirmed. Anatol settled into the rifle, let out half a breath, and said "ready" once more. "Range 1,173 meters. Hold over 2.5 mils, hold left 0.2 mils, send it."

Anatol made the final adjustment using the Horus illuminated reticle, holding the enemy's shoulder at an illuminated dot under and to the right of the center crosshair. The Horus reticle revolutionized long-range shooting by etching a grid of mil and ½ mil marks underneath the crosshair. Instead of dialing in a complicated wind and movement solution using the scope turrets, the sniper simply centered the target on the right grid reference, and the reticle did the rest. This was like having a ballistic computer superimposed on the scope image, which made wind calls stupid easy. Anatol was already applying pressure to the second stage when the rifle recoiled once more.

From an altitude of 3,000 feet above the ground, the Watchkeeper WK450 drone saw the second sentry fall through its thermal imager. The live feed was transmitted down to Viktor Fedorov's DS11 tablet. As the drone circled above, the South side of the Schloss came into view just in time to see another sentry fall to one of the Sierra sniper teams. Even from this altitude, the enemy's blood splatter could be seen, white and hot against the cold, dark grey of the gravel courtyard. Fedorov could see one more sentry walking around the South corner of the building. The man paused and looked to the tree line; he must have heard the supersonic crack of the bullet as it struck the sentry behind him.

A moment later, Fedorov saw the sentry fall. *"That was the last of the sentries,"* he thought as he picked up his radio to call the incoming aircraft. "Rattler One," Fedorov said into the radio, "this is Copperhead Actual; how copy over?"

Stefan smiled as he heard Viktor's voice in his headset. "Copperhead actual, this is Rattler one, I read you five by five."

Stefan lowered the collective and pushed the cyclic left and forward to bring the EC155 down into a wide channel carved through the forest for the road to Schloss Drouin. The flight plan called for the approaching helicopters to use this road as a causeway to fly beneath treetop level, popping up at the last moment to alter course and bring them to the LZ on the East side of the palace. Stefan looked at the mirror mounted to the doorframe. Rattler Two was right behind him. Suddenly, car lights illuminated the road in front of Stefan. The appearance of light blazed brightly in his night vision goggles. The car was traveling fast, and the distance to the vehicle closed quickly. The two aircraft passed over the car in a thunderous whoosh as Stefan called Fedorov once more. "Copperhead Actual, this is Rattler One; we have overflown a passenger car coming down the causeway; request any change to target status; Rattler Flight is forty seconds out."

Fedorov looked at his MilDef DS11 tablet to view the IR feed from the Watchkeeper. "Negative Rattler One; no change to target status. Be advised, there is an armored vehicle parked on the South courtyard, engage that target first, no sign of enemy AAA or SAMs."

"*Good,*" Stefan thought. The only real threat to the gunships was some kind of anti-aircraft artillery or a surface-to-air missile.

Stefan intended to fly so fast over the target area that nobody with a rifle would stand a chance of hitting him. The aircraft were twenty seconds from the schloss. Stefan called Rattler Two on the radio, "Rattler Two, this is Rattler One; come to echelon right formation and cover me while I engage the courtyard target."

This formation would place Rattler Two between Stefan and the Schloss itself, allowing an unobstructed shot from Rattler Two's guns if a threat engaged Rattler One from the palace. Stefan spoke into the intercom to his co-pilot, "Master Arm ON."

Nikolai flipped a covered red switch on the EC155 instrument panel that activated the firing switches on Stefan's control stick. He pulled back on the cyclic and pulled up on the collective to climb out of the causeway, leveling out the aircraft to skim the tops of the trees. He banked the helicopter into a tight left-hand turn and flew as low as he dared to keep the enemy from seeing the gunship. The grass LZ and the schloss were coming up fast, and Stefan could see the glow of the interior lights of the palace through his NVGs. As the grass field came into view, Rattler One banked to the left as Stefan followed the contour of the terrain, with Rattler Two matching his maneuver.

The towering form of the schloss rushed at them as Stefan turned the nose of the EC155 and pulled back on the cyclic and raised the collective to climb over the East wing. The courtyard opened in front of him. "Rattlers on station," he said into the radio, "ground target ahead."

Stefan lined up the vehicle in the crosshair on the EC155's heads-up display and pressed the button on the back of his control stick. Four 70mm Hydra rockets shot out of their pods. The rocket motors traced their way to the armored vehicle and exploded, sending a greasy orange flame into the night sky. Rattler One overflew the wrecked vehicle, banking to the left to come around for a strafing run on the schloss.

Major Aubert had taken his last sip of cognac when a flash of light was seen outside the windows of the lounge rattled. He dropped the glass and ran to the window. The burning hulk of the armored vehicle Legion Services used for patrol of the grounds could be seen across the courtyard. The whole front of the castle was bathed in orange light as the vehicle burned, its fuel alight and flames reaching towards the sky. Fighting through the fog of inebriation, he ran towards the security office to find out what happened and coordinate an emergency response.

Rattler Two finished its turn when the pilot spied a helicopter on its pad near the castle. The pad was dark; if it were not for the NVGs the pilot was wearing, he would have missed it altogether. "Snake One, this is Rattler Two," the pilot said into his radio, "Enemy helicopter spotted on a pad to the west; request permission to engage."

In the TOC, an operator shifted the image from the drone's IR feed. Petrov nodded to the man and he and called the pilot back. "Copy, Rattler Two; permission granted; light 'em up."

Rattler Two brought his nose to bear on the enemy helicopter, an Agusta A109. The pilot pressed the trigger on the control stick and a ripping noise came from the M134 miniguns mounted to the EC155 weapon pylons. A line of tracers shot ahead of Rattler Two as the pilot moved the cyclic and pedals to walk the streams into the target. The A109 was ripped to shreds by hundreds of 7.62mm rounds. The fuel tanks ruptured, and a tracer ignited the jet fuel, once again bathing the Schloss in orange light. As Rattler Two passed over the burning aircraft, the pilot saw soldiers running on the North side of the property near the pool. He moved the nose of the EC155 with his pedals and pressed the trigger again. Red tracers shot ahead of the gunship once more, and the soldiers disappeared in a cloud of dust kicked up by the 7.62mm rounds tearing through the soldiers and into the stone patio. Within a second, Rattler 2 disappeared into the night, coming about to attack the Schloss again.

This time, Major Aubert heard the report from the miniguns. The deafening roar of ripping fabric was unmistakable. The EC155 roared off into the night, and the Fenestron tail fan shrieked its high-pitched whine as the aircraft passed. Aubert had reached the security office and picked up a radio. "All sentry units report in!" He shouted into the radio as his thumb mashed the PTT button.

After a second of static, he heard a lone voice come on the radio, "This is unit two, we are moving outside..."

The voice on the radio was abruptly cut off as Aubert heard the miniguns fire again. Major Aubert swore loudly in the security office and turned his attention to the monitors on the wall that showed the security camera feeds. *"Gunship,"* he thought, *"Had to be. No wonder Pogi was so rushed to get out of here."*

He wished he had not transferred the Stinger missiles back to the CIA, as his brain tried to produce a plan for an effective aerial defense. They had access to light machine guns, but there were only two. Aubert did not even consider trying to engage the gunship with an M4 rifle. He looked at the monitors again, this time noticing a flaming pile of wreckage where Drouin's helicopter used to be. *"Using the A109 as an aerial platform was out too,"* he thought.

"All units, we are under attack by at least one armed helicopter," he said into the radio. "Stay inside and guard the doorways."

Aubert heard his team leaders begin to report in and acknowledge his order. He had another thought and lifted the radio to his mouth once more. "Security detail, move the principal to the safe room, and lock yourselves inside until I say otherwise."

Drouin stared out of his bedroom window, dumbfounded. He had seen the tracers from Rattler Two's miniguns destroy his helicopter. His shock was interrupted by the sound of his bedroom door being kicked in. Two guards from his security detail barged into the room. Each soldier grabbed him by the arm and dragged him out of the bedroom before he could protest. Overcoming his surprise, he said, "What is this? Let me go at once!"

The soldier holding his right arm said, "You are going to the safe room, your excellency. Orders from Major Aubert."

Drouin voiced his protest the whole way to his office, but the soldiers ignored him. Inside the office, there were two more guards waiting. One of them had swung the bookshelf away from the wall that concealed the heavy steel door to the safe room. The guard captain looked at the retina scanner, and the electronic door lock made a hollow "thunk" as it actuated and opened the door. The two soldiers hustled Count Drouin inside the room as the other two followed and locked the door behind them. Drouin sat in one of the chairs, fuming at his treatment. The guard captain spoke into his radio, "Major, this is the security detail, principal secure."

Fedorov heard Viper One call him on the radio, "Copperhead Actual, Viper flight is sixty seconds out, request an update of LZ status." He looked at his DS11 tablet and saw no threats or enemy personnel in the immediate area. "Viper One, LZ is secure, winds four knots at three one five, clear to land. Rattler One and Two, Vipers incoming, hold station to the West of the structure," he said back to the pilots over the radio.

The big H215 transport helicopters streaked down the causeway, the pilot of Viper One pulling up at the last minute to follow the terrain as the gunships had only minutes before. As the grassy field opened before the lead helicopter, the H215 pilot slowed the big aircraft. The rotors beat the air as the transport helicopter flared and unfolded its landing gear. A moment later, the pilot gently set the H215 down on the grass lawn and flipped a switch on the instrument panel that activated a green light next to the doors. "Soldiers! Out the door! Go! Go! Go!" the crew chief shouted over the screaming engines.

The knights needed no encouragement as they hustled out the door with their G36C rifles at high ready. From the cockpit, the pilot could see the IR laser beams dancing around as the soldiers ran to their objective. The Crew chief's voice came over the aircraft intercom. "Pilot, soldiers offloaded," he said. The transport aircraft unloaded, Viper One's pilot lifted the collective and the helicopter took off into a hover. The pilot eased the cyclic forward, and the H215 began to move forward to the safety of the designated holding pattern to the North.

On the ground, Captain Diego, Captain Ivan, and Captain Andrei led their men at a run. The door was just ahead of them. "Demo up!" Diego shouted over the roar of the departing transport helicopters. His combat engineer ran up to the door with one of the shooters to cover him while the blocking teams took a knee on the grass next to the building, watching for movement in the windows. The combat engineer placed a large explosive charge on the door and ran a command wire back around the corner to where his captain was waiting. "Demo set," the combat engineer said to his commander. Diego nodded at the man and said, "Blow it."

Inside the schloss, five Legion soldiers guarded the North door to the East wing. The squad leader looked behind him, there was another team to the south. *"Good,"* he thought. "We have the first floor secured." The man by the door heard movement outside and flashed a warning to the rest of the squad with a hand signal. The soldiers flipped the safeties off on their M4 rifles as they waited for the door to open.

Outside, the combat engineer shouted to the crouched soldiers, "Fire in the hole! Fire in the hole! Fire in the hole!" He pressed the firing lever of the M57 electrical firing device, and the entire doorframe on the North side of the Schloss was turned into splinters and white smoke. The whole building shook as the pressure wave from the explosion thundered down the first-floor hall.

Chapter 22

Three knights pushed through the smoking hole in the building, their G36C rifles at the ready. Another step, and they were past the smoke; the IR laser beams from their PEQ-15 laser emitters could be seen with the GPNVG-18's panoramic NVG tracing bright green lines down the hallway. The frontman in the stack saw movement in the darkness at the end of the hallway and illuminated the area with his IR illuminator. Enemy soldiers could be seen trying to shake off the effects of the explosion. The knight flipped his G36C's selector from **SAFE** down to the **FULL AUTO** pictogram and pressed the trigger. A five-round burst of 5.56mm rounds flew down the hall, striking the enemy in the sternum and head. The man fell as the other knights brought their weapons up and dispatched the other Legion soldiers. Forcing himself to break away from the previous threat and look around, Diego spied a fallen enemy trying to reach for his pistol. He lowered the G36C and fired three fast rounds into the man's face. "Clear!" he shouted, hearing the same word repeated as the men under his command indicated their sectors were clear of threats.

Diego turned to see Ivan coming in through the ruined door. There was a service stairwell just ahead on the right. The knights from blocking team three stacked up at the door and quickly opened it. The stairwell was empty. The knights poured in through the doorway, taking positions to cover the stairwell. Once the men were in place, the first group from blocking team one rushed up to the second floor, where they again took up positions to cover the stairs from the third floor.

Free from their task, the men of blocking team three ran up the stairs, bounding to the level above and stacking once more at the door to the second floor. This time, the man at the door had M85 flashbang grenades ready in his hands. The door was pulled open, and he threw the flashbangs into the hallway. He heard the detonations and rushed into the space, turning to the right, the number two man in the stack right behind him. Ten feet in front of him, he saw a guard with his hand over his eyes, trying to shake off the effects of the flash and noise.

The two men brought their G36C rifles up and pressed the triggers, sending 5.56mm rounds into the enemy's upper torso. They heard gunfire behind them; the rest of Blocking Team One was engaging another Legion Soldier. Diego was the sixth man through the door; his team had eliminated the enemy in the second-floor hallway. *"Okay,"* he thought. *"Time to secure the objective."* He saw the arch in the hallway that led to the grand gallery, the hall team one had to hold while the I.T. and search teams did their work.

Team one ran to the gallery and took positions along the sides of the hallway, taking whatever cover was available as he saw his light machine gunners begin to set up the H&K MG4 and the ballistic shield. Ivan watched the gunner slap the top cover of the MG4 down and charge the action. He looked down the hallway; his position gave his team a commanding view of the gallery. An enemy would have to run no less than thirty meters to reach any member of his team; this was a good position to hold and easy to defend, so long as the MG4 could keep firing. The rest of the team's job was to defend the machine gunner at all costs.

At the top of the grand staircase, Captain Andrei and team two were setting up to defend the top of the stairs.

Victoria was jolted awake by the detonation of the flashbang grenade. *"What was THAT??"* she thought. A second later, ears still ringing from the explosion, she heard the unmistakable sound of automatic gunfire. She ran to the windows and looked outside just in time to see a massive helicopter lift off and armed men in green camouflage combat fatigues run towards the schloss. A bolt of realization hit her. The order had found her and was coming to take her home. With tears in her eyes, she ran to the door and began pounding on it with all her strength. "I'M IN HERE!!! PLEASE, OPEN THE DOOR!!!" she shouted through the door at the top of her lungs, hoping someone outside could hear her.

Jan ran through the ruined door, his G36C tucked in the pocket of his shoulder, ready to bring his weapon up and fire at any enemy who crossed his path. Ahead, he saw the door to the stairwell, guarded by some of the team members from team three. He led his team up the stairs unopposed; Captain Diego, with team three, had made sure that there was an easy and secure way in and out of the schloss. Echo and his team were right behind Jan and his men. The I.T. team exited the stairwell and ran to the opposite end of the hall, where the architectural drawings indicated the server racks would be found.

The knights assigned to guard Echo Stacked up on either side of the door. They nodded to each other, and the man closest to the door knob brought his leg up ad delivered a solid kick to the door right underneath the lock. The fine wood that made the door frame could not withstand the strike of the man's boot, and the wood splintered as the lock was forced through the brass strike plate. The door swung inward as the other knight forced his way inside the room. Seeing the room was unoccupied, the knight waved Echo inside.

Echo slung his MP-7 and took off his backpack, beginning to connect ethernet cables to the server rack. He opened a laptop that was sitting on a cluster of external hard drives and booted the machine up. The operating system came alive, and Echo started the program that would force the password to the servers and allow him to copy data from every hard drive attached to the network. The Count's network did not have a difficult password, and this process took less time than expected. He soon had administrator access to the network and began the process of copying the data. The progress bar inched toward completion painfully slowly; the estimated time to completion was sixteen minutes. While inside the network, Echo began to look around and noticed the schloss had an extensive security system with hundreds of cameras. *"I'll have to do something about that,"* he thought. There was no sense in allowing the enemy that kind of tactical advantage.

In the security office, Major Aubert watched the monitors showing the security camera feeds. He saw the H215 transport helicopters land and the effects of the explosive breach on the East wing of the Schloss. He saw heavily armed soldiers with odd night vision equipment efficiently eliminate his soldiers. *"Who was attacking us?"* he thought. *"And why were they concentrating their attack on the East wing? Drouin's apartments were on the West side of the building."*

Aubert saw, yet another H215 come in for a landing and discharge enemy soldiers. *"How many men were attacking us?"* he thought. He counted what had to be at least eighty. As he watched the soldiers enter the second floor, he saw the flashbangs detonate. As the soldiers poured out of the stairwell and into the hallway, he saw ballistic shields being moved around. *"Why all this firepower for assaulting Drouin's harem?"* Aubert thought. This attack cannot be about stealing a few women; that made no sense. A moment later, the video feed died. He called the IT specialist on the radio. "Louis, what's happened? I've just lost the security camera feed for the entire property."

A panicked reply came back on his radio. "Major, it's the enemy, they're in our network!"

Aubert swore, "Well, kick them out of there!"

Louis waited a moment to get his anger under control. "Major, you don't understand. They have physical control of the server; I can't kick them out!"

Aubert looked dumbfounded at the radio as the specialist continued with the unwelcome news. "What's worse is that I am detecting a file transfer in progress; they're taking all our data!"

Aubert's knuckles went white around his radio. "All of it?" he asked.

"Yes, sir. Hard drive data, network history, even smartphone data. If a device is connected to the wireless network, they are copying it – and I cannot stop them."

A slow realization came over the Major. The enemy would know of Drouin's plans for Europe, the digital currency, the ISIS cells... Aubert had to stop the enemy, or his employer would never be able to show his face in Europe again. *"That's why there are gunships outside,"* he thought. *"They are there to limit our movement and prevent us from flanking the enemy while they do their work; clever."*

He picked up his radio once more. "All surviving Legion soldiers, come to the security office. Do not, I repeat, do not go outside the Schloss under any circumstances." It took only three minutes for the Legion soldiers to assemble. Most of them were concentrated here in the West Wing anyway.

Major Aubert stepped forward and addressed his men. "Soldiers, the enemy who attacked us tonight came here to steal electronic data. Right now, they are copying every bit of information inside the schloss; even the data stored on the smartphones in your pockets."

A concerned murmur broke out among the assembled men. Aubert held up his hand and continued. "Right now, the enemy is concentrated on the second floor of the East wing, providing cover for someone who has physical control of the network server. We must stop them and secure the data they are trying to steal. Video surveillance has been cut off, but the enemy will mass here at the East end of the gallery, and here, at the top of the East staircase. By holding these two points, they control the first and second floors of the East wing. This is our plan; two small teams will engage the blocking forces at the gallery and the staircase. These teams will distract the enemy while the bulk of our force attacks from the third floor. The third-floor team will bring grenades and use them to dislodge the blocking force at the staircase. Once we control that point, we will have trapped the other blocking force in the gallery. Time is then on our side, Gentlemen." Aubert looked over at Lieutenant Lapointe. "Lieutenant, you will lead the third-floor team. Sergeants

Allard and Lacroix, you will lead the teams to harass the blocking forces. We have two FN MAG-58 machine guns, take those with you. We also have ten ballistic shields. Two shields will go to each of the harassing teams, the final six will go with Lapointe." Aubert could see that some of his men were not convinced this mission was worth the danger.

"Remember that our information is part of this download, men. Our home addresses, next of kin, personal information and everything Legion services has done in Somalia, Sudan, and Syria." That last bit got their attention, Aubert saw.

Legion Services had engaged in conduct that, if released publicly, would be considered war crimes. Most of the men here would rather fall in battle than face the humiliation of a tribunal at The Hague. Others worried about their families. Regardless of personal reasons, Aubert could see that he had no issues with motivation. Every single man here would fight to the death.

Captain Ivan looked down the long, dark hallway of the gallery. Light from the burning vehicle outside created a bright spot towards the end of the hall, and the contrast made it difficult to see anything beyond. He thought he saw movement at the end of the hall. He flashed a hand signal to his gunner, who nodded. Suddenly, a star-shaped flash appeared at the opposite end, and incoming rounds began to impact the ballistic shield.

"Snake One, this is blocking team one. We have enemy contact," Ivan said on his radio. Needing no direction, team one's gunner opened fire with his MG4, sending a twenty-round burst of 5.56mm ammunition down range.

"Team one, watch for runners and smoke," Ivan said on his radio. "Gunner, keep fire on the enemy machine gunner." The two machine gunners exchanged across what instantly became a two-hundred-foot no-man's land.

Andrei warned his team to get ready; the enemy was sure to attack their position as well. As if on cue, another MAG-58 started firing at the bottom of the grand staircase, the gunner taking cover behind a massive granite column. "Blocking team two reports enemy contact on the first floor," Andrei said on his radio. They had to hold their position until the IT team and search teams were done.

Lew and Aleksy went to each locked door along the East side of the hallway and gently pushed a fiber optic camera underneath the door. The first three rooms were empty. When Aleksy got to the Fourth room, he could hear someone pounding on the door from the inside. The fiber optic camera confirmed his suspicions; the search team had found Victoria. "Captain!" Aleksy shouted, "I've found her!"

Jan slung his rifle and ran to the door. "VICTORIA!" He shouted at the door.

Victoria heard a voice from the grave. It could not be him! "Jan? JAN!!! It's me, please get me out of here!" she shouted back at the door.

"*Thank God,*" Jan thought. "We must blow the door with explosives! Get away from the door and behind something solid!" She looked around; the bathroom would do.

"Okay!" she said.

Jan looked at Lew and pointed at the door lock. Lew took off his backpack and removed a small brick of C-4 plastic explosive and detonation cord. He mashed the brick against the lock and the door frame and pushed a blasting cap into the explosive. He quickly connected one end of a command wire to the blasting cap and the other to his M57 firing device. "Ready," he said to his captain.

"Blow it," Jan said as he waved for Diego's men to get back from the door.

"Blocking teams," he said into his radio, "This is search team, we are blowing the door." Lew crouched along the East wall of the hallway and shouted, "Fire in the hole! Fire in the hole! Fire in the hole!" He mashed the firing lever of the M57, and the explosives detonated with a thundering crack. The force from the explosion blew a gaping hole into the steel of the door and mangled the door frame. Aleksy ran along the wall towards the door, kicking it open with his boot when he got there, Jan right behind him. Both men scanned the room for targets but found none. "Victoria!" Jan shouted as he flipped up his GPNVG-18 goggles, "Where are you!?!"

She appeared in the doorway to the bathroom and ran to him. Jan slung his G36C and held out his arms as Victoria ran to his embrace. His strong arms held her firmly as she started sobbing from the emotional release of being saved once more by this brave knight. She quietly thanked God that he had yet again sent a guardian angel to save her from an awful fate. His gloved hand cradled her head as she cried in his arms. *"Everything was right again with the world,"* he thought. *"Thank you, Lord for this opportunity to save her once more."*

He took her by the shoulders and said to her, "Victoria, can you walk?"

She nodded. She could run three miles if she had to. Jan looked down at her bare feet, "Put a pair of shoes on, there's lots of debris downstairs."

Victoria ran to the wardrobe to get her athletic shoes as Lew came in the door. Jan walked over to her. "We need to wait here for a few more minutes," he said.

"Echo is snatching data from Count Drouin's computer network." He was interrupted by an impossibly loud bang from an explosion nearby that made Victoria's ears ring.

"Snake One, this is team two!" Andrei shouted into the radio. "We are taking fire from the third floor; my gunner is down from a grenade explosion." He looked at the shield. The gunner's leg was gravely injured, and the MG4 was wrecked. The loader was working on his gunner, trying to place a tourniquet on what was left of the man's leg. Andrei looked up just in time to see another grenade falling toward him. "Grenade!" he shouted, "Get down!!"

The M67 grenade bounced once on the marble floor and detonated, peppering some of his men with shrapnel. He was taking casualties here, and his team was in grave danger of being overrun.

"Fall back to the hallway!" he shouted at his men. Into the radio,

Andrei yelled, "Diego, BLOW THE STAIRS!!"

Diego nodded at his combat engineer, who flipped down the safety lever from the M57 firing device. After he shouted out the warning on his radio, the combat engineer mashed the firing lever of the M57. An electrical signal raced down the command wire to two satchel charges that the combat engineer had placed in a broom closet located under the stairs.

BOOOOOOOOOMMMMMMM!!!!!

Fifty pounds of C-4 explosive detonated, turning the staircase into rubble in a yellow flash. The pressure wave traveled upward, destroying the marble staircase and sending rock shrapnel everywhere. The thunderous roar of the explosion droned out the groaning and creaking of the structural members that held up the walls inside the room that contained the grand staircase.

The staircase structure partially held up the third floor and with the lower half of the staircase annihilated by the explosion, part of the East wing began to collapse. The Legion soldiers on the third floor ran for their lives as the stairs and balcony gave way, raining tons of rubble down into the first floor. The team on the first floor screamed as the building fell on them.

Outside, Stefan could see the explosion throw building debris out through the roof and saw the building start to collapse in on itself. "Dear God..." he said aloud over the intercom. Stefan mashed the PTT button and said, "Snake One, This is Rattler One, do blocking teams require assistance?"

Petrov called Andrei on the radio. "Blocking team two," he said, "do you need air support?"

Captain Andrei choked on the dust, fighting off the effects of the explosion. His gunner was dead, and he had three wounded men from the grenades. "Yes," he said into the radio, "We cannot hold them if they rush our position. Have Rattler one and two concentrate fire on the third floor, repeat third floor only."

Andrei found Diego in the hallway and said, "Captain, I need your help. I need to get my casualties to the first floor, and I cannot hold my position. Can you replace our losses with your men here?"

Diego nodded, "Yes, Andrei. We shouldn't have to hold for long."

He pressed his hand to his throat. "I.T. team, this is blocking team three, how long to complete your task?" Echo turned away from the monitor. "Team three this is I.T. team," he said into the radio. "Ninety seconds until download complete."

Major Aubert heard the massive explosion from the two satchel charges and felt the building shake under his feet. He knew he had lost many men in that blast. "All teams report in," he said into the radio.

"This is Sergeant Allard," the Major heard first, "We are at full strength, still engaging enemy forces at the end of the gallery."

A voice came over the radio right after Allard, choking. *"This is Lapointe, we lost eight men in the blast, I still have twenty-two."* Major Aubert thought about the tactical situation. Twenty-two men were still a sizeable force.

"Lacroix, report status," the Major said into the radio. There was no response. Aubert thought fast, and he could redeploy Lapointe's men to engage the helicopters from the third floor. From the East windows, they would be able to engage the helicopters once they returned to pick up the enemy. Aubert's thoughts were interrupted by a series of booming explosions as he raised the radio to call Lapointe.

"Rattler one and two, this is Snake One," Petrov said on the aerial frequency, "blocking team two requests immediate air support. Attack the third floor with rockets." From the drone feed, Petrov could see the enemy scurrying around in the darkness on the third floor from the gaping hole in the building's roof. "Concentrate fire on the South end of the hole in the roof," he added.

"Snake One, this is Rattler flight," Stefan said into his microphone, "starting attack run now." He looked out of the aircraft window and spied Rattler two.

"Rattler two," he said, "Form up on me in line formation and proceed to target."

Stefan pressed the cyclic forward and gently lifted on the collective as he increased speed towards the building. Rattler two turned hard to intercept him and line up on his right side. As the two helicopters raced in towards the building, Stefan lined up his HUD crosshair on the South edge of the smoking hole in the building. When he and Rattler two were three hundred meters out, the gunships began firing their M70 Hydra rockets. Twelve rockets raced in towards the building and began impacting in rapid succession. The exposed interior walls offered no resistance to or cover from the rockets, and they shredded the remaining soldiers under Lapointe's command.

"Snake One, this is Rattler One," Stefan said over the aerial frequency, "target destroyed, Rattler one and two continuing to orbit target area." The gunships banked to the left and right, coming about and searching the area for additional targets.

"Lieutenant Lapointe," Major Aubert called into the radio, "Report in!" Nothing but static answered him. The Major went pale; twenty-two men were dead. He realized now he could not recover the data. Ten men simply could not resist one hundred elite enemy soldiers with air support. He had no power to stop them, and they would have evidence of serious crimes. It was time to think about the survival of his remaining men and Count Drouin. They could flee to a non-extradition treaty country and rebuild. Major Aubert picked up a hardline phone that connected to the safe room. "Protection detail, this is Major Aubert. We have lost the bulk of our forces in action. Prepare to move the principal to the lodge and escape from there."

In the safe room, the guards on the protection detail raised an eyebrow and looked at Count Drouin. When he returned their stare with a questioning expression, the bodyguards addressed him, "Sir, we are leaving the Schloss."

Back in the security office, Major Aubert picked up his radio. "Sergeant Allard, disengage from the enemy and fall back to the safe room. Assist the protection detail with extraction of the principal and provide additional security when they get to the lodge. Use the escape tunnel; it's too dangerous to move in the open."

Sergeant Allard tapped the gunner on the shoulder and gave the signal to fall back to his men. They hastily retreated and ended the gunfight in the gallery. The walls were scarred with bullet holes, and the paintings were ruined. The ten men assigned to Allard ran back to the safe room as fast as they could, kicking the door open to Drouin's office once they arrived. Sergeant Allard pounded on the safe room door with his fist and looked at the security camera. The lead bodyguard opened the door to the safe room and ushered the Legion soldiers inside. There was a hatch in the floor that one of the bodyguards opened. The hatch made a metallic creak as it swung up to reveal a ladder and a lit room far below. The lead bodyguard went down first, followed by his number two man. The rest of the bodyguards muscled Drouin down the ladder, the gentile aristocrat protesting with every step. Once Allard's men were down, the lead bodyguard flipped an industrial disconnect switch to the **ON** position. Yellow caged lights flickered on, revealing a long tunnel that stretched North for over two kilometers.

The lead bodyguard addressed the group, "We have a long walk, let's get moving." The group hustled down the long, cold tunnel towards the lodge. The earth over the tunnel was no thinner than three meters, and it provided protection from the attack helicopters circling overhead.

In the solitude of the security office, Major Aubert threw the radio on the floor. He put on a black plate carrier and a helmet. On the way out the door, he picked up an M4 rifle and ten thirty-round magazines. Aubert had no intention of fleeing with Drouin. His men had died here, and he was going to join them like a true commanding officer. "Honneur et Fidélité," Major Aubert said as he walked towards the East wing of Schloss Drouin.

"Snake One, this is team one," Ivan said over the radio. "Enemy has broken contact and pulled back."

Petrov looked at the IR feed from the Watchkeeper. He could not see any men outside the building, and the third floor of the East wing was wrecked; no one could have survived that. "Snake One copies, Team one. Hold your position until IT team is finished with their task." Echo's voice came in over the radio as if on cue.

"This is IT team, task complete." Petrov let out a slow breath.

"*Time to go,*" he thought. "Snake One copies, IT team. Search team, do you have the hostage secure?"

Jan's voice came in over the assault frequency, "Roger, Snake One. One hostage ready to go, and she is ambulatory."

Captain Fedorov switched to the aerial frequency and called the H215 transports in a holding pattern to the North. "Vipers one through four, request extraction for all teams." The pilot of Viper

One heard him and hit the PTT button in the cockpit to respond. "Copy Copperhead Actual, this is Viper one. ETA to LZ sixty seconds, request status of LZ."

Fedorov looked at the DS11 tablet once more to scan for threats. Seeing none, he called Viper one back. "LZ secure Viper one." Fedorov switched back to the assault frequency and called the teams inside the school. "All teams, we are extracting. Transports inbound." He got to his feet, picked up his rifle, and put the tablet away in his backpack. He started running towards the tree line. Just beyond it was the grass field where the H215 transports would land. He took a knee and waited; in the distance, he could hear the sound of approaching helicopters.

Inside Victoria's room, Jan heard the radio call from Viktor. "Time to go, gents," he said to his men. Lew walked over to Victoria. "Put your hand here on my plate carrier, just like before," he told her with a smile. "I'm going to take you out of here." She kissed Lew on the cheek, and he blushed. He readied his G36C and got ready to move as he nodded to Jan.

"Okay team, let's MOVE!" Jan said to his men. He and Aleksy led the way, with Lew and Victoria close behind. Jan could see Echo running to the stairwell door as Jan filed in behind the IT team. Diego's men followed, careful to cover the team's escape. Jan followed the IT team out of the stairwell and took a knee just inside the wrecked door to the outside to wait for the helicopters.

Major Aubert walked by the pile of rubble on the first floor that had entombed his men. The grand staircase was unrecognizable; what once were beautiful carvings and mason work were now worth nothing but scrap. A pile of stone sat where the staircase once stood. Half the walls were missing in this room, exposing adjacent rooms on the second and third floors. Aubert climbed over the rubble pile and continued. He had to get to one of the East windows before the transport helicopters arrived.

The pilot of Viper One came in quickly, flaring his aircraft and gently setting it down on the grass field. The landing was repeated by Viper two, then three, then finally four at the end of the field. The engines of the four helicopters screamed on the ground, and the stench of burned jet fuel soon filled the air. One of the Rattler gunships flew overhead as Viper One's pilot looked toward the

Schloss. He could see soldiers running towards him as he waited, holding the aircraft at full power. The crew chiefs of the H215 transports had run outside the helicopters, holding up one, two, three, or four IR glowsticks, depending on which Viper they were assigned. The blocking teams piled onto the transports; blocking team three was assisting team two with moving their wounded. Inside the doorway, Jan nodded to Victoria. It was time to go. He ran outside the school and onto the field. Viper four was close, just a few dozen meters away.

Major Aubert had made it to one of the rooms that faced the East lawn. He saw the helicopters on the ground; their main rotors were spinning as they loaded the enemy. As he walked up to one of the windows, he brought his M4 rifle up and looked for a target. *"Wait,"* he thought, *"That's the girl we brought back."* He took careful aim at the two soldiers in front of her and pressed the trigger.

Jan felt something strike the back of his head, and he fell to the ground hard. Aleksy fell to the ground beside him, seeking cover in the dirt. Lew grabbed Victoria and forced her down. He pressed his body down on top of her, hoping his armor plates would shield her from the gunfire. Ivan had heard the shots as he was supervising security for the boarding of the helicopters. He yelled to his gunner, and the man brought his MG4 out and readied the light machine gun for action once more. "First floor windows," Ivan said to his gunner, "Watch for flash."

"Did I hit them?" Aubert thought.

He knew he had shot one enemy in the head but was unsure of the other shots. The Major flipped the selector on his M4 to "AUTO" and tried to look for the girl. It was dark, and he was having trouble seeing clearly now that the targets were not moving. He saw something lighter in color on the grass, aimed just in front of the object, and pressed the trigger again. The M4 bounced against his shoulder as he fought to control the muzzle. Aubert fired short bursts, trying to walk the rounds into the target, hoping for a hit.

Ivan saw the flash. "Gunner, enemy contact first floor, seventh window from the right of structure." The gunner saw the flash and looked through the Aimpoint optical sight mounted to the MG4. He put the red dot just underneath the flash and pressed the trigger. The light machine gun recoiled and filled the gunner's nostrils with acrid smoke as it fired. The gunner sent a twenty-round burst into the window where he saw the flash; the point of aim naturally rose as the gunner suppressed the enemy. When the recoil force brought the point of aim up to where the average man's head would be, he stopped, adjusted his aim, and fired another twenty-round burst.

Major Aubert collapsed to the floor in a heap. One of the SS109 5.56mm penetrators had struck his throat and blew out his neck vertebrae. His body no longer responding to commands from his brain, he dropped to the floor like a marionette whose strings had been cut. The round had yawed a bit when it entered Aubert's neck, and a large pool of blood was forming underneath his head from his severed Carotid artery. "*It was a good death,*" he thought as he bled out on the fine wood floor of the palace he used to rule with Count Drouin. He had fallen in battle fighting the enemy, and he was grateful that his end was here, weapon in his hand. His last thought was the motto of the Legion, the proud group of soldiers who had defended the interests of France for over one hundred years. "*Honneur et Fidélité,*" he thought as the blackness closed in around him.

Chapter 23

Aleksy looked over at Jan. It was obvious his helmet had taken a round, and Jan was unconscious. Aleksy waved to the knights assigned to the IT team to help him get Jan on Viper four. The three men lifted Jan carefully as Echo cradled Jan's head. They awkwardly carried the fallen captain to the waiting helicopter and set him down on the cabin floor. When Lew and Victoria boarded the H215, she could see how badly Jan had been hurt. "JAANN!!" she screamed as she rushed to his side. He was not moving, and Victoria feared he was dead. She looked up at Aleksy, her eyes asking if he was alive.

"He's alive," he said, "but he took a round to the head and he is badly injured." Lew looked at Jan again. One of the other knights on the IT team was working on him, immobilizing the captain's neck and restraining him to a spinal board. Federov jumped on board the aircraft last, followed by the crew chief. Viper four was ready for departure. The pilot gently raised the collective and input small corrective movements to the cyclic and pedals. In a moment, the big H215 was airborne and on its way to staging area Snake One.

Stefan was worried about Jan, but one would never tell from his flying. His control of the EC155 was rock solid as he flew overwatch for Viper Two as it picked up the November sniper teams. The snipers had to run through the woods to a small clearing where a McGuire rig was lowered through the canopy. One by one, the four men of November one and two slung themselves into the rig for their ride underneath the helicopter. Although they did not expect any resistance for the pickup, overwatch and security were taken seriously. Stefan had seen what happens when flight crews let their guard down on the last extraction, and it usually ended in disaster. He diverted his attention between the instruments, the pickup, and the trees below them. Nikolai did not have to fly the aircraft, and he kept his full attention on the task of looking for threats.

Drouin's bodyguards and the surviving soldiers of Legion Services had reached the end of the tunnel. Like at the tunnel entrance, there was a ladder leading up to a hatch. The lead bodyguard climbed the ladder, slid the locking bolt over, and pushed open the hatch into the space above. The other men who made up the protection detail climbed up the ladder after him into a cold hunting lodge. The lodge was made of stone, with a kitchen in the corner and a large table in the center. Beds lined one wall of the one-room structure. This lodge was used by the game wardens of the Drouin estate when a guest wished to hunt for game animals.

The Legion soldiers pushed Drouin up into the space, and they followed right after. Sergeant Allard ordered one of his men outside to start the waiting Mercedes-Benz G550 four-wheel-drive vehicles. There were two forest green vehicles outside, fully fueled and waiting here in the event the Schloss was attacked and they needed to get Drouin out. As Allard heard the vehicles start and begin to warm up, the bodyguards consulted a map of the estate. They had practiced this extraction plan before and now was the time to put it in place for real.

The G550 wagons would drive along the forest road until they came to an old railway that used to run through the property. The tracks had been removed long ago, but the bedrock and clear path through the woods made an efficient escape route that appeared on no public maps. At the border of the property was a tunnel. That tunnel led to the highway. If they could get on the highway, they could disappear into traffic and get Drouin to an airport. They decided that they would load Drouin into the first vehicle, and the Legion soldiers would pull security in the trailing vehicle. Sergeant Allard walked over to Drouin, picked him up by the arm, and led him outside despite his protests. Allard put him into the first G550, and he got into the front passenger seat of the second. The forest was dark and smelled of pine. The G550 started rolling, and pine needles crunched under the tires. As they left the lodge, the driver saw that the road was too dark to drive safely, and he switched on the headlamps.

Nikolai saw a light in the trees to the South of their position. "Pilot, I have a light at two three zero at approximately two thousand meters."

Stefan whirled his head to look in that direction. Viper two had just finished its pickup, and four men were dangling underneath the aircraft. If they were attacked now, the four knights hanging from the McGuire rig would be as good as dead. "I see it," Stefan said over the intercom.

The light blazed brightly in the dark green phosphorescent image of his night vision goggles. He lifted the collective a bit to increase altitude and get a better view. They looked like vehicle headlamps; he turned the EC155's nose in the direction of the light to take a closer look. He was careful to approach the light from the rear to mask his signature. Through the trees, Nikolai could see that there were two four-wheel-drive vehicles slowly making their way down a trail through the woods. Stefan hit the PTT button to call it in. "Snake One, this is Rattler one, we have two vehicles trying to escape target area two clicks to the south of the November sniper team pick up point, requesting permission to engage, over."

Back at the TOC, Petrov heard the call. They weren't expecting to find civilian vehicles in this part of the estate. "Rattler one, this is Snake one," Petrov said into the radio, "do not engage any civilian vehicle unless fired upon."

Stefan scowled in the gunship cockpit. He and Nikolai suspected that the vehicles were carrying Count Drouin, but the rules of engagement were clear regarding civilian vehicles in the target area. This could be Drouin, or it could be two cars full of maids and cooks. There was no way to tell from the air...or was there? Stefan gave Nikolai a wolffish grin. Nikolai nodded; he was thinking the same thing.

Corporal Lavigne had his torso protruding from the sunroof of the trailing G550, and the FN

MAG deployed on its bipod in front of him. As the vehicle moved, the bipod feet carved deep scratches in the G550's green paint. *"I'm glad it's not my car,"* Lavigne thought as the vehicle went around a corner.

He was doing his best to pay attention in the chilly night air. The vehicles slowed to ascend the steep bedrock of the abandoned railroad. The rear tires of the trailing G550 lost traction as the driver tried to follow the first vehicle, causing Lavigne to stumble as he tried to keep from falling. The G550's traction control system took over and allowed the big vehicle to roll up onto the mound of gravel. Free of the trees and driving on a straight road, the lead vehicle increased speed. The tunnel was less than a kilometer ahead.

Lavigne heard an odd whistling noise over the sound of the wind blowing past his ears. He strained to hear this new sound, it was a high-pitched buzz and whistle that was not coming from the vehicle; whatever it was, it was getting louder. Suddenly, a large grey helicopter screamed over the vehicles, its shape becoming visible in the headlights of the lead vehicle. *"OH MY GOD,"* Lavigne thought.

He panicked at the sight of the rocket pods and miniguns hanging off the weapon pylons mounted to the EC155 and reacted by sending a forty-round burst of 7.62mm ammunition down range. The tracers chased after the retreating gunship as it disappeared back into the night.

"Snake one, this is Rattler one, we have just been fired upon by the vehicles," Stefan said into the radio.

"Snake one copies, Rattler," Petrov replied. "Permission granted to engage hostile enemy vehicle." Stefan turned the helicopter to line up for a strafing run on the rear vehicle.

"Pilot, the enemy vehicles are heading for a tunnel, we have time for one attack pass," Nikolai said over the intercom.

"Roger," Stefan said in reply, "We fire on the rear vehicle only." He wanted to engage both vehicles, using the EC155's miniguns to rip both vehicles into expensive tinfoil, but the first vehicle did not fire at them, and the rules of engagement did not permit an attack. Stefan pulled back on the cyclic, raising the nose of the gunship to gain altitude for the strafing run.

Once he had enough, he gave the EC155 some right rudder to turn the gunship into a steep dive. The helicopter raced to the ground; the two vehicles were just ahead of them. Stefan smiled, *"This was just like two medieval knights in a joust competition,"* he thought.

The comparison pleased him to no end as the EC155 passed into weapons range. He lined the aiming point up on his HUD with the rear G550 and pressed the firing button. Two streams of red tracers raced towards the target as the miniguns made their menacing roar that sounded like a low buzz. Stefan saw the vehicle gunner try and return fire, but it was too late. In the two seconds, Stefan had shot at the G550, two hundred rounds of 7.62mm ammunition had flown down range. The rounds tore the German-made SUV to pieces, shredding the vehicle. Dozens of rounds hit the fuel tank, spraying gasoline over the wreckage. As more tracer rounds hit the target, the fuel ignited, sending an orange plume of fire and black smoke skyward.

Stefan rotated the cyclic left to bank the EC155 out of the path of the explosion as the first G550 accelerated towards the tunnel. A second later, the vehicle entered the safety of the opening in the rock, the driver gripping the steering wheel so hard it nearly bent under pressure.

Stefan called Petrov back on the radio and flew away from the flaming hulk of the destroyed G550.

He looked to the south and saw Rattler two escorting Viper one out of the area, the Sierra sniper teams dangling below the aircraft's belly. Less than two minutes later, all aircraft exited the battlespace and had crossed the border of the Drouin estate. Free of his overwatch duties, Stefan's thoughts turned to Jan. It came in over the aerial frequency that Jan had been shot in the head. He worried about the young captain and hoped that he could return to duty soon.

Stefan looked over at Nikolai. He liked his new co-pilot and would be proud to fly with him again if the order called. Stefan felt a feeling of contentment as he flew towards the landing pad at Snake One. The men today had lived up to the legend of their pedigree; they had stormed a castle and rescued a kidnapped maiden. Stefan even got to challenge the enemy to a modern version of the joust. At one point in time, wine would be drunk, and songs to celebrate the battle would be written. Today, however, the chronicle would be buried under some version of a "state secrets" clause. *"Such is the state of the uncivilized age in which we live,"* Stefan thought as he scanned his instruments.

St. Anthony's Hospital, Zurich, Switzerland

Jan awoke suddenly in his bed. He felt the roughness from the heavily starched cotton sheets, and a strong clean smell of chemical disinfectant filled his nostrils. Bright morning light streamed through his hospital window, and Jan winced. The light was giving him a headache.

"My head," Jan thought as his hand felt where he had been struck. He felt the effects of pain medication as he felt a big knot, but no crushed bone or stitches. Next to his bed, a young blond woman covered with a blanket dozed in a comfortable lounge chair. Jan recognized her immediately.

"Victoria," he whispered. She gently woke up, and he smiled at her.

"Oh Jannn!!" she cried out, instantly at his side.

"Don't worry," he said. "I'm all right... at least I think I'm all right." Victoria was relieved beyond words.

The thought that Jan gave his life for her a second time was too much to bear. Her tears started flowing as she held his hand. "You came for me," she said quietly. "Thank you."

Jan had something to ask. "Did they hurt you in there?"

Victoria wiped the tears away and told Jan the story about how the servants of Count Drouin had put her through a regimen of psychological abuse, how they intended her to be one of Drouin's sex slaves, and how she had nearly lost hope. "I've been talking a lot with Father Matthew," she said. "It's been helping."

Jan was thankful to hear that. From what he just learned, Victoria had undergone a mental shock equally as severe as what happened to her at the farmhouse. She needed to talk this out with a professional familiar with combat operations and the Order of Saint John, and there was no one better than Father Matthew. Petrov and Aleksy walked into Jan's hospital room a moment later. Tears of joy welled in Aleksy's eyes as he rushed to the other side of the bed. Petrov stood at the foot of the bed, grinning with pride from ear to ear. "How do you feel, captain?" Petrov asked.

"I am well sir," Jan said in response. "Did I get shot in the head?" The innocence of the question broke the group into quiet laughter.

Aleksy recovered first and said, "You sure did, captain. You scared all of us for a while; but don't worry, we got the bastard that shot you."

The doctor came in next. "It's good to see you awake, Jan," he said with a smile. "You gave us a bit of concern; you have been unconscious for three days."

Jan sat up a bit before he spoke. "Thank you, doctor. Is there..." Jan paused a moment before continuing, "any permanent injury?"

The doctor smiled, "No, son. You have a concussion, and a nasty welt on your head. You will have a headache for the next few days, and you need to take it easy, but after a week of rest you're cleared for combat operations."

Jan exhaled in relief; it was like getting a second chance, and those did not come often in a gunfight. Jan remembered a phrase that was the favorite of one of his British combat instructors. The instructor always said, *"Who dares, wins."*

He and the knights on his team had dared and won. Even if Jan had died on the grass that night, the team still would have won because the mission was successful. The Doctor broke Jan's train of thought. "I need to continue my rounds, is there anything further, son?" he asked.

"No, doctor. Thank you." The doctor smiled and left Jan with his friends. Jan looked at Petrov. "What happened after I got hit?" he asked.

"MI-6 went in afterwards with the Politzei to collect intelligence... and to smooth things over with the Germans. Legion Services has been annihilated as an organization. You and the rest of the teams killed nearly all of their members. Stefan saw Drouin trying to escape in a small convoy of two civilian vehicles. One of the vehicles foolishly shot at him, and he destroyed it. Examination of the wreckage showed that it was full of Legion soldiers, and the second vehicle escaped. It is a one-hundred percent certainty that Drouin was on this second vehicle."

Jan had another question. "What did we get from the data?" he asked.

"A treasure trove of misdeeds," Petrov said. "The locations of the ISIS cells working in Britain were just the tip of Drouin's plan. He had spent considerable resources buying off politicians to implement a digital currency and overhaul of the banking system that would have turned every UK subject into a serf, and Drouin planned to do the same in every single country of the EU. He intended to use fear as a weapon to force a political outcome, and this plan was underway for over a decade. The migration of refugees from Iraq and Syria was orchestrated, Jan. Years ago, the CIA created ISIS from the turmoil in Iraq, and the whole point of the migration was to provide cover to move these operatives into Europe. Drouin was able to buy support in the United States as well. We even saw evidence that he wholly funded the campaign of the current President."

Jan whistled at the scope of Drouin's power and influence. "After he fled the estate," Petrov continued, "MI-6 was watching for private aircraft departures leaving Europe and traveling to destinations known to be frequented by Drouin. They found a charter Boeing 737 that left Frankfurt on Monday and landed at Chhatrapati Shivaji Maharaj International Airport the next day."

Jan raised his eyebrows and asked, "Where is that; India?" India was a long way off from Europe. Drouin no doubt wanted to be far away from MI-6, but a former British colony was an odd choice.

"Correct, Jan. It's in Mumbai. Technically, there is an extradition agreement between the United Kingdom and India; but over the past few decades the UK has not honored its side of the agreement. This has led to political tension in India's foreign services office every time the UK makes a request to extradite a fugitive from India. MI-6 is trying to call in a favor with India's Research & Analysis Wing, but with Drouin's propensity to purchase the help of local politicians and officials, it is unlikely that they will succeed."

Jan thought about this for a moment. "Then we were successful in forcing Drouin away from his home turf, and we were able to separate him from the protection of Legion Services?"

Petrov nodded, "We were; Legion Services currently does not exist as a force capable of posing any threat. Right now, Drouin is reliant on a local security company. That company is simply not the peer of Legion, but it was the only option available in Mumbai."

Jan smiled and said, "If I'm hearing you correctly, sir this means that MI-6 is looking for help in the recovery of an international fugitive?"

Petrov looked back at Jan and answered him. "They are, Captain. How would you like to pay Drouin a visit and send MI-6's warmest regards?"

Chapter 24

The Oberoi Resort, Mumbai

Drouin looked out at the ocean from the patio of his top-floor suite at the luxurious Oberoi Hotel. The climate was warm here, even in February. He could see the lights of ships offshore, bringing their wares to the port city from the far corners of the world. Drouin was dressed appropriately for the climate. He sported a pair of khaki trousers and a white linen shirt. He hated being dressed so casually, but the tropics were too humid for his preferred choice of clothing. Drouin could not wait for Hans to get here and tailor some proper clothing for him; he felt like a peasant in these "rustic" fabrics. He looked over at the table in his suite. *"At least I didn't have to eat like one,"* he thought.

The remains of a five-star meal were there, awaiting room service to take the dishes away. Drouin thanked providence that a descent Italian restaurant was on the resort grounds; he despised Indian food. He was still in a bit of shock from the attack on his family's ancestral home. Drouin shuddered at the memory of the attack helicopter destroying the vehicle behind his. Thanks to Sergeant Allard, he was still alive.

Allard had decided it made more sense to arm the second vehicle with the machine gun; in the event of an attack, the vehicle without Drouin would draw fire. *"That's exactly what happened,"* Drouin thought. *"That's why I have servants; they take my place so I can continue on with my plans."*

Those plans had been irrevocably altered; he knew it would take years to rebuild the terrorist network to properly frighten European citizens into voting themselves into subjugation. Still, the network of politicians and government officials was still intact; he would have to remember to make the necessary election donations when the time came. Perhaps now that his plans were sidelined, he would focus on producing an heir for his title and fortune. There were plenty of eligible daughters from the finest families in Europe; in fact, some of those families were already trying to court Drouin as a son-in-law. He was the proper age now, in his fifties; the same age as his own father was when Drouin was born. The door to his suite opened, breaking his ruminations. A man in a hotel uniform walked into the room and headed to the bar in Drouin's suite. He remembered that he had asked room service to send up a barman to fix an after-dinner cocktail. Tomorrow would be a busy day, even for an aristocrat in exile, and he wanted something to help him sleep.

The barman quietly began to mix his drink. Drouin's assistants had coordinated with the resort to have his favorite beverages and food on hand, so he did not have to ask or explain anything. Drouin ordered a drink, and his favorite cocktail appeared without saying another word. He ordered food, and the finest French or Italian dishes were served.

Drouin was shocked when the barman opened his mouth and began to speak. "Did you know a young girl named Katreesa, Anton?"

Drouin's anger was ignited, and it began to smolder within him. A slow burn of indignation began to rage at the familiarity this servant was showing him. He walked inside from the patio, his eyes blazing with hatred. "In my language," the barman continued, "Katreesa means 'graceful' and 'elegant.' You did not treat her in a way worthy of her namesake, Anton."

Who was this man? It was slowly dawning on Drouin that the barman was not a hotel employee. This man looked like all the other employees. He was from India, of course, but the man was enormous. He did not look like a simple hotel employee; the man looked more like a soldier. "Before she died of sepsis, humiliated and alone, Katreesa found a maid in the brothel and begged her to get word to me. Against all odds, that maid found me and told me of your crime."

Puzzlement was giving way to fear in Drouin's mind. How did this man know about the brothel? The client list and arrangement he had with that criminal enterprise was a closely guarded secret; no one knew about this! Drouin opened his mouth and shouted a single word as he backed away from the bar. "Security!" Drouin called.

The suite doors opened immediately, but the men who walked inside were not the two assigned to Drouin's security detail. Instead, Jan and Aleksy strolled into the suite, dressed in their grey combat uniforms with the white cross on their shoulders and armed with Heckler & Koch MP-7 personal defense weapons. The bartender looked over at the two, who nodded at him. "Make it fast, brother," Jan said to the man. "The Mumbai police are on their way. Someone in the hotel heard us shooting Count Drouin's guards."

Drouin could not move; he was immobilized with fear. The order had found him, despite all the precautions that were taken. "How did... It's not possible," Drouin began to speak, but Jan cut him off.

"The order can be found in every country that Christendom touches, Count Drouin. Although he may appear different, Captain Rakesh here is a knight like Aleksy or myself. We all serve the same God and Order; therefore, I call him my brother." Before Drouin could respond, Rakesh grabbed him forcefully by the arm and led him back to the patio. Rakesh threw Drouin to the ground and began to tie a noose with a section of laundry line he had concealed under his hotel uniform. He slipped the noose around Drouin's neck, the aristocrat begging for mercy.

"Please," Drouin whined, "I'll give you whatever you wish, my wealth is vast, and I will give you more than you could ever count."

Rakesh stopped and lifted Drouin to his feet. "Do you know what I want, Anton?" he said to the trembling Count as he tied the rope to the balcony railing, "I want my daughter Katreesa to come home. I know you have great power, Count Drouin. But there is only one man who lived on this earth who had the power to raise the dead from the grave...and you're not him."

Rakesh grabbed Drouin by the neck and leg, easily lifting the shrieking man off his feet and over his head. He held Drouin there for a full second before throwing the Count off the edge of the balcony. Drouin screamed as he fell. His cry of terror was abruptly cut off with a sickening crack as Drouin's neck vertebrae snapped, killing him instantly. In the quiet, Rakesh looked out at the Indian Ocean as he remembered his daughter. *"It's done now,"* he thought as his Polish brothers joined him. The warriors said not a word, and gazed out at the sunset, pondering the horizon.

THE END

THE KNIGHTS WILL RETURN

Made in the USA
Monee, IL
18 September 2023

42924105R00284